GUACAMOLE
The LGBT Collection

David Gerrold

TABLE OF CONTENTS

INTRODUCTION

On July 19, 1969, I had an epiphany.

I hadn't planned to have an epiphany. It just kinda happened—

It was a golden afternoon and I had fallen into the arms of a beautiful redheaded man.

We were young and foolish and horny. What had started as a momentary fling, an hour or two of diversion had slowly and deliciously become something else. The lazy conversation had evolved into something more intimate. Chatting became sharing. Curiosity became discovery, and after a while, delight. We got caught up in the sheer joy of each other's enchantment.

He said he liked my body. Nobody had ever said that to me before. We shared an ice cube, passing it back and forth in our kisses until it was nothing more than a cool memory. He sang to me, "You're just too good to be true, can't take my eyes off of you." He sang what he was feeling. I surrendered to the moment and let him lead.

We'd both had sex before. But neither of us had ever truly made the connection that goes beyond just connecting, had never joined so intimately with another human being—and now, here we were, two joyous naked young men wrapped up in each other, amazed at what we had become. He lay on top of me, both of us just resting, and I could feel our hearts beating together, the waves of sensation pulsing outward from our mutual center. Neither of us spoke, we didn't need to. We'd never felt this before.

The day had become rapturous. We were enchanted with each other, and later, when I was on top of him, as I lifted up and stared into his sparkling eyes, both of us overwhelmed with emotion, I burbled, "God must love us a lot, to have given us a gift this good." It was connection. Intimacy. Completion.

That was the transformation, a life-changing epiphany.

I hadn't known that such a moment was possible. It was the explosion of overwhelming new feelings. Joy, like a physical wave, surged up through my body and out my eyes in tears. I fell into love. I wanted to run out naked into the street and shout to the world what I'd discovered—that such a glorious ecstatic soul-filling connection was really possible. It was so silly that people could feel this good, I had to laugh. In one of those moments of sheer exuberance, I realized just how emotionally impoverished the rest of the world had become. I babbled, "If Adolf Hitler had ever had sex like this, World War II would never have happened."

I mean, really, when you're feeling that good, that connected, that joyous, that delighted, you don't have room to hate.

Or feel ashamed.

Yes. That.

Remember the context of the time?

Outside of that sparkling moment, outside of that room, if you were gay, you were a target, deserving only abusive contempt. You were supposed to be ashamed.

Suddenly, that was over.

In that moment, that transformative, life-changing, soul-exploding instant of joy, that conversation evaporated in a shower of silliness. The question was no longer, "What's wrong with me?" The question was now, "What's wrong with them?" Why don't they know that this is possible?

Whatever happened after that, I was a different person.

In July of 1969, American culture held that homosexuality was a disgusting aberration, a detestable abomination, a sickness, a degenerate act. Straight priests had declared it a sin. Straight lawmakers had legislated it a crime. Straight psychiatrists diagnosed it as an emotional disorder. Straight people had defined the sexual attraction of millions of men and women as simply wrong.

All of the experts on homosexuality were straight—but nobody was asking gay people who they were or what their experience was.

But that day, that moment, that was where I began.

I had written stories. A lot of stories. But I hadn't sold any yet. Something was missing.

But after that day, after that moment, I began to write from my own experience. It took a while to find the words, I had to learn how to evoke the feelings. But I began to write about the joy of connection and the devastating pain of loss. I wrote about rage and I wrote about redemption. I wrote from my heart. The more I wrote from that place where everything had awakened, the more honest and authentic my writing became.

And eventually, I began to write about the gay experience as I knew it. I had to because it was necessary. Because it was part of who I am.

The first stories were tentative explorations. But that was because the entire gay community was still trying to figure out how to define itself. That conversation was occurring in an environmental vacuum. So was I.

Nature abhors a vacuum. The painter abhors a blank canvas. The writer abhors the empty page. Silence must fall.

The best of us, the ones who make a difference, the ones who set the standards of excellence for the rest of us—they go to the other side of the mountain, take a good look around, then come back and report what they saw, what they felt, what they experienced. That is the aspiration. That is the life.

The human condition is a vast continent, most of it still unknown. Each of us explores only a small part of it. There's so much to discover and learn. If there is meaning to life, then a large part of it has to be the search for meaning—until we learn that we can create our own meanings.

So this isn't just a collection of stories, it's the fragmented record of an incomplete journey.

And not just my journey, it's a reflection of the journeys of a whole generation of men and women discovering themselves, learning to say, "This is who I am. Deal with it."

I had my epiphany, and it still resonates in my soul. Gay men and lesbians, bisexuals, transgender people, and all the other categories—in the past few decades, we have created a cultural epiphany. Because we have created pride in ourselves, we have changed the world. We've made it a little safer. We've made it a little better. We've made it easier to have a golden afternoon of discovery.

Oh, one more thing.

About the title.

My favorite sandwich is a BLT. It's crunchy and sweet and savory, all in the same bite. My mother used to add slices of hard-boiled egg to what she called a "club sandwich." And, to be honest, this is one of the few sandwiches where even a smidge of mayonnaise is acceptable to me. But more than that, I like to add a shmear of guacamole. So that's the perfect LGBT sandwich, right? Lettuce, guacamole, bacon, tomato, and an assortment of other flavors too. Crunchy, sweet, and savory. Yum!

Here's the ironic part, a delicious smidge of salaciousness:

The word "avocado" comes from an Aztec word for "testicle" Guacamole is therefore "testicle sauce." I can't say that these stories are testicular—but a couple of them are definitely ballsy.

Enjoy.

—David Gerrold

The orphan trains ran from 1854 to 1929. There's not much about them in the history books, but once I learned about them, I couldn't get the images out of my head.

250,000 children were shipped west to escape the poverty of the overcrowded cities I started with that thought—and the darkness beyond. The story grew from there. The Magazine of Fantasy & Science Fiction published it in 2004, and it became a Sturgeon award finalist.

DANCER IN THE DARK

When Ma finally died, they said they didn't have a place for me and it wasn't safe in the city anymore, so they decided it would be best to send me somewhere west where I could live on a farm. They said I would like it. Hard work and sunshine. And I'd get over Ma's death in no time. You'll see. They said.

They put me on a train with a whole bunch of other tight-faced people and went away. The train sat in the station for half a day, all of us waiting scared, before it finally chugged out. It was cold and shivery in the car, and there wasn't much to eat. You could get a drink from the faucet, but the water tasted funny.

Out the window, there was a lot of smoke, and where there wasn't smoke, there was burnt-out buildings, some old, and some still smoldering. I never been on a train before, I thought they went faster than this, but no, this was all stop-and-go, mostly stopping and waiting. And when we did go, we went slow, like the driver was being careful to watch the tracks to make sure they was still there. Once we went real slow through a corridor of burning buildings.

I was stuck way in the back behind a family, sort of, with a couple of older sisters and a lot of young-uns, except they weren't a real family because they wasn't related. They was just traveling together, and the older sisters weren't sisters at all, they was just supposed to keep the little-uns together. The kids all stunk real bad, they didn't have any clean clothes, and they'd pissed and crapped themselves, more than once. And they cried a lot, trying to keep warm. So I just turned to the window and stared out at whatever there was to see, which wasn't very much because once we got away from the big towns, the dark was spread real thick in a lot of places.

Mostly the dark looked like black fuzziness floating in the air. I'd never been inside the dark, but I heard stories. Everybody heard stories. It's like being shoved inside a thick blanket, you can't see, you can't hear, you can't breathe, and you just stumble around blind. It has something to do with the dark making it hard for things to move, like light or air or blood through your veins. You lay down a couple miles of dark around something and nobody can get through, no matter how much tinfoil they're wearing on their head.

Somebody else said that the whole country was sectioned off now. Dark everywhere. The trains ran through special corridors with walls of dark on each side, just enough room for the tracks and nothing else. You could maybe jump off the train, it wasn't going very fast, but so what? You couldn't get through the walls of dark, you couldn't go anywhere except follow the tracks. So you might as well stay on the train.

Sometime in the middle of the second night, we got to our first stop and they took some of the people off. There was all kinds of dark here, all around everything, even above so we couldn't even look up and see the stars. We didn't know where we were. Even though everybody was real tired, they woke us all up while all these men in different uniforms came marching through. They looked like soldiers from five or six different armies. They pointed at people in their seats. You, you, not you, not you, yes, yes, no, no, and so on. Another man in a different kind of uniform, I think he was the train conductor, came running after them, shouting about how they couldn't just take only the workers, they had to take a balanced cross-section, otherwise it wasn't fair.

I was hoping they'd take me, I wanted off the train real bad, I didn't care where we were. I even asked one of the soldier-men to pick me, but he shook his head and said I was too skinny. I tried asking a couple of the others, but they ignored me, so I slumped back down and pulled my blanket up and tried to go back to sleep. There wasn't nothing else to do. I was hungry and cold and stinky and not feeling too good inside. But at least there was some empty seats now and if you had one next to you, you could stretch out.

We had two more stops the next day, one just before noon, and the other late in the afternoon. Each time, another bunch of soldiers came through and took off some more people. After the last stop, there was almost nobody left on the train so they made us all move to the last car. They didn't say why. But probly because it was easier to watch us all in one place.

When they woke us up again, it was still dark. Darkfield dark. I couldn't tell what time it was, somebody said it was 3:30 in the morning. They made us gather up all our things, I didn't have much to gather, and then they herded us off the train and into a fluorescent station. The light hurt my eyes and the room smelled real strong of that disinfectant they use everywhere now. There was a red line across the room and we weren't allowed to cross it. On the other side, there was a line of grumpy-looking people, farmers and townsfolk. I guess they didn't like getting out of bed at this hour either. They looked us up and down like we were something bad-smelling. I guess we were. Every so often, I sort of got a whiff of myself. I felt dirty and itchy, and I wanted a bath or even a shower. My feet hurt and I was shivering in my blanket.

The guy who looked like the conductor read a statement to the folks on the other side of the line, something about what they was agreeing to and how they had to treat us, stuff like that. They all looked bored, like they'd heard it all before. Then he read another statement to us on this side of the line, about our rights and stuff and how we didn't have to go if we didn't want to, but we couldn't refuse either. Which didn't make any sense.

And then they started letting people pick us. A big farmer pointed at one of the skinny girls and asked her if she could cook and clean. She nodded, and he grunted and said, "Okay, come along," and she picked up her little suitcase and followed him. There was a sad-looking man and woman, they looked at the two littlest children and whispered together for a while, and then crossed the line and picked them up and left real quick, like they feared someone wouldn't let them take the babies.

It went like that for a while, until there weren't many of us left. There was this hard-looking woman standing across from me. She looked like she'd been baked in the sun until all the juice had been burned out of her and all that was left was this dry crunchy thing. She was looking at me like she couldn't make up her mind if I was worth the trouble. Finally, she said, "Boy? Are you gonna work, or you just gonna eat?"

"I can work," I said.

She walked over to the conductor and they talked together for a bit. He shook his head a lot. I got the feeling that I wasn't the first kid she'd picked out. And maybe the other one didn't work out. But finally, whatever, she came back and pointed at me and said, "Get your things." And that was it. I followed her out through the big double doors to a dirty parking lot surrounded by dark. A couple of tall light poles showed a few cars and the building we'd come out of and not much more than that.

"You got a name?"

"Folks call me Em."

"Em?"

"Yeah."

"Short for Emmett?" she asked.

"Em for Michael."

"Michael, yes. That's better than Em. You can call me Miz."

"Yes, Miz."

She pointed toward a beat-up old flatbed truck. She tossed my duffel into the back. I started to climb up after it, but she opened the door for me and said, "Get in."

We drove west on a road that was lined with dark. There might have been stars above, I couldn't tell. We had headlights, but they was mostly useless. They picked out the line of the road and that was all. She didn't say much and I didn't feel like talking either. I was too cold. I bunched up part of my blanket like a pillow and tried to rest my head against the window. It was worse than the train. We must have driven two hours. By the time we got where we were going, there was a feeling of light behind us. Hard to tell though, with all the dark.

Then there was a hole in the dark and she turned right and then left and then right again, and then we came out onto a big gray slope leading up to an old gray house. Behind it there was a dirty barn that had once been red, real tired-looking and leaning to one side, like it wanted to lie down, like if you gave it a good hard push, the whole thing would collapse, except there were a bunch of boards jammed in at an angle, propping it up so it couldn't. The old woman pointed. "You'll sleep in there. There's straw for a bed, and some old horse blankets. You can wash in the horse trough. Don't bother the cows. I start milking at six. I want you up and mucking out the stalls every morning. As soon as the cows are turned out. There's a couple barrels of disinfectant. You keep those stalls clean, you hear? As clean as you want your own bed—or your dinner plate. It's almost six now, so wash yourself up, you stink like a pig. Then get started. After milking, I'll bring you a plate. Don't want you in the house, boy. Lord knows what you're carrying."

"Yes, ma'm."

She stopped the car in front of the house, yanked on the parking brake real hard, like she was angry. "You like eggs? You ever had fresh eggs? Don't look like it. You're thinner than a ghost. When was the last time you ate?"

"Day before yesterday. I think. On the train, they gave us some leather to chew on."

"Damn fools. That's no way to treat anyone. Even deepies."

"Deepies?"

"Displaced Persons. DP's."

"Oh." Remembered my manners. "Thank you for takin' me in. I'll work real hard for you, ma'am."

She grunted. "Damn right you will. No free meals out here. Well, don't just sit there. We got work to do."

After milking and mucking, we pulled down a couple of bales of hay from the loft and broke them open for the cows. There was only three cows and they looked kinda sickly, but I don't know much about cows, so they coulda been fine too. But they walked real slow and stupid, like some of the people I'd seen in the city, the sick ones that they'd herd away every so often. But maybe that's how cows are. One of them looked at me for a bit, but she didn't look dangerous or anything, I didn't think you could make friends with a cow, so I just kept on shoveling cowshit.

Then there was the chickens, there was too many to count, they kept moving around all the time, bobbing their ugly little heads and clucking like old ladies. Miz poured out some corn for them and they all came cackling up. They was funny to watch. Later, after they'd finished the corn, they wandered around the fenced-in part of the yard, scratching for bugs and worms.

The biggest part of my job was feeding the refiner. This was three or four big metal tanks in a row, all piped together like a connected series of garbage disposals. I had to dump all the garbage into it every day, and everything else that wasn't nailed down—old corn stalks, dirty straw, stinkweeds, whatever. I had to scrape up the chicken guano and dump it in, plus wheelbarrow loads of cow manure and pig shit. Miz had indoor plumbing, but we both had to use the outhouse, because it pumped right into the refiner too. The methane that came off the top was piped around to fuel the stove at the bottom. The refiner was a big stinky stew pot, simmering and bubbling, sometimes grinding and chewing. But I didn't mind working the refiner, except for the smell, it was the only time I was really warm.

At the far end, out came oil. Enough for the truck, enough for the water heater, enough to power the refiner for another few days. Sometimes there was even enough to sell the extra in town. What didn't get turned into oil, came out as mulch. And a scattering of metal bits and rock. The metal bits we saved for town. I had to check the refiner when I got up, twice during the day, and again before hitting the straw. Miz said if we had two more pigs, we'd be fat. But we didn't have enough corn to feed any more pigs. We were already too close to the bone, she said.

Out back of the house, Miz had a garden for vegetables, mostly stuff like tomatoes and potatoes and cucumbers and things like that. Some pumpkins and watermelons too. She also had a big patch of corn. Not a whole field, but enough to feed us and the chickens and even some for the cows. Like everything else though, the corn had a sickly look. "Hard to grow things when there isn't enough light for them. Not good for plants, not good for people either. Still, it's better'n dyin'." She sniffed. "One good thing about the dark, though. We don't get as many rabbits or foxes sneakin' in. They don't like the dark anymore than anyone else. But you still have to watch out for burrows, because sometimes they will dig under. Saturdays, we go to town and get whatever supplies they still got. Sometimes there's a movie, but don't be expectin' it. Sundays, we go to Meeting. When we get back from Meeting, you can have time by yourself. But you stay outta trouble. Stay away from the dark. Don't go darksniffin' like the last damnfool I had out here. And no, I ain't sayin' nothin' about that. And don't you go askin' no questions neither, if you're smart."

But I didn't have to ask no questions. There was plenty enough people willin' to tell me everthin' they knew. First time we went to town, while I was loadin' sacks of chemical fertilizer into the back of the truck. Town wasn't much, just a scattering of old buildings on one side of the old highway, like someone just dropped them there any which way. Surrounded by dark, of course. Only way in or out is through the corridors, that's three roads and the train tracks. So there's not a lot to see. Funny lookin' kid with a broken tooth comes up and says, "You Miz's new boy?"

"Guess so."

"You wanna be real careful. Not like Doey. She tell you what happened to him?"

"I know what I need to know," I said, pretending to ignore him.

"No, you don't. You're a city-boy. You don't know shit."

"I know enough to keep my nose outa other folks' business." I hefted the last sack in.

"You just stay out in the barn, boy, you know what's good for you. Come winter, she's gonna want you to come in and warm her bed, you'll see. Keep yourself, bad-smellin', that's what Doey did. Till he ran away—ran into the dark, he did."

Miz came out of the feed store then, saw the kid and her face got real fierce. He saw her the same time and skittered off like the rat he was. Miz came up to me and stared at me hard. "What'd that boy say?"

Already knew better than to lie. Miz wasn't easy even on the best of days. I just sorta shrugged. "He said you had another boy named Doey. He ran away."

"That all he said?"

"Yes, ma'm."

She sniffed like she didn't believe me, but she didn't push it. "Well, you stay away from that J.D. boy. He's bad news. That whole family is. Now get to work. Help me load all this."

Miz explained that the train had come through again, so today was a good day. Some of the stores had new things on the shelves, even some new magazines in the racks. Miz bought a couple, bought one for me too. "Readin' is good for you, as long as you don't do too much of it. Puts funny ideas into your head. You start daydrea-min', you won't get your chores done."

She bought me some new jeans and a couple of work shirts, a pair of boots and some thick socks. For herself, she stocked up on spices; she was starting to run low, she even bought a bottle of vanilla. "Might try makin' a cake or something. When was the last time you had cake?"

"Had a birthday party once, when I was little. My Ma bought a cake."

"Store-bought cake? Ain't the same. You get your chores done, I'll make you a cake so good you'll think you died and went to heaven."

Second time I heard about Doey was the next day at Meeting.

Meeting was a ways off, I couldn't tell how far, but we were driving for at least an hour, maybe more, down a long corridor of dark, all twisty, up and down, with a couple of sharp turnoffs into passages that felt even darker. When we got there, we weren't really anywhere, just a wide open space with an old school-looking building in the center of a hard-dirt clearing. The dark around was cut by seven different openings, but one of them was walled off with tall orange cones and Miz told me to stay well away from that one. I didn't ask why, she wouldn't have said anyway.

Inside, the room was gloomy, lit by kerosene lamps. No generator here. But it was warmer than outside and it was a chance to sit quiet-like and almost doze. It was kind of like church too, so you had to keep your eyes open. There were these old ladies up top all singin' real faraway and soft like they was a choir of angels or something. The music was real old-fashioned, but it wasn't too painful.

Then the mayor got up and talked about living the hard life and staying clean and trusting God and following the rules because the reason that things had gotten so bad was that so many people had stopped following the rules, and we'd all made a big mess of things, so now we had to do penance for a thousand years or more while we tried to put things back together the best we could, but the only way to do that was to stay away from the dark and follow the rules. He went on and on like that for a long time. Then there was some discussion of chores that had to be done in the coming days, including putting down some new dark lines just to the west. He asked for volunteers for a work crew.

After Meeting, some folks climbed back into their trucks and drove off right away. But most folks gathered for tea and little sandwiches and even a cake. It looked real pretty. And everybody stood around in their clean clothes and talked polite and pretended everything was going fine, which it wasn't, but nobody would say so, because nobody wanted to be accused of doing the devil's talk. But you could see it in their faces, all hard and narrow and pinched. The sandwiches and cake disappeared fast, some of these folks was hungry. Miz stopped me, wouldn't let me go to the table. She whispered, "You let that food be, son. It's not for us. It's for them that hasn't any. We have food at home. Some of these folks, this is their only meal today." So I went outside and stood around by the cars with the other men, just stood and listened.

"Hey you, new boy!" One of the men turned around and pointed to me. A big man. Beard. Overalls. A broken eye.

"Yeah?" I answered the good eye.

"You coming out with us, tomorrow? Help lay some dark lines?"

I shrugged. "Dunno. Whatever Miz says."

"Miz'll say yes. If I ask her. Can I trust you to work? Not stand around?"

"I can work."

"You have to promise to stay away from the bright. And keep your glasses on. And don't take off your silver. That's how we lost the other one. Whatsisname. Doey. You heard about that?" He peered at me.

Didn't answer, just sorta shrugged again. Safest way. Better to have them think I'm stupid than wrong. You can get killed being wrong. That's a city lesson. But it might be true out here in the dark lands as well.

"He don't know shit," said someone else. "Just another dumb city-boy."

"He can carry. I'll talk to Miz. We need the hands. Besides, if we lose him, nobody'll care. Not even Miz. She'll just hook another one off the train."

And that was how it was decided that I should work on the dark team one or two days a week. I think Miz was glad to not have me around so much. There wasn't enough work to keep me busy every day. Or maybe she was just glad not to have to feed me. Sometimes the food was a little thin, even at her place. There just wasn't enough light. Somebody said that made everybody sad all the time. Depressed, he said. And then someone else told him to shut up. That was the devil's talk. Next he'd be complaining about the dark lines and the lines were the only things keeping *them* out. And then somebody said, "Not in front of *him*," meaning *me*, and that was the end of that conversation.

A few days later, an old truck pulled up in front of the house and a couple of workmen I didn't know got out and paid their respects to Miz. She handed them a paper bag with a bit of lunch in it, nowhere near enough to feed one hungry man, let alone three, but it was all she could spare. I climbed into the back of the pickup and made myself comfortable among the tools and wires.

We drove for half an hour, through the town, up the old highway for a while, and then off to the right where the corridor ended in orange cones. The workmen got out then and we all put on heavy black goggles and breathing masks and shiny silver capes and heavy work gloves. Then we drove on. The driver steered the truck carefully around the cones and up the passage to where the dark lines simply stopped. Beyond the lines, the ground rolled away like a rumpled gray bedsheet. There were already two other trucks here and five other men. One of them had a map rolled out on the hood of his truck and he was drawing lines with a crayon.

When nobody was looking, I lifted my goggles just a bit and snuck a peek at the brightlands. Immediately, I wished I hadn't. It knocked me backward. It was like being slapped in the face with a red-hot splash. I stumbled into the side of the truck, I fumbled the glasses back into place. My eyes were watering, I held them shut tight and tried to wipe at them without being blinded again. I felt really stupid, then I heard the men laughing at me and I got angry. They could have warned me. But then, one of them, a big soft guy everybody called Tallow, came up and put a black cloth over my head. He reached under the hood, pushed my goggles back, and mopped my face with a damp rag. It smelled faintly of disinfectant. He said quietly, "Don't take it bad. You only done what everybody else here did their first time too. We was all watching you. You got it over with quick. Now that you've seen a little bit of what's out there, you know what we all got to be careful about. Your eyes will stop hurting in a bit."

"You looked too, your first time?"

"Yep. Worse than you. I wasn't much older than you neither. I went out with my cousins, they said it wasn't nothing to be afraid of, you just take off the gloomies and look, see? So I did. That was real stupid. I stepped in it as deep as anyone could. It was most of an hour before I could see again. You got off easy, boy." Then he leaned in close and whispered, "It was real pretty, wasn't it? After a while, you're gonna start thinking that you'd like to take another look. Don't you be tempted, you hear? Don't you even think about it."

"I won't," I said. "I really truly won't." And I meant it. My eyes were still hurting bad. But then, I asked, "What was all that? What did I see?"

"You never mind that. It wasn't nothing."

"It must have been something. It damn near knocked me down."

"Don't you get too curious, boy. It ain't safe. You just follow the rules."

"Just tell me what it was, that's all. So I'll know. And then I won't ever ask again. Promise."

Tallow sighed. "You can't ever talk about this to anyone, you hear? You're not supposed to know. Nobody is. They don't want folks going out to see it for themselves." He lowered his voice. "They call it colors. It's what happens when light gets too bright. Your brain can't handle it. It's called overload or something like that. It's a little piece of madness, is what it is. You don't want to get sucked into it. You won't never get back. You'll just wander out there into the brights and die of your own hallucinations. That's what happened to — never mind."

"Doey?"

"Yeah, that was his name. Damn fool was too smart for his own good. Don't you go getting too smart now, you hear? You just keep remembering how much your face hurt."

"I will."

"You do that. Now that you know, you keep your gloomies on, you hear? And that breathing mask too, so you can't smell anything either. The air is just as bad. And don't say nothing to no one. No matter what. If you know what's good for you."

Tallow felt around under the hood, pulled my goggles back down over my eyes, and then made me to check to see that they were properly seated. And the breathing mask too. When we were both satisfied, he pulled off the hood. I blinked and looked around. Everything was safely gray again. As long as I didn't think about what was really out there, I was okay. As long as I didn't say what I'd seen, I was okay. I didn't even tell Tallow about the after-image still burning in my eyes. It looked like a naked boy. But he wasn't there when I put the gloomies back on, and I looked around everywhere. And I didn't tell him about the honey-smell either. Through the glasses, the brightlands looked flat and hard and empty. But I didn't have a lot of time for looking. There was too much work to do.

Putting down darklines wasn't hard. Just tedious. Mostly, it was boring.

First, we pounded stakes. The stakes were heavy Y-shaped things anchored in an iron base. The base was pointed like a bee sting. It had to be pounded deep into the ground, three feet or more; then the long leg of the Y part was stuck all the way into it. Then, after all the stakes were in place, we strung the wire, hanging it from one stake to the next.

I didn't do any of the actual stringing, that was done by the others. They had the strength for it, I didn't. I held cable, feeding it out from a big roll so it didn't hang up while the crew manhandled it into position. They used pitchforks so they wouldn't have to touch the line themselves. It was a thick naked braid of wire. The outer threads were deliberately broken and frayed, so the line looked like it had silvery scraggly hair. The wire was supposed to be fuzzy, so the dark would be deeper and stiffer, so I had to wear thick gloves, because the frayed bits had sharp ends. Even with the work gloves, I still got a few pokes and jabs and had to pull a couple of wire splinters from the heel of my palm.

When it was lunch time, we all hiked up the corridor a ways, far enough so that none of the bright could get in, so we could finally take off our gloomies and airmasks. Even here, safe between the dark lines, it still felt too bright. Or maybe that was an after-effect. I didn't ask. There wasn't much to eat, and what there was, wasn't very good. Stale bread, dried up cheese, wilted lettuce. Everything felt tired. Still, it was better than hunger. There wasn't much talk among the work crew. Everybody seemed to have something personal to think about. I thought about the naked boy. Was he really there? No, probly not. How could anyone stand naked in the bright? We finished eating as quickly as we could and pulled our goggles and capes back on, then hiked back out into the bright.

When the line was all strung, it was a chest-high fence. Not enough to stop anybody or anything. Least, not until it was turned on. The end of the line split into three separate wires that were fed into a terminator box. They put a terminator box at each end of the line, then they threw first one switch, then the other.

I pointed at the line. "How's it work?"

He waggled his hand. "It's what's called a seduction current. Something like that. It's powered by ambient photons. That's a fancy way of saying it sucks the extra light out of the air. The more light it sucks, the thicker the dark it makes."

"But nothing's happening," I said. The cable hung limp between the stakes.

Tallow grunted. "It takes a while. In a month, there'll be another patch of land safe to grow on. It'll go to the Martins. They might be able to get some winter wheat in. Might be enough to make it to spring."

"Why does it take so long?"

"It has to be slow. Otherwise, it would only make dark during the daytime, and we need the dark at night too. It usually takes a month or so for a line to suck enough light to get up to full strength, but after that, it only gets darker and stronger. Some of the older lines around here have enough residual in them to go for a year or more. Enough time to replace them if they go down. We'll come back out next week and see if it caught. Sometimes the terminator boxes are bad." He stepped over and peered closely at the wire. So did I, but I couldn't see any difference.

"Can I ask you something?"

"What?" Tallow seemed annoyed, like he was getting tired of me.

"How does the line know how much light to suck? What you said about the older lines getting stronger — do they ever suck too much light? Could they make it *too* dark?"

"Eh?" Tallow squinted, suddenly angry. "Don't you go anywhere with that. We got enough talk already."

"I was just asking—"

"You was just asking too much. That's not safe, boy. Don't ask questions, just follow the rules, you hear?" He strode away from me, began loading his tools into his truck. The other men too. Like they couldn't be away from here fast enough. Pretty soon, we all piled into our separate pickups and headed back down the corridor. They dropped me back at Miz' place and that was that.

I worked on the line crews off and on all summer long, when I wasn't mucking out stalls for Miz. Tallow didn't talk to me much, probably afraid he'd already said too much. None of them ever talked to the city-boy, so I mostly kept to myself. Every so often, I thought about the colors I'd seen, I wondered if there was a safe way to look at them, a safe way to be naked; but I didn't ask those questions. I didn't ask any questions at all anymore, and I didn't answer any either. I pounded stakes and unrolled wire. One day, I looked at myself in the mirror, I actually had muscles. But I was still hungry all the time. And cold. Miz managed to keep food on the table, but it wasn't a lot. Sometimes we had cornbread. Sometimes just mush. We had eggs too, but the hens weren't laying regular. A couple of times we even had chicken. That was pretty good. We didn't starve, but nobody was getting fat either.

One Sunday, while we were at Meeting, one of the cows wandered into the dark; either she didn't have enough sense to keep away or maybe she was daydreaming the way cows do and the dark just pulled her in. She wasn't in her stall and she wasn't in the field either. I finally found her, ass-end sticking out of the dark, and went running up the hill to the house. It took both me and Miz to drag the cow out, but she was never the same. She wobbled on her feet. She looked like she'd been smacked in the face with a shovel. That night, she fell down in her stall. She wouldn't get up, so the vet came out to look at her. He did some doctor stuff, then took Miz off for a talk.

I didn't hear what they said, but Miz looked angry and frustrated. Finally she nodded her head. The vet came back into the barn and put the cow down. Put a gun to her head and *thump*, just like a street-killing, execution style. It took all three of us to jack the cow up with a block and tackle. We hung her by the hind legs and cut some veins to drain the blood. The vet opened up her belly and the organs spilled out onto a canvas tarp. Some of it, Miz fed to the hogs, the heart and brains and tongue, she put into a big tub for pickling. I got the feeling she'd done this before, especially the way she stripped off the hide and stretched it out for tanning. We left the cow hanging so the meat could age two-three days, you can't eat it right away, it's too tough; hanging makes it more tender. Two days later, the vet came back early with a couple of helpers, and we all started hacking and sawing. We were a week smoking the meat. We pickled some of it too, in great big jars. We didn't eat much of it ourselves though. It didn't taste very good. Like it was old and stale. Even when you put gravy on it. Miz said that was the effect of the dark.

Finally, on Friday, we wrapped and boxed everything we could. On Saturday, Miz and me packed as much as we could fit into the truck and she drove into town, where she traded that cow for hard goods, spices, and even some jars of fruit from somewhere up north. Some people would eat it, she said. Just not us.

Miz didn't take me with that day, she wanted me to stay behind, in case anybody came wandering by. Word was that some brightlanders had wandered through town recently and nobody was sure if they'd moved on yet. I hadn't seen them, but I'd heard about them at Meeting. They all wore long black capes, just dark enough to keep them from going mad, except maybe they were a little mad from all that time in the bright. And maybe they'd come through looking to see if there was anything worth stealing. Maybe they were out there now, just waiting on the other side of the dark. But I didn't think it was the brightlanders Miz was fearing. I think it was our own neighbors. Some of them were real hungry, even eating tree bark. Miz had a big pot of stew simmering on the stove for Sunday's Meeting. Maybe some of them folks wouldn't wait. So I stayed behind, sitting on the front porch, watching the chickens scratching through the remaining patches of grass.

Moments like this, I watched the dark. Sometimes, if you watched it close enough, you could see it move. It looked like it was flowing real slow, like a river of slow time. Sometimes it wasn't all dark, sometimes it was dark gray; that was mostly at night. The dark leaked. It couldn't hold all the light it sucked and some of it seeped back out. Just enough to make everything look like moonlight.

But the closer you got to the dark, the worse you felt, like it wasn't just sucking light, but life as well. Everything close to the dark looked bad, all dusty-dull and shabby, turning gray and old in the gloom. I tried to stay away from it, especially now that I knew how it worked. But there was something about it, something I couldn't explain. I always felt like it was pulling me into it. Miz called it dark-sniffing. I had to watch myself. I wondered if someday I'd get so lost in some dream that I'd wander right into it, not even realizing what I was doing. That's what happened to the cow.

That's when the colored boy appeared.

First I smelled flowers. Yellow and pink flowers. Bright red flowers. I stood up, looking around, wondering where the flowers were. Then I saw him.

He stepped out of the dark at the bottom of the hill and started up the path to the house like he lived here. I saw him instantly. He stood out like a flash of the brightlands. Where everything else was gray, he was all the different colors a person could be. He glowed like he was lit from within. He was gold all over. His hair flashed in shades of red and blond; his skin shimmered like sunset. He was shining and naked. I'd never seen anybody so beautiful. He could have come from the far side of the sky. Wherever he'd come from, I wanted to go there. I wanted to glow too.

He came all the way up to the porch. He put one foot on the bottom step, then stopped. I knew who he was. "You Doey?"

He nodded. He held out a hand to me, like inviting me to dance. I was real tempted to take it, he was so beautiful. But I didn't. After a moment, he lowered his hand.

"Was that you I saw in the bright?"

He smiled, a dazzle of happiness. I'd never seen anything like that. It just made me hurt with longing all the more. He was insane, of course. He had to be. How could he not?

"Do you talk?" I asked.

He laughed. A gentle chuckle of sound, like a shared secret. "Yes, I talk. I also sing. I dance. I laugh. Do you?"

Shrug. "I dunno. Never tried. Never had much reason to try."

He stepped up one step. He reached out with his hand. I took a step back. He drew his hand back, then took another step up, this time onto the porch. And this time, when he extended his hand, I didn't move away. With outstretched fingers, he touched my shirt, my chest. Through the faded cotton, I felt a hot rush of feeling, I couldn't explain. His eyes met mine. His eyes were green and blue and violet. Not the sad shabby colors of the faded flowers around the edges of the old gray house, but the glistening sparkle of the deep edge of the rainbow. His eyes were bright. Everything about him was bright. The touch of his fingers—it felt like he was pumping energy into me. I felt *alivened*. Was this the magic of the bright? Is this how people went crazy? I didn't want the moment to end. I wanted to fall helplessly into it, dissolving into a bath of color, just like Doey.

I reached up with my own hand, took his in mine, held it, felt the warmth, both strong and soft at the same time, released it, reached across and touched his chest as he'd touched me. Placed my palm flat against his hot and glowing body. There was nothing I needed to say, there was everything I wanted to say. There was perfect understanding and a thousand thousand questions. I'd never known a moment like this. Never felt a hot surge of feeling like this. I thought I was going to faint. Or fly apart in pieces.

"Yes," he said, finally.

"Yes?"

"Yes, you know how to sing and dance and laugh. You just haven't had a place to do it."

My mouth was dry as dust. "Will you—can you take me there?"

He smiled and leaned forward. Close enough to kiss. "When you learn to glow."

"How do I—?"

He touched my lips with a golden finger, silencing my question.

"Hush," he whispered. "Not yet. Not yet."

And then he whirled and spun, a twirl of light and color. He leapt and danced and flew, arms outstretched, all the way down the hill and back into the wall of darkness that surrounded the house. And then he was gone. Leaving only the fading scent of color. The afternoon was dull and gray again. I felt tears on my cheeks. Both joy and despair at the same time.

I almost ran after him, almost. Something held me back. All the words, all the warnings, all the gloom that wrapped the world. He was right. I wasn't ready to let go. Not yet. Not yet. Oh, that bastard boy of color. How did he do that? How could he flirt and fly? How did he live? Where had he gone?

Sank down into a chair, an old wooden chair that creaked in pain as it accepted my weight. A faded cushion, hard and flat as cardboard. What mad thing had just happened here? Damn that Doey! I hated him, I loved him, I envied him, I feared what he was, and I wanted to be him more than anything.

I was comfortable here. Working for Miz. Working on the lines. I was comfortable, wrapped in dark. I didn't have to care. I didn't have to think. I only had to follow the rules. I could do that. Okay, I wasn't happy, but I wasn't unhappy either. I was comfortable and after being hungry and tired and cold and uncomfortable for so long, comfortable was a good place to be. It was enough. I didn't need happy. Happy didn't exist anyway. Certainly not here. And then the glowing boy stepped out of the dark and looked in my eyes and touched my heart and left me gasping with desperation. Because now that I knew what happy was, now that I knew it did exist, how could I ever be comfortable again anywhere?

Now that I knew what happy felt like, I also knew I didn't have any. Instead, now I knew what lonely felt like.

Did he know how cruel his words were? "Not yet. Not yet."

I felt so torn up inside I didn't know what I felt. I put my head into my hands and started sobbing, I don't know why. Cried for Ma, cried for me. Cried for the whole stupid everything. Who made up this stupid world anyway? Why do we have to put down all these walls of darkness? What's on the other side that everybody is so afraid of they won't even talk about it? And why did I feel so awful?

After a while, I felt all hollow and empty. So I got up and went to the barn. Stood around for a bit, then finally started mucking out stalls. Not because I wanted to, but it was something to do. And if I didn't do it, Miz would have words, lots of words. I hated all her words. I just never knew it until now.

When Miz got back, she sniffed the air and looked at me sharply. "What happened here?" she asked.

"Nothing," I said.

"Don't lie to me, Michael. Something happened here. I can see it in your face. You're all hot and flushed. Your cheeks are red." She put a hand on my forehead. "You're burning up. You have a fever."

"It's nothing," I said. Maybe too loud.

She grabbed me by the arm and dragged me to the horse trough. "Take off your shirt," she demanded. I did so and she pushed me down to my knees, pushed me head first into the sour brown water. She picked up a horse brush and began scrubbing my back with it. I couldn't scream and I couldn't breathe and I was trying to do both at the same time. She yanked me up, gasping. Before I could stop myself, I called her all those words she'd made me promise never to say again. She didn't even hesitate, she just whacked me across the head with the heavy wooden brush, knocking me backwards. "You're still an evil old bitch! And beating me to death ain't gonna change that."

"You think I'm stupid?" Miz shouted. She was loud. "You think I don't see what you're turning into? You want to go out there and get colored? You want to glow? You want to turn into some kind of fairy-dancer? You want to die in delirium? Why do you think we put up all the darklines? Because we like the dark? You think we like being cold and hungry and miserable all the time? No, we do it because we don't have any choice. We have to protect ourselves. All of us. Even you—you stupid cityboy."

I didn't say what I was thinking. She made me feel angry. But what if she was right? Everything was all confused. If the dark was so good, why did it feel so bad. And if the bright was so bad, why did it feel so good? I pulled myself bitterly back to my feet. Already, I was trying to figure out how I could get away from here. I could probly get a loaf of bread out of the kitchen, maybe some vegetables, put them in an old potato sack or something. But where could I go? And how could I get there? Walk the roads? Maybe, but to where? And if anybody else came down the road, they'd see me for sure. No place to hide in the corridors. Follow the train tracks? Maybe. But where did they go? Just to another place like this. I didn't know. I needed a map or something. But there had to be someplace somewhere better than this. I shook the water out of my hair, brushed it back with my hand. My arm and shoulder hurt where she'd slammed me against the trough. My back hurt from the scrubbing of the brush. And my head was throbbing like a nightmare. I hurt all over. And I stunk of the foul water. And I was cold. Evening was coming on, and the dark was expanding.

Out in the barn, wrapped in a blanket, shivering against the night, listening to the wind scrabbling against the old wood, all the voices argued back and forth. Evil old bitch. I don't care what she thinks. This is sick. Everything is sick. These people are dying. I don't want to die with them. They're all sick and dirty and dead inside. I don't want to be like this. But there's no way out. It's a trap. All the darklines, all the rules, all the walls everywhere.

And just what's out there on the other side of the lines anyway? What's so horrible that you can't look at it direct, can't see it without being eye-poisoned? Doey wasn't wearing any gloomies. He was naked like one of those angels in the old books. He was as beautiful as a girl with long flowing red hair, but he was stallion-cut like a prize. He was both at once. I'd never seen anyone or anything like that. How did he live out there? How did he see without being blinded? What did he say? Learn to dance. No. Learn to glow. How do you glow? How do you learn? All those questions and nobody to ask. Nobody to trust.

Next morning was Meeting. I wasn't going to go, but Miz didn't take no arguments. She just told me to clean myself up, put on a clean shirt, and not go around smelling like a pig. But once we were in the truck, she did say one thing. She said, "I didn't want to hurt you yesterday, Michael. What I did, I had to do. I had to break the spell. You were all glassy. I had to dunk you in the water and scrub your back hard and smack you to put you in all that pain to pull you back from wherever it was you were drifting off to. I've seen that look before, saw it on Doey. Didn't act fast enough with him. He danced away one night. Ain't going to lose you too. I see you starting to glow, I'm going to beat you—not because I want to hurt you, but because hurting you is the only way to pull you out. You understand that, don't you?"

"Yes'm. Whatever."

We pulled up at Meeting early, but we wasn't the first ones there. Bunch of folks all clustered by their trucks, talking. They looked over as we drove up, and a couple of them walked over to talk to Miz. She glanced at me, then moved off a ways so I couldn't hear what they were all saying. I pretended like I didn't care anyway and wandered down to where the older kids were scratching in the dirt with sticks. J.D. was there, the kid with the broken tooth, the kid from town who'd first told me about Doey. Nobody had names out here, only initials. He stopped what he was doing, tossed his stick aside, and said, "You hear?"

"Hear what?"

"'Bout the Trasks?"

"What about them?"

"They went out."

"Out where?"

"You stupid, cityboy? Out."

"Oh. Out."

"Doc drove over to see if they was all right, if they had enough food. He had a couple spare bags of beans and rice. He got there, they was all gone. The whole family. Ever single one. Even the baby. And one of their fields was starting to glow. Big hole in the darklines—all snapped, like somebody cut 'em. Doc didn't have no gloomies. He got out of there fast. Scared-like. That's what I heard, anyway. They're going to send out a hunting party, I bet. Go shoot some bright-eyes. They're going to need every gun in town. You know how to shoot, cityboy?"

"I can shoot," I said.

"Then you'll get to go, for sure. They won't let me go. I already asked. They said I was too small. That's a damn lie. They just ain't forgiven my pa for losin' a gun last hunt. They say he stole it. But he din't. The brighties did. Turned it into something weird, I bet."

"How would you know?"

"I know lotsa stuff. More than you."

"Yeah? You think so?"

"I know so."

"Yeah? How do you know anything? You ever been out there?"

He shook his head. "Not gonna say what I know."

I wanted to tell him about the bright-eyed boy. I wanted to ask him if he'd ever seen the naked colors. But something told me that probly wasn't a good idea. So I just shrugged. Whatever. Drop it. Turned away, back to the others. More folks was arriving now. I hiked up the hill to where Tallow was standing, waited behind him for a bit until no one else was talking. He finally noticed me. "You want something?"

"You going hunting?"

"You got a gun?"

"Miz does, I think."

He scratched his neck thoughtfully. "Probly not a good idea. You being a city-boy. And we're going out deep. Miz won't like that. But maybe you can hold the wire at the safe end. Might could use you that way. You just don't say nothing right now. You talkin' about it just makes a bad idea seem worse."

Then Miz came over with Doc. He looked at me, took my chin in his hand, turned my head side to side. Looked into my eyes. Put a hand on my forehead. Asked me to stand on one foot, put my arms out, and shut my eyes tight. Stuff like that. Turned to Miz. "He looks all right to me. You probly got to him in time. But if you want me to wrap him in darkline for a bit, suck some of the brightness out of him, bring him by one day, and we'll give him a bit of treatment."

"I'll do that, thanks," she said. "You be in tomorrow?"

"Better wait till the end of the week," he said. "It's going to be a busy few days. Let's get this Trask business taken care of first. I think this lad will be fine for the moment."

Eventually, we all got inside and got settled, but nobody was thinking about Meeting. Everybody was still whispering. It was like the room was full of bluebottle flies. The mayor said that he was sorry about the bad news, everybody had probly heard it anyway, but he had to officially confirm it. The darklines had broken by the Trask farm and it looked as if the Trasks had been enchanted. And yes, there would be a committee meeting to decide what to do next. Volunteers should make themselves known to the usual folks.

After that, there wasn't much else to say, because nobody was listening anyway, so we broke up early. Folks didn't eat much, they was mostly too upset. The whole family was gone, even the baby. Not even bodies left for a proper funeral. Lots of talk floated around. Somebody was going to have to get out there and take care of the livestock. Miz said she could take the cows and the chickens if nobody else needed them, but she didn't want no more pigs right now. They ate too much. A couple of the other folks spoke up, laying claim to tools or dishes or furniture. Blankets and quilts. Pots and pans. A little of this and some of that. Eventually, it was all sorted out, who was going to go out and pick stuff up. Tallow opened his truck and passed out gloomies to the folks who were going to need them.

Miz collected goggles and masks for us and some capes too, shiny on one side, black on the other. And gloves, just in case. We didn't even head home, just straight out through town and off around the hill to the Trask place. I don't know how Miz knew the way. All the corridors looked the same to me, just narrow twisty roads through the dark. But I tried to pay attention anyway, just in case. Miz kept talking, the whole trip. She was angry about everything. "Should never have let the Trasks settle so far out, way out on the borders with nothing between them and the bright. Damn fool stupid idea from the start. And now a whole family is lost. And the farm. And it's not like we have families or farms to spare. Lord knows what shape the poor animals are in. Put your goggles and mask on, boy. We're almost there. And you put that cape and gloves on before you get out of the car, you hear?"

She pulled up short of the farm and pulled on her own cape and goggles and gloves and breathing mask. She pushed the goggles up on her forehead and inched the truck forward, a little bit at a time. I pushed my gloomies up just enough to see under the frames. We came around the last curve and there was the brightness leaking in around the edges of the broken dark. We both pulled our goggles down at the same time. "I told you to keep those things on. You're susceptible. You can't take any more chances."

We pulled up in front of the barn. It was old and saggy. It leaned to one side and it looked like it was ready to collapse, even worse than Miz's barn. Miz looked off toward the bright before getting out of the truck. Half the darkline was down, the dark just faded off into filigree wisps. Beyond, the fields glowed harsh and stark in our gloomies. Without the goggles, they would have been impossible to look at.

Miz made a clucking sound of disapproval. I followed her into the barn. There were three cows tethered, all of them lowing uncomfortably. Miz told me to load up the sacks of feed, while she set about milking the cows. Afterward, I loaded the cans into the truck. Then she blindfolded the cows and led them out of the barn, tying their tethers to the back of the truck. Then she went and found a stack of empty crates and we began collecting the chickens. Some of them were clucking quietly in the barn, those we crated; but others were lying stunned on the ground outside. A few were wandering around dazed. Those she picked up and swiftly broke their necks.

"Can't they be saved?" I asked.

Miz shook her head. "Too dangerous. Too much bright in 'em. This is better. Safer." There were a few little chicks too, all safe in the incubator. She put these in a crate, dropped a canvas over it, and I loaded the crate into the back of the pickup. We walked around the barn then, looking to see what else we could find. The two pigs in the back were both gone. Miz shook her head at that. "Probly ran into the bright. Pigs are like that," she said.

Then we saw it. The fourth cow. It was staggering, all glassy-eyed and confused. It looked bright—not as bright as the brightland, but brighter than it should be. Miz said one of those words I'm not supposed to. She went to the truck and pulled out her shotgun from the back window.

"Don't you want to walk it into the barn?"

"What for?"

"That's a lot of meat—"

"Nobody's going to eat this beef. It's sick. You want to get sick too?"

"Can't you have Doc wrap it in darkline and drain the bright out of it?"

"You can't drain it. Draining takes the flavor out. And you can't let people eat meat that's been brightened either. That's even worse. No, this cow is gone." She lifted the shotgun, moved closer, then moved closer again, until the barrel was almost touching the cow's skull. I didn't want to see it, but I couldn't look away either. The rifle flashed. The cow dropped to the ground with a thud. She stepped closer and fired the second barrel. Just to be sure.

Miz checked the house then. She wouldn't let me go in, but she came out carrying a pillow case full of spices and other things from the kitchen. Even a small jar of honey, I found out later. That was a surprise. The Trasks weren't supposed to be doing that well.

Back in the truck, barely inching along the road, not moving faster than the three tethered cows could follow, Miz started talking again. She looked old. Older than the first day. And tired too. Like she'd been drained a few times. "This isn't right," she said. "Letting cows and pigs and chickens and corn go bad like that. And all those vegetables. Nobody should have been out this far, with only one line of dark between them and that—that brightmare. Now look what it's gone and done. A family gone, a cow gone. Two pigs running loose in the bright. All those chickens. All that food. What a waste. What a waste."

It took most of the day to bring the cows in. It was a long drive and we couldn't go very fast. But we were back before dusk settled in. I was glad of that. I didn't like being out in the dark. Not any kind of dark at all.

I slept badly. Tossed and turned in the straw all night. Finally, just before dawn, I got up and walked out of the barn. I tried to look up at the stars. Once in a while, you can still see them, some of them, but not tonight. Everything was black. Just dim shapes of black against blacker. I thought about lighting a lantern, but I didn't want to wake Miz, so I just stood barefoot and listened. Nothing much to hear. Just wind. A lonely cricket. Not a lot of insects anymore. I heard that one in town. That was the real reason everything was dying. The insects couldn't get through the darklines. No bees, no ants, no bugs, no spiders, nothing.

Not even a glimmer of bright from over the hill. Sometimes you can see it, mostly its reflection off the clouds. But not tonight.

Finally, I went back into the barn, back to my straw. Pulled my blanket around me and just sat with my arms wrapped around my knees, rocking softly. I used to do that when I was little. I don't remember much from when I was little, we moved around so much. But I remember I spent a lot of time sitting in the dark and rocking. Sometimes Mom would come and sit with me, wrapping her arms around me, and we'd sit as quiet as we could, not making any noises, so they wouldn't find us.

Thought about what I'd seen. Everything. All the bright leaking over into the fields. Miz didn't know, but while she was milking the cows, I'd lifted up the edge of my gloomies and snuck a quick peek—not at the bright directly, but at the fields it was just creeping into. That didn't hurt so much. I could see the colors, all the dazzling colors, everything at once—the rustling golden corn in the field, the crisp green stalks so clear it was like they cut the air, the rich dark soil like a warm bed, even the sky above glowed blue. I'd never even known such colors were possible. I wanted to see more. But then, I heard a noise behind me and just as quick-like I pushed the goggles back down over my eyes. I didn't want to get caught. Not by Miz. Because Miz wanted to take me to Doc. And wrap me in darkline. And drain the bright out of me. Like the beef. Drained beef. "You ever taste drained beef? You won't like it." Maybe that's what's wrong with these people. They've all been drained.

But what if Miz hadn't made a noise right then? Would I have kept looking until it was too late, until I was sucked away into the brightland too? I wondered what that might feel like—to dance naked in the stars. To whirl and dazzle and laugh. Madness, yes. But even madness looked better than this life. Miz wanted to wrap me in dark and make me just like everybody else. My stomach rumbled and I wondered what people ate in the brightlands? Magic corn? Enchanted beans? I didn't know. Nobody knew. Anybody who knew hadn't come back to tell. Maybe they was all dead, lying bright and starved? Maybe the bright pigs was eating them. Maybe this and maybe that and maybe some of the other. Nobody knew. Or if they did, they wasn't saying.

Finally, I just rolled over, curled up and tried to sleep. Thinking about stuff doesn't do any good. It doesn't work. It just makes my head hurt. Enough. Enough already. I wrapped myself tight in my blanket and eventually shivered myself to sleep.

For the next couple days, Miz didn't say anything more about getting me dark-lined, but I knew she was still set on the idea. She kept giving me these looks. But maybe she also felt bad about having to do it, because she made some honey-corn-bread and cut me an extra thick slab with lots of butter. Or maybe she just felt I had to have my strength up so I could survive being drained. She didn't say. And I didn't ask. I was starting to think about running again. We still had the gloomies and the capes in the truck. Maybe if I could find my way to the Trask farm, I could go outside the darklines and cross the bright to some other place. Supposedly, the town council had some maps somewhere, but nobody was allowed to see them.

Tuesday evening, Tallow came driving up unexpectedly. He talked with Miz a bit, then told me to get into the truck. Tomorrow morning, we were going out to fix the darkline at the Trask farm. And maybe do a bit of hunting too. Miz sniffed unhappily. I could see she disapproved. She didn't trust any of this. She came right out and said it. "That boy's got too much bright in him. He ain't been drained. If you don't tie him down good, you know he'll just get sucked into the colors. I swear, you lose him and I'll skin you bad, Tallow, I will."

"Nah, you'll just get another one off the next train. Like you always do." Tallow grinned back.

Miz didn't think that was funny. She sniffed again in that funny way she had. "Oh, hell. Wait a minute." She went to her own truck and pulled the rifle down out of the back window, and the box of shells next to it. She cracked it open and popped the two shells out, dropping them into the box. She walked back over, and motioned me to open my door. She handed me the shotgun and the box of shells. "Don't you load this thing unless you need it. And you bring it back clean, y'hear? Tallow, you teach him how to use it. It's on your head now."

Tallow grunted and climbed into the truck. He pulled his door shut and put the engine into gear. We rolled down the hill and into the corridor of twisted dark. Tallow laughed. "Miz is good folks, but some folks say she's been drained one too many times."

I thought about that. It kind of made sense. "You ever been drained?" I asked.

"Most folks around here have. For their own good."

"Oh," I said.

"It doesn't really hurt. It just makes you queasy, a little. Like having the runs, sort of. After a couple days, the feeling goes away. And the bright can't get to you as easy."

"Did the bright ever get to you? I mean, before you were drained?"

Tallow's face tightened. "Y'know, boy. This ain't really anything you want to talk about. You don't want to go asking too many questions. Folks'll start talkin'."

"Just curious, that's all."

"Yep, that's all. That's what they all said. Just curious. You don't want to get too curious about the bright. You want to stay away from it. That's why we smacked you with it the first day on the lines — so's you'll know. You've seen all you need to see. Right?" When I didn't answer, he repeated himself. *"Right?"*

I shrugged. "Whatever."

Tallow stopped the truck with a screech. I jerked forward with the suddenness of the stop. He turned to me and grabbed my shoulder hard. "Listen up, cityboy. You don't know what you're dealing with here. That ain't a question. It's the truth. You don't know shit. So when I tell you how it is, I'm not just running my mouth 'cause I like hearing my jaw flap. I'm telling you what you need know so you don't get sucked away like all the others. We used to be three times as many people and ten times as much livestock and crops. Where do you think all those folks went? All those animals? They didn't listen and they didn't take care and now they're gone. You want to be gone too? Just keep asking questions. You ask too many questions, we'll open the dark and toss you out in the bright ourselves. This is for your own good, cityboy. If you want to live, you better learn to listen."

"I thought you liked me," I said. I didn't know why I said that.

"This ain't about liking. Even if I didn't like you, I wouldn't want to see you turn into one of them damn fairy-dancers."

"You've seen them?"

Tallow didn't answer. He let go of my shoulder and turned away and put the truck back into gear. I rubbed where he'd grabbed me so hard.

"You didn't answer my question."

"That's right. I didn't." Tallow didn't say anything else for the rest of the drive. That left me with lots of time to think about all the things he wasn't saying. I got the feeling he knew more than it was safe for anyone to know. And maybe he didn't want anyone else to know how much he knew. But it was only a feeling and he'd made it real clear that he wasn't going to answer any more questions of any kind. I felt bad about that. Because maybe if he'd said he'd seen a fairy-dancer, I could tell him I'd seen one too. And maybe then we'd each have someone we could trust enough to talk about it. Except I didn't dare tell him, because he might tell someone else; and he couldn't risk saying anything to me either, because I was just another stupid cityboy.

"We going out tonight?"

"Tomorrow. Early morning. But I don't have time to drive out and pick you up then, so you'll sleep behind the feed store tonight with some of the other boys. You keep your hands to yourself, you keep your mouth shut, and you don't ask any questions. I'll keep Miz's shotgun in my truck. No sense in having you shoot yourself in the foot, or anybody else either."

Behind the feedstore, it was just a big empty space under a sagging roof. A few bags of feed, here and there, just enough to make a rough bed. It wasn't much, but it was better than straw. Four or five others talking together, nothing important. I recognized two of them, but J.D. was the only one whose name I knew. They glanced at me, but didn't say anything. Just another cityboy, using up space, eating up food. I grabbed a stretch of canvas to use as a blanket and made myself comfortable off in a corner, away from the others. They had a kerosene lamp, but that was all. The light pretended to warmth, but the night was just as cold here as anywhere else.

After a while, J.D. wandered over, wrapped in a blanket. "Hey, cityboy. Can I sleep by you?"

Shrugged. Not yes, not no. J.D. pushed a couple of feed bags into position and stretched out on top of them. "You know something you're not saying." It wasn't a question.

I didn't answer.

"If you tell me what you know, I'll tell you what I know."

I rolled over on my side, turned away from him. I trusted him less than anybody. J.D. liked to talk, liked to pretend he knew stuff. Safest not to tell him anything.

"Aw, c'mon—"

"Fine. Okay. You go first."

"No, you," he insisted.

"Forget it then." I settled myself again.

Silence for a bit. Just enough time for me to figure out what was going on. They'd sent J.D. over to find out what I knew, if I'd ever seen anything.

A minute more and I figured out the rest of it. It didn't matter what I said. J.D. was going to make something up for me.

"Okay," he said. "I'll tell you. Folks keep seein' Doey. Miz's other boy. He's a fairy-dancer now. We're goin' out to find him. Hunt him down like a blind pig. That's what my maw says—"

I sat up and looked at him. "J.D. Go away. Get away from me. You got devil-talk inside you and I don't want to hear it. Get away from me or I'll punch you." I said it loud enough for the others to hear. That was enough. J.D. gathered up his blanket and went scuttling back to the others.

He hadn't told me anything I didn't know already. It wasn't that hard to figure out. Even the rest of it, the part he hadn't said. Not just Doey, but the Trask family too, if they were still alive. Anyone and anything in the brightlands. Didn't need to be smart to figure that out. Just scared and angry and tightened up inside.

But something about this didn't feel right. Going out and shooting people. Even if they were all colored. No matter how little you felt inside. Just fix the darklines, that's all. Put up more lines if you have to. But going out into the bright. That didn't sound like a good idea. Not for this reason, not for any reason. Not unless you were planning to never come back. I just wish I knew more about what was out there. But if anybody around here knew, they weren't saying, and it sure wasn't safe to ask.

Next thing I knew, Tallow was kicking me awake. "Time to go, cityboy. Move your ass." I rolled off the sack of feed onto the hard black dirt. It looked as dark in here as it was out there, but Tallow was waving a lantern, and that outlined everything in brown gloom. Two other men were kicking the rest of the boys awake. I didn't see J.D. anywhere. I pulled myself to my feet, scratching and aching and hurting all over. My stomach hurt the worst. "Is there anything to eat?" Nobody answered.

I followed them all around the building to the front, where six or seven trucks had pulled up. Somebody had set up a table with a big plate of hard biscuits and even some hot coffee, seven or eight men just lining up. I fell in line behind them, then got pushed even further back when three more arrived. "Wait your turn, cityboy. Let the men eat first." Pigs.

Bitter coffee and a couple of biscuits later, they formed up teams. I recognized most of the men from the darkline team, plus a few folks from Meeting. And a couple of the big stocky women too. Some of them had guns. This wasn't any darkline crew.

After a bit of discussion, people figuring out who was going to ride with who, that kind of stuff, Tallow pointed me toward one of the trucks, and I climbed into the back with two other boys. I said hello, but they ignored me. After a few last minute instructions, the trucks all headed out toward the Trask place. The headlights of the ones following us made an ominous line snaking through the dark.

We couldn't drive very fast, it wasn't safe, so by the time we arrived, the sky was just starting to show an edge of gray—or maybe it was the glow off the distant brightness. I couldn't be sure, and I wasn't going to ask. We stopped down the hill from the Trask place and safely behind the bend in the road, so no one would accidentally get a glimpse of brightness before they got their goggles on.

We bumbled around in the gloom for a while, while the Sheriff and a couple of others organized everybody into teams. I was pushed over to stand with Tallow. He was carrying Miz's gun as well as his own, but he made no move to give it to me. I wasn't sure why I was even here, nobody was talking to me.

Finally, everything was sorted out and we all put on our shiny capes and our gloomies and our breathing masks and we started off. We trudged up the last of the road, around the bend of the corridor of dark, and finally up the hill to where the ground was starting to glow. And beyond that, we could see where the glare was leaking into the air from the brightlands. Kind of like the dazzle of light from an open refrigerator in a midnight kitchen.

Two of the men rolled a cart with three huge spools of darkwire on it. For some reason, everybody kept close to the cart. Even though the wire wasn't powered, folks still acted like they were safer staying close to it. Once we got to the top of the hill, I looked around for the dead cow, but where I thought it should be, I saw only a hump, covered with little white flowers. We all waited while the Sheriff and his deputies looked out across the brightland through special binoculars. They whispered to themselves for a bit, pointing and nodded and finally agreeing. After some more conferences, the guys with the cart installed one end of the wire to a convenient post; they hooked up a terminator box to it, there was another terminator connected to the end of the wire inside the big drum.

Then, when that was done, we all headed out into the bright, with the cart leading and the men unspooling the wire as they went. We didn't install any posts, we weren't putting up a darkline. This was only a safety line. All you had to do was follow it back. You could do it with your eyes closed, if you had to. I hoped I wouldn't have to. Just the little bit of leakage around the edge of my goggles was painful.

Nobody told me where we were headed, so I just followed Tallow. At least, I thought it was Tallow. In the harsh glare, with all of us caped and goggled, everybody looked alike, all different shades of gray and white and whiter. To keep from stumbling, I spent most of the time watching the ground directly in front of me, following in the footsteps of the man I thought was Tallow. We hiked into the brightness where the ground turned white like salt—that's what it looked like through the gloomies; it must have been glittering gold without them.

We hiked through scorched fields, abandoned to the bright. An old dirt road cut straight through, but it was already starting to get overgrown. On either side, twisted trees groped in the glare. They looked like they were alive, their limbs slowly moving, waving, even reaching. We kept clear of them. And the bushes too—they looked like they were all burning. They were so bright, even the gloomies couldn't keep out all the color. They looked burnished with a hint of red and gold, like they were all wrapped in shivering flame. Everywhere else, I saw stalks of something that might have been corn once, but was something else now; they looked like torches.

None of this made much sense to me. How was anybody going to hunt anything in a place like this? Ten feet away, everything blurred out in yellow and white. It was like fog on fire. And nobody was saying much either. If they knew what they were doing, they weren't telling.

Finally, someone in front of me stopped and pointed. A couple of others stopped, so I did too. At first, I couldn't see what they were looking at, but finally I made it out, way out there, way beyond the place where the road just dazzled out, there was a tall old house, an outline of a house, a glimmering hint of a house. I guessed that was where we were heading, I tried to make it out clearer—but then somebody punched me in the back and growled, "Keep moving, bait." So I pushed on.

It was hot out here. Once, I tried looking off to the east, tried to see the sun, the source of all this brightness, but the gloomies just went black. They overloaded and shut down. And I had to walk blind for a few moments until they reset themselves.

Eventually, we reached the house. It was in a field of grass so bright that the goggles showed it black, they didn't even try to resolve it. The house itself looked like it was made out of glass. The walls had gone glistening and transparent, and all we could see clearly was just the structural outlines, the edges and corners. It looked like it had been here forever, standing tall and stately, with porches and gables and even a widow's walk around the front and sides. And a tall cupola. It was almost a castle. Even Miz's house wasn't this big.

The two men with the cart cut the wire and tied one end of it to one of the porch posts. Once they did that everybody felt safer. A few folks started to go up onto the porch, but Sheriff stopped them, said the house was off-limits to everybody. Except the lure.

Then everybody busied themselves, separating into three teams. Each team had a cart and a roll of wire. Each team tied one end of their wire to the porch, connected a terminator, then headed out a bit and waited. One team was pointed straight out south, the other two east and west.

Tallow was on the western team, but when I went to follow, he grabbed me by the arm and walked me back to the house. "No, your job is to wait here and make sure nothing happens to the wires."

"By myself?"

"Nothing's going to happen. You're perfectly safe. You have four active dark-wires terminating here."

"Then why do you need me to stay here? I thought I was going with you."

"I promised Miz."

"Then give me the gun."

"You won't need it."

"Then why'd she give it?"

"Stop asking so many questions. Go sit up on the porch. You'll be able to see farther."

"Can't see anything in this bright. Neither can you. And why'd he call me 'bait?' I'm the lure, aren't I?"

Tallow grabbed my shoulder. Hard. Just like last time. "Listen to me, cityboy. If we take you out there, you'll get sucked away so fast you won't have time to scream for help. You stay here because I say you stay here. And if you want to argue about it, we can tie you down with darkline. And that won't be just an hour of draining, it could be a day or two or forever. You want that?"

I didn't answer. Not right away. "You say nothing will happen?"

"Nothing will happen."

"You sure?"

"Get up on the porch. Oh, wait—" He fumbled under his cape, passed me a sack. "Here's some more biscuits and a bottle of water. In case you get hungry."

"How long are you going to be out there?"

"As long as it takes." And then, he added. "Probly back by afternoon, certainly before nightfall. We don't want to spend the night out here, that's for sure; this place glows in the dark. You just stay awake and make sure those wires stay tied." He started to turn away, then turned back. "You'll be all right."

And then he was gone. All of them were gone. They hiked out into the bright and faded away in the distance like wavering shadows.

Tallow said I could go up on the porch, but I wasn't sure it was safe. The Sheriff hadn't let anybody else go up there. But maybe that was just because he didn't want anything disturbed. What the hell. I put one foot on the glassy first step. It held. Another foot on the next step. It held too. One more step and I was on the porch. It felt yellow everywhere. Dusty yellow. And it smelled of sweet sharp lemons. Even through the mask. And honey. And honeysuckle. And green melons. It was wonderfully delicious. Could the men out in the fields smell it too? What kept them from ripping off their masks and rolling around in the delicious air?

And the sounds—now that I wasn't surrounded by hulking men with their three-day sweaty stinks, the underfoot crunching of dirty boots, the lumbering hooves of upright beasts, the clatter of machinery and the stink of gun oil—now that all of that was gone, I could hear the tinkling music of translucent leaves, rustling in the delicate touch of the breeze. The wind sang like a distant chorus, very faint and far away. Silvery insects rattled and buzzed. And now, much nearer, something soft and small kept calling, *"Hoo-hooo, hoo-hoooo."* I wanted to go looking for it, whatever it was—bird or cricket or owl, I didn't know, but it sounded like the voice at the edge of the world, but so close by now that I wanted to find it, wanted to peer over the edge and see what was there on the other side. It felt like it was just around the corner.

This probably wasn't a good idea, thinking like this. I wondered if I would be safer inside the house? Maybe inside, I'd be out of the wind and away from all the flavors sweeping across the fields. Cinnamon and musk and jasmine. How did I even know all those different scents?

The doorknob glittered like diamond. I turned it and the door swung open. Inside, the house was silent, still, and empty. No furniture here, only an empty shell, a suggestion of a life once lived, exploded outward into solar dazzle and flare. The windows glowed with the creeping brightness of the world outside. The light felt muted here. I wondered if it would be safe to take off my clothes and dance in here.

I wandered from room to room, touching each wooden or metal or glass surface. The doors, the walls, the glass of the mirrors. Everything tingled. My fingers caressed. I didn't remember taking off my gloves. I wasn't even sure where I'd left them. This wasn't good. I shouldn't be doing this. All the voices in my head were screaming. Run away, now! Grab the wire and head back into the dark. Don't get sucked away. But all the songs were singing even louder. The music whirled and roared. Come dance aloft, be free. Be clear. I cowered shivering under my cape. Eyes clenched shut against the fiery noise. The seductive smells of sweet apricots and cream and gently scented candles. Overwhelmed by influx, I held myself and counted, one and two and three and breathe and one and two and three and breathe—

No. No. I wouldn't succumb. Not going to get sucked away. Never. Ever. Didn't come this far to be a golden bird fairy dancer. All the walls are here for a reason. The carefully constructed dark, the comfortable black essence of nothing at all.

Upstairs, the house is wide open. Tall windows with billowing white drapes, open to the balcony surrounding the house. Outside, the view went on forever. So bright below, so clear up here. Out to the horizon, the sparkling fields, the waves of rippling air, the colors sparkling and dancing. If I take off my cape, I can feel it like the comforting radiance of the refiner. I stand, arms outstretched to feel the heat, the delicious soul-filling heat. It soaks into my flesh, heals my bones, warms my spirit. I giggle at the wash of sensation. I can feel myself glowing.

In the cupola, I twirl alone. Naked and free. Finally warm, and finally here. The frozen winter of my past retreats before the blasting sun. I thaw and come alive. Joyously alive. I laugh with silly pleasure. I am enchanted. The delight of heat.

Am I ready to see? Can I take off the goggles?

Here on the fenced roof of the cupola, the highest part of the house, I can see the world as far as the darklands, the carefully drawn boundaries of exclusion, every tiny little line etched into the face of the land like the wrinkles of time. The gloom of fear.

In the other direction, out toward the east, the south, the west, the land sparkles and shimmers. It dances with light and aliveness. Why would anyone try to hide from all this laughter?

I peeked under the glasses. It wasn't pain I felt, it was color, bright color, brightness overwhelming. It wasn't pain at all, just the sudden shock of coming alive after being dead so long. An awakening from the grave of gloom.

Lift the glasses slowly. Eyes ready to clench. At first, the dazzle startles. A splash of intensity. Hold my hand in front of my eyes — I can see through my fingers — I am translucent. Pink and gold and glistening. I have taken on the colors of the world. The crimson of my blood gives my skin a rosy blush. The blue of my veins resonates. I am a roseate glow of violet and vermilion. I lower my hand, and all the rest of the colors of the world flood in. All the smells and sensations. All the wonderful noises.

All the heat and the light and the delicious flood of everything roiling together in a cascading symphony of being.

As I focus, I see...*them*. They've been there all along. Waiting for me. I just couldn't see them until now. Laugh and wave in radiant delight. They recognize me as one of them now. The dancing one is Doey. The others, also dancing, used to be the Trasks. I can hear the children singing.

And then, without passing through the intervening space, I am down among them, laughing with them. A moment of pause. Doey and I, face to face. Can I dance with you now? What a silly question. We're already dancing.

There are men with guns, hunting you. Hunting us. I wave toward the horizon. Doey laughs. He holds up the ends of the darkwires. The terminator boxes have been removed. The wires are dead—no, not dead, coming alive, infusing with clarity. Even metal can be bright.

Doey sparkles. Laugh with me and we'll dance the ends of these wires out to the distant south, out into the solar dazzle. Anyone who follows these lines will end up enchanted in the luminous day. The men will either dance or die. Whatever they choose. Doey twirls and passes out the tingling wires. I join him singing.

I was invited to write a Sherlock Holmes story, one where he might have a case involving a famous person of the era. I chose Oscar Wilde. The first challenge was to evoke the writing style of Dr. John Watson, while still capturing the voices of both Holmes and Wilde. The second challenge was the research. The more I dug into the facts surrounding Wilde, Lord Alfred Douglas, and the Marquis of Queensberry, the more the story narrowed to a specific moment of time. The backstory of all these men put everything into a new light, and I included as much of it as I could in the story. And then, of course—but read it for yourself.

THE CASE OF THE GREEN CARNATION

Despite the impression that some readers may have gained from my occasional articles in the *Strand* Magazine that Sherlock Holmes and myself were regularly plunged from one frantic adventure into another, we actually spent many quiet evenings alone in our rooms at 221B Baker Street.

This evening in particular should have been one such. London had finally shaken off both the gloom of winter and the muddy storms of spring. The lengthening evenings of May promised pleasant opportunities to stroll through the awakening gardens of nearby Regents Park. I enjoyed these outings much more than Holmes. To see children shouting and running or young couples walking together and enjoying each other's company always restored my sense of balance in the world. It reminded me that not every circumstance must have a dire element.

While Holmes often grumbled that such walks were a waste of both his time and his energy, it was evident that the outings did bring him a measure of peace, mellowing his mood enormously. He often paused to examine the leaves on the trees, the insects, and even the occasional bit of discard.

Back in our flat, Holmes would immerse himself so completely in the latest scientific journals from Europe, and lately even America, that he would often forget to eat. While he read, occasionally arguing loudly and vigorously with what he felt was faulty logic on the part of one author or another, I would concentrate on translating my hastily scribbled notes of our most recent adventure into a much more detailed account. Usually, I forwarded the more interesting narratives to the *Strand* Magazine, but not always. Some cases, especially the most delicate ones, were held apart for my private files.

This case, for instance, the one I am about to relate, is one that I shall not allow to be published in Holmes' lifetime or my own. Perhaps one hundred years after we have both passed on, the custodians of my literary estate will feel it is appropriate to share this chronicle with an audience capable of a greater understanding.

As I said above, we were spending a quiet evening in our rooms, not by choice however. May had brought warming weather, but also a quite unexpected and horrendous thunderstorm of astonishing proportion. The unpleasant weather enforced a necessary confinement. We had a choice between keeping the windows tightly shuttered or open to the elements. Closed, we would endure the stuffy atmosphere of our enclosed quarters and the stifling heat of the roaring fireplace. Open, we would suffer chilly dampness and the first encroachments of a vague odor of mildew. This evening, unable to find a suitable compromise, we alternated between one unpleasantness and the other.

It was not the most productive night. Holmes had been reading a somewhat vitriolic commentary on Mr. Darwin's theory of natural selection, written by a certain archbishop whom I shall not identify, and it had put him in a very sour mood. Holmes had grown angrier and angrier as he read, finally throwing the magazine into the fire with a furious outburst. "What unmitigated nonsense," he declared loudly. "The man is illiterate in the ways and means of science. He should stick to his wine and wafers, lest he hurt himself trying to think."

To soothe himself and restore his emotional balance, he took up his violin and attempted a thoughtful exploration of Camille Saint-Saens' Violin Concerto No. 2. Although written in 1858, it had been presented to the public only recently. Holmes had been deeply affected by the same composer's third symphony which made effective use of an aggressive organ line in the fourth movement. Afterward, intrigued by the composer's melodic sense, Holmes had ordered the sheet music for the Violin Concerto directly from the publisher, but on this evening the incessant crashing and banging of lightning and thunder continued to interrupt his concentration, and when he finally threw down his violin in exasperation I feared for a moment that it would follow the unfortunate magazine into the fire.

My concern must have shown. "Watson," he announced. "There is nothing worse for the mind than the lack of challenge. We need a case worthy of our attention,"

"But we have been offered many cases," I remarked. "Inspector Lestrade has called several times in the past few weeks—"

"And none of those cases were challenging at all. The hairless man, the unkempt one-eyed American, the obsessive monk, the ill-mannered doctor—Lestrade could have solved those cases by himself. It might have taken him a few days, perhaps even a week or longer, but in every one of those situations, the author of the crime was obvious. The Inspector is getting lazy. He has become too dependent on us, Watson."

"Well, hm, yes." I busied myself lighting my pipe. "You may be right." It was the safest response.

"There is no 'may' about it." He hesitated a moment, listening, then remarked, "If I'm not mistaken, we're about to have a visitor."

I had long since learned that Sherlock Holmes was rarely mistaken. I gathered up my notes from the rather gory episode of The Fatal Lozenge and pushed them all into my leather case. I would have to put it aside for the evening, leaving the completion of the tale for another time. I had barely finished when there was a frantic knock on the door of our flat.

Without waiting for either of us to call out, Mrs. Hudson pushed in. "Mr. Holmes," she said, very crossly. "You simply must tell your visitors that it is *not* appropriate to call at such a late hour, and certainly not without informing me in advance."

Holmes and I exchanged a glance. "We weren't expecting anyone," I started to say, but Mrs. Hudson would hear none of it.

"Well, this *gentleman*—" She sniffed at the word. "—is quite insistent that he see you right away. I tried to tell him that you were busy and couldn't be disturbed, but he refused to leave."

Indeed, even as Mrs. Hudson continued to express her justifiable irritation, the unseen caller shoved his way into the room. "Sherlock Holmes?" He looked from me to Holmes, decided I was not the detective and addressed Holmes instead. "Apologies are tedious, so I won't bother. I have brought you a small conundrum to consider. Small for you, tiresome for me." He was an odd-looking fellow, dressed in an unconventional manner, such as one might see moping about in Leicester Square in the evenings. His coat had a broad fur collar that extended over his shoulders, and he wore a bright silk cravat. He was clearly an upper class man, but obviously one who had dallied with the fancies of the aesthete movement. He had a longish face, clear penetrating eyes, and a fair complexion, all surrounded by shoulder-length black hair parted in the middle. He wore a gaudy ring on the smallest finger of his left hand—and he appeared quite anxious.

Mrs. Hudson threw up her arms in despair or disgust, either meaning could have been assigned to the gesture, and returned downstairs. "I suppose I should thank you," the strange caller said, "but gratitude is generally tedious and boring. Only the most common people engage in it. May I sit."

"Please do, Mr. Wilde," said Holmes. "Would you like some tea? I'm certain Mrs. Hudson could not possibly be more annoyed than she already is."

"No, no, thank you. I'm quite fine, although I wouldn't turn down a spot of brandy." The anxious gentleman looked suddenly surprised. "You know who I am?"

I busied myself with the brandy while Holmes explained, "Of course, I do. You are Oscar Wilde, playwright and author, a gentleman currently held in very high regard in London's literary circles." Before Mr. Wilde could ask how Holmes had deduced his identity, Holmes continued, "Your hands are exceptionally clean, except that the index finger and thumb of your right hand are stained with various colors of ink, mostly black, but also some blue, purple, and green. This suggests that you do a great deal of writing, so much so that it has become difficult for you to keep your fingers clean. The evidence of the purple and green ink suggests private correspondence not part of your regular pursuits."

Holmes continued methodically. "You have an Irish accent, Dublin I believe, but overlaid with a hint of Oxford education. It is commonly known that the famous Oscar Wilde affects the attire of an aesthete or even a dandy, and speaks in phrases that reverse the normal course of language with the intention that the shock should be clever and entertaining. It is also known that Wilde cannot control his wavy hair, despite liberal applications of pomade. Now, here you are, your hair still damp from the storm, but shining with oil, some of which has dripped down onto your purple coat. You are wearing a brocade waistcoat quite lavish in nature, also known to be an affectation of the author. Add to that the overly sweet scent you wear and the well-remarked green carnation in your lapel, and the deduction was obvious." Holmes peered across at Wilde. "That was the easily discernible part. Shall I go on?"

Wilde lifted both his hands in an extravagant gesture of surrender. "You have me, Mr. Holmes. Fame is a much sought-after curse."

Holmes nodded in that perfunctory way he has when others acknowledge his skills. He added, "Yes, but even without the foreknowledge of your appearance, I would have recognized you. There was a very unflattering caricature of you in last week's issue of the *Strand*."

Wilde looked startled at the admission, then laughed out loud. "Oh, yes, that," he said. "How terribly clever of you."

Holmes was not insulted. "The obvious is what we overlook. Not all deduction needs to be intricate. In that same issue, you would have also seen Dr. Watson's report on the events surrounding The Willowdale Handcar and that would have called your attention to my skills at deduction, so you came to me not only expecting brilliance, you came demanding it—the same way that your audiences come to your plays. Should I have disappointed you? Would you disappoint your audiences?"

Holmes' words had their intended effect. Oscar Wilde, the extraordinary playwright, did not seem so extraordinary this evening. Indeed, he seemed quite abashed, one might say even humble. But he took the proffered brandy from my hands and downed it with a generous flourish, as if he felt obligated to live up to his flamboyant reputation. The immediate warmth of the liquor had its intended effect, because Wilde quickly recovered himself. He remarked, "I am quite grateful for any libelous effort. That scandalous caricature will have all of London talking for a week. Of course, then I shall have to do something else to keep them talking. Perhaps I shall sue someone. The only thing worse than being gossiped about is not being gossiped about."

Holmes waved that away impatiently. He peered across at Wilde, "Now then, as to the matter at hand. You did not come out so late on such a rainy evening to discuss your reputation."

"On the contrary, my dear fellow. Reputation is the only thing worth discussing. It is so ephemeral, one must make the most of it while one can."

Mr. Wilde's clever flippancies might have been appreciated in a more literate arena but in that moment I found him quite tiresome. Although grateful for the interruption in what had promised to be one of Sherlock Holmes's less notable tirades against the obstinacy of the universe, I was not at all amused by Oscar Wilde's extravagant pretense of shallowness. Clearly there was a matter of some urgency here and Mr. Wilde had yet to address it. "Now, see here," I interrupted. "This is all very amusing but—"

Holmes held up a hand to silence me. "Watson, please. Oscar Wilde has something quite urgent on his mind. Unfortunately, it is in the nature of his character that he must come around to it in his own way. In that he is not unlike most authors, holding out the pertinent details for as long as possible for the artificial creation of suspense. Mr. Wilde is not here on his own behalf or on behalf of his family either," Holmes remarked. He peered intently at Mr. Wilde. "In fact, this is a matter that you wish to keep quite confidential."

Wilde's expression changed. His whole demeanor changed. He sagged in his chair and seemed to become an entirely different man, one far more serious and without any of his previous affectations. Holmes's words had clearly struck home. "You are appallingly correct," he admitted.

"Of course, I am," said Holmes. "If this were a matter of personal danger to you or your family, you would have gone directly to the police. Therefore, this has to involve some aspect of your life, or the life of someone close to you, that you do not wish to expose to public scrutiny. A matter of personal extortion, yes?"

"That too is correct," Wilde said, this time without any attempt at cleverness in his elocution. He was not happy at having his dilemma so quickly unraveled by Holmes.

Holmes continued with uncharacteristic delicacy. "Now...the green carnation in your lapel. Men of a certain nature wear a green carnation to identify themselves to other men of the same nature, is that not so?"

Wilde allowed himself a rueful smile. "It was not so until I made it so. I chose the green carnation because it clashed so well with my purple coat. It became a signal of nature because others of similar nature chose to emulate me. Obviously, imitation is the sincerest form of style."

Holmes ignored the conversational tangent. "So I am correct. This is a matter regarding the intimacies that occasionally occur between such gentlemen...and if such intimacies were to become public, it would be a disastrous matter for all involved? Yes?"

"And their families as well," agreed Wilde. "The law is notoriously unkind in some matters...."

"Quite," said Holmes.

"Can I trust you, sir? Can I depend on your discretion? I would have to reveal to you certain situations that present no real harm to any individual, but which the law has defined as existing outside the boundaries of respectable commerce. I would need your assurance that this information will go no further than yourself and Dr. Watson."

Holmes sat back in his chair, steepling his hands in front of his face in a posture of thoughtfulness while he considered the man across from him.

"What you ask, Mr. Wilde, were it to become known, would severely damage my relationship with Scotland Yard, a relationship I do value quite highly, despite Dr. Watson's occasional published insinuations otherwise."

Wilde hung his head. "I understand."

"I cannot agree to any restrictions on my investigations, Mr. Wilde, nor will I operate outside the law. You do understand that I cannot and will not function in alliance with any criminal endeavor." Then he added, "But insofar as a case may be without physical harm or financial assault, a crime without a victim as they say, I will make every effort to respect the confidence of my clients. That is the best I can offer you."

"Then you will help me with this problem, sir?"

"I am contemplating it. I admit the situation intrigues me."

Wilde looked across at Holmes with desperate hope in his expression. Holmes continued to study the playwright's unraveled appearance. I surmised that he was arguing within himself the wisdom of taking such a case, one that would provide enormous intellectual challenge, but might also present some risk to his personal reputation, Wilde's own remarks about the ephemeral quality of reputation notwithstanding.

I had never known Holmes to consider his personal reputation as a factor in any investigation, but this was clearly a much different matter. He would be cooperating with what the law regarded as a secretive culture of continuing criminal behavior. As he had already acknowledged, such an involvement, were it to become known, would certainly damage his relationship with the Yard, so it was not his personal reputation that he would be endangering here, but his professional credential. It was an enormous risk—and that perhaps was probably what intrigued him the most.

But for poor Mr. Wilde, sitting opposite while Holmes continued to study him, the prolonged silence must have been unnerving. Finally, Wilde could stand it no longer. He spread his hands wide, almost a gesture of supplication. "Mr. Holmes, I am a clever man. Indeed, I am far more clever than I pretend to be—clever enough to recognize the difference between a precarious situation and a delightful one. I fear that my precarious situation has now become a deliciously delightful one, so much so that I need someone of your intellect to share it with."

Holmes kept his face deliberately without expression. I recognized that look. It was the closest he came to ever revealing his annoyance with someone. Wilde did not notice or he chose not to notice. Very curious. Was Oscar Wilde pretending to be more intelligent than he actually was?

The playwright leaned forward now, almost imploring. "Sherlock Holmes, I believe you are the only person in all of London capable of understanding. I have a situation rather more serious than a lost manuscript or a carelessly misplaced infant.

I rarely ask anyone for assistance, but after much reflection, it seemed obvious to me that you and your *companion*..." He glanced sideways at me with a meaningful expression. "...would surely bring a certain sympathetic understanding."

"Excuse me—?" I put down my brandy snifter. "What are you implying?"

Wilde looked at me surprised. "I am implying nothing at all, Dr. Watson. I'm saying it outright."

I came to my feet in outrage. "I beg your pardon—"

"Oh, please, do sit down, Dr. Watson." Oscar Wilde said firmly. "Your performance of indignation is unconvincing. I have seen far better performances among the speakers at Hyde Park corner. Certainly, you cannot be deaf to the whispers about yourself and the great detective. You are two gentlemen, sharing quarters together, acting as partners in all of your endeavors together. There are lifelong married couples behaving with less affection. Given your own accounts of your relationship in the *Strand* magazine, Doctor, even the most innocent of minds will have entertained the occasional salacious thought. Indeed, life would be quite dull without them."

"There is no such relationship between Sherlock Holmes and myself!" I was quite near to shouting now. "I am a married man."

"Yes, many of us are." Wilde said it with a knowing smile. He paused, carefully choosing his next words. "But...if the delicious hint of scandal is misapplied here, then the failure is yours, Doctor Watson. If you and Sherlock Holmes have never expressed your genuine feelings for each other, then you will have not only failed yourselves, but a great many admirers who simply cannot believe that two such magnificent minds are incapable of any passion beyond the pursuit of criminals. Surely, there must be more to your lives than the continuing quest for the most dreadful elements of society."

I turned to Holmes. "Would you please speak up!"

The great detective was already rising from his chair, holding up a hand. "Watson, please forgive Mr. Wilde his presumption. It is an understandable mistake. I will explain it to you later, perhaps." He turned his attention back to Wilde. "So where is it you wish to take us?"

Wilde looked startled. "How did you know I have a cab waiting?"

Holmes said, "It is not all deduction. A great deal of it is simple observation. The window was open. I heard the cab arrive. I did not hear it depart. Therefore...." He gestured to me. "Watson, get your coat. It's going to be a damp evening and if you catch another chill, Mrs. Hudson will take it out on me."

For reasons that will shortly become clear, I shall not relate the details of our journey nor the location of our destination, except to say that the cabby took us to a handsome neighborhood bordering a large greensward. It was, as I shall soon demonstrate, a very incongruous setting for the covert enterprise we were about to visit. Wilde told the cabby to leave us off at the bottom of the avenue and directed us around a corner to a much darker and quieter street, defined by dark hedges and overarching trees already thick with leaves. Whatever light might have come from the gas lamps on the street was immediately swallowed up by the surrounding foliage. It was not a foggy evening, the rain had marvelously cleared the air, replacing the ever-present haze of coal-dust with the cleaner smells of spring, yet despite the seeming clarity of the night it was still possible for a person to disappear into the gloom in a few short steps.

We arrived at the front of a house very much like all the other houses along the street, quite indistinguishable from any of them. "Say nothing," Wilde instructed. "No matter what you see or hear, keep silent until I tell you it's safe to speak." Wilde then escorted us both to the door and tapped quickly, almost furtively. A peephole opened and an eye peered out at us. It closed and the door opened. We were admitted to a dark foyer. A tall stern-looking man, dressed all in black, stood in our way. He had thin aquiline features. His black hair was combed straight back, with a distinguishing bit of gray at both temples. He wore a small ring on the last finger of his left hand, much like Wilde's but nowhere near as gaudy. He moved with deliberate grace, such as might be seen on the stage of the ballet. His demeanor had a quality that some would have called feminine, but no, he had a distinct air of masculine strength. The contradiction was immediately apparent and disquieting. He eyed both Holmes and myself with ill-concealed disdain, then turned back to the playwright. "Mr. Wilde, you are well aware that our membership policy—"

"—is quite tedious, yes I know." Wilde cut him off. "But these are not prospective members. At least not yet, anyway. They are my guests. This is the great detective, Sherlock Holmes, and his constant companion, Dr. John H. Watson, and they are here on a matter that affects the entire membership and very possibly the continuing existence of this club." Wilde turned to us. "This is Mother Clap, not his real name, but that's what he prefers to be called, and he runs this establishment."

"Hm. An interesting choice of words." Holmes nodded a greeting.

"I suppose I should say I am honored to meet you, sir," Mother Clap responded. "But to be quite candid, I am not. I do not want you here." He looked to Wilde. "But Oscar is correct. There is...a situation. Oscar, I thought we agreed that we would handle this ourselves."

Wilde spread his hands wide and inclined his head with a smile. "As much fun as it is to handle it ourselves, it's far more fun to have someone else handle it."

Mother Clap was not amused. He turned to Holmes and myself. "Come with me, please."

We followed the tall dark man through a series of lavishly-decorated rooms. Though not exactly to my taste, there had been no shortage of expense. The wainscoting was a dark-stained oak, complemented by richly textured red velvet wall-dressings, a look that had become popular in many of the finest homes since Queen Victoria had taken the throne. The paintings on the walls were mostly portraits of handsome young lords, none of whom I recognized, but based on the clothing styles, most of the portraits were at least a century old. The gas lamps were held in gilded sconces, of course, and here and there alcoves within the walls displayed various pieces of classical Greek statuary. Almost all were naked male figures or torsos, a few were busts, although one notable piece displayed two well-muscled wrestlers angrily caught in a most disturbing conjugation.

In one of the rooms, a pretty young man in an outlandish brocade coat and apparently nothing else underneath—at least that was how it appeared to me, the brightly-colored garment was sleeveless and open to the waist—sat at a piano pounding out an aggressive sonata. A small cluster of well-groomed men stood around the instrument, listening appreciatively. "Beethoven's *Pathetique*," I remarked. "An excellent performance."

Holmes glanced sideways at me and said, "Yes, I'm sure all those men are connoisseurs of the musical arts and are there only to appreciate that young man's skill at the keyboard."

"Of course. What else?" And then, I realized that Holmes' remark had been laden with irony, and as I realized *what* else, I flushed red with embarrassment and resolved to say nothing more, a belatedly wise but still practical decision on my part. Other rooms were arranged similarly to the first, with comfortable chairs facing elegant fireplaces and a variety of well-dressed upper-class gentlemen sharing brandy and cigars. Several of them glanced casually in our direction as we passed, then returned to their previous pursuits.

But one room in particular revealed a startling scene. I had just begun to suspect we were being led deliberately through the entire premises when we passed through a ballroom with a gleaming chandelier and a polished floor. To one side, a string quartet played an energetic Strauss waltz, but it was not the music that caught my attention this time. No—it was the dancers. They were all men, paired off in graceful couples, sweeping stylishly around the dance floor. Perhaps those men thought themselves sophisticated. My reaction was less agreeable. I saw the dancers as a grotesque parody of the higher manners of English fashion.

Holmes placed his hand uncharacteristically on my arm. "Watson," he cautioned, and that was enough for me to regain my composure. Despite the warnings of Oscar Wilde that we would see things that might startle or shock us, I could not help myself. I felt a continuing confusion, an alarming rush of conflicting emotions and feelings that I could not identify. I took a deep breath and realized abruptly that it was not the dancing gentlemen that bothered me, but the obvious pleasure they took from the exercise. These male couples were looking into each other's eyes and studying each other's expressions with the kind of intensity that a prospective groom brings to a serious courtship—an uncommon and unnatural interest.

But at last we arrived at a curtained doorway opening onto a secluded private study that apparently served as an office for the gentleman who called himself "Mother Clap." He directed us to an arrangement of comfortable red leather chairs and without asking, brought out a handsome silver tray bearing an ornate cut-glass decanter and several brandy snifters. He poured for all of us, including himself. Wilde reached immediately. I started to, as well, but hesitated when I noticed that Holmes made no move of his own.

"Thank you, but no. I need to keep myself focused on the matter at hand," Holmes said. He glanced around at the furnishings of the room and I knew his calculating mind was already discerning things an ordinary person would overlook.

I had to admit to myself that this room was much better maintained than our own disordered apartment, which was usually filled with scattered piles of books and papers, samples and specimens, newspapers and journals, bottles and jars and beakers, and various scientific tools and devices of all kinds, including my own medical supplies and instruments. Mrs. Hudson often complained of the messiness and the smells. The poor woman suffered from the terrible affliction of chronic housekeeping, a mental-illness that infected neither Holmes nor myself. Indeed it had often seemed to me that most men found more meaningful and important activities with which to engage themselves than the pursuit of trivial tidiness, so the exceptional elegance of this room, and even the entire establishment of which it was a part, struck me as somewhat unusual for a gentleman's club, even for a club of unusual gentlemen, but I did not speak the thought aloud for fear of giving offense. I was becoming increasingly uncomfortable. The rules of behavior here were beyond my experience.

Holmes, however, seemed quite at ease, unruffled by our surroundings and the uncommon behavior of the club members. "Mother Clap," he said. "That is obviously not your given name." Holmes took out his pipe and began to pack it. "The original Mother Clap was Margaret Clap and she ran a Molly house in Holborn from 1724 to 1726. The establishment was raided and three men were hanged at Tyburn for the crime of buggery. Sodomy has been illegal in this country since the Buggery Act of 1533. The act is still in force and sodomy is still a capital offense before the Crown."

"Hmpf," sniffed Wilde with a deliberate show of annoyance. "If this is how Her Majesty intends to treat her sodomites, she doesn't deserve to have any."

Holmes ignored the remark, never taking his eyes from Mother Clap. He finished packing his pipe and lit it carefully. "Your use of the name Mother Clap is a deliberate homage to Margaret Clap."

Mother Clap smiled. "Indeed, Mr. Holmes. You are, as your companion has represented you in his articles for the *Strand* magazine, quite knowledgeable. But I must admit a bit of surprise at your familiarity with Margaret Clap and her Molly house. It is not a commonly repeated history, except of course, among those who have a specific need to know about such things."

Holmes' reply was impatient. "It is my business to be well-informed. Particularly in this line of work, where I come into contact with all kinds of people from all classes of society. Were I to accept without question the judgments of society, I would be denying myself the opportunity of observing the actual facts in the matter."

Mother Clap regarded Holmes with skepticism. "Yes. Be that as it may," he said, "Oscar here has violated my trust in him by bringing you here. I am not at all pleased by this unwelcome visit. As a consulting detective, you are well-known as an asset to the law, in particular Scotland Yard. Your presence here represents an enormous risk to all of us. You could very easily put this establishment and all of its members in great danger. What is to keep you from reporting this house to your friend, Inspector Lestrade?"

"Nothing at all," replied Holmes, puffing on his pipe. "Nothing at all. But I see no reason to do that." He explained slowly, "For me to go to Inspector Lestrade, I would have to have evidence of that a serious crime has been committed. If I see no crime, then I have no evidence, and I have nothing to report. Does that calm your mind?"

"Not in the slightest, sir. I do know the law. I know it quite well. The simple existence of this house would be evidence enough for some people."

"Sherlock Holmes is not *some* people," I said, with ill-concealed annoyance. Holmes gave me a warning look and I fell silent.

Mother Clap put his brandy snifter down. He had not taken a sip. He spread his hands and said, "Whatever the case, you are here, Oscar is here, I am here. We are all at your mercy."

Holmes lowered his pipe and looked at Mother Clapp through the blue haze of smoke. "Let us attend to the immediate matter, the reason why Oscar Wilde has brought us here at such a late hour. Someone is being blackmailed. Someone important."

"Someone *very* important," said Wilde, with deep emotion. "Someone very important to me."

"Yes. That part was obvious." Holmes turned back to Mother Clap. "I need to ask you some questions."

"Please."

"Your establishment here—your club for gentlemen—you remain open all hours?"

Mother Clap nodded. "Our clientele prefers a later evening than one finds elsewhere. That service is provided here. This is a place where gentlemen may gather among those of their own kind and be free of the peculiar customs of the age. Here, we remember and honor the heritage of the classical age of Greece, a culture that recognized the profound relationships that can occur between men."

"Ah," I said. "That explains the statuary."

Mother Clap looked at me. "Yes. How very observant of you, Dr. Watson."

Holmes ignored the interruption. "And this club has been here for how long?"

"We've been in this location just under a year. Previously, we had a much smaller house in the West End."

"I see. And what is the cost of membership here?"

"It...ah, depends on the member. The young man playing the piano, for instance. He is here on what you might call a scholarship. But yes, our other gentlemen pay handsomely for the privilege of attending."

"And you have several members of the peerage among your clientele." It was not a question.

Mother Clap hesitated, considering his words carefully. "Among others, yes." He finally admitted. "Obviously, I will not disclose any names. Our members depend on my discretion."

"I have no interest in your other members," Holmes said. "Only the young lord who has not yet arrived." He nodded toward Wilde. "Our esteemed playwright's notable companion."

"How did you—?" Wilde started to ask, then stopped himself. "Of course. You are Sherlock Holmes."

"Thank you, yes. But it should have been obvious to anyone paying attention. This club is expensive. Your anxiety about the situation is palpable. A blackmailer would choose the greater target, not the lesser, therefore your companion must be someone with a much higher social status than yourself, a member of the peerage, obviously an heir to a title, otherwise you would be the subject of the attempted extortion."

"Excellent! Excellent!" said Wilde, obviously delighted. He looked to Mother Clap, "We shall have this resolved in less time than it takes to sneer at a critic." Mother Clap looked unconvinced.

"But Holmes," I asked, "Why do you say an heir and not the lord himself? How do you know that we're waiting for a young man?"

"Isn't it obvious, Watson? The blackmailer's target must be someone who has been careless in his behavior. A man with some years of experience would have a well-developed sense of discretion and would not be so vulnerable to blackmail. He would also be much less likely to be looking for an evening of this particular sport."

Wilde laughed. "You're confusing maturity with exhaustion."

Holmes ignored the interruption. "A young man, however, is much more likely to foolish and immodest in his behavior, assuming that his own lack of concern for public morality will be shared by others. If that's the case, then the young man might not realize just how much is at risk. Obviously, there is much at stake here or the blackmailer would have no leverage—so where is the real danger? That's the question.

"Let's consider. If this young man's nature were to be revealed, it would be an enormous disgrace, not just for a single season of gossip, but a permanent stain on the family name. Therefore, we are talking about a family with hereditary honors and rights. A shame of this magnitude would be disastrous. It's likely that the young man's father is still alive and the young man fears his wrath. And that is the threat the blackmailer has made—evidence presented to the parent, correct? The young man must comply or face disinheritance, perhaps even an exile to the Americas on a minimal stipend. He would lose everything that defines his place in the world, a house, a title, a fortune, various land holdings, and even a seat in the House of Lords.

"But perhaps we're dealing with a reckless young lord. Perhaps he doesn't see the danger, perhaps he doesn't care, or perhaps his relationship with his father is so strained that he wishes to strike back at him somehow. A public embarrassment would accomplish that, of course—but that personal foolhardiness would present a great danger to anyone closely associated with the fellow, wouldn't you agree?" Holmes looked across at Wilde with a questioning expression.

"Bravo," said Wilde. "Bravo."

"I am not yet done," said Holmes. "Perhaps the relationship with the father is more than strained—perhaps it has escalated into overt hostility. And perhaps the father has not only made his disapproval known, perhaps he has done so with great ferocity. And perhaps the son continues in his immoderate ways as an act of open rebellion. This would suggest he is not directly in line for the title, knows it, and has little care for the reputation of the family name."

Wilde nodded. "Quite correct, Mr. Holmes."

"Let me continue. The father in question is probably frustrated by the insolence of his son. He is likely a stern man with strongly held convictions about right and wrong, even to the point of publicly advocating strict standards of behavior for others. Because most people have a spotty relationship with rules and authority, this man must spend a great deal of time being frustrated and probably takes it out on those around him. He likely has a temper and may even be known for displaying his wrath in public. The most obvious choice would have to be the Marquess of Queensberry who has lent his name to John Graham Chambers' rules for boxing.

"But the Queensberry family has had a difficult history. Last year, Lord Drumlanrig, the heir to the title, died and the Marquess must have taken that loss very hard. There were rumors of an illicit relationship." Holmes steepled his hands in front of himself thoughtfully. "Given such a circumstance, the Marquess must have become deeply invested in the behavior of his third son." He looked across at Wilde, "So when may we expect Lord Alfred Douglas' arrival?"

Wilde was shaken. "Good lord," he whispered. "Is it all that obvious?"

"Not all of it is deduction, Mr. Wilde. Remember what I said about observation? Last year, a novel was published called *The Green Carnation*. Although published anonymously, many believe that the work is about you and Lord Douglas and was written by someone with considerable access to both of you. The words put in the mouth of the primary character have a style consistent with your own. The book is impudent, bold, and ultimately scandalous. So I am probably not the only person to put all the pieces together."

"And now you lower yourself to the depths of literary criticism?" Wilde said.

"No," said Holmes. "Let us call it the forensic of language. You have had an enormous impact on the world of letters these past few years—"

"Thank you."

"—and for that, you are paying a price for your celebrity. You have been careless yourself. For instance, there is also the suspicion that you had some hand in the authorship of the ensemble novel called *Teleny*, a work of considerable eroticism."

"Please," said Wilde. "It was *not* erotic. It was deliberately pornographic. What is the point of having standards of decency if you cannot violate them from time to time? But I'm surprised that you're familiar with the work."

Holmes shrugged. "As I have already said, it is my business to be familiar with all classes of people and all classes of criminal enterprise. Some time ago, I was asked to review the manuscript for the Crown to deduce the actual authorship of the work."

Wilde looked surprised, so did Mother Clap, but neither was as startled as I was. "Holmes, you never told me of this!"

"Forgive me, old friend. I did not wish to expose you to something that might disturb you so profoundly."

"I suppose I should be grateful," I said, miffed. "But I thought we were partners."

"And we are," Holmes reassured me. It wasn't enough, not at that moment.

"May I ask, sir?" Mother Clap studied Holmes intensely. "What was the outcome of your review?"

"Inconclusive. It was obvious from the difference in styles that several different authors were responsible for the work. It struck me as not impossible that Chapter 7 and a long passage of chapter 8 might have come from the pen of our playwright here. There were some interesting similarities of style, but when I considered the serious outcome that might befall any individual if I were to report that conclusion, I could not declare the evidence compelling enough to justify the accusation. While the exercise of literary detection may be a useful pursuit for others, but it is not my specialty. Perhaps my brother, Mycroft. He enjoys that sort of thing. In any case, Watson and I were shortly called away on another matter, you may remember, Watson—that messy adventure with the giant rat."

"Oh yes. Yes, indeed. Very unpleasant, indeed. Very."

"Upon our return, a letter was waiting, plus a cheque for full payment of my services. The letter stated that no further investigation into the authorship of the manuscript was necessary. No explanation was given. At the time I assumed that someone in authority had finally come to his senses, recognizing the whole matter as unimportant and not worth pursuing. I was happy to oblige. We had more interesting cases to pursue."

"More interesting than a chapter written by Oscar Wilde?" The author looked peeved. "I am wounded."

"One that was only *assumed* to be written by Oscar Wilde," Holmes corrected. "Unless you are prepared to claim authorship now."

Wilde waved the opportunity aside. "I think not. The world deserves its literary mysteries. Who am I to deny future historians the joy of conjecture? Imagine how impoverished their world would be if they were to finally discover the true author of the works of William Shakespeare. They would have so little to argue about. Although," he added, "I suppose they could make up something. That's what I would do. If I were an academic. I would do it for the sheer joy of confounding other academics."

"That might be wise," said Holmes. "No, not the creation of a literary puzzle. Those can be quite entertaining, if occasionally facile. True detective work usually involves gathering a great deal more evidence than ever suggested by Dr. Watson's superficial reports to the *Strand*. He makes every effort seem much easier than it really is. But no, the advisability of keeping your name a discreet distance from that pornographic book should be obvious. You are already under severe inspection and there are many in government who find even the hint of such activities to be...." Holmes paused, considering the right word to use. He frowned. The language was not well-suited for this discussion. "...lacking in the masculine virtues."

"You mean *unmanly*?" Wilde asked. He did not look offended.

Holmes nodded. "That is one word for it, yes."

"Tell me, Sherlock Holmes. What could be manlier than the total rejection of the female sex? What could be manlier than exploring the profound bonds of companionship possible between two men? You cannot tell me that you are unaware of how deeply two men can feel for each other. That some men feel that bond so completely and so intensely that they are able to actually express it—what could be manlier than one man honestly acknowledging his affection for another man? And if such affection crosses into the realm of the physical, with both partners giving and sharing pleasure, what could be manlier than that?"

Holmes opened his mouth to speak, but Wilde raised a hand to cut him off. "Yes, I know that there are many who believe that all relationships have a male and a female role and that a physical relationship between two men would require one of them to take on a submissive role. An *unmanly* role." Wilde nodded a small admission. "And yes, there are relationships like that among this community of men, where one partner seems dominant and the other submissive, appearing to all intents and purposes as a shallow imitation of the common masculine and feminine identities— but that is a hasty misconception, a profound misunderstanding. It is the submissive partner in that relationship who is in charge. By his compliance, he presents the dominant partner with the experience of power. It is a gift that is returned by the tender exercise of that power.

"But to suppose that the emotional relationship between two men is an imitation of the ordinary masculine and feminine roles is a supposition rooted in profound ignorance. Only those with no personal experience of what is possible would subscribe to such an unenlightened view. This is why I came to you this evening, Sherlock Holmes. I expected you to understand. Your relationship with Dr. Watson—it seemed evident to me that, between the two of you there must exist some of those same profound feelings and an intimation of the same profound relationship I have just described."

I was ready to speak up and tell Oscar Wilde just how wrong he was, but Holmes held up his hand and as always I deferred to his authority. "Watson, do sit down. That's a good fellow." He turned back to Oscar Wilde. "Mr. Wilde, I do believe that you are projecting your own feelings onto the world at large. Are you familiar with the term 'projection?' It is a psychological thesis proposed by Doctor Freud."

"The middle-aged Viennese Jew obsessed with sex? Yes, I've heard of him."

"Yes, that Doctor Freud," said Holmes. "He suggests that what we see in others is only what we see in ourselves. Allow me—" Holmes began to summarize. "Doctor Freud considers intimate affections to be the most profound of all human interactions. He has considered the matter of men who choose to be intimate with other men and come to the conclusion that while it is not an advantage, it is nothing to be ashamed of either. He considers it to be a variation of the sexual function. Personally, I am not sure that I agree with his assertion that it is produced by a certain arrest of sexual development. In fact, I'm not even sure I agree that it conveys no advantage. The advantage may very well occur as a strategically significant difference in perspective—just as Vincent Van Gogh's madness allowed him to see the starry night or the wheat fields of France in a way that shocked and startled those who could not see in the same way.

"It is my own feeling that Doctor Freud's error lies in seeing all human behavior as an issue of the mind, while ignoring the possibility of biological or chemical or even genetic influences. Charles Darwin has postulated that traits emerge and continue because they provide adaptive value to the species. So in this situation, I wonder if there might be many other factors that Dr. Freud has not yet recognized.

"One of the basic principles of good detective work, Mr. Wilde, is that we should not stop asking questions just because we have found an answer. It may be that there is more to any answer than is immediately apparent. Never mind that right now. My point is that I do not regard your nature as a disability."

Oscar Wilde was not taken aback by this remark, as I expect any other man might have been. He replied, "Thank you for that, Mr. Holmes. And I in turn will not regard the condition of you and your partner Doctor Watson as a disability either."

Holmes nodded. "My point, sir, is that you may be speaking from a position of advantage. Like myself, you stand outside the commonplace boundaries of society. Like myself, you have a perspective unavailable to those living within the commonplace."

"I have often felt that way myself," said Wilde. "The commonplace is boring."

"But—" said Holmes. "Your presumption about my relationship with Dr. Watson is as misspoken as the presumptions you just described that some people hold about the relationships between men."

"Nevertheless," replied Wilde. "I am not completely wrong. There is a genuine affection demonstrated between the two of you, whether you acknowledge it or not. In my view, the failure to acknowledge your affections is a disability." He looked ruefully at the empty brandy snifter still in his hands, then put it aside and continued in a much more serious manner, "I have lived with this all my life. I have listened to what all of the experts have had to say on the matter—but all of the experts who have had their say on the matter are themselves detached from personal experience of the issue, and so their remarks have to be taken as little more than eloquent but misguided guesses. Much of what they have had to say simply does not match the experience of myself and others who have shared their confidences with me.

"As for the possibility of the advantage inherent in the condition—I'm afraid that the current state of our society does not really allow for the exploration of that thought. However, if we look to the evidence of history, we can easily see that philosophers like Socrates and Aristotle and Plato certainly made their mark on our thinking. Painters like Michelangelo and Leonardo da Vinci have influenced our art. And even that Russian composer, the one with that squalid little Christmas ballet— I'm told his work has some pleasing effect on audiences. Perhaps the advantage is that because one is not burdened with the task of raising children, such a man is able to put the same energies into creative tasks. But Johann Sebastian Bach fathered twenty children and it did not seem to slow down his creativity. I myself also have a family and two marvelous sons, and yet I too have some small measure of creative ability—no, modesty does not become me. I have established a known measure of brilliance in the theater, so perhaps that thesis of advantage may not have universal validity. And it does not counter the hostility of society. Nevertheless, *my* point is that I do not trust the words of the experts. This is because I am an expert myself and I know that I am not trustworthy. Now then, shall we return to the specifics of this case?"

Holmes was not amused. "Oscar Wilde, you are not fooling me. Your cleverness conceals your true intelligence. What a shame that is. You have a genuine aptitude for examining ideas in depth. And with considerable passion. But your wit tends to eclipse your insights."

Wilde smiled broadly. "That is exactly the kind of compliment I seek. Thank you, sir. I would not want to be known as a wise man, for that would be a terrible burden to carry. It would keep me from saying what I think for fear of damaging my reputation."

"The opportunity to be wrong is also the opportunity to learn." Holmes' expression grew darker. "You speak of the hostility of society. Now I see why the inquiry into the authorship of *Teleny* was dismissed. It was no longer necessary. The publication of *The Green Carnation* made it irrelevant."

Oscar Wilde opened his mouth to say something, then closed it again abruptly. The conversation had turned suddenly serious.

Holmes continued patiently. "The book engendered a great deal of rumor, speculation, and unfortunate gossip. Despite having my energies focused on far more interesting puzzles, the book did not escape my attention. It was clear that the novel had a darker intention, a libelous one—so it would not have needed a great detective to predict this immediate situation. It has been simmering for a long time. The publication of this scandalous *roman a clef* has only brought the matter to a boil. That you have taken so long to recognize the danger is unfortunate. It suggests that you—as well as Lord Alfred—have been heedlessly inappropriate and others are taking notice. In their eyes you are no longer deliciously gay and carefree, you have now gone beyond the boundaries of acceptable public behavior."

"What other people think has never been my concern," said Wilde. "Quite the contrary. It is what I think that concerns them. That so many pay for the privilege of reading my stories and attending my plays shows that they have more interest in my thoughts than I have in theirs."

"So you say," said Holmes. "And that is why you have behaved so recklessly. Apparently, you made the mistake of believing that your celebrity conferred a degree of immunity. To a small degree, Mr. Wilde, you may have been correct, but it is a very small degree. You are finally and reluctantly acknowledging that. Why else would you have come seeking my assistance?" Before Wilde could offer another annoying quip, Holmes added, "That it is *you* who came to me, and not Lord Alfred—that is also revealing. It suggests he does not have the same concern as you."

I took out my watch and popped it open. "It is getting quite late," I said. "Perhaps he isn't coming."

Wilde shook his head. "Ah, Dr. Watson, you are a man of a much simpler world. Here, in this club, it is still quite early. Bosie, that is my name for him, will be here shortly or eventually. Either way it will be a surprise. Dear Bosie is an unrestricted spirit. He will not be controlled by simple machineries." Wilde indicated my timepiece.

I snapped my watch shut in annoyance. "In my opinion, that is a very rude behavior, making others wait."

"Yes," agreed Wilde. "That is your opinion. And a charming one it is. I'm sure Bosie will ignore it as elegantly as he ignores everyone else's opinions. Including mine." He turned back to Holmes. "Is that the sum of your observations so far?"

"Of course not," said Holmes. "Seeing as how Lord Douglas does not consider this attempt at blackmail as seriously as you do, let me continue."

A sudden noise from outside the room distracted all of us. A foppish-looking young man came bustling into the room, flinging hat, coat, scarf, and baggage in all directions, without any regard for where they landed.

Wilde stood up to greet him. "Bosie," he said, grabbing him affectionately. "My dear Bosie." He turned the young man to face the rest of us. "I want you to meet Sherlock Holmes, the consulting detective. And his... *companion*, Dr. John Watson."

Companion? I did not like the stress he put on the word. "I say," I said, but before I could say more, Holmes looked across to me with a warning expression. He slightly raised one hand as a signal to say nothing else.

If Wilde noticed, he gave no sign. He turned his attention to us said, "Gentlemen, please meet Lord Alfred Douglas."

Holmes rose and offered his hand. Reluctantly, I rose as well. Lord Alfred looked at both of us with ill-concealed skepticism. "A pleasure, I'm certain," he said as he stripped off his very expensive gloves. The tone of his voice made it clear he did not consider much of anything to be a pleasure. He looked around for a table on which to set his gloves, saw nothing close to hand, and tossed them casually in the direction of his coat.

"Ah, brandy," he said, going to the table. He poured an inordinate amount of liquor into one of the empty snifters. "Anybody else?" he asked. "No? Good. More for me." He flung himself down on a settee. "So who are we talking about?" he asked. "What did I miss?"

"We're talking about you, Lord Alfred," Holmes said, returning to his chair. The rest of us resumed our previous seats as well.

Lord Alfred looked across to Holmes as if seeing him for the first time. "Really? Why? Should I be flattered?"

"You're being blackmailed, are you not?"

"Oh, that?" Lord Alfred waved a hand dismissively. "Just a rent-boy needing a handout. Oscar will pay him—" He shrugged, drank deeply of the brandy, then added, "He always does. I don't see why he bothers."

"I daresay he bothers out of his affection for you."

"Affection? What a tiresome affair. Am I right, Oscar? It's about breaking the rules, isn't it?"

Wilde, who had been silent for a bit, shook his head—it was not a denial of Lord Alfred's assertion as much as it was a disinclination to answer. I could not tell if he was embarrassed by the young man's behavior or angered by it. I assumed it had to be anger. I found it hard to believe that anything would embarrass Oscar Wilde and Lord Alfred's demeanor seemed unconscionably boorish, but for no reason that I could see Wilde still seemed genuinely fond of him.

"Oh, Oscar—do say something. I hate it when you pout like that."

Wilde shrugged. "Rent-boys have a tolerable charm, but ultimately it's a tawdry distraction. They have so little to talk about." He was already fumbling in his coat. "How much does this one want?"

Holmes held up a hand. "Wait a moment, please." He turned to Lord Alfred. "Why should Mr. Wilde pay this rent-boy anything at all."

"It's a favor really," Lord Alfred replied, pouring himself more brandy. "I gave the boy an old waistcoat. Terribly out of fashion. Or did I sell it? I forget. But Oscar doesn't mind—"

"Excuse me for interrupting," I said. "Why should Oscar Wilde mind?"

"Oh, because he bought it for me. He would be embarrassed if I showed up to the theater in anything less than the latest style. He bought this coat for me—oh, where is it? That one—" He pointed toward the corner where the coat in question lay in a heap on the floor. "The boy is merely doing me a favor. I can be so careless. Oscar writes me the fondest notes. I think I have one here—" He patted his pockets. "Oh, never mind. Later. But sometimes I forget to empty my pockets. The boy wants to return the letter, that's all. He simply feels he deserves something for his trouble. And I agree he's entitled to a reward for his thoughtfulness. Nothing much. A small sum, really."

"How much is a small sum? May I ask?"

"A hundred pounds."

I'm afraid I let my surprise and my indignation show. "A hundred pounds is *not* a small sum!"

Holmes lifted his hand, this time in a gesture of caution. "Perhaps not to you, Watson. Perhaps not to most people. But we are not dealing with most people here. We are dealing with Oscar Wilde and Lord Alfred Douglas." He turned back to

Lord Alfred. "Mr. Wilde asked us here tonight because he felt that you were in some trouble. Apparently, you do not see the situation in the same light."

"The letters are irrelevant distractions. I don't know why you're making a fuss."

Holmes looked to Wilde. "The cause of your problem is clearly apparent. Lord Alfred neither sees the danger nor cares about it. But—" Holmes rose abruptly, a move I recognized. It meant that he was finally putting the last few pieces of the puzzle into place. "You are in a dangerous situation, Oscar Wilde. There is danger here. But not just for you—danger for everyone who frequents this Molly house."

Mother Clap looked up sharply. "Mr. Holmes? Really! Your accusation is unwarranted!"

"It's all dreadful piffle," said Lord Alfred. He turned himself away, faced the wall, and studied his brandy morosely. "This has grown quite boring."

Holmes stood apart, frowning in momentary contemplation, pursuing one last insight down the dark corridors of thought. When he did return to the conversation, his expression was severe. "Mother Clap, you are not the owner of this house." It was not a question.

The accusation startled him. He was immediately taken aback. "Why do you say that?"

"The neighborhood here is expensive," said Holmes. "The furnishings throughout this club are lavish. Everything, even your brandy decanter and the tray it sits on, and I assume the quality of the liquor as well, demonstrates an enormous investment of time and money. When we arrived, you walked us through the main floor of this building. I counted the rooms. I counted how many men I saw as well. Even if your total membership is ten times the number of men I counted, you cannot possibly be making a profit. The costs of maintaining this club in such a lavish style far outweigh even the most exorbitant membership fees you could charge. Anyone can do the math. It's a shame that none of your members have done so or the conclusion would be obvious. You have a silent partner."

Mother Clap took a deep breath. "I have an investor, yes."

"Precisely. And the identity of this investor is...?"

"I am not at liberty to disclose."

"There is no need. I already know."

"Sir?"

"There is an office, an agency, within the government. It engages in clandestine operations. One such operation occurred several years ago. It was not well publicized but I was involved in the effort, so I have some knowledge of how it went down. Do you know what a 'fence' is? It's a slang term for a man who receives and sells stolen goods, jewelry and the like. Oliver Twist's mentor, Fagin, for instance, was a fence. But the individual I'm about to mention was nowhere near as notorious. He was quite successful in his own quiet way and would have continued on for many years, had I not pointed out certain obvious pieces of evidence that Scotland Yard had unfortunately overlooked. Upon my recommendation, the gentleman in question was discreetly apprehended by Inspector Lestrade and given a choice. He could go to prison or he could return to his previous employment, but this time with an assistant, an undercover detective. Scotland Yard funded the operation. Stolen goods were purchased from thieves as before, but this time stored away as evidence. In less than a year, the Yard had assembled a comprehensive list of the most notorious thieves in London. One evening, all of those thieves were invited to a secluded warehouse for a party to celebrate the success of the season. The party was held not by the fence, but by the police—and as the guests arrived, they were arrested and handcuffed and quietly locked in cells at the back of the building. Seventy criminals were arrested that evening and the crime rate in London dropped for many months after. The operation was seen as an enormous success, and from time to time, it has been repeated as necessary. Let us call such an operation a 'honey-trap' because it is intended to entice those with a hunger for sweetness."

Mother Clap did not speak. His face had gone pale.

"Yes, you see what I am getting at. This place, this club, this establishment—it's a honey-trap for homosexuals, is it not?"

Still, Mother Clap remained silent. He folded his hands into his lap.

"Let me repeat," said Holmes. "Last year, Lord Drumlanrig, heir to the marquessate of Queensberry, died in a suspicious hunting accident. Suicide? Homicide? I was not called in to investigate, otherwise I would have the answer. There were rumors that Lord Drumlanrig had been having a homosexual affair with Prime Minister Rosebery, thus the suspicion of either suicide or murder. Those rumors would have provided all the motivation a secretive agency would need to set up a honey-trap, in this case a Molly house for the purpose of discovering the identities of upper-class homosexuals in London. Perhaps the original intention was a noble one—to keep the highest levels of government informed against future scandals, or even to provide a secure venue for such scandalous activities so as to keep them discreetly contained, but there could be darker purposes as well. Such a tool is easily misused. The same knowledge can also be used for blackmailing the clientele. No, not for money, but for political favors—votes, or appointments, or simply a bit of influence in the right places. Yes, there is very likely a dossier on every single man who has passed through the doors of this establishment."

Mother Clap had gone immobile.

"I am correct, yes?"

Mother Clap nodded. "May I ask, what gave it away?"

"Well, aside from the obvious costs involved, your name. Mother Clap. It's a brazen reference to an unfortunate history. Any endeavor that depends on discretion for survival would avoid such a direct reference. Only a honey-trap would want the connection and feel safe enough to make it." Holmes continued, "There is one person who funnels money to you for the upkeep of this house, correct?"

Again, a nod.

"And that person is—?"

"You already know who," said Mother Clap.

"Of course," said Holmes. "It would have to be John Douglas, the 9th Marquess of Queensberry, the father of Lord Drumlanrig and the father of Lord Alfred Douglas, Oscar Wilde's intimate friend. He is your contact. You pass your information through him."

"I do," Mother Clap admitted sadly. "Yes."

"So the Crown funds this house for its own purposes, but Lord Douglas has a purpose of his own—discovering the truth of the relationship between Lord Alfred and...." Holmes looked to Wilde. "I am afraid, sir, that the damage is done and may be irreparable. Lord Alfred is correct, the letters are an unnecessary distraction. You have already given Lord Douglas all the evidence he needs."

Wilde looked alarmed. He turned to Lord Alfred. "Bosie?"

Lord Alfred shrugged. "This is all very interesting, I suppose, if this is the kind of thing you're interested in." He paused for dramatic effect. "But I am not."

"You're not going to do anything at all?" I asked.

"Of course, I'll do something. I'll do what I always do. I will ridicule my father. Perhaps I will do it in public. I will call him a silly old fool."

"Oh, please—" said Oscar. "Surely you can do better than that."

"Of course," said Lord Alfred. "That will be the nicest thing I'll say to him."

Holmes looked to me with an expression of profound sadness, then he turned back to the two men. "Perhaps you should reconsider that course of action. Given the volatile temperament of Lord Douglas, what do you think he will do?"

Wilde looked surprised that anyone would even ask the question. "I doubt he will take it with as much aplomb as I would. Some people have far too little enthusiasm for their own denunciation. Condemnation from your child is marvelous evidence that you have done your job well."

"He will succumb to his own rage," said Holmes. "A man enraged is not a man in control of his actions."

"Then he will only discredit himself," said Wilde, brushing off an imaginary crumb from his sleeve.

"He intends to expose you."

"Nothing I cannot handle. I am Oscar Wilde."

"And I am Sherlock Holmes. I see things that you do not."

"Lord Douglas enjoys being angry. It is the only happiness he knows. Perhaps I will sue him and make him even happier."

"That would be a mistake, sir. You might find that your own behavior will not withstand the scrutiny of the court."

"I'm not afraid."

"Perhaps you should be."

"What is it you are advising?"

Holmes spoke slowly and carefully. "You have several options, sir. I would advise them all. First, you must break off your relationship with Lord Alfred Douglas. If you can. That alone will satisfy the Marquess' anger. Second, you must end your attendance at this Molly house. And third, you will have to be more discreet in your behavior. If you cannot do that—and it is apparent that you cannot—then you must remove yourself to a jurisdiction where your excesses will not incur the dangerous attention of the authorities. I assure you, prison is no place for a man of your nature. You should consider going abroad. I would suggest Paris. The French do not share the same English abhorrence of the love between men. You would not have to fear prosecution by the law."

"Sir?" Wilde held his hand dramatically to his chest. "You are advising me—Oscar Wilde—to be discreet? Surely, you jest. And failing that, you are advising me to flee? Whatever else I may be, and I am quite a few things, I am not a coward. If I were to do as you suggest, it would be an admission of wrongdoing. It would be an admission of guilt. It would be an admission of *shame*. No. I cannot and will not."

"Then I cannot help you, Mr. Wilde."

"Obviously, you cannot. I am England's most successful playwright. The Crown will not dare."

"I have given you my best effort, sir. I wish you well." Holmes gestured to me. "Come along, Watson. Our work here is finished."

"You may send me your bill in the morning," said Wilde, an obvious dismissal.

"No, I will not. You will need every penny you have for the legal battles to come."

Mother Clap started to rise. "I'll show you out."

"No need. We will see ourselves away."

I followed Holmes back through the maze of richly-decorated passages and rooms, until we reached the ballroom where men still waltzed in each other's arms. Holmes stopped and studied them for a long moment. "One almost has to envy them...."

"Holmes?" I asked.

"In the face of massive disagreement, they are still courageous enough to be true to their nature. It is a fleeting victory, to be sure, but a victory of the soul nonetheless. I admire their courage, I pity their destiny."

"Holmes?"

"Wilde was wrong," Holmes said abruptly. "Terribly wrong. And I fear he will suffer an appalling fate. He refuses to see beyond his own cleverness. He deprives himself of the wisdom of others." Holmes fell silent again. Then, abruptly, "And he was wrong about something else as well."

I waited for him to explain. At last he turned to face me. He looked at me as if seeing me for the first time.

"Watson. I promised you an explanation. Here it is. That some men do not express their affection openly does not mean it does not exist, nor does it mean that it is not deep and profound. For some men, the affection is so understood, it does not need a demonstration."

"Yes, of course. Of course."

"In such a relationship, a demonstration of affection would therefore be unseemly and out of place."

"Certainly."

"But that is not a denial of the affection."

"Of course not." I wasn't sure what point he was trying to make.

"Indeed, in such a relationship, the mutual trust would be absolute, no matter what the circumstance."

I nodded my agreement.

"So, Watson, looking out at this ballroom, listening to this music, still one cannot deny the emotional aspect of the circumstance—that this is a place where a demonstration of affection could be appropriate, even for those who do not need it."

"Of course, of course."

"So...if I were to ask you to take a waltz with me, your answer would be...?"

"Sherlock!" After the initial instant of surprise, I realized that this could only be another of his experiments. But to be fair, I had to consider his request in the context of the entire discussion. I looked into his face, his curiously expectant face.

"If you were to ask me to dance, Sherlock. Holmes, I would be honored by the invitation. But before I could say yes, I would have to ask—which of us shall lead?"

"I would, of course." Holmes laughed softly. "Thank you, Watson. That was all I wanted to know. Shall we take our leave now?" And he offered me his arm.

I wrote this in 1978 in angry reaction to a whole load of bullshit I had read somewhere about "disorders" and "choices" and "cures." Despite some nice words from editors, I couldn't sell it, so it's never been published anywhere until now.

THE CURE

And then one day, the last piece fell into place.

It was inevitable, of course.

There was the one piece and the other piece and they fit together in such a way that the shape of the piece missing between them was obvious and it was just a matter of time. After a while that piece was filled in too and they announced that they had found the cause of it. Well, not exactly the cause, because it wasn't something that was caused, but at least the reasons why it occurred. And why it expressed the way it did.

It was a little bit of this and a little bit of that; something in the genes and something in the hormones, something in the way your parents raised you and something in the way your head was put together too—but there was an equation now, and if all these little pieces came together in just that certain way, then you would be homosexual.

And that was the source of it.

Now that the elements of the equation were known, now that they could be measured as precisely as the distance to the known edge of the universe, or the diameter of an atomic particle, now that this secret was no longer secret, at last people could do something about it.

What they meant was—now they could "cure" it.

Oh, they were very careful to say that it wasn't a sickness. Even dysfunction was too strong a word. No, they were calling it "an expression of sexual attraction, brought on by the confluence of specifically definable conditions." But no matter—now that the conditions could be accurately defined, whatever judgment anyone might care to make was irrelevant. Because now it was possible to do something about it.

And they did.

Parents first. You couldn't blame them. There it was: "The Seven Warning Signs of Homosexuality." They could have their children immunized as easily as if it were measles or mumps or chicken pox. it was their duty. They only wanted the best for their children, that's all.

Some people argued that maybe it wasn't a good idea to tinker with biological destiny; we didn't know what the side effects might be. But there were people— politicians, religious leaders, even some limousine liberals—who argued that not all parents were ready or able to deal with a homosexual child, and they had the right to want the best for their children—

The best.

The implication being that everything else was second best.

And that's what this was really about. The right to feel superior to others. It didn't matter who or what the others were, as long as some folks could define them as different. Alien. Not as good.

I'm old enough to remember what it was like before, back when there was no definable cause. People like me could demand acceptance, because nobody knew for sure. So we argued that we were like every other human being on this planet and we were entitled to be who we turned out to be—especially when there hadn't been any choice in the matter.

But now that's not the case any more. Now there is a choice—they can fix it—so when I say to a person, "I'm gay," they look at me as if to say, "But why? Now you can be happy. Now you can be normal. Why do you continue?"

Shit. I've given up trying to make them understand.

The answer is Forrest. Forrest, with the childish face and the slightly receding hair, dustyred and frazzly. When he wakes up in the morning, all grumply and rubbing sleep from his eyes, he looks like Bozo the Clown.

The last time I saw him was in front of the University library.

I saw him across the grass, like an island in a sea of frozeninwax summer greenery. I called him, but he didn't hear me. I had to run across the lawn after him. He was wearing that corduroy Englishstyle hat he liked so much and a matching jacket, and when I came charging up beside him, breathless and looking perhaps a little like an overweight madman, he blinked in sudden recognition and said in surprise, "Why, Dove—?" But he did not smile, nor did he seem glad to see me, as if I was something embarrassing from his past and I knew immediately that he had become one of them. He had let himself be convinced. Converted.

He had bought the lie.

They were very persuasive. They hot-boxed him. They love-bombed him. They invited him to experience "a new way of being."

"If you aren't happy," they said, "we can change you back. But, of course, you won't want to. You'll feel so much more complete. That's part of the process—the sense of completion." And because so many of them were "formers" he listened. He trusted. They were very convincing, and I think, he wanted very much to be convinced.

I begged him, pleaded with him, cried on his knees for him not to go. I told him that this thing he was contemplating was wrong and horrible. Everybody feels broken inside; it's the normal condition of humanity—that paranoid sense that something isn't right.. It's the residual impact of the birth trauma, compounded by the submersion of the juvenile mind into the linguistic maps that our culture imposes on the experiential self, further exacerbated by the cascading angst of puberty, peer group anxiety, and adolescent depression, finally expressing itself in the adult as an unformed but impacted alienation—and that all those people walking around claiming to be "transformed" and "complete," that was the real lie. That false sense of self—that's not human, that's inhuman—they were all plastic pod people, wired for permanent slow-drips of dopamine and endorphins and God knows what else. They're in a conversion-induced haze of "I feel fine" and there's no room for any other emotions—like fear or grief or anger—even when the plane is crashing or the building is on fire.

"But that's what I want," he said. "They're happy. They are so happy. All the time. Is that so wrong? I want to be happy too?"

"But we're happy—" I argued. It was a desperate claim. Unconvincing. But I insisted anyway. "Forrest, our relationship is real. It's honest. All right; yes, we have fights. So what? That's part of living with another person. And making up is always so much fun—"

He shook his head.

I was raised not to cry. Big boys don't cry. Men don't cry. So I've never let myself cry. Not out loud. I didn't cry when my father died. I stood stiff and immobile as the casket lowered into the ground. And I didn't cry that time I was caught and beaten and publicly shamed. I stood stiff and immobile then too, not meeting anyone's gaze. They couldn't hurt me. Not inside, not where I really lived.

But when Forrest said he had a brochure from the clinic, that he was considering it, I went into the bathroom, sat down on the floor, wrapped my arms around my knees, buried my face in my arms—and wept. Forrest came to me. He sat down next to me. He put his arm around my shoulders. I thought for a moment that he had been so moved, so touched by my anguish, that he would give up the whole idea.

But no. He pulled me close against his shoulder, stroked my hair, and said, "Maybe we should do it together—"

A man my age should not have to cry on his lover's knees and beg him, but it happened and I knew no other way to show him just what he meant to me. I'd never poured my heart out so completely to anyone.

I asked him to reconsider, to remember all those times when all we had was each other. Remember, Forrest?

There was that night we sat up till four-thirty in the morning, just talking about all the different things we wanted to do with our lives. There was the afternoon we hiked up to the highest peak overlooking the city and sat there at the top, holding hands, looking at the view and then looking into each other's faces with such joy we could not believe we were real. And there was the morning I awoke before him and snuck into the kitchen and ruined his birthday breakfast and we laughed all the way to the restaurant instead.

And yes, there was that awful night he woke up crying and wouldn't tell me why and clung to me close, and when I begged him to share what it was that scared him, he didn't say anything for the longest time, and then finally, he blurted out, "I was thinking about our future," he said. "All our days together, and I realized that forever isn't really forever. Not really. What if something happened to you? I'd be so alone and lost, Dove. I couldn't go on without you, I couldn't!"

And I held him close and said, "Oh, Forrest—is that what's troubling you?" And he sniffed and shook his head and wiped his nose with the back of his hand, and said, "And then I started thinking what if I died first, Dove, what would you do without me, and I couldn't stand the thought of leaving you to be alone and hurting like that. The last thing I ever want to do is hurt you—"

I reminded him of that. He shook his head. This wasn't the same. He held me, not close, but firm, and looked at me with dreadful sorrow in his eyes. "That was then, Dove. This is now. I love you. I have always loved you, and perhaps I'll still love you, in whatever way I can, afterward. But they have the weight of proof on their side, and—and I can't go on like this anymore. I just can't."

And then, with words that stabbed like knives, he added, "I have to know what it's like to be normal."

There really wasn't anything else for me to say. I'd given him all the logical, rational, arguments. I'd given him all the emotional ones. I had nothing else to say. I said it anyway. "Forrest, don't let them cut pieces out of you. Don't let them take away the part that makes you special."

He listened, but he didn't hear me. And I knew he'd already made up his mind. He went into the bedroom and closed the door against me.

"Forrest, please—"

He opened the door again. "Dove, please stop. I'm sorry I brought it up. I knew we couldn't have a rational discussion about this—"

"Rational?!" I exploded. "What the hell is ever rational about two people loving each other—?"

"That's the point."

"Love is supposed to be irrational! Crazy! Wonderful!"

But he was right, I'd run out of rationality, and this argument ended the same way all the others did—with me thinking that we'd mastered the crazy part, but still missing the wonderful.

I argued that it was just the momentary bumps and bounces that occur when any two individuals live together, that we just hadn't learned how to finetune ourselves to each other; I tried to tell him that he was blaming the wrong thing—

But it wasn't enough. Not for him. One day I came home, feeling beaten and exhausted, having fought another small part of the good fight, another desperate piece of the neverending battle for truth and justice. I walked in, feeling tired and frustrated and very much needing his gentle voice and his comforting arms, and instead I found only his note that he would be gone for a week or so, perhaps a little longer, and I knew, even though he hadn't said a word about it for weeks, where he had gone, and I went into the bathroom and opened up all the bottles of pills and poured them all out into a cup and took the cup into the kitchen and took down a tumbler and filled it with alcohol and something else to hide the taste of the alcohol and then I went into the living room and sat down in my comfortable chair with the pills and the booze and I sat there and sat there, trying to order my thoughts and the more I thought, the more I realized that if I did do this, it would only prove everything they had been saying all along, that I wasn't normal, so I went into the kitchen and poured the pills and the booze down the garbage disposal and turned it on. It gurgled and clanked, it chewed for a moment, and then—appropriately—it died.

And now, here, Forrest was in front of me, the first time I'd seen him in six weeks and it was as if he had been resurrected from the dead, except he hadn't. I don't know why I thought he might still be Forrest. Perhaps I was foolish and desperate and silly, perhaps I still had a tiny piece of hope in my heart, but I looked into his eyes and it was like looking into a vacuum. Whatever had lived there in those beautiful bright blue eyes, that thing that had always struck sparks in my life—it was gone. I searched his face and there was nothing I could find that was mine.

In that moment, I hated them.

I swallowed and I said, "Forrest? Are you happy?"

He smiled, a warm genuine smile. "Yes, Dove. I am very happy." I searched his face—but no, if the expression was plastic, it was perfect plastic. I couldn't find the flaw in it. I had to believe it was real. It was real. I knew him too well—

So I smiled back at him, my reassuring smile number two, the one I hide behind while scrambling frantically for poise, "I'm glad. I'm really glad. Because I want you to be happy, more than anything. Whatever it takes, Forrest, that's what I want for you. Your happiness is essential to my own, you know, and even if that means we have to be apart, I can be happy knowing that you're happy—" And I stopped suddenly because I realized how stupid I sounded. It was true and it wasn't true, and we both knew it.

Forrest looked at me pityingly. "You really should go ahead with the treatment, Dove," he said. "It doesn't hurt. "Not at all. In fact, parts of it are very pleasant. You'll discover parts of your soul you didn't know existed, and you'll be surprised to find they're really very nice." He was so stiffly formal that I blinked in surprise and cleared my eyes to look again.

He still looked like Forrest. And he didn't. He was wearing the salmon sweater he had bought himself in one wild impulsive shopping spree in London, and his heavy wingtip shoes as well. He was looking quite dapper, but then, he always did. But, no—it wasn't Forrest, only a stranger who looked like him, but held himself so differently I couldn't imagine how I had ever mistaken him for my Forrest.

There was pity written on his face and hunger on mine. I wanted to hold him and I was holding myself back, but finally, I had to ask it, I said, "Forrest—tell me, is it gone? All of it?"

He looked puzzled.

"Do you feel anything at all for me? Do you remember—?"

"I remember," he admitted. "But Dove, it's like something on the other side of a dream. I remember it as if it happened to someone else, as if I wasn't there."

"And—" I had to ask, I had to explore the hole in my mouth where the tooth had been. "What do you feel now?"

"Nothing," he said. "Nothing."

The numbness crept up around me, but I pushed on anyway. "If I said I wanted to kiss you, Forrest, what would you feel?"

He looked uneasy, but he said, "I would probably feel nothing."

"Would you kiss me goodbye anyway?"

And he looked at me and asked, "Why?" Before I could answer, he said, "I have different feelings now, and these are the feelings I want, Dove. You have to accept that."

I leaned forward anyway and brought my lips to his, I touched my mouth to his and waited for his response. I pressed to him and I put my hands on his shoulders. He let me kiss him. He even let my tongue nip quickly across the threshold of his mouth, and yet, despite it all, he never kissed back, and when I broke away and looked into his face, all he said was, "I'm sorry, Dove. I'm sorry. I really am." And then he stepped back and looked down the walk, "Oh, I'd like you to meet Anne."

She must have seen, but she gave no sign. She was sweet and pretty and pleasant. Even as I hated her, I knew I couldn't hate her, I envied her. But I shook her hand and smiled. She said, "Oh, I'm so glad to meet you, Dove. Are you here for the treatment too? You'll be so much happier. Forrest is."

I looked at Forrest, and there was that look on his face, the way he used to look at me, but now it was for her. That smile, that sparkle—in that instant, if I'd had a gun, I would have killed them both, but no, I wouldn't, because that would have only proven what all those others had been saying all along, and it would be one more argument why the treatment should be mandatory. It was just a matter of time anyway. The bill was already moving to the Senate floor.

I'd have to renew my passport. There were still a few places I could go. But I hurt all over.

I said to Anne. "No, I'm not going to have the treatment." I turned and walked away. Behind me, she asked Forrest, "But why not?"

And Forrest said, "I don't know. There's a lot about him I never understood."

He was right about that. He never understood.

I wouldn't let them steal it from me. If I cooperated willingly with their soul-death, then that would only prove their argument—that it was never true love at all.

Maybe it is just a little piece of this and a little piece of that, something in the genes and something in the hormones; maybe it really is all those things they say—but whatever it was, I felt it and it was real to me.

They could take it away from Forrest and they could even take Forrest away from me, but they cannot take away the fact that it happened. They can deny it—I won't. Never.

But, Forrest, oh, damn you, damn you, Forrest—I'm so angry!

What magic lies within that we deny? Offer me a wild dance and rescue me from the dreariness of days.

THE GREEN MAN

The dark of spring. We were driving.

Michael and I and the smell of wet fog. A corridor of trees, a green gothic cathedral. A winding twilight road somewhere in northern California. Or maybe Oregon. Occasional headlights from passing cars, stabbing luminous fingers through the air. Neither of us talking. Nothing to say anymore.

Finally, he pulled the old Mustang over to the side of the road. We sat there in silence for a while. After a moment, he got out of the car. I wondered if I should follow. He stood in the middle of the road, arms outstretched as if he were going to embrace the inevitable logging truck that would surely run him down.

I sighed and got out of the car. I put my arms around him from behind, held him for a moment in a hug of peace, then walked him to the side of the road. He came willingly, he wasn't suicidal. He was just...whatever.

He stopped at the car. He leaned on the warm hood and stared at nothing in particular. "What's the point?"

I boosted myself up onto the fender, so I could sit and look at him. "What do you want me to say?"

He looked at me, a sour expression of annoyance.

"Michael," I said. "What can I say to you that you haven't already said for both of us?"

He shook his head and stared off into space. "It's not that," he said. "It's...everything else. What's the point?"

I shrugged. I could listen better than I could speak. That's why Michael included me in his life. I was his audience. I didn't mind. He was an interesting show—except when he got like this, which was about once a month. Or whenever something happened that he couldn't control.

I'd hoped that this trip would be a chance to get away from this, but somewhere between the first rest stop and the end of the beef jerky, it became obvious that we'd brought it with us and I was going to have to sit next to it for the next four hundred miles. Or longer. Because we weren't driving anywhere in particular. We were just driving to drive. Except when we weren't driving. Except when we were parked by the side of the road and Michael was staring off into space wondering why the universe existed in the first place. It must have seemed like a good idea at the time, but not to Michael.

"Maybe we should start looking for a motel?" I suggested.

He didn't answer. He was still looking into the trees. Finally I turned around to see what he was staring at.

A slender figure, silhouetted in fog. He looked naked. Hard to tell. He was just standing, watching us. A tableau. Michael and him—eyes locked. And me, looking back and forth between the two of them.

"Hello?" I said tentatively. I slid down off the fender, turned and waved. "Hello...?" To Michael, I whispered, "How long has he been watching us?"

Michael didn't answer.

And then I realized— "Oh, shit." I tugged Michael's arm. "It's one of *them*."

"Yeah," he said softly. I wasn't sure if he was speaking to me...or *him*.

"Get back in the car, Michael. Let's get out of here." I tried to pull him toward the door.

He resisted. "They're not dangerous."

"Then why did they tell us to keep away from them?"

Michael ignored the question.

"Remember what the Ranger said? 'If you see one of them, keep your distance. Don't try to talk to them.' Remember that?"

The man-boy stepped out of the fog. He was naked. And he was green. All shades. Deep green hair. Lighter green skin. Shiny green highlights. He shimmered in green. He had turquoise eyes. Piercing.

I was trying to remember everything the Ranger had said. "You're entering a restricted area. For the next fifty miles, don't stop. Just drive straight through." He'd given us a pamphlet, one of those not-very-informative government things that explained about the reservation. The elves, the morphs, the greenies, the forest dancers, *them*. They weren't dangerous. Mostly they stayed away from people. Only sometimes they didn't.

Sometimes people went looking for them. Out of curiosity. Or to study them. Or to take their pictures. Or even to hunt them, trap them, hurt them—because they weren't likely to fight back. But sometimes, the people who went looking for them didn't come back.

Every so often, there'd be an article in the news. Someone else's abandoned car had been found. Or their clothes. Or there'd be stories about another green person seen dancing in the forest. The Rangers tried to keep a tally of them, but they were the first to admit they had no idea how many faerie folk were in the hills. But the number was growing.

The green boy was closer now. He moved with the grace of a breeze. He stepped onto the roadway just in front of the car. He looked to us expectantly.

"Michael, please—? Let's get out of here."

"Wait—"

"Michael, this is freaking me out."

Michael turned to look at me. "Jay. Nothing's going to happen. It's just a green boy. I want to see. Relax. You're not going to end up dancing with moonbeams. I won't let it happen." He turned back to the man-boy. They were close enough to touch. I felt like an outsider in my own life.

The boy reached out a hand, slowly—as if listening to Michael's feelings with his palm. His hand moved up and forward, stopping just in front of Michael's face. His azure eyes searched innocently. He looked lost and wise, both at the same time.

I gulped and stepped up beside Michael. "Don't let him touch you," I said.

For the first time, the boy's glance slid sideways to rest on me. His expression was bemused. His hand floated toward me now. As if tasting the moment. His fingers traced the line of my cheek. They weren't human, they felt like doll fingers, made of satin. For an instant, I heard distant voices, a chorus faint and far away, and little silvery bells—something familiar and mysterious, both at the same time. Beckoning. A chill in my gut, both sensual and scary. A flood of desire and panic—

All the memories.

A taste of something like butterscotch, but more magical and elusive. A moment of the time before birth. A touch like flavored silk. A waterfall of colors, azure, verdant, aqua, violet, lavender, all bright and rosy in the luminescent air.

I heard music. Like harps and violins and the wail of distant horns. Alluring, elusive, beckoning, comforting, blue and enveloping. Underneath, I heard *the heartbeat* of the Earth.

I turned around to look. The trees were bright. The forest glowed like home. And I could see a thousand years in all directions. Every line, every curve, every branch and leaf and needle. Every moth and bird, every blossom, every beetle. Everything that crept and crawled, slithered and slid, flapped and glided—everything that sang and croaked, squeaked and chittered. I felt it all as if it were my own body, my own naked skin open to the silvery air. As if the madness of rationality had finally fled, leaving me as free as starlight.

Moments fell away like baggage dropped from a bridge, splashing into oblivion. A thousand little hurts. The burdens of a mumbled life. Evaporated into blue eyes. Met mine like a kiss. *Get naked. Dance with me.*

All that. Just from a single touch—

I caught his wrist in my hand. *What are you doing to me?* The boy looked startled and puzzled. *Don't you want me to?* I released his wrist in shock. He didn't pull it back.

I looked to Michael.

Michael wasn't there.

I looked back to the boy—and he was gone too.

I was standing on the road, alone. Naked.

High up the slope, I could see the headlights of the car. I didn't remember walking down here into the fog. "Michael?" I started running back to the car—

It was where we'd left it. Lights still on. Doors still open.

"Michael?"

I looked at my watch. It was gone.

Where were my clothes? Where was Michael?

"Michael!"

No answer.

I leaned into the car to look at the dashboard clock. 3:17 am. Five hours.

Oh, shit.

"Michael!" I started back down the road, back to where I'd found myself. Looking for my clothes. Looking for Michael. Looking for the boy.

Oh, shit. Oh, shit. Oh, shit.

They'd gotten away from me. Michael had promised he wouldn't let me go—

I plunged into the woods. Everything was still luminous. I could still taste the silvery flavors. The songs still circled and danced. The music whirled. I flew toward the magic. "Michael—? It's Jay! Come back! You promised!"

The flavors. My god, the flavors. My feet tasted the leaves of the forest floor. My hands swirled through sweet currents of the night. My legs, my thighs, my belly, my skin—everything flooded with sensation. Everything inside, unfamiliar feelings. Emotions. Passions. Lust and fear, desire, panic, madness, hunger, emptiness, longing—fulfillment beckoned. Following the light. Too fast, too far away, like rainbows in the fog. Please Michael take me with you don't leave me behind not like this oh shit

Cold. Naked.

Sunlight filtering through trees.

Ugly noises.

Men and dogs.

Rough blankets. Wrapped around.

Noises. Guttural. Familiar. Meaningless. Words.

"Can you hear me, son? Do you understand what I'm saying? Look at my hand. How many fingers am I holding up?"

Go away. What are you doing here? I want to dance.

Something bites my arm.

I float away.

But not into the forest.

All white.

Then colors. Drab colors. Green, but not really green. Pink, but not really pink. Smells like walls. Ceilings. Floors. Curtains. Tubes. Beeping.

The woman smiles at me. She's wearing rubber gloves. "How are you feeling this morning? Do you know where you are?"

Another planet. *Wrong answer.* "Somewhere on Earth?" I venture.

She smiles. It is meant to be comforting, but it isn't. She does things, touches my body here and there. But her touch is dead. No magic. No music. The feelings are fading. I am shaking awake, she is dragging me back into rationality. I can still sense the flavor of the forest, deep inside; but it is too far away for me to reach.

"We're here to help," she says. I can feel the hooks sliding in. They sound like words. Feelings turn into sound. Language ensares.

"Not magic at all," she says. "Pheromones and hallucinogens."

Explanations. Polymorphic kinesthesia.

Wrapped in the cold sheets of rationality, I come back. I've had a bad experience. But I'm feeling much better now. Just ask me.

"You were fringed by a morphic entity. It lives in the green people. It's in their breath. The particles in the air intoxicate you. It's on their skin. Their touch infects you. You were lucky. We found you in a week. We cleansed you with anti-psychotic agents until the effect wore off. If we hadn't found you before the change became infused, you would have become a reservoir of your own intoxication."

"What about Michael?"

"Who?"

"Michael. Did you find him too?"

"There was no one with you."

"Michael was driving. He's the one who stopped the car. He's the one who saw the green boy."

Her look says I'm crazy.

"Did you look in the car? Did you see his luggage?"

"There was only one bag in the car."

"The black one was his. The brown one was mine."

"There was no black case." More words. More explanations. Transitional hallucinations. False memories. There is no Michael. The Ranger remembers me. I was alone. He warned me not to stop, he didn't think I was listening. When I didn't arrive at the exit station, they alerted the patrols.

"You're feeling a great loss. That's common. Listen to me. Your name is Jay Michael. You've personified your loss."

Language ensnares.

The woman speaks, day after day, webbing me with all the little insects of her mouth. Her words. They scurry across my brain, trying to muffle the great green heartbeat. They swarm. They chitter. They chew. But for all their itching and chewing, I could still hear the heart of the Earth booming inside me.

And then — it was winter, and the heartbeat was wrapped in cold sheets. My own heart as well. Hardened in ice. Shining.

It was over.

I thanked the counselors for all their help. For killing the glow inside. I promised to check in every week. I promised to call if I needed to talk. I promised to stay away from hallucinogens and pheromones and dreameries. I promised not to do anything tribal. I waved goodbye and put the car in gear.

And I kept my promises too.

I went to the sessions and I sat on the couch between two strange men and I shared what had happened. And they shared their stories. We all told the same story. "For a while...I *belonged* to something. That's all I ever wanted." We all shared the same feelings. Desire. Hunger. Longing. Emptiness. Loss.

One day I asked, "Why is it so wrong—to belong? Why do they think they're doing us a favor taking it away from us? Where's the good in coming back here? What's the point?"

The group leader, the facilitator, looked at me sharply. "Michael, do you really want to disappear?"

I didn't answer.

"That's what happens to people who turn green. They give up their sense of self. It isn't just the death of the ego—it's the death of individuality."

"Is that so bad?" I demanded. I slapped my head with both hands. "Can't you feel it? The walls are made of bone! Don't you ever want to get out?"

"You're still feeling the after-effects. They told you, didn't they, that the recovery period could be as long as a year? Your body is going through a profound physical depression. You were elevated through a series of transformational plateaus. Then you crashed and burned. You're still ringing like a bell. You probably hear echoes every night, lying alone in your bed, don't you? Do you think you're the only one? Every person in this room—*myself included*—feels it! We understand it, Michael. This is a place where you *do* belong."

Afterward, afterward, Jay and I go walking through the dark satellite sky. Glittering noises everywhere.

"Do you believe that?" Jay asked.

At first, I didn't want to answer. But I knew that Jay liked hearing me work things out. "If they know better than me, then I should accept what they say. Shouldn't I? But how do I know that they know better what's best for me. Who's responsible for my life? I am. And if this is a choice, then it's my choice to make. And what if they don't know better than me? What if they're just as confused? Then why am I making someone else's mistake?"

"You want to go back, don't you?"

"Don't you?"

"Everyone does." And then he added. "But you can't. They've sealed off the whole north coast. You can't even drive through anymore."

I shrugged. "You could hike into the area."

He nodded agreement. "You could." He adds. "It would be a long hike, though. Twenty-thirty miles. Two or three days."

"Yeah. Probably."

"They'll catch you, you know. They have patrols now. And cameras."

"Yeah, I heard that too." I glance over at him. "Are you coming with?"

"I think we should wait."

"For what?"

"To see if the feeling will pass."

"And if it does? Then what have we gained?"

It's his turn not to know. "I just think we should wait."

"Some people say...that the green people are the next step in evolution. A symbiosis with Gaia. You get chlorophyllins in your skin. You stand in the sun, naked, and the light feeds you, energizes you."

"And winter kills you," said Jay.

I look at him sharply.

"That's what they say," he adds. "The Rangers say that every spring, when the snows start melting, they find the decomposing bodies of the ones who didn't survive."

"We can wait till spring."

Jay looked relieved.

"Spring is the best time. You have all summer to glow. In the winter, you go dormant. You go deep into the Earth, deep down into the heartbreath, where the soil is warm and nourishing. You wrap yourself up and sleep until the sun returns. It's the ones who don't use the summer for glowing who don't survive."

"How do you know all this?" Jay asks.

I shrugged. "I just know." I look at him with azure eyes. "How do you know that rocks are hard and water is wet? How do you know gravity and sky and sun? You just do."

Dawn seeps over the eastern edge of the world. We crawl back into the coffins of our lives and wait for spring.

The dark of spring. And we will go driving. Jay and I.

This is the first story I ever wrote with a gay hero—well, not quite a hero. I wrote it in the early 70s. It's an uncomfortable glimpse into possibility. None of the magazines wanted it, so I put it into my first collection of short stories. It turned out to be more predictive than I expected, and it has since been picked up twice for reprint anthologies.

HOW WE SAVED THE HUMAN RACE

```
TEST TRANS CODE
ALPHA ALPHA TAU
QWERTYUIOPASDFGHJKLZXCVBNM1234567890
THE QUICK BROWN FOX JUMPED OVER THE LAZY DOGS.
END TEST
MESSAGE BEGINS HERE
DATE/2037.05.14
FROM/THE UNITED STATES AMBASSADOR TO BRAZIL
TO/ THE PRESIDENT OF THE UNITED STATES
FILE/BRZ9076THX
CODE/ALPHAALPHATAU/20370514.475FGH
STATUS OF DOCUMENT/CLASSIFIED/CODE 475FGH
```

MR. PRESIDENT, IN PLAIN TERMS, THE ANSWER IS NO. THE GOVERNMENT OF BRAZIL ABSOLUTELY REFUSES TO RELEASE THE BODY. THERE CAN BE NO POSSIBLE NEGOTIATION ON THIS. THIS IS AN INTERNAL MATTER— THEY CLAIM—AND NO OTHER POLITICAL BODY WILL BE ALLOWED TO INTERVENE. OF COURSE, THIS IS A BLATANT GRAB ON THEIR PART, BUT THERE IS NOTHING WE CAN DO ABOUT IT. I AM AGAINST MAKING ANY KIND OF FLAP.

FIRST OF ALL, WORLD OPINION GENERALLY FAVORS THE BRAZILIANS. ANY ATTEMPT BY US TO PRESSURE THEM WOULD ONLY PRODUCE HOSTILE REACTIONS, AND THAT'S THE LAST THING WE WANT NOW. SECONDLY, THEY WANT TO TAKE CREDIT FOR LEDGERTON'S CAPTURE. THEY FOUND HIM AND THEY EXECUTED HIM. OR RATHER, THEY ATTEMPTED

TO. IT WAS UNFORTUNATE THAT THE CROWD BEAT THEM TO
IT. THERE ARE THOSE WHO SUGGEST THAT THE POLICE
DELIBERATELY LET THE LYNCH MOB IN, BUT I WOULD
DISCREDIT THAT STORY. THEY LOST TWELVE OF THEIR OWN
IN THE DISORDER.

I THINK WE OUGHT TO LET THE BRAZILIANS HAVE THE
CREDIT. THIS IS NOT TO SUGGEST APPEASEMENT, BUT
WISDOM. THIS GOVERNMENT IS THE FRIENDLIEST ONE
BRAZIL HAS HAD IN TWELVE YEARS AND WE WANT TO KEEP
IT THAT WAY. ANY PRESSURING ON OUR PART WOULD
DEFINITELY COOL RELATIONS, AND PRESIDENT GARCIA
WON'T BEND TO PRESSURE ANYWAY. POLITICAL REASONS.
THE MILITANT RIGHTISTS WOULD USE SUCH ACQUIESCENCE
AS A LEVER AGAINST HIM. SO I THINK WE'D BETTER
JUST MAKE INEFFECTUAL NOISES FOR NOW, LOUD ENOUGH
TO PLACATE OUR OWN PEOPLE, BUT NOT LOUD ENOUGH TO
ANNOY JUAN PABLO GARCIA.

BY THE WAY, THE BODY WILL REMAIN ON PUBLIC DISPLAY
FOR ANOTHER DAY AND A HALF. YES, STILL HANGING FROM
THE GALLOWS, BULLET HOLES AND ALL. I'VE SEEN IT AND
IT'S A GHASTLY SIGHT. NOT EVEN LEDGERTON DESERVED
WHAT THEY DID TO HIM. YOU KNOW OF COURSE THAT THEY
CASTRATED HIM TOO.

IN ANY CASE, I HAVE IT FROM GARCIA HIMSELF THAT IT
WILL BE TAKEN DOWN TUESDAY AND CREMATED. THE ASHES
WILL BE SCATTERED AT SEA. NO, WE CAN'T STOP THAT
EITHER.

I WISH I COULD BE MORE ENCOURAGING AT THIS TIME,
BUT ALL I CAN DO IS SAY THAT IT'S A ROTTEN
SITUATION ALL AROUND. I'LL HAVE A MORE DETAILED
REPORT LATER. DESPITE OUR CLAIMS TO THE CONTRARY,
THERE ARE STILL TOO MANY PEOPLE DOWN HERE WHO
BELIEVE THE WHOLE THING WAS A C.I.A. PLOT.

FOR GOD'S SAKE, THIS IS ONE TIME WHEN I HOPE OUR
OFFICIAL POSITION COINCIDES WITH THE TRUTH.
SINCERELY,

2057.05.14/DATELINE: BRAZIL.

    CARDINAL SILENTE TODAY DEDICATED THE MONUMENT AND ETERNAL FLAME COMMEMORATING THE MARTYR DANA LEDGERTON. THAT SUCH A HIGHRANKING MEMBER OF THE CATHOLIC CHURCH SHOULD TRAVEL TO BRAZIL FOR THE CEREMONIES SUGGESTS IMMINENT BEATIFICATION OF THE MARTYR. THE CARDINAL HIMSELF SAID ...

PSYCHIATRIC INDEX REPORT
COMSKOOL TWELVE, MANWEATHER COMPLEX, CA 91405-0932
May 1, 2003
Dana Ledgerton, DL 551-69-5688, age nine.

    Child is unfortunately too smart and too pretty for his own good. Male, age nine, fair skin, pale hair, thin, undersized for age (poor nutrition again, damn these comskool minimums), lives in Comskool Creche. Unfortunately, subject also has advanced intelligence. (Tests enclosed.) Presently enrolled two grades above average. for his age level. This physical discrepancy between him and his classmates generates extreme feelings of inferiority, coupled with strong motivation to succeed. Success on mental level increases antagonism between himself and peers, but it is the only arena in which he is fairly matched with his classmates. The kid takes a lot of teasing about being a sissy, and his sense of masculine identification is weak. I'll give odds of ten to one that he's a fag by the time he's twenty. RECOMMENDATIONS: None. There's nothing we can do. Tough.

    SUPERVISOR'S REMARKS: *Dammit, Pete! Can't you be a little more clinical than this?* (signed) H.B.

MAY 9, 2011
LABOR POOL STATUS BOARD, CA 99-5674
UNIT MONITOR FORM JHX-908
DANA LEDGERTON, DL 551-69-5688

    Subject is thin, very fair, blond hair. Small for his age. Required to perform eighteen hours of Class IV labor per week in, order to support educational demands. Assigned to manual labor in University CafCom. Designation: busboy.

    REMARKS:

    Subject discovered in Comskool Personal committing homosexual act with fellow student at age twelve. Referred to PsychStat who confirmed unit's sexual outlook. No recommendation made. In accordance with Federal Civil Rights Amendment, subject's sexual preference has no bearing on his ability to perform Class IV labor.

    RECOMMENDATION:

    Leave to discretion of local supervisors.

MAY 45, 2035
FROM: FIELD OPERATIVE JASON PETER GRIGG
TO: F.B.I. DIRECTOR WARREN J. HINDLER,
       HOOVER CENTER,
       WASHINGTON D.C.
FILE: LEDGERTON, DL 551-69-5688

Chief,

Sorry for the sketchiness of this report; I'll have to do a complete rundown when I get back. This thing is a mess to the nth power. The Manweather records only go back twelve years. Before that, it's incomplete and often sketchy. Yest, I know that's hard to believe, but Manweather was one of the hardest hit during the sex and protein riots, and, a lot of their records were wiped clean by the activists.

Attached are copies of the working papers. Here's the summary:

Ledgerton's birth was an accident. He wasn't wanted, not by his parents, not by the local board. When he came along, unannounced and unwelcome, the parents were sterilized and sent to Labor-Module 14, Manweather. The child was transferred to the Comskool Creche, which had only been open two years at that time and still had elbow room. However, due to shifting population pressures, Manweather became one of the densest concentrations in CA. Within five years, it was a behavioral sink.

Competition wasn't Ledgerton's big thing. He preferred to withdraw into himself. Because his teachers and psychstats kept telling him how smart he was and how he should be proud of himself, he became narcissistic and introverted. He took a lot of fag-baiting from his classmates, too.

There's a full psych-profile in here somewhere. I was lucky to find that. According to the shrink, "Little Dana" wasn't as self-assertive as he should have been and too many of his life-choices were made because population pressures forced him into them and he didn't feel like fighting back.

His college career tends to bear this out. He went into bio-chem strictly by accident. It was the only classification still open that he was qualified for. And it was either that or the unskilled labor pool. Nuff said about that.

MAY 24, 2014
UNIVERSITY OF CALIFORNIA AT INDIO
REAGAN HALL
FLOOR MANAGER'S MEMO
SUBJECT: REASSIGNMENT OF ROOMS,

Dana Ledgerton DL 551-69-5688 and Paul-John Murdock PJM 673-65-4532 have been reassigned (at their request) to room 12-32, the "lavender hills" section. This leaves rooms 6-87 and 7-54 with only one person in them. Immediate reassignments available for each.

MAY 3, 2015
UNIVERSITY OF CALIFORNIA AT INDIO
PSYCH-STAT REPORT,
CONFIDENTIAL SUBJECT: PAUL-JOHN MURDOCK PJM 673-65-4532

Subject is tall and husky. 6'1", 186 lbs. Fairly well built. Dark hair, curly. Thin face. "Penetrating" eyes—an illusion produced by deep-set sockets and heaviness of eyebrows. Prone to long periods of moodiness and introspection. Theatre arts major.

He has been living for the past year with another male student and the relationship is apparently sexual. However, subject's emotional involvement tends to be shallow. He has a long history of casual sexual encounters with his fellow students, both male and female, and probably would not grieve if this relationship were to end abruptly.

I suspect the continued use of mildly narcotic drugs, including such illegal agents as "Spice," "Pink," and "Harrolin." (No definite proof here.) Subject's manner is lackadaisical and uncaring. Selfish, introverted, narcissistic. Typical T.A. major: more concerned with things on a "higher plane" than with the exigencies of everyday life.

Subject's strongest motivation for continuation of education is the avoidance of the labor-draft.

RECOMMENDATION: 1A status.

STATE OF CALIFORNIA, INFORMATION DUP-OUT
APPLICATION FOR CONTRACT TO ENTER STATE OF LEGAL MARRIAGE
DATE: MAY 12, 2015
APPLICANTS:
DANA LEDGERTON DL 551-69-5688
PAUL-JOHN MURDOCK PJM 673-65-4532
LENGTH OF CONTRACT: THREE YEARS.
PURPOSE: MUTUAL INTERDEPENDENCE.
CONDITIONS: INDIVIDUAL PROPERTY MAINTENANCE, DISSOLUTION TERMS NON-NEGOTIABLE. MUTUAL INHERITANCE. RESIDENCE: REAGAN HALL, UNIVERSITY OF CALIFORNIA AT INDIO, ROOM 12-32.
DISPOSITION OF APPLICATION: GRANTED.
WILLIAM APTHEKER, COUNTY CLERK

HARDCOPY FRAGMENT IN FILE, dislocated page, thought to be part of report by investigating agents. (Nature of agency not known.)

"...after his marriage broke up, he remained at the University for another three years. He tried to reconcile the contract several times, but twice he couldn't get in touch with Paul-John and the third time, Paul-John was vague in his reply.

"After that, he concentrated heavily on his studies. He earned a Ph.D. in bio-chemistry and an M.A. in medicine. They were (in the words of the department head) 'Uninspired degrees'. Meaning he was qualified, but not exceptional.

"Somehow he landed a teaching position and was able to hold onto it for several years. They had him giving the freshman science classes, something nobody else wanted to do.

"What he did on his own time during those years is beyond me, though I suspect he spent a lot of time at the boy-shows."

———————————

MAY 32, 2027
COLORADO COLLEGE OF SCIENCE
DENVER, COLORADO
FROM: Dr. Margaret James-Mead
TO: Dept. Head Harlan Sloan

Hal,

If I have to look at that "wispy little thing" wandering around the halls of this college one more day, I think I'll puke. You know who I mean. That man is a disgrace to the institution.

I don't care how you do it, but you've got to get rid of him. If you can't find something on him, make something. If you don't ask him for his resignation within a week, I'll give you mine instead.

Love, Maggie.

———————————

May 34, 2027

Dear Dr. Ledgerton,

It is with deepest regret that I must ask you to resign your position with the Denver College of Science. Your record here has been without blemish; however, we find that there is no longer any need for your services and are forced to take this rather unfortunate step.

I assure you that it has nothing to do with your personal life, or the incident with Dr. James-Mead. It is instead a question of ....

———————————

MAY 3, 2029
INTERBEM CHEMICAL RESEARCH
PORTION OF SUPERVISOR'S REPORT

"...the Ledgerton group seems, to have come closest to a workable solution of this problem. They have generated an experimental strain, temporarily designated

NFK-98, which appears to combine the functions of both DFG-54 and DFS-09 into one continuous process, rather than the two separate steps we have today.

"Suggest further experimentation along these lines to substantiate the findings and put them into production. The Ledgerton group should be commended. Despite his unappealing manner, Ledgerton is a tireless worker. Morale of the technicians working under him is not as good as it could be, but they do produce usable results.

"The viral research teams should be expanded as soon as possible in order to . . ."

INTERBEM CHEMICAL RESEARCH
MAY 9, 2029
TO ALL EMPLOYEES:
COMPANY FACILITIES ARE NOT TO BE USED FOR PRIVATE
RESEARCH PROJECTS WITHOUT FIRST SECURING PERMISSION
FROM DEPARTMENT HEADS. IT IS UNDERSTOOD THAT
INTERBEM RETAINS THE RIGHT OF FIRST OPTION ON ANY
COMMERCIAL APPLICATION OF PRIVATE DISCOVERIES
PRODUCED BY INTERBEM EMPLOYEES. REMEMBER, THIS
PRIVILEGE IS CONDITIONAL UPON FULFILLMENT OF
MINIMUM QUOTAS AND WILL BE REVOKED IF THEY ARE NOT
MET.

MAY 1, 2030
FIRST DORIAN CHURCH OF AMERICA
OSCAR WILDE CONGREGATION
CONFIDENTIAL MEMBERSHIP REPORT:

Dr. Dana Ledgerton, employee of InterBem Corporation, age thirty-six. Unmarried.

Dr. Ledgerton was interviewed by the membership committee whose discussion follows. J.M. commented at length that Dr. Ledgerton is thirty-six and physically unappealing. He suggested that the only reason Ledgerton wants to join is because he cannot find sexual partners anywhere else.

K.R. found J.M.'s attitude and phrasing undignified and demeaning.

L.N. said that Ledgerton's primary purpose in joining the church is probably loneliness.

J.M. agreed, but said that loneliness was just another way of saying "horniness."

L.N. insisted that the applicant was basically good intentioned. Lots of people join churches because they are lonely. Why should the Dorians be any different?

K.R. interrupted both of them to speculate on whether or not Ledgerton really did embrace the principles of Dorianism.

Ledgerton was called back into the room then and further questioned. He responded at length and the discussion continued again, while he waited outside.

A.S., visiting minister from the Bay Area, cast his support in favor of Ledgerton. Most people, he said, are not aware of all the precepts of Dorianism when they join, and it would be unfair to hold that against Ledgerton.

A vote was taken then, and Ledgerton was admitted to the membership by a count of 4-1. He was readmitted to the room and sworn to uphold the church and the principles upon which it was founded, that overpopulation is a sin and that all Dorians will devote their whole lives to zero population growth.

Dr. Ledgerton will be presented to the general congregation at the next open meeting.

———

MAY 39, 2031
INTERBEM CHEMICAL RESEARCH
SUPPLY REQUISITION

Need: Forty hours use of electron microscope for viral research. Private project. After hours use will be okay. Would appreciate available time as soon as possible.

(signed) D. Ledgerton

———

MAY 14, 2032
INTERBEM CHEMICAL RESEARCH
SUPERVISOR'S MEMO

Spoke to Ledgerton again today about his after-hours research. He's been working on this one project for nearly a year now, and he has spent nearly thirty-five thousand dollars on it. When questioned how much longer this line of research would continue, Ledgerton declined to say, but seemed to indicate that it would not be much longer.

I asked if he were close to a solution. He replied that he was closer to finding out that there was no solution, but would not go into any further detail. I suspect he does not want to discuss his project. A complete report on the objectives of his program and his findings has been ordered. He has until the end of the month to submit it, at which time it will be evaluated and decided whether or not he will be allowed to continue.

He was upset, but not as much as I expected. Perhaps he is nearing the end of his research after all. He mentioned something about a possible sabbatical later in the year. If he requests it, it is my recommendation that it be granted. His lapse in work has been only recent and may be due to personal problems. Ledgerton has always been a good worker, although his personal manner does leave something to be desired.

———

MAY 50, 2032
INTERBEM CHEMICAL RESEARCH
REQUEST FOR LEAVE OF ABSENCE
APPLICANT: DANA LEDGERTON DL 551-69-5688
REASON: VACATION, INDEFINITE LENGTH
DISPOSITION OF APPLICATION: GRANTED
REMARKS: (Scrawled in pen.) Good. I never liked him anyway.

MAY 50, 2032
FIRST DORIAN CHURCH OF AMERICA
OSCAR WILDE CONGREGATION
CONFIDENTIAL MEMBERSHIP REPORT:

The membership committee then considered a motion to expel D.L.

J.M. wanted to go on record as being opposed to D.L.'s membership in the first place. It was duly noted.

L.N. inquired as to what the charges against. D.L. were.

J.M. said that D.L. has not been faithful to the principles upon which the credo is based.

K.R. noted that D.L. has been observed almost nightly in the company of "paid female prostitutes."

L.N. requested amplification of this charge.

J.M. presented receipts made out to D.L. from the Xanadu Pleasure Corp.

L.N. wanted to know how J.M. got the receipts, but he was ruled out of order. The issue at hand is D.L.'s transgressions, not J.M.'s source of information.

L.N. disagreed, saying that we should not be "spying on our brothers." He was ruled out of order again.

The vote was taken and D.L. was expelled by a count of 4-1. The general membership will be informed at the next open meeting.

MAY 7, 2036
FIRST DORIAN CHURCH OF AMERICA
OSCAR WILDE CONGREGATION
CONFIDENTIAL MEMBERSHIP REPORT:

L.N. called the special meeting to order at 8:00 p.m. The first order of business was the reconsideration of the expulsion of D.L. four years ago. In light of recent events, it has become obvious that D.L.'s actions at that time were not in violation of the basic principles of Dorianism.

If anything, D.L., more than any other member, has done the most to further the cause of zero population growth.

K.R. noted some additional facts about the situation and a vote was taken. D.L. was unanimously readmitted to the congregation. He has not been notified because his whereabouts remain unknown.

It was decided not to apprise either the public or the general membership of this decision, because of the adverse publicity this might bring to the church.

MAY 27, 2033
FILE: 639 RADZ
SUBMTTED BY: RESIDENT PHYSICIAN JAMES-TAYLOR RUGG

Mr. and Mrs. Robert D____ came into my office on May 6 of this year. They have been trying for six months to start a baby and have had no success. I initiated the Groperson tests as well as a routine physical examination of each.

Mrs. D____ is in excellent physical condition and well-suited for child-bearing. Mr. D____ tests out with a normal sperm count and is in no need of semination-cloning. I'm sure that the rest of the tests will also turn out negative. I admit it, I'm stumped, and I pass this case on to the board with all the rest.

WRITTEN IN INK ACROSS THE BOTTOM: Dammit! This is the twenty-third one of these I've seen in the past two months. What the hell is going on?

(signed) B.V.

2033.05.21/TIMEFAX

... SURPRISINGLY, THE ONLY PLACE WHERE THE POPULATION GROWTH HAS KEPT WITHIN ITS PROJECTED LIMITS HAS BEEN SOUTHERN CALIFORNIA, THE DENSEST URBAN COMPLEX IN THE COUNTRY. THE STATE SURGEON GENERAL OFFERED NO EXPLANATION FOR IT, BUT USED THE OCCASION TO CONDEMN ARTIFICIAL ADDITIVES IN THE YEAST CULTURES. HE NOTED AN INCREASE IN THE NUMBER OF MARRIED COUPLES CONSULTING DOCTORS ABOUT THEIR INABILITY TO CONCEIVE AND HINTED THAT THERE MIGHT BE A CONNECTION.

IN CLEVELAND, DR. JOYCE FREMM DISCOUNTED THIS, SUGGESTED INSTEAD THAT THE CALIFORNIA SLOWDOWN WAS A RESULT OF ITS BECOMING "ONE GIANT BEHAVIORAL STINK." WHEN ASKED IF SHE DIDN'T MEAN "BEHAVIORAL SINK," DR. FREMM REPLIED, "I KNOW WHAT I SAID."

2034.05.03/TIMEFAX

CONCERN OVER THE SO-CALLED "INFERTILITY PLAGUE" HAS SPREAD EVEN TO THE EASTERN BLOC NATIONS. THE LATEST CITIES TO REPORT DECLINING BIRTH RATES INCLUDE MOSCOW,

PEKING, HONG KONG, TOKYO, OSAKA, HANOI, NEW DELHI AND MELBOURNE. EARLIER IN THE WEEK, THE PARIS COUNCIL MET AGAIN TO REPORT STILL NO SUCCESS IN FINDING THE CAUSE OF THE DECLINE.

DR. JOYCE FREMM, WORKING OUT OF SOUTHERN CALIFORNIA COMPLEX, UNIT HOSPITAL 43, ADMITTED THAT HER TEAM WAS NO CLOSER TO THE CAUSE THAN THEY HAD BEEN A YEAR AGO. "ALL WE KNOW ABOUT IT, WHATEVER IT IS," SHE SAID, "IS THAT IT KEEPS PEOPLE FROM STARTING BABIES."

SHE GAVE NO INDICATION WHEN A SOLUTION MIGHT BE FOUND. WHILE SHE WAS SPEAKING, THE WORLD HEALTH ORGANIZATION RELEASED A LIST OF AN ADDITIONAL FOURTEEN NATIONS WHOSE BIRTH RATES HAVE BEGUN TO SHOW THE INITIAL SLOWING THAT INDICATES THE PRESENCE OF THE SYNDROME.

MAY 9, 2034
MEMO TO: DR. JOYCE FREMM
FROM: DR. VICTOR-WEBB KING

Joyce,

I don't know how important this is, but it wouldn't hurt to track it down. Out of the last three hundred couples I've interviewed, nearly sixty per cent of the men have met their wives and been married only in the past eighteen months. Out of this group, nearly half report occasional premarital visits to a joy house, and nearly a third of all the men we interviewed have had some kind of professional contact.

More important however, is that *at least one partner in every couple has had at least one pre or extramarital contact with a partner other than wife or husband.*

The former fact is way out of line with the statistical average; the latter implies a definite connection. Could the Xanadu Pleasure Corp be an active vector of the disease?

MAY 11, 2034
MEMO TO: DR. VICTOR-WEBB KING
FROM: DR. JOYCE FREMM

(1) We don't know yet that it's a disease.

(2) Make no public announcement of this—especially do not suggest that Xanadu or any other company may be connected with it.

(3) Check it out immediately.

MAY 11, 2034
MEMO TO: DR. JOYCE FREMM
FROM: DR. CARLOS WAN-LEE
Dr. Fremm,

I believe my section has come up with a clue as to the nature of the syndrome. Sperm from one hundred affected men has been compared with the sperm of one hundred unaffected men; i.e. men whose wives have been impregnated within the past two months.

There is a minor but definite difference in the enzyme output of the affected sperm cells. All of the affected men (excepting three with very low sperm counts) had this qualitative difference in their enzyme production. Ninety-three of the unaffected men had normal enzyme production.

We're exploring this further and we'll have a more detailed report at the end of the week.

~~~~~~

MAY 30, 2034
REPORT TO THE WORLD HEALTH ORGANIZATION
BY DR. JOYCE FREMM
TRANSCRIPTION OF REMARKS—MOST CONFIDENTIAL
Gentlemen,

We have discovered the cause of the infertility plague, and we believe that it is only a matter of time until we discover the cure.

The cause of the plague is simple: We have been hit by a new kind of venereal disease— a benevolent tyrant, so to speak. It has an incubation period of less than twenty-four hours, and its immediate effects are so mild as to be negligible; perhaps a headache or a mild sense of nausea, that's all; but after that, the victim will pass the infection on to everyone he or she has intimate contact with.

Both males and females are carriers of the disease, creating an ever-increasing reservoir of active infection, with promiscuity its vector.

The disease has no effect on females of the species. To them, it is a benevolent parasite. It lives in the female reproductive tract and minds its own business. Unfortunately, its business is to infect that woman's every male contact.

And each time it does that, it effectively castrates the man. Viability of the sperm cells is reduced to 7% of what is considered normal.

The causative agent is a virus. It is a new strain and related to nothing we have seen before. Were it not for the fact that artificial virus tailoring is still such an infant science, I would suspect a vast campaign of virological warfare is being waged against the human race.

The viral bodies live and breed in the cells lining the vaginal wall. During intercourse, the release of certain hormones cause them to become active, and the viral bodies migrate into the male organ—usually through the urethra, but occasionally through a mild, almost unnoticeable rash.

The virus then migrates to the testes, specifically to the sperm-forming cells. The viral DNA chains attack these cells, burrowing into the cell walls, throwing off their protein sheaths and becoming just another hunk of DNA within the cell. Impossible to discover.

The result is small, very small—but very noticeable. The sperm cell no longer "cares."

The average human male ejaculation contains three hundred million sperm cells. Ideally, each of these sperms has the capability of being the one that fertilizes the waiting egg; but after being infected by the virus, the quality of the whole ejaculation is changed. The sperm cells still race madly up the fallopian tubes to meet the ovum—but when they get there, they can't fertilize.

It's this: Each sperm cell carries a tiny amount of an enzyme called hyaluronidase. Hyaluronidase sub-one, that is. No matter what the enzyme is called, though—what does matter is that the virus changes the male so that he no longer produces that enzyme. Instead, he produces something else, some other enzyme. The virus adds a few little acids of its own to the amino chain of the enzyme, and instead of hyaluronidase1 we get hyaluronidase2—a very different creature altogether.

Hyaluronidase2 is not as active as hyaluronidase1. It takes longer to do its work. Much longer.

Although only one sperm cell is needed for fertilization to occur, three hundred million are provided in order that one will succeed. But because only one is needed, the other two million, nine hundred ninety-nine thousand, nine hundred and ninety-nine sperm cells must be resisted. For that reason, the cell wall of the human ovum is too strong for any individual sperm cell to break down. Hyaluronidase is the enzyme that breaks down or softens the cell wall, and it takes the combined effort of all the sperm cells to provide enough of the enzyme to soften the wall enough for just one sperm cell to break through. Immediately upon fertilization, a change takes place in the cell wall to prevent other sperm cells from breaking in, a calculated resistance to their pressure,

But, if all those sperm cells are producing hyaluronidase2 instead of hyaluronidase1, fertilization will never take place at all. (Except in very rare cases—statistically insignificant.) The changed enzyme is still an enzyme, and it still works to soften the cell wall of the human egg—but it takes at least ten times longer to do it. And by that time, most of the sperm cells are already dead, dying, or too weak to complete the task of fertilization.

In addition, the ejaculation will also have introduced enough viral bodies into the woman so that if she weren't already, now she too will be infected and will pass the disease on to every subsequent male contact.

Insidious, isn't it?

Other than that, the virus has no effect at all on living human beings—only on the unborn. They stay that way. Unborn.

MAY 47, 2034
SUPPLEMENTARY REPORT, VIRT 897
W.H.O. FILE BVC 675

SUMMARY: The virus, designated VIRT 897, seems to have made its initial appearance on the western coast of the American continent in June or July of 2032, specifically in the area of the Southern California Urban Complex known as Angeles. (colloq. L.A. or "Ellay.") From there it migrated along the heaviest tourist routes, traveling eastward to Denver, St. Louis, Chicago, Dallas, Miami, and scattered parts of the eastern seaboard Urban Complex.

Within six months, it had also appeared and made its effects known in Seattle, Portland, Detroit, Pittsburgh and scattered areas surrounding. It extended the complete length of the western coast, being specifically virulent in Frisco and Diego counties, as well as in the areas already noted. It spread to Tijuana, Mexico City and Acapulco. The same trend occurred simultaneously on the eastern coast, with scattered pockets of sterility spreading out from the Boston, York, Jersey, Philadelphia and D.C. areas of the Urban Complex. Also affected were Toronto, Montreal and Quebec, as well as scattered areas surrounding.

At about the same time, it leapt both oceans simultaneously. Tracing the path of the falling birth rate, the disease showed up in London, Paris, Rome, Berlin, Warsaw, Munich, Belgrade, Dublin, Saigon, Seoul, Hanoi, Tokyo, Okama, Osaka, Beijing, Honolulu, Hong Kong, Melbourne, Sidney, Buenos Aires, Caracas, Panama City, Havana, and scattered points on the east African Coast as well as in the Mediterranean and Mid-East areas.

It is obvious that there are too many active vectors by this time, making it increasingly difficult to trace the spreading waves of infection. Not only does the disease move too rapidly, but once, the waves of infection overlap, their directions blur.

There is no way to tell at this time whether the origin of the disease was deliberate or accidental or a combination of both.

Detailed analysis charts are enclosed.

~~~~~~

MAY 50, 2034
INTERBEM CHEMICAL RESEARCH
MEMO TO: DR. LEON K. HARGER
FROM: SECTION SUPERVISOR VANCE

Dr. Harger,

I've just finished reading the WHO report on the sterility plague and a rather curious anomaly has caught my eye. I'm forwarding it to you to see if you catch it too. If you do, give me a buzz. If not, then forget I said anything.

~~~~~~

MAY 50, 2034
INTERBEM CHEMICAL RESEARCH
MEMO TO: ALL DEPARTMENTS
FROM: DR. LEON K. HARGER

Urgent! I need all data pertaining to Dr. Dana Ledgerton DL 551-69-5688 and any and all research that he might have been involved in while he was employed here. Also, anyone knowing his whereabouts or the itinerary of his sabbatical trip, please contact me immediately. I cannot understate the importance of this information!

~~~~~~

MAY 1, 2035
TO: SUPREME COURT JUSTICE DOUGLAS JOSEPH WARREN
FROM: UNITED STATES ATTORNEY GENERAL ALFRED G. WYLER

Dear Doug,

This is strictly *off* the record, and you might want to burn this note after reading it.

I've been talking to the President, and he and I concur that it would be extremely unwise to allow the InterBem Company to be sued merely because Ledgerton was an employee of theirs at the time he constructed the Ledgerton Virus.

Yes, I've studied the briefs in the case. I know that the appealing lawyers make a good case for the company's negligence in not keeping tighter reins on their employees' after-hours research. They also make a good case that Ledgerton would have been unable to construct his artificial venereal disease without the company's research facilities.

However, no matter how good their case is, both the President and I agree that at this time it would be best for all parties if the appeal were turned down. The InterBem Company has been most cooperative with us in *every* area of our investigation, especially in our efforts to develop the artificial enzymes. To allow them to be sued now might destroy them as a viable corporation and would cost us a valuable ally in our fight against this thing.

I don't know if you're familiar with the fact, but my office has registered more than five hundred thousand separate actions against InterBem. That corporation can't afford to be embroiled in this kind of legal feeding frenzy. If you allow this first appeal to be granted, you will be setting a dangerous precedent that might cost the United States a valuable natural resource—i.e. a commercially healthy corporation.

Yes, I know this smacks of pressuring, but this case is too important to allow you to make a decision without knowing the administration's views on it. If you have any questions, don't hesitate to call me.

(signed) Alfred

~~~~~~

MAY 7, 2035
FROM: FIELD OPERATIVE JASON PETER GRIGG
TO: F.B.I. DIRECTOR WARREN J. HINDLER,
       HOOVER CENTER,
       WASHINGTON D.C.
FILE: LEDGERTON, DL 551-69-5688

Chief,

It's my guess that the Paul-John Murdock lead is going to be another dead end and we'll probably have to start digging backward. (I'll try to get up to Manweather Complex before the end of the month, though I don't think I'm going to find much up there.)

We located Murdock in South Frisco, where he's working as a shoe salesman. He has neither seen nor heard of Ledgerton since their post-college days. Apparently, he doesn't miss him either. I get the impression that the only reason they married was so that Murdock could avoid the labor-draft. The full interview tape is enclosed.

On the other side of it, there's some evidence that there was an emotional involvement on Ledgerton's part and that he's been trying to contact Murdock, but without success. We'll continue to monitor Murdock on the off chance that Ledgerton is still trying.

Oh, one more thing. The latest word on Ledgerton hints that he is somewhere in Africa and heading south. But I doubt it. Last week, he was in Scotland.

MAY 14, 2036
THE CONGRESSIONAL RECORD
CONGRESSMAN JOHN J. HOOKER; DEM, GEORGIA

Gentlemen, we are presented today with a unique opportunity. The development of the artificial enzyme insures that the human race will not die out—and it gives us the chance to end, once and for all, the population explosion.

We need not manufacture the enzyme indiscriminately, nor need we make it available to every member of the world's population. In fact, even if we wanted to, it would be beyond our technology to service twenty billion individuals.

We are not geared for rehabilitating the human race; we can only provide enough enzyme for a fraction of the people. Dr. Fremm has stated that even if we began a massive synthesis program right now, we would never be able to reach all of those who are infected.

According to Dr. Fremm and others, it is only a matter of time until every man, woman, and child on this planet has the disease. When that happens, the only people who will be able to procreate will be those to whom we provide the enzyme.

Gentlemen, I say to you—here is an opportunity we cannot pass up—historians will condemn us if we allow this golden moment to slip out of our grasp—the chance to optimize the human race, to remake humanity. Therefore, I wish at this time to introduce this bill which would give the government the right to withhold the enzyme from those individuals who are judged to have undesirable genes ...

(The rest of Congressman Hooker's speech was drowned out.)

MAY 20, 2036
BERKELEY NEW PRESS:
U.S. PLANS RACIAL WAR

Hooker (The Aardvark)'s plan would be only the first foot in the door. For instance, what would keep the establishment slime from declaring Negro-ness an "undesirable trait"?

In cities across the nation, Freedom Now groups are planning urban disturbances to demonstrate their opposition to any form of "optimization," which would be only another word for genocide. The right to bear children is a right, not a privilege—and certainly not something that should be legislated. All right-thinking citizens are urged to come this weekend to the Free People's Plaza ...

MAY 3, 2037
FROM: FIELD OPERATIVE JASON PETER GRIGG
TO: F.B.I. DIRECTOR WARREN J. HINDLER,
      HOOVER CENTER,
      WASHINGTON D.C.
FILE: LEDGERTON, DL 551-69-5688

Chief,

The monitor on Murdock has turned up an interesting postcard (fax herewith enclosed) postmarked Brazil. Although there's no name signed to it, the content and phrasing could be a code of some sort. Or perhaps a reference to a personal experience known only to Murdock and Ledgerton. It should be checked out by one of our Brazilian operatives as soon as possible. I would appreciate being kept informed on this lead.

2037.05.09/TIMEFAX

... THE RIOTERS FOCUSED PARTICULARLY ON THE SYMBOLS OF ESTABLISHMENT CONTROL. FOUR BIRTH CONTROL CENTERS IN HARLEMTOWN WERE SACKED AS WELL AS ALL BUT ONE OF THE AREA'S TEN ENZYME CONTROL CLINICS. THIS OUTBREAK WAS THE WORST RIOTING TO HIT THE CITY IN SEVEN MONTHS, AND ACCORDING TO MAYOR GILBERT ROCKEFELLER, "IT DOES NOT LOOK AS IF THE END IS IN SIGHT." MEANWHILE, IN WASHINGTONTOWN, THE PRESIDENT DEPLORED THE NATION'S

GROWING TREND TO VIOLENCE AND PROMISED IMMEDIATE
STEPS TO HALT IT IN THE FUTURE. WITH THAT, HE SIGNED INTO
LAW THE CONTROVERSIAL MANPOWER CONTROL BILL...

2037.05.11/DATELINE:BRAZIL. RIO DE JANEIRO. PRESIDENT
GARCIA TODAY ANNOUNCED THE CAPTURE OF THE NOTORIOUS
RACE-CRIMINAL, DANA LEDGERTON (DL 551-69-5688) AT RIO DE
JANEIRO, AIRPORT. LEDGERTON WAS ATTEMPTING TO BOARD AN
AFRICAN-BOUND FLIGHT WHEN BRAZILIAN AGENTS SCOOPED
HIM UP. HE IS BEING HELD IN RIO INDEFINITELY.

THE BRAZILIAN GOVERNMENT HAS ANNOUNCED IT
INTENDS TO TRY LEDGERTON FOR THE CRIME OF GENOCIDE, AS
WELL AS OTHER CRIMES AGAINST HUMANITY. ANGRY CROWDS
HAVE BEEN MILLING IN THE STREETS OF RIO EVER SINCE THE
ANNOUNCEMENT OF LEDGERTON'S CAPTURE WAS MADE.

WORLDWIDE REACTION TO THE ANNOUNCEMENT WAS
IMMEDIATE. IN THE UNITED STATES, THE PRESIDENT SAID...

MAY 5, 2040.
REPORT TO THE WORLD HEALTH ORGANIZATION BY DR. JOYCE
FREMM
MOST CONFIDENTIAL—TRANSCRIPTION OF REMARKS

Gentlemen,

Our recent studies on the enzyme synthesis program suggest that there is just no way to do what you ask—at least not without massive appropriations—and I, for one, am opposed to it.

(Pause)

If I may continue... If I may continue... I'll wait...

If the delegate from Nairobi will stop calling me a racist slime long enough to listen, I will explain my position. Any appropriations for the enzyme synthesis would have to be made at the expense of other programs and the amount of money needed to do what the delegate from Nairobi wishes us to do would necessitate the closing down of almost every other United Nations Program now in existence, with the exception of the pollution board. And the pollution board is far more important than this!

If I may continue ... I believe that there is a way to save the human race, but enzyme synthesis is not it. In any case, a few years of minimal breeding will not hurt this planet any. There are about nineteen and a half billion too many people on Earth already.

2041.05.11/TIMEFAX

THE IRISH CIVIL WAR, WHICH HAS BEEN SMOULDERING FOR MORE THAN TWENTY YEARS, BURST INTO THE NEWS AGAIN TODAY WITH THE BURNING OF DUBLIN. THE CATHOLIC FACTION IN IRELAND CONTINUES TO CHARGE THAT THE NEO-PROTESTANT GOVERNMENT IS WITHOLDING THE ENZYME FROM CATHOLIC MOTHERS IN AN ATTEMPT TO REDUCE THE NUMBER OF CATHOLICS IN THE NATION. THAT CHARGE WAS ECHOED ACROSS THE GLOBE BY OTHER MINORITIES IN OTHER NATIONS. IN ISRAEL, ARAB NATIONALS CHARGED THE ISRAELI GOVERNMENT WITH DELIBERATE BIRT'H-CRIMES. THE JEWISH MINORITY IN RUSSIA LEVELED THE SAME CHARGE AGAINST THE KREMLIN. THE CHINESE MINORITIES IN MALAYSIA AND INDIA HAVE ALSO CHARGED THOSE TWO GOVERNMENTS WITH WITHOLDING THE ENZYME.

THIS BRINGS TO A TOTAL OF FORTY-THREE, THE NUMBER OF COMPLAINTS REGISTERED WITH THE U.N. MINORITY PROCREATION CONTROL OFFICE.

MAY 19, 2041
TO: THE PRESIDENT OF THE UNITED STATES
FROM: WARREN J. HINDLER, HOOVER CENTER
Mr. President,

The situation is becoming more and more serious every day. I have reports coming across my desk to indicate that the activists are planning to step up the number of urban disturbances within the next two months. This nation is headed for civil war unless some way is found to take the steam out of the Anti-Enzyme movement.

I recommend immediate action along the following lines....

MAY 20, 2041
POLICE REPORT, MANWEATHER COMPLEX

At 7:45 pm, Officers J.G. and. R.F. investigated a complaint at 1456 Rafferty Avenue, Block 12, Apt 56789. Investigating Officers found Donald Ruddigore in process of assaulting his, wife, Alice. Woman had already sustained minor injuries.

Ruddigore explained that his wife had told him she was pregnant As he had been infected with the Ledgerton Virus some years earlier, he knew that he could not be the father of the child, and he had only begun beating her when she refused to tell him who the real father was.

When questioned, Mrs. Ruddigore insisted that she has never copulated with anyone but her husband. Officer G. Suggested that both Ruddigores see a County Clinician before the week was over.

Mr. Ruddigore became abusive at this and had to be forcibly restrained. He was booked at Station 12 (preventive detention) and released the following morning on his own recognizance. Mrs. Ruddigore spent the night at her sister's after being released from the Emergency Hospital, where she was treated for minor scalp injuries.

As he was being taken into custody, Mr. Ruddigore noted that he was "glad that whoever the bastard is, now he's got it too!"

MAY 38, 2041
TO: DR. JOYCE FREMM
FROM: DR. CARLOS WAN-LEE
Joyce,

I've had four physicians call me in the past two days wanting to know if someone is bootlegging enzyme or something. All of them report a number of women (with previously infected husbands) turning up unexpectedly pregnant. Yes, I know it sounds like adultery, but I suspect it is something more. I'd like to talk to you about it in detail. I think we should investigate this. Are you free for lunch?

2042.05.14/DATELINE:BRAZIL. IN RIO TODAY, A CROWD OF MORE THAN TEN THOUSAND FORMED IN FRONT OF THE LEDGERTON GALLOWS TO HOLD A MEMORIAL SERVICE FOR DANA LEDGERTON, WHO DIED FIVE YEARS AGO ON THIS SPOT. WHILE LEDGERTON'S NAME IS STILL REVILED IN MANY PARTS OF THE GLOBE, A GROWING NUMBER OF PEOPLE ARE BEGINNING TO REALIZE THAT NOT EVERY EFFECT OF THE LEDGERTON VIRUS IS NECESSARILY EVIL. THE BRAZILIAN BIRTH RATE, FOR EXAMPLE, HAS DROPPED TO A COMFORTABLE...

MAY 20, 2042
REPORT TO THE WORLD HEALTH ORGANIZATION BY DR. JOYCE FREMM
TRANSCRIPTION OF REMARKS—FOR PUBLIC RELEASE

... what has happened is this: The virus has mutated. It wasn't stable. Few viruses are.

We have, in the laboratories, taken the virus through a total of seven different mutations, each of which has a different effect on human fertility. At present, we have no way of stopping the virus completely, but if our early tests hold true, the human race will be able to stop worrying about its birth rate.

Ledgerton Virus sub-one reduces fertility to a scant 7%. Variety sub-two, which is currently sweeping the globe, raises that percentage to 53%. Certainly not what it was before, but high enough for two very determined people to to start a baby, if they wish. The other varieties, which we've produced through careful bombardment of radiation (and other techniques), produce fertility levels ranging from 89% normal to 17%.

We can expect the virus to keep mutating at least once every four years. This is often enough to keep humanity from developing any kind of immunity to it. Also, it will hold the birth rate down, without keeping it dangerously depressed.

Gentlemen, without knowing it, Dr. Ledgerton seems to have stopped the population explosion.

~~~~~~~~~~~~~~~~~~~~~~

MAY 43, 2045
TO: THE PRESIDENT OF THE UNITED STATES
FROM: THE SECRETARY OF INFORMATION
Mr. President,

Enclosed are samples of the publicity releases you requested.

You will note that we have taken great pains to minimize Ledgerton's homosexuality. As you said, "It wouldn't do to have an effeminate American hero."

Motivational Research indicates that the need for a new American hero is greater than ever now, especially since the recent Mexican defeat. For that reason, I urge that we initiate this program as soon as possible.

~~~~~~~~~~~~~~~~~~~~~~

MAY 49, 2045
MINISTRY OF INFORMATION PAMPHLET #354657-098

...Single-handedly, this determined little man stopped the population explosion, stopped it dead with a biological brake—then he set that same brake so that it would release gently, allowing the race to maintain itself, but to cease its cancerous growth. When the death rates level off in the next few generations to match the new birth rates, the Earth will enjoy an era of peace and prosperity such as it has never known before....

~~~~~~~~~~~~~~~~~~~~~~

MAY 4, 2046
TO: THE SECRETARY OF FINANCE
FROM: THE PRESIDENT OF THE UNITED STATES
Dear Jase,

Sorry, but I'm going to have to ask you to quash your economic report on the primary causes of the current depression.

You're probably correct that the economy's continued growth is a direct factor of the nation's population spiral—but we can't suggest that fact publicly without starting a minor panic. (Besides, anything which would reflect negatively on the Ledgerton Program would not be welcome in certain circles.)

I agree with your recommendations though, and if you will circulate copies of your report (privately) to the Vice President and to the Secretary of Commerce, and also to the Secretary of the Treasury, between us we can initiate some of the steps you recommend to keep our financial heads above water.

And the sooner the better. This is an election year and we want to retain control of the House.

MAY 19, 2049
EXCERPT FROM *TODAY'S PSYCHOLOGY*

...one of the effects is the disappearance of the term "unwanted child" from the language. There is no such thing any more as an unwanted child. All children are wanted. Just look at the crowd of adults standing by the fence at any playground today.

Of course, not all the cultural changes are so beneficent. For instance, in the past, the pregnancy of an unmarried girl could quite likely have been the result of a mistake. Today, it can only be the result of several nights of steady "mistakes."

However, now that the onus of pregnancy has been removed from intercourse, certain other moral conventions are vanishing. Women are enjoying a sexual freedom even greater than that of the late twentieth century, when use of oral contraceptives first became widespread.

In general, the population of the nation is more birth-conscious than ever before, and one of the side effects has been a reduced tolerance for social and sexual deviants. Homosexuals have been driven out of several cities, and there is reason to believe that this trend will continue for some time....

2050.05.06/TIMEFAX

...FOUND BEATEN TO DEATH IN AN ALLEY. THE MAN WAS LATER IDENTIFIED AS PAUL-JOHN MURDOCK, A VAGRANT. POLICE SUSPECT THE BEATING DEATH IS JUST ONE MORE IN A SERIES OF "ANTI-FAGGOT" INCIDENTS THAT HAVE RACKED URBANA IN RECENT MONTHS.

2053.05.10/TIMEFAX

...THE PRESIDENT ANNOUNCED TODAY A NEW STAMP COMMEMORATING THE WORK OF DR. DANA LEDGERTON, CONSTRUCTOR OF THE FERTILITY VIRUS. THE STAMP WILL GO ON SALE IN FOUR DAYS, TIMED TO COINCIDE WITH THE SIXTEENTH ANNIVERSARY OF HIS DEATH....

Mike Resnick invited me to submit a story for an anthology of science fiction noir, called Down These Dark Spaceways. *The limit was 30,000 words. Somewhere around the 25,000 word mark, I realized I was still a long way from the ending. Resnick told me I could go to 40,000 words. The final draft was 46,275 words, half a novel. It got mostly good reactions and Gardner Dozois selected it for the* Best Science Fiction Of The Year #23 *anthology.*

Even so, I felt like I had rushed to the end, and hadn't gotten as deep into these characters as I'd wanted, so someday I may return to this story and let it become the novel it wants to be—so the characters can become the people they need to be.

IN THE QUAKE ZONE

The day after time collapsed, I had my shoes shined. They really needed it.

I didn't know that time had collapsed, wouldn't find out for years, decades—and several months of subjective time. I just thought it was another local timequake.

Picked up a newspaper—*The Los Angeles Mirror*, with its brown-tinted front page—and settled into one of the high-backed, leather chairs in the Hollywood Boulevard alcove. There were copies of the *Herald*, the *Examiner*, and the *Times* here as well, but the *Mirror* had Pogo Possum on the funny pages. "Mighty fine shoes, sir," Roy said, and went right to work. He didn't know me yet. I snapped the paper open.

I didn't have to check the papers for the date, this was late fifties, I already knew from the cars on the boulevard, an ample selection of Detroit heavy-iron: the inevitable Chevys and Fords, a few Buicks and Oldsmobiles, the occasional ostentatious Cadillac, a few Mercurys, but also a nostalgic scattering of others, including DeSoto, Rambler, Packard, Oldsmobile, and Studebaker. Not a foreign car to be seen, just a bright M&M flow of chrome-lined monstrosities growling along, many of them two-toned. The newer models had nascent tailfins, the evocation of jet planes and rocket ships, giddy metal evolution, the hallmark of a decade's misguided futurism and an industrial dead-end.

The Mirror and *The Examiner* both disappeared late '58, maybe early '59, if I remembered correctly, the result of a covert deal by the publishers. Said Mr. Chandler to Mr. Hearst, I'll shut down my morning paper if you'll shut down your afternoon. "Let us fold our papers and go."

A new Edsel cruised by—right, this was '58. But I could already smell it. The Hollywood day felt gritty. The smog was thick enough to taste. The Hollywood

Warner's theater had another Cinerama travelogue—the third or fourth, I'd lost track. I was tempted; not a lot of air conditioning in this time zone. A dark old theater, cooled by refrigeration, I could skip the sweltering zenith. But, no—I might not have enough time.

The papers reported that timefaults had opened up as far north as Porter Ranch, popping Desi and Lucy seven years back into the days of chocolate conveyer belts and Vita-meata-vegamin; as far east as Boyle Heights where ten years were lost and the diamond-bright DWP building disappeared from the downtown skyline, along with the world famous four-level freeway interchange; as far south as Watts, they only rattled off a couple years, but it set back the construction of Simon Rodilla's startling graceful towers; and all the way west to the Pacific Ocean. Several small boats and the Catalina Ferry had disappeared, but a sparkling new Coast Guard Cutter from 1963 had chugged into San Pedro. The big red Pacific Electric streetcars were still grinding out to the San Fernando Valley. I wondered if I'd have a chance to ride one before the aftershocks hit.

Caltech predicted several days of aftershocks and the mayor was advising folks to stay close to home if they could, to avoid further discontinuities. The Red Cross had set up shelters at several high schools for those whose homes had disappeared or were now occupied by previous or subsequent inhabitants.

Already the looters and collectors from tomorrow were flocking to the boulevard. Most of them were obvious, dressed in jeans and T-shirts, but they gave themselves away by their stare-gathering unkempt haircuts and beards, their torn jeans and pornographic T-shirts. They'd be stripping the racks at World Book and News, buying every copy they could find of *Superman*, *Batman*, *Action*, and especially *Walt Disney's Comics* with the work of legendary Carl Barks. And Mad Magazine too; the issues with the Freas covers were the most valuable. Later, they'd move west, hitting Collector's Books and Pickwick's as well. The smart ones would have brought cash. The smartest ones would have brought year-specific cash. The dumb ones would have credit cards and checkbooks. Not a lot of places took credit cards yet, none of them recognized Visa or Mastercard. And nobody took checks anymore; not unless they were bank-dated; most of the stores had learned from previous timequakes.

The Harris Agency—there was no Ted Harris, but he had an agency—was just upstairs of the shoeshine stand; upstairs, turn left and back all the way to the end of the hall, no name on the glass, no glass. The door was solid pine, like a coffin-lid, and painted green for no reason anyone could remember, except an old song, *"What's that happenin' behind the green door...?"* The only identification was a small card that said, "By appointment only." That wasn't true, but it stopped the casual curiosity seekers. My key still worked, the locks wouldn't be changed until 1972; there was no receptionist, the outer office was filled with cardboard file boxes and stacks of unfiled folders. Two typists were cataloguing, they glanced up briefly. If I had a key, I belonged here.

Georgia was still an intern, working afternoons; she'd started when she was a student at Hollywood High, half a mile west and a couple blocks south. Now she was taking evening courses in business management at Los Angeles City College, over on Vermont, a block south of Santa Monica Blvd. A few years from now, she'd be a beautiful honey-blonde, but she didn't know that yet and I wasn't going to risk a bad first impression by speaking out of turn. I pretended I didn't know her. I didn't, not yet.

I brushed past, into the cubby we called a conference room. More old paper and two old women. Pinched-faced and withered, they might have been the losers in a Margaret Hamilton look-alike contest. Sooner or later, one of them was probably going to demand, "Who killed my sister? Was it you?!"

Opened my wallet, started to flash my card, but the dustier of the two waved it off. "I recognize you. Wait. Sit." But I didn't recognize her. I probably hadn't met her yet. Some younger iteration of her had known an older iteration of me. I wondered how well. I wondered if I would remember this meeting then. The other woman left the room without saying a word. Just as well; some folks get uncomfortable around time-ravelers. Not travelers—*ravelers*. The folks who tend the tangled webs.

I sat. A dark mahogany table, thick and heavy. A leather chair, left over from the previous occupant of this office, someone who'd bellied up early in the thirties. She disappeared into a back room, I heard the scrape of a wooden footstool, the sound of boxes being moved on shelves, a muffled curse, very unladylike. A moment later, she came back, dropped a sealed manila envelope on the table in front of me. I slid it over, turned it around, and scanned the notations. Contract signed in 1971, backshifted to '57. Contract due date 1967. It had only been sitting here a year, and the due date was still nine years away.

A noise. I looked up. She'd put a bottle on the table and a stubby glass. I turned the bottle. It said Glenfiddich. I didn't recognize the name. I gave her the eyebrow. She said, "My name's Margaret. Today's the day you acquire this taste. You'll thank me for it later. Take as much time as you need to read the folder, but leave it here. Here's a notepad if you need to copy out anything. That contract's not due for 9 years, so the best you can do today is familiarize yourself, maybe do a little scouting. There's an aftershock due tomorrow morning, about 4:30 am; go to West Hollywood and it'll bounce you closer to the due date. Oh, wait—one more thing." She disappeared again, this time I heard the sounds of keys jingling on a ring. A drawer opened, stuff was shuffled around, the drawer was closed. She came back with a cash box and an old-fashioned checkbook. "I can only give you three hundred in time-specific cash, but it'll still be good in '67. There's a bank around the corner, you've got two hours until it closes, I'll give you a check for another seven hundred. You can pick up more in '67. But be careful, your account doesn't get fat for awhile. How's your ID?"

In the past, my personal past, I'd renewed my driver's license as quickly as I could after every quake, but a DL expires after three years, a passport is good for ten. The lines at the Federal Building were usually worse than the DMV, especially in a broken time-zone, but except for a gap of three years in the early 70's, I had valid passports from now until the mid-eighties.

"I'm good," I nodded. I signed my name and today's date to the next line on the outside of the envelope, then broke the wax seal. It was brittle; it had been sitting on the shelf for a year, waiting for today, and who knows how long before it got to this time zone. I didn't have a lot of curiosity, most of my cases were small-timers. The big stuff, the famous stuff, most of that went to the high-profile operations, the guys on Wilshire Boulevard, some downtown, some in Westwood. There was a lot of competition there—stop Sirhan from killing RFK, catch Manson before he and the family move into the Spahn movie ranch, apprehend the Hillside Stranglers, find out who killed the Black Dahlia, help O.J. find the killers of Ron and Nicole ... and so on.

The thing about the high-profiles, those were easy cases. The victims were known, so were the perps. The big agencies had a pretty good idea of the movements of their targets long before the crimes occurred. But most of the laws had been written before time began unraveling and the justice system wasn't geared for prevention, only after-the-fact cleanup.

Then one hot night in an August that still hasn't happened, Charles "Tex" Watson gets out of the car up on Cielo Drive and someone puts a carbon-fiber crossbow bolt right through his neck, even before he gets the gun out of his jacket. The girls start shrieking and two more of them take bolts, one of them right through the sternum, Sexie Sadie gets one in the head. The third girl, the Kasabian kid, goes screaming down the hill, and some redheaded kid in a white Nash Rambler nearly runs her down, never knowing that the alternative was having his brains splashed across the front seat of his parents' car. I didn't do it, but I knew the contract, knew who'd paid for it. Approved the outcome.

That was the turning point. After that, the judicial system learned to accommodate itself to preventive warrants, and most of the worst perps will be safe in protective custody weeks or even months before they have a chance to commit their atrocities. The question of punishment becomes one of pre-rehabilitation—is it possible? When can we let these folks back out on the streets? If ever. Do we have the right to detain someone on the grounds that they represent potential harm to others, even if no crime has been committed? The ethical questions will be argued for three decades. I don't know yet how it resolves, only that an uneasy accommodation will finally be achieved—something to the effect that there are no second chances, it's too time-consuming, pun intended; a judicial review of the facts, a signed warrant, and no, they don't call it pre-punishment. It's terminal prevention.

Meanwhile, it's the big agencies that get the star cases—save Marilyn and Elvis, save James Dean and Buddy Holly, Natalie Wood, Sal Mineo, Mike Todd, Lenny Bruce, RFK and Jimmy Hoffa. Stop Ernest Hemingway from sucking the bullet out of his gun and keep Tennessee Williams from choking to death on a bottle cap. Save Mama Cass and Jimi Hendrix and Jim Morrison and Janis Joplin and John Lennon. And later on, Karina and Jo-Jo Ray. And Michael Zone. Kelly Breen. Some of those names don't mean anything yet, won't mean anything for years; the size of the up-front money says everything—but we don't get those cases. The last one we bid on was Ramon Novarro, beaten to death with his own dildo by a couple of hustler-boys, and we didn't get that job either; later on, after the Fatty Arbuckle thing, and that was a long reach back anyway, all of those cases went through the Hollywood Preservation Society, funded by the big studios who had investments to protect.

No, it's the *other* cases, the little ones, the unsolved ones that fall through the cracks—those are the ones that keep the little agencies going. Most families can't afford five or six figure retainers, so they come to the smaller agencies, pennies in hand, desperate for help. "My little girl disappeared in June of '61, we don't know what happened, nobody ever found a trace." "I want to stop the man who raped my sister." "My girl friend had a baby. She says it's mine. Can you stop the conception?" "My boy friend was shot next November, the police have no clue." "I was abused by my step-father when I was a child. Can you keep my Mom from ever meeting him?"

There were a lot of amateurs in this business—and more than a few do-it-your-self-ers too. But most folks don't like to go zone-hopping; it's not a round-trip. You don't want to end up someplace where you have no home, no family, no job. Just the same, some people try. Sometimes people clean up their own messes, sometimes they make bigger ones. Some things are better left to the professionals.

The Harris Agency had three or six or nine operatives, depending on when you asked. But some of them were the same operative, inadvertently (or maybe deliberately) time-folded. Eakins was a funny duck, all three of him, all ages. The Harris Agency didn't advertise, didn't have a sign on the door, didn't even have a phone, not a listed one anyway; you heard about it from a friend of a friend. We took the jobs that people didn't want to talk about, and sometimes we handled them in ways that even we didn't talk about.

You knocked on the door and if you knocked the right way, they'd let you in. Georgia would sit you down in the cubby we called a conference room, and if she liked your look, she'd offer you coffee or tea. If she didn't trust you, it would be water from the cooler. Or nothing. She conducted her interviews like a surgeon removing bullet fragments, methodically extracting details and information so skillfully you never knew you'd been incised. Most cases, she wouldn't promise anything, she'd spend the rest of the day, maybe two or three days, writing up a report, sending an intern down to the Central Library or the *Times*' morgue to pull clippings. She'd pull pages out of phone directories, call over to the Wilcox station to get driver's license information (if available), and even scanned the personal ads in the *L.A. Free Press* a couple times. For the most part, a lot of what the outer office staff did was "clipping service"—pulling out data before, during, and after the events; the more complete the file, the easier the job. Working with Margaret, the jobs were usually easy. Usually, not always.

Georgia replaced Margaret in '61, right after Kennedy's election; Margaret retired to a date farm in Indio, as soon as she felt Georgia was ready; she'd managed the agency since '39, never missing a beat. She trained Georgia and she trained her well. The kid had been a good intern, the best, a quick-study; after graduation from Hollywood High, she stayed on full time while she picked up her degree at L.A.C.C. The work wasn't hard, but it was painstaking; Margaret had been disciplined, but

Georgia was meticulous. She relished the challenge. Besides, the pay was good and the job was close enough to home that she could walk to work. And at the end of the day, she'd satisfied her spirit of adventure without mussing her hair.

The files demonstrated their differences in approach. Margaret never wrote anything she couldn't substantiate. She wasn't imaginative. But Georgia always added a page or two of advice and suggestions—her own feelings about the matter at hand. Margaret didn't disapprove. She'd learned to respect Georgia's intuition. I had too.

This envelope was thin, thinner than usual. Inside, there were notes from both, I recognized Margaret' crimped precise handwriting, Georgia's flowing hand. A disappearance. Jeremy Weiss. Skinny kid. Glasses. Dark curly hair. Dark eyes, round face, an unfinished look—not much sense yet what kind of adult he might be. A waiter, an accountant, an unsuccessful scriptwriter. Seventeen and a half. Good home. Good grades. No family problems. Disappears summer of 68, somewhere in West L.A. Not a runaway, the car was found parked on Melrose, near La Cienega. But no evidence of foul play either. Parents plaster the neighborhood with leaflets. Police ask the public for help. The synagogue posts a reward for information. Nothing. Case remains open and unsolved. No clues here. Nothing to go on. The file was a list of what we didn't know.

Two ways to proceed with this one—shadow the kid or intercept him. Shadowing is a bad risk. Sometimes, you're too late, the perp is too fast, and you end up a witness instead of a hero. Agents have been sued for negligence and malpractice, for not being fast enough or smart enough, for not stopping the murder. Interception is better. But that means keeping the vic from ever getting to his appointment in Samarra. And that means the perp never gets ID'd either.

The easiest interception is a flat tire or even an inconvenient fender-bender. That can delay a person anywhere from 15 to 45 minutes. That's usually enough to save a life. Most cases we get are events of opportunity. Take away the opportunity, the event doesn't happen—or it happens to someone else. That's the other problem with preventive interception. It doesn't always stop the bad luck, too often it just pushes it onto the next convenient opportunity. I don't like that.

Give me a case where the perp is known ahead of time, I can get a warrant. I don't have a problem taking down a known bad-boy. I don't have to be nice, I don't have to be neat. And there are times when I really don't want to be. But give me an unsolved case, it's like juggling hand grenades. Sometimes the victim is the real perp. It's messy. You can get hurt.

But this one—I listened for the internal alarm bells—they always go off when something smells wrong. This one felt different, I'm not sure why. There's a flavor. I had a hunch, a feeling, an intuition, call it whatever—a sense that this case was merely a loose unraveled thread of something else. Something worse. Like the red-headed kid who didn't die on August 9th was merely a sidebar.

Think about it for a minute. Hollywood is full of manboys. They fall off the buses, naïve and desperate. They're easy targets for all kinds of opportunists. Old enough to drive, but not old enough to be street smart. They come for the promise of excitement. Ostensibly, it's the glamour of the boulevard, where the widescreen movies wrap around the audience; it's the book stores rich with lore, shelves aching with volumes of forgotten years; it's the smoky jazz clubs and the fluorescent record stores and the gaudy lingerie displays; it's the little oddball places where you can find movie posters, scripts, leftover props, memorabilia, makeup, bits and pieces of costumery—they come in from all the surrounding suburbs, looking for the discarded fragments of excitement; sometimes they're looking for friends, for other young men like themselves, sometimes they're unashamedly looking for sex. With hookers, with hustlers, with each other. With whoever. A few years from now, they'll be looking for dope.

But what they're really looking for is themselves. Because they're unformed, unfinished. And there's nobody to give them a clue because nobody has a clue anymore. Whatever the world used to be, it hasn't finished collapsing, and whatever is going to replace it, it hasn't finished slouching toward Bethelehem. So if they're coming down here to the boulevard to look for themselves, because this looks like the center, because this looks like where it's happening, they're looking in the wrong place; because nobody ever found themselves in Hollywood, no. Much more often, they lose whatever self they had to start with.

You can't save Marilyn and Elvis because they don't exist, they never existed—all that existed was a shitload of other people's dreams dumped on a couple of poor souls who'd had the misfortune to end up in front of a camera or a microphone. And you can't save anyone from that. Hollywood needs a warning label. Like that pack of cigarettes I saw up the line. "Caution, this crap will kill you."

Jeremy Weiss wasn't a runaway. He didn't fit the profile. And he didn't end up in a dumpster somewhere, his body was never found. He wasn't a hustler or a druggie. I doubted suicide. I figured he was probably destined for an unmarked grave somewhere up above Sunset Boulevard, maybe in the side of a hill, one of those offshoots of Laurel Canyon that wind around forever, until they finally turn into one lane dirt scars. Someone he met, a casual pickup, I know where there's a party, or let's go to my place—

So yeah, I could probably save this kid from the Tuesday express, but that wouldn't necessarily stop him from lying down on the tracks again on Wednesday night. Or if not him, then maybe Steve from El Segundo or Jeffrey from Van Nuys. Most of the disappearances went unreported, unnoticed. Not this one, though.

Margaret sat down opposite me. She put a second glass on the table and poured herself a shot, poured one for me.

I knew Margaret only from her work—the files that Georgia had passed me, up the line. Margaret was compulsive; she annotated everything on every case, including newspaper clippings, police reports when she could get them, and occasionally witness interviews. Reading through a file, reading her notes, her advice, her suggestions, it was like having a six-foot invisible rabbit standing behind every moment.

But today was the first time I'd actually met Margaret, and I held my tongue, still gauging what to say. Should I thank her for the cases yet to solve? Did she want to know how these cases would play out? Would it affect her reports if she knew what leads were fruitless and which ones were pay-dirt? Do we advance to Go or do we go directly to jail? The real question—should we put warnings into the files? Watch out for Perry, a harmless little pisher, but an expensive one; stay away from Chuck Hunt, the chronovore; don't go near Conway, the bigger thief; and especially watch out for Maizlish, the destroyer.

Should I ask—?

"Don't talk," she said. "There's nothing you have to say that I need to hear. I've already heard it. I'll do the talking here because I have information that you need." She pushed the glass toward me.

I took a sniff. Not bad. Normally, I don't drink scotch. I prefer bourbon. But this was different, sharper, lighter. Okay, I can drink scotch.

"Something's happening," she said.

I waited for her to go on. There's this trick. Don't say anything. Just sit and wait. People can't stand silence. The longer you wait, the more unbearable it becomes. Pretty soon, they have to say something, just to break the silence. Leave an unanswered question in the air and wait, it'll get answered. Unless they're playing the same game. Except Margaret wasn't playing games.

She finished her scotch, neat, put the glass down, and stared across the table at me. "The perps are starting to figure it out." She let that sink in for a moment. "The timequakes. The perps are using public quake maps to avoid capture. Or to commit their crimes more carefully. Bouncing forward, back, sideways. They call it the undertime railway. LAPD has taken down the Manson clan three times now. Each time, earlier. Now they're talking about maybe legalizing preemptive abortion. Just stop them from being born. Nobody's sure yet. The judges are still arguing. The point is, you'll have to be careful. Especially with cases like this where we don't have any information. The perp always knows more about the crime than the investigator. The more the perp knows, the harder the job becomes. If the case gets any publicity, the perp gets dangerous.

"Here's the good news. Caltech has been mapping the timequakes. They've been putting down probes all over the county for thirty years now. We have their most recent chart. The one they didn't make public. It cost us some big bucks and a couple of blow jobs." She unrolled a scroll across the table—it looked like the paperback edition of the Torah, smaller but no less detailed. "It stretches from 1906 all the way to 2111, so far. All of the big quakes and aftershocks are noted, those are the public ones, the ones the perps know. But all of the littler ones are in here too." She tapped the scroll. "*This* is your advantage.

"Most people don't notice the little tremors, the unnoticeable ones. You know that feeling when you keep thinking it's Monday when it's really Sunday? That's a dayquake. Or when you've been driving for an hour and you can't remember the last ten miles? Or when you've been at work 8 hours and you still have 7 hours to go? Or when you're out clubbing and suddenly the evening's over before it's really started? Those are all tremors so small you don't even feel them, or if you do notice, you figure it's just you. But Caltech has them charted, has the epicenters noted, can tell you almost to the second how far forward or back each quake bounces. See the arrows? You can chart a time-trajectory from here to forever—well at least up to 2111, depending on which of the local trajectories you choose. They probably have even more complete charts uptime, but we can't get them yet. We expect Eakins to send back copies, but nothing's arrived yet, not this far back. But it should have reached '67 by now. So as soon as you get there, come back to this office. I won't be here, I'm already retired in '67, but Georgia will have what you need. We start bringing her up to speed right after Kennedy's election.

"The point is, this timeline gives you more maneuverability. Protect it like it's gold. If a perp gets it, it'd be a disaster. That's why it's on proof paper. It goes black after twenty minutes' exposure to UV." She rolled it up, slid it into a tube, capped it, and passed it over to me. "Right. Get to the bank, get yourself some dinner, then get out to the quake zone. You've got a reservation at the Farmer's Daughter Motel. That puts you half a block from the epicenter. You can get a good night's sleep. Georgia will see you here in '67."

Picked up some comics at the Las Palmas newsstand and shoved them into my briefcase, I do a little collecting myself, on the fringes, mostly just for my retirement. But not only comics. Barbie dolls, G.I. Joe, Hot Wheels cars, Pez boxes, stuff like that. And I'm saving up for a trip back to '38, I hope to pick up some IBM stock.

The Farmer's Daughter is better than it sounds. On Fairfax, walking distance from Farmer's Market. Of course, it isn't the Farmer's Daughter yet, but it will be in '67

I check in, check the room, check the bed, think about a hooker, I have the number of an escort service, they'll be in business for another year or so; but it's not a good idea. There might be a foreshock. Almost certainly, there will be a foreshock. Not fair to the girl.

So I content myself with a nightcap in the bar. It's almost deserted. Just the bartender and me. His name is Hank. I ask him what time he gets off, he thinks I'm hitting on him, he gives me a big friendly grin, but I say, no thanks. Close up and go home. Timequake tonight, an aftershock. He shrugs. He's already been caught in two quakes. He won't even keep a cat now. Everything important, he keeps in a bag by the door. Just like me.

Not a lot of out-of-towners visit L.A. anymore; they don't want to risk the possibility of time-disruption, finding themselves a year or ten away from their families. But some folks deliberately come to L.A., hoping to ride a quake back so they can prevent some terrible event in their lives. Some succeed, some don't. Others have meticulous lists of sporting events and charts of stock fluctuations; they expect to get rich with their knowledge. Some do, some don't.

I fall asleep in front of the TV, watching Jack Paar on the tonight show. I wake up and it's the last week of April '67. The smog is the same, the cars are smaller and more teenage; on the plus side, the skirts are a lot shorter. But my old brown suit is out of style. And my car is visibly obsolete—a '56 Chevy. Obvious evidence that I'm a wandering time-raveler.

Caught breakfast in the market, fresh fruit, not too expensive yet, then headed back up to the boulevard. Santa Monica Boulevard was now a tawdry circus of adult bookstores, XXX theaters, and massage parlors. The buildings all looked like garish whores.

Hollywood Boulevard was worse. The stink of incense was almost strong enough to cover the smog. Clothing had turned into costumes, with teens of both sexes wearing tight pants and garish shirts—not quite hippies yet, but almost. The first bell-bottom jeans were showing, the Flower Children were just starting to bloom. The summer of love was about to begin.

Several store fronts had signs for time-tours and maps of the quake-zones; probably a better business than maps to the homes of the stars. I noticed several familiar faces—a small herd of comic book collectors—heading toward the newsstand on Cahuenga; they were probably the first customers of the quake-maps.

Roy was still shining shoes, twelve years older, but just as slick and just as fast. "Shoes look good, Mister Harris," he said, as I walked in. He called all of us Mister Harris. Nobody ever corrected him. Maybe it was his way of keeping track. He knew who we were, but he never asked questions, and he never offered advice. He kept his own counsel. But sometimes, he steered the right people to the office and sometimes he turned other folks away. "What you lookin' for ain't up those stairs, mister." Every so often, Georgia would march downstairs and hand him an envelope. She never said why. I assumed that was something else she'd learned from Margaret.

The office had been redecorated; it felt more like Georgia now. All of the typewriters were IBM Selectrics. New lateral filing cabinets, a Xerox photocopier, even a fax machine. The cubby had been painted light blue with white trim and the stacks of boxes and files had disappeared, replaced by dark oak bookshelves. Most of the files had moved into the offices next door, which we'd leased in '61, when the accountant finally died. It'd be another few decades before we would have all that information on hard drives and optical discs. The same heavy mahogany table and leather chairs remained in the center of the room, but looking a lot more worn.

Georgia was expecting me. She tossed the same manila envelope on the table, brought in another bottle of Glenfiddich, one glass, and a new pocket-Torah. I passed her the old one, as well as the few collectible treasures I'd picked up in '58. She'd put them in storage for me.

"Lose the brown suit," she said. "I bought you a new one, dark gray. It's in the closet. Already tailored. Read the file, there's some new information." She reached for the bottle.

"Not this early, thanks." I was already signing the envelope. The file had been accessed only three times in the last twelve years. Margaret twice, Georgia once. But it was significantly thicker.

This time there was a bundle of newspaper clippings. Not about Jeremy Weiss, but about a dozen *others*. I checked the dates first. June of '67 to September of '74.

Georgia had typed up a chart. At least thirteen young men had disappeared. Jeremy Weiss was the third. The third that we knew about. I wasn't surprised. I'd had a hunch there were more.

We weren't obligated to investigate the disappearances of the others; Weiss was the only one we had a contract on. But if the disappearances were related … if they had a common author, then finding that author would not only save Weiss, but a dozen others as well. Preemptive action. But only if the disappearances were connected. We'd still have to monitor—*save*—Weiss. Just in case.

I read through the clippings, slowly, carefully. Three times. There was a depressing similarity. Georgia sent out for sandwiches. After lunch, she sat down next to me—she was wearing the Jasmine perfume again, or maybe still, or maybe for the first time—and walked me through the similarities she'd noticed. The youngest victim was fifteen, but big for his age; the oldest was twenty-three, but he looked eighteen.

Last item in the envelope was a map of West Los Angeles with a red X at the site of each vic's last known location; his apartment, his job, where his car was discovered, or the last person to see him alive. There were no X's north of Sunset, none south of Third. The farthest west was Doheny, the farthest east was just the other side of Vine Street. It was a pretty big target area, but at the same time fairly specific.

"I want you to notice something," she said. She pointed to the map, tracing an area outlined by a yellow highlighter. All of the red X's were inside, or very close to the border of the yellow defined region, except for the one east of Vine. "Look at this." She tapped the paper with her fingernail. "That's West Hollywood. Have you seen it?"

"Drove through it this morning."

"Ever hear of *Fanny Hill*?"

"Isn't that a park in Boston?"

"Not funny. Don't quit your day job. It's a book, by John Cleland. *Memoirs of a Woman of Pleasure*. It has redeeming social value. Now."

"Sorry, I'm not following."

"John Cleland was born in 1710. He worked for the East India Company, but he didn't make much money at it. He ended up in Fleet debtors' prison from 1748-1749. While there, he wrote or re-wrote a book called Fanny Hill. It's written as a series of letters from Fanny to another woman, and it is generally considered the first work of pornography written in English, its literary impact derives from its elaborate sexual metaphor and euphemistic language."

"And this is important because…?"

"Because last year—1966—the Supreme Court declared that it is not obscene." She didn't wait for me to look puzzled. "In 1957, in Roth versus the United States, the Supreme Court ruled that obscenity is not within the area of constitutionally protected freedom of speech or press, neither under the first amendment, nor under the due process clause of the fourteenth amendment. They sustained the conviction of a bookseller for selling and mailing an obscene book and obscene circulars and advertising.

"In 1966, in Cleland versus Massachusetts, the court revisited their earlier decision to clarify the definition of obscenity. Since the Roth ruling, for a work of literature to be declared obscene, a censor has to demonstrate that the work appeals to prurient interest, is patently offensive, and has no redeeming social value. It's that last one that's important, because it could not be demonstrated to the court that *Fanny Hill* has no redeeming social value. The case can be made that the book is an historical document, presenting an exaggerated and often satirical view of the mores of 18th century London, just as the *Satyricon* by Petronius presents an exaggerated and satirical view of ancient Rome; so a very strong case can be made that pornography represents a singular insight into the morality of its time. Thus, it has redeeming social value. Therefore, it cannot be prosecuted as obscene."

"Redeeming social value...."

"Right."

"Since the *Fanny Hill* ruling, pornography has become an industry. If a publisher can claim redeeming social value, the work is legal. A book of erotic pictures with a couple quotes from Shakespeare. A sex-film with a preface by a doctor—or an actor playing a doctor. It's a legal fan dance—you don't go to the fan dance to see the fan. The pornographers will be testing the limits of the law for years. The fans are going to get a lot smaller."

"Okay, so what does all this have to do with West Hollywood?"

"I'm getting to that. For the next decade, enforcement of obscenity laws will be left to local communities. There will be years of debate. Nothing will be clear or certain, because the definition of obscenity will be determined by local community standards. Until even that argument gets knocked down. At some point, the whole issue of redeeming social value becomes moot because it becomes unenforceable. How do you define it? And that'll be the end of anti-smut laws. But right now, today—it's all about local community standards."

"And West Hollywood is a local community...?"

"It's an *unincorporated* community," Georgia said. "It's not part of Los Angeles. It's not a city. It's a big hole in the middle of the city. L.A.P.D. has no authority inside this yellow area. There's no police coverage. The only enforcement is the L.A. County Sheriff Department. So there's no community and there are no standards. It's the wild west."

"Mm," I said.

"Right," she agreed. "None of the city ordinances apply. Only the county ones. And the county is a lot less specific on pornography. So you get bookstores. And more. The county doesn't have specific zoning restrictions or statutes to regulate massage parlors, sex stores, and other adult-oriented businesses. The whole area is crawling with lowlifes and opportunists. Here—" She pulled out another map. This one showing a corridor of red X's stretching the length of Santa Monica Boulevard, with a scattered few on Melrose.

"What's this?"

"A survey of sex-businesses in West Hollywood. Red for hetero, purple for homo, green for the bookstores. You get clusters. Here, all the way from La Brea to La Cienega, this used to be a quiet little neighborhood where seniors could sit in the sun at Plummer Park and play Pinochle. Now, there are male hustlers in hot pants, posing at the bus stops.

"Take a drive around the neighborhood. You'll see things like massage parlors advertising specific attention to love muscle stiffness—Greek, French, and English massage. Or sex-therapists who will help you work out your inhibitions with sex-fantasy role-playing. Here, here, and here, these are gay bars, this is a bath house, so is this. This place sells costumes, chains, things made of leather—and realistic prostheses."

"Prostheses—?" And then I got it. "Never mind."

"If you can imagine a sexual service, you'll find it here. This is the land of negotiable virtue. It's a sexual carnival, the fun zone, the zoo. This is the reservoir of licentiousness. This is where AIDS will start. You'll need to start carrying condoms. Anyway—" She stretched out the two maps side by side. "Notice the congruence? I'm going to make a guess—"

"These kids are horny?"

"And gay."

"Is that a hunch, or—?"

She didn't answer immediately. "Okay, I might be wrong. But if I'm right, then the police will be useless to us. Ditto the Sheriff's department. They don't care. Not here. They won't take this seriously. And we can't talk about this with any of the parents. And probably not even with the kids themselves. This is still the year of the closet ... and will be until June of '69. Stonewall," she explained.

"I know about Stonewall. We bid on a contract to videotape it. The problem will be getting cameras onsite."

"Eakins is working on that. There's a thing called...never mind, I don't have time to explain it." She tapped the table. "Let's get back to this case. We've got six weeks until the first disappearance. This is as close as you can get by time-skipping. You'll have to live concurrently, but that'll be an advantage. You can familiarize yourself with the area, locate the victims, make yourself part of the landscape. Let your sideburns grow. We've found an apartment for you, heart of the district, corner of N. Kings Road and Santa Monica, second floor. Here, wait a minute—" She stepped out of the room for a second, came back with a cardboard filebox, and a set of keys. "We bought you a new car too. You can't drive a '56 Chevy around '67 L.A. It attracts too much attention."

"But I like the Chevy—"

"We bought you a '67 Mustang convertible. You'll be invisible. There are a hundred thousand of these ponies in California already. It's in the parking lot behind. Give me the keys to the Chevy. We'll restore it and put it in storage. Another forty years, it'll be worth enough to buy a retirement condo. A high-priced apartment."

She popped the top off the box. In it were another dozen envelopes of varying thicknesses. "Everything we've got on the other disappearances. Including pictures of the vics. It's the first two you want to focus on."

I sorted through the reports. "Okay, so we have an approximate geographical area and a pretty specific age range. Is there anything else to connect these victims?"

"Look at the pictures. They're all twinks."

"Twinks?"

"Pretty boys."

"And based on that, you think they're gay?"

"I think we're dealing with a serial killer. Someone who preys on teenage boys. Yeah, I know—lots of kids go missing every year just in L.A. County. They hop on a bus, they go to Mexico or Canada, they go underground to avoid the draft. Or maybe they just move without leaving a forwarding address. But these thirteen don't fit that profile. The only connection is that there's no other connection. I don't know. But that's what it smells like to me." She finished her drink. Neat. Just like Margaret. "I think if we find out what happened to the first victim, we unravel the whole string."

I finished my drink, pushed my glass away, empty. Put my hand over it in response to her questioning glance. One shot was enough. If she was right, this was big. Very.

Took a breath, let it out loudly, stared across at her. "Georgia, you've been working these streets long enough to know every gum spot by brand name. I won't bet against you." I gathered the separate files. "I'll check them out." I thought for a moment. "How old am I now?"

Georgia didn't even blink. "According to our tracking, you're 27." She squinted. "With a little bit of work, we could probably make you look 21 or 22. Put a little bleach in your hair, put you in a surfer shirt and shorts, you'll look like a summer-boy. What are you thinking? Bait?"

"Maybe. I'm thinking I might need to talk to some of these kids. The closer I am to the same age, the more likely I'll get honesty."

Something occurred to me. I turned the maps around and peered back and forth between them. Pulled the disappearance map closer.

"What are you looking for?"

"The dates. Which one of these was first?"

"This one, over here." She tapped the paper. The one east of Vine. "Why?"

"Just something I heard once about serial killers. Always look closest at the first vic. That's the one closest to home. That's more likely a crime of opportunity than premeditated. And sometimes that first vic and the perp—sometimes they know each other."

"You've never done a serial killer before," Georgia said.

"You're thinking about bringing in some help?"

"It might not be a bad idea."

Considered it. "Can't bring in L.A.P.D. They have no jurisdiction. And County isn't really set up for this."

"Bring in the Feds?"

I didn't like that idea either. "Not yet. We might embarrass ourselves. Let me do the groundwork first. I'll poke around for a few days, then we'll talk. See if you can get anything from uptime."

"I've already put a copy of the file in the long-safe. I'll add your notes next week. Then we'll look for a reply."

The long-safe was a kind of time capsule. It was a one-way box with a time-lock. You punch in a combination and a due date, a drawer opens and you put a manila envelope in. On the due date—ten or twenty or thirty years later—the drawer pops open, you take the file out and read it. Usually, the top page is a list of unanswered questions. Someone uptime does the research, looks up the answers, writes a report, puts it in another manila envelope, and hands it to a downtime courier—someone headed backwards, usually on a whole series of errands. The downtime courier rides the quakes until he or she reaches a point before the original memo was written. The courier delivers the envelope, and it goes into the long-safe, with a due date *after* the send date of the first file, the one with all the questions. This was one of the ways, not the only one, that we could ask the future for help with a case.

Sometimes we sent open-ended queries—what should we know about that we don't know yet to ask? Sometimes we got useful information, more often not. Uptime was sensitive about sending too much information back. Despite the various theories about the chronoplastic construction of the stress-field, there weren't a lot of folks who wanted to take chances. One theory had it that sending information downtime was one of the things that triggered time-quakes, because it disturbed the fault lines.

Maybe. I dunno. I'm not a theorist. I'm just a meat-and-potatoes guy. I roll up my sleeves and pick up the shovel. I prefer it that way. Let somebody else do the heavy thinking, I'll do the heavy lifting. It's a fair trade.

I didn't set out to be a time-raveler. It happened by accident. I was in the marines, got a promotion to sergeant, and re-upped for another two years. Spent eighteen months in Nam as an advisor, mostly in Saigon, but occasionally up-country and twice out into the Delta. The place was a fucking time-bomb. Victor Charlie wanted to give me an early retirement, but I had other plans. Rotated stateside the first opportunity.

Got off the plane in San Francisco, caught a Greyhound south, curled up to sleep, and the San Andreas time-fault let loose. It was the first big timequake and I woke up three years later. 1969. Just in time to see Neil Armstrong bounce down the ladder. Both Dad and the dog were dead. I had no one left, no home to return to. Someone at the Red Cross Relocation Center took my information, made some phone calls, came back and asked me if I had made any career plans. Not really, why? Because there's someone you should talk to. Why? Because you have the right set of skills and no close family connections. What kind of work? Hard work. Challenging, sometimes dangerous, but the money's good, you can carry a gun, and at the end of the day you're a hero. Oh, that kind of work. Okay. Sure, I'll meet him. Good, go to this address, second floor, upstairs from the shoeshine stand. Your appointment is at three, don't be late. And that was it.

My first few months, Georgia kept me local, bouncing up and down the early '70's, doing mostly easy stuff like downtime courier service. She needed to know that I wouldn't go off the rails. The only thing the agency has to sell is trust. But I wasn't going anywhere. The agency was all I had—they were a serendipitous liftoff from the drop zone of '69, and you don't frag the pilot. A lieutenant maybe, but never a pilot—or a corpsman.

I'd thought about corpsman training early, even gone so far as to sit down with the Sergeant. He just looked across the desk at me and shook his head. "There's more to it than stabbing morphine needles into screaming soldiers. You're better where you are." I didn't know how to take that, but I understood the first time mortar shells came dropping in around us and voices all around started screaming, "Medic! Medic!" I wouldn't have known which way to run. And I just wanted to keep my head down as low as possible until the whole damn business was over. It was only later, I got angry enough to start shooting back. But that was later.

After the courier bit became routine, Georgia started increasing my responsibilities. When you pass through '64, pick up mint-condition copies of these books and magazines. Pick up more if they're in good condition, but don't be greedy. Barbie dolls, assorted outfits (especially the specials), and Hot Wheels, always. Buy extras if they have them. Sometimes she just wanted me to go someplace and take pictures— of the street, the houses, the cars, the signs.

After a couple months, I told Georgia that the work didn't seem all that challenging. Georgia didn't blink. She told me that I had to learn the terrain, I had to get so comfortable with the shifting kaleidoscope of time that I couldn't be rattled. That's why the '60's and the '70's were such a good training ground. The nation went through six identifiable cultural transitions in the course of 16 years. But even though the '50's were supposed to be a lot quieter, she didn't think so. They weren't all that safer, it was just a different kind of danger. Georgia said she wanted to keep me out of that decade as much as possible. "You've got tombstones in your eyes," she said. "You'll scare the shit out of them. And frightened people are dangerous. Especially the ones with power. Later, after you've mellowed, we'll send you back. We'll see."

After a bit, she started passing me some of the little jobs, the ones where clients bought themselves a bit of protection, or closure, or prevention.

For instance, "Here, this file just came up. Here's fifty dollars. Go to this address, give it to this person. Find a way to make it legit, tell him you're a location manager for Warner Brothers, you're shooting a pilot, some TV series, a cop show, lots of location work like Dragnet, you want to measure the apartment, photograph the view from the balcony, and here's a few bucks for your trouble." That one was easy. A struggling young writer with no food in the house, desperate and waiting to find out if he'd sold his first book, all he needed was another week—his future self was giving him a lifeline.

Another one, "The mail carrier delivers the mail to this address between 1 and 2pm. Nobody will be home before 5. Open the mail box and remove any letters with this return address. Do this every day for the next two weeks." A fraternity at USC. That one didn't make sense until a year later when that same fraternity was thrown off campus for a hazing scandal. Somebody didn't get the invitation to rush, didn't pledge, didn't get injured, and didn't have his college career stained.

And a third, "Tomorrow afternoon, this little boy's pet dog gets out an open window and wanders away from the house. Nobody's home until three. Pick up the dog before it gets to the avenue, come back at seven, knock on the door, and ask if they know who the dog belongs to, you found it the next block over." Right. No mystery there.

"Tuesday evening, Lankershim boulevard, across the street from the El Portal theater. There's a blue Ford Falcon. Somebody sideswipes it, sometime between 6:45 and 9:30. Get the license number, leave a note on the windshield."

After those, I started getting the weird jobs. Some of them made no sense, there was no rational explanation; but the client doesn't always give reasons. Our rule is that we only take oddball cases on the condition that no physical or personal harm is intended.

Here's one, "Take this copy of *Popular Mechanics*, thumb through it so it looks used. Tomorrow afternoon, 1:30, go out to Van Nuys, 5355 Van Nuys Boulevard, Bobs #7. Sit at the counter near the front, near the go-order window. Order a Big Boy hamburger and a Coke. Read the magazine while you eat. Fold it so the ad on page 56 is visible. Leave a dollar tip. Leave the magazine on the table."

And another, "Friday night, just after the bars close, stand in front of the door at this address, like you're waiting for a ride. That's all. Nothing will happen. You can leave at 2:30."

And one more, "Take this package. No, don't open it. At 4:25, catch the 86 bus at Highland. Get off at Victory and Laurel Canyon. Cross the street and wait for the return bus. Leave the package on the bench."

And the weirdest, "Here's a white T-shirt, blue jeans, and a red jacket; right, the James Dean look. You've got the face for it. Tomorrow afternoon, Studio City, corner of Ventura and Laurel Canyon. When this kid comes out of the drugstore, you stop her and say, 'When you are ready to learn, the universe will provide a teacher. Even when you are not ready to learn, the universe will provide a teacher.' Hand her this paper. It has a poem by Emily Dickinson. Don't answer questions. Go into the drugstore, go all the way to the back and out to the parking lot, turn right and duck around the corner of the building, she won't follow, but she mustn't see you again. Walk west till you get to the ice cream store. You can park your car behind it."

Finally, when Georgia was satisfied that I could follow orders, she gave me a tough one. "Do you trust me? Good. Go to this address and kneecap this son of a bitch."

"Kneecap?"

"Slang term. Shoot him in the kneecap. Both kneecaps. We want him in a wheel-chair for the rest of his life. Oh, and rip the phone off the wall. Wear these gloves, wear these shoes—use this gun, here's ammunition, here's a silencer, put everything in this plastic trash bag, bring it all back here for disposal."

"You're kidding."

"We don't joke about things like this."

"Shoot him in the kneecaps—y'know, that's a tricky shot. Especially if he's moving."

"If you can't manage it—"

"I can manage it."

"Would you rather just kill him?"

Thought about it for two or three seconds. "What'd he do?"

"You don't like being hired muscle, do you?"

"I just need to know—"

"It's righteous," she said. "He's a rapist. He rapes little girls. The youngest is six. And then he kills them. He goes off the rails tomorrow. Cripple him tonight and you'll save three lives that we know of, probably more if he starts time-walking."

"Can I ask you a question? Who makes these decisions?"

She shook her head. "It's a need-to-know thing." Then she added, "Think of it this way. The perps choose it when they choose to be perps. We try to provide permanent solutions. This guy tonight—he's a dangerous asshole. Do your job and tomorrow, he'll just be an asshole." She shrugged. "Or a corpse. Either is part of the contract. Whatever's easiest for you. Or most enjoyable. Your call."

"I'm not a psychopath."

"That's too bad. We really do need one. For the big jobs."

I let that pass. "Do we have a preemptive warrant?"

Georgia shook her head. "That law hasn't been passed yet. But we can't wait. Here, ease your conscience. After you do him, drop this envelope out of the plastic bag, leave it on the floor."

"What's in it? Cash?"

"Clippings. About how he'll torture his victims. Leave it for the cops, they'll get it. Don't touch anything, don't leave prints."

There were other jobs like that. They never got any easier.

In real life, you don't shoot the gun out of the bad guy's hand. The bad guys don't drop the gun, say ouch, and reach for the sky—no, they shoot back. With everything they've got, with bullets and mortars and mines that take your best buddy's legs off. They just keep coming at you, spraying blood and fire, hammering explosions, hail-storms of dirt and flesh and bone. You have to keep your head down and your helmet tight and hope you have a chance to lay down a carpet of fire, burn them alive and screaming, just to buy those moments of empty dreadful silence while you wait to see if it starts up again. In real life, you beat them senseless just to slow them down. And if that doesn't slow them down, you kill them, you blow them away, you turn them into greasy red gobbets.

On TV, everything is neat. Real life is messy, ugly, scabrous, squalid, festering, putrid, and painful. In real life, the bad guys don't think they're bad, they think they're good guys too, just doing their stuff because that's the stuff that a man's gotta do; but in real life, there are no good guys, just guys, doing each other until everybody's done. And then maybe afterwards, while you're picking up the pieces of your corporal or your radioman, you get a chance to sort it out. Maybe. And that's when it doesn't matter if anybody's a good guy, they're still dead.

Because in real life, there are no good guys. They don't exist and neither do you. That's the cold hard truth. You're not there, you're just another TV death, consumed like a TV dinner, until it's time to change the channel. You think you have a life? No. You're just the space where all this shit is happening. That cascade of experience— you don't own it, it owns you. You're the bug in the trap. The avalanche of time, the pummeling of a trillion quantum-instants, second after second, it pounds you down into the sand, and whatever you think you are, it's an illusion—you exist only as a timebinding hallucination of continuity. And after long enough, after you realize you can't endure anymore of this senseless pummeling—whether its mortar shells or rifle bullets or cosmic zingers so tiny you don't know you've taken one in the heart until you get to the third paragraph—you just continue anyway. Waiting. Sooner or later, the snipers will get your range.

You don't survive, you just take it a day at a time, a moment at a time. You pick your steps carefully, always watching for the one that might go click. And you don't think ahead, don't think about when it's going to be over, because it's never going to be over. You look, you listen, and you never move fast—until you have to. And when you do, you take the other guy down first, and keep him down, and you don't worry about nice and you don't worry about pretty; the whole idea is to keep him from ever getting up again. So you do what you do so he can't do what he does. And once in a while, somebody tells you it was worth it, but you know better, because you're still carrying the ruck through the hot zone, not them. In real life, real life stinks.

So I took him down. Him and the next three. And I learned to drink Glenfiddich straight from the bottle.

Until one morning, Georgia dragged me out of bed, still covered in vomit and stink, rolled me into a tub and filled it with cold water. Grabbed me by the hair, dunked me until I screamed, then poured cold black stale coffee down my throat until I was swearing in English again. My head hammering like a V-8 with a broken rod, she dressed me, drove me to the gym and handed me over to Gunter, the personal trainer. After that, 7am every day. In the afternoon, language classes at the Berlitz. Monday evenings, firing range—hands-on experience with weapons from here to flintlocks. Tuesday, world history class. Wednesday, Miss Grace's Academy of Deportment, I'm not kidding. Thursday, meeting—friends of Bill W. Friday, movie night. With Georgia. Not a date—cultural acclimatization. Saturday, assigned

research and dinner at Georgia's. Not a date—a full report on the week. Sunday ...
breakfast with Georgia.

She didn't save my life. She made it worth enduring. Especially when we started
sleeping together. Not at her place, not at mine, she wouldn't have that. We went to
one of those little cardboard motels out on Cahuenga, where it turns into Ventura,
halfway between here and the San Fernando Valley. She needed danger and I needed sex. So we rumpled the sheets like a war zone for three months regular, every
Saturday night—until the next timequake and I had to go to Sylmar and bounce
forward three years, and even though I was up for it, even thinking maybe I should
buy her a ring, she'd already moved on, and that was the end of it. That was the zinger
right through the heart.

I found something else to do on Thursday nights and let myself have one glass of
scotch every time I finished a dirty job. Sometimes the clean jobs too. It didn't help.
And I told her why.

No, it wasn't her. It was that other thing. The good-guy thing. I didn't feel like
one. Killing for peace is like fucking for chastity. It doesn't work.

She offered to buy out my contract, send me off somewhere to retire, I'd certainly earned it. But no—I don't know why I said no. Maybe it was because there was still
work to do. Maybe it was because I still wanted to believe there was something to
believe in. What the hell. It was better than sitting on my ass and poisoning my liver.

So I took the envelope and left the bottle. Maybe someday I'd figure it out, but
for now, I wasn't looking anymore.

Picked up the first vic at his job, tailed him to his place. Brad Boyd. He lived in
a courtyard apartment on Romaine, just east of Vine. In two and a half months, the
bitchy neighbor who hates his dog and his motorcycle will be the last person to see
him. She'll scream at him about the bike being on the walk, in everybody's way; then
she'll push it over. He'll pick it up, get on it, turn it away from her so both exhaust
pipes are pointing in her direction, and rev it as loud as he can, belching out huge
clouds of oil-smelling smoke; then he'll roar away. 9:30pm on a hot Thursday night
in July. It's a blue Yamaha, two-stroke engine, 750cc, a mid-sized bike; it'll never be
found. Left this vic at home, watching TV. The blue glow is visible from the street.

Headed out to the valley and drove past the Van Nuys home of the Weiss kid.
He still lives with his mother, his dad died a year ago; he's in his last year at San
Fernando Valley State College in Northridge. His room is in the back of the house,
I can't see any lights. But his car is in the driveway.

The fourth vic lives on Hyperion in the Silverlake area, catches the bus downtown, where he works for a bank. I ride the bus opposite him, sit where I'm not in his
line of sight, and study him all the way to Hill Street. Randy something. Skinny little
kid, very fair complexion, too pretty to be a boy; put a dress on him you can take him
anywhere. They must have teased the hell out of him in school.

After that, I check the locations, the last known sightings. I'll start working on
the other vics next week; I want to read the neighborhood first. Weiss's car will be
found on Melrose Ave, two-three blocks east of the promising lights of La Cienega.

Carefully parked, locked up tight. He went someplace, he never came back. I park across the street. I lean back against the warm fender of the Mustang and study the street. At first glance, it seems innocent enough.

This forgotten little pocket of West Hollywood is a time-zone unto itself, with most of its pieces left over from the twenties and thirties. In '67, Melrose is dotted with tacky little art galleries, interior decorators, and a scattering of furniture stores hoping to get trendy. It's a desolate avenue, even during the day.

At night, the street is dry and deserted, amber streetlights pockmark the gloom; a few blocks away, the bright bustle of life hurtles down La Cienega, but here emptiness, the buildings huddled dark and lonely against themselves, waiting for the return of day and the illusion of life. Bits of neon shine from darkened storefronts. Occasional redlit doorways hint at secret worlds.

Few cars cruise here, even fewer souls are seen on the sidewalks—only the occasional oasis of a sheltered restaurant, remaining open even after everyone else has fled; departing customers move quickly from bright doorways to the waiting safety of their automobiles, tuck a bill into the valet's hand, and whisper away into the night.

There's this thing they do in the movies, in a western, or a war picture, where someone says, "It's quiet, too quiet." Or: "Listen. Even the birds are silent." That's how they do it in the movies, but that's not how it works in the hot zone. In the zone, it's more like a little timequake. There's this sense, this feeling that you get—like the air doesn't taste quite right. And when you get that feeling, sometimes the little hairs on the back of your neck start tickling. You stop, you look around, you look for the reason why those little hairs are rising. Sometimes, it's just a shift in the wind and the way the grass ripples across the hillside, and as you watch the ripples, you realize that one of those ripples isn't like the others. And you wake up inside your own life in a way that makes the rest of the day feel like somnambulism.

Sometimes the feeling isn't anything at all. Sometimes the feeling is just too much coffee. But it's a real feeling and you learn to respect it anyway because you're out there in the hot and the guy who drew the pretty pictures on the chalkboard isn't. You hit the dirt—and the one time you hit the dirt and hear the round go past just over your head instead of through your gut—that one time makes up for all the times you hit the dirt and there's nothing overhead.

You learn to listen for the feeling. You never stop. Years later, even after the Delta has receded into time, you're still listening. You listen to the world like it's ticking off, counting down. You listen, not even knowing what you're listening for anymore.

Standing on Melrose, I got something. Not the same feeling, but a feeling. A sense there's something *else* here. Something that comes out, late at night. And good folks don't want to be here when it's up and about.

Get back in the car. Lean back and disappear into the shadows. Sit and wait, not for anything in particular. Just to see what comes out in the darkness. Picket duty. Eyes and ears open; mind catching forty. Watching. Reading the street.

The avenue has a vampiric life of its own. Every so often, motion. A manboy, sometimes two. Sometimes a girlboy. The children of the night climb out of their daytime coffins and drift singly through the shadows, flickering briefly into existence for a block or two, then disappearing just as ephemerally. It isn't immediately obvious what's happening here.

Finally, got out of the car and went for a walk. West, where Melrose angles in toward La Cienega. Where are the manboys going? Where are they coming from? Ah.

Half a block east of the lights. A darkened art gallery with an unpaved parking lot. The lot is dark, unlit. At the back is a fenced-in covered patio. Discreet. Unobtrusive. Inconspicuous to the point of invisibility. You could drive by a thousand times and never notice, even if you were looking for it. It's furtive. Like Charlie. Things that hide are either frightened or stalking. Either way, dangerous.

Two-three teens standing in the lot, smoking, chatting. Only room for a few cars here. I fumble around in my pockets for a pack of cigarettes. I stopped smoking when Ed Murrow died, again when I left Da Nang, and a third time when I got off the plane in San Francisco; the third time it stuck; but it's still convenient to carry them. Pull one out of the pack, approach the girlboys, ask for a light, say thanks, nod, wait.

"You new?"

Shrug. "Back in town."

"Where were you?"

"Nam."

"Oh. I heard it's pretty bad."

"It is. And getting worse."

The boys have no real names. The tall thin one with straight black hair is "Mame." The shorter rounder one is "Peaches." The blond is "Snoopy."

"You got a name?"

"Solo."

"Napoleon?"

"Han."

"What'd you do in Nam?"

"Piloted a boat. Called The Maltese Falcon." Almost added, "Went upriver to kill a man named Kurtz." But I didn't. They wouldn't get it, not for twelve years anyway. I doubted any of them had ever read either Conrad or Chandler. Mame was more likely a Bette Davis fan than Humphrey Bogart. The other two ... hard to tell. Shaun Cassidy probably.

"You goin' in?"

Took a puff on the cigarette. "In a minute." Hang back, listening. The girlboys are gossiping, overlapping dialog, about someone named Jerry and his unrequited crush on someone else named Dave, except Dave has a lover. Jerry has a secret too. Honey, don't we all? Oh, guess what? Speaking of secrets, Dennis' real age is 23, he's a chicken hawk, he's dating Marc. Marc? That's funny. Marc has the crabs, he got them from Lane. Lane? That sissy? Lane isn't even his real name. He's cheating on his sugar daddy, you know. Hey, have you met the new girl? With the southern accent? You mean, Miss Scarlett? More like Miss Thing. She's way over the top. She's just a sweet ole Georgia peach. I thought she said Alabama. Whatever. Do you believe her? Honey, I don't even believe me. She says she went to her senior prom in drag. With the Captain of the football team. In Alabama? Girl, I'll believe that when I hear it from Rock Hudson Jr.

Mame turns to me abruptly. "Getting an earful?"

Shrug again. "Doesn't mean anything to me. I don't know any of those people."

Satisfied, Mame turns back to the others. Did you hear about Duchess and Princess? I only know what you've told me. They were arrested—in drag—for stealing a car. Has anybody heard anything else? Not me. Have you ever seen them out of drag? No, have you? I have. Princess puts the ugh into ughly. Her and Duchess, it's Baby Jane and Blanche. I wonder who'll get their wardrobe. Honey, just one of Princess's gowns is big enough for all three of us. If we're friendly. I'm friendly, very friendly. Honey, get real. What are you and I going to do together—bump pussies, try on hats, and giggle?

Gossip is useful. It's a map of the social terrain. It tells you which way the energy is flowing. It tells you who's important. It's the quick way of tapping into the social gestalt. Find me three gossips and I can learn a community. Except this isn't a community. This is a fragmentary maelstrom of whirling bodies. A quantum environment, with particles flickering in and out of existence so fast they can only be detected by their wakes.

Eventually, I go in. There's no sign, but the place is called Gino's. Admission is 50 cents. The man at the door is forty-five, maybe fifty. This is Gino. He has curly black hair, a little too black. He dyes it. Okay, fifty plus. He looks Greek. He hands me a red ticket from a roll, the anonymous numbered kind they use at movie theaters. Good for one soda. He recites the rules. This is a club for 18 and up. No drugs, no booze. If the white light goes on, it means the vice are here, stop dancing.

The outdoor patio is filled with jostling teens, all boys, some giggling, some serious. Several are standing close. Some make eye-contact, others turn away, embarrassed. Others sit silently, sullenly, on heavy benches along the walls. Potting benches? Perhaps this used to be a nursery.

The patio connects to a second building, tucked neatly behind the art gallery. Invisible from the street. Perfect. Inside, it's darker than the patio. A quick survey reveals a bar, sandwiches and Cokes; in one corner a pool table, another a pinball machine. There's a jukebox playing a song by Diana Ross and the Supremes; several of the boys are singing falsetto-accompaniment. Baby Love. And an area for dancing. But no one's dancing. The same embarrassment in the high school gym.

A slower survey of the inhabitants—almost no one over the age of 25. Most of the boys here are high school girls, even the ones of college age. A few pretend to be butch, others don't care. Every so often, two or three of them leave together. I listen for conversations. More gossip. Some of it desperate. Longings. Judgments.

Hopes. And the usual chatter about classmates, teachers, schools, movies … and Shaun Cassidy.

Someone behind me says to someone else. "Let's go to the Stampede." "What's the Stampede?" "You've never been there? Come on." I follow them out. Discreetly.

The Stampede is on Santa Monica, near the corner of Fairfax. It's a beer bar. Inside, it's decorated to look like a western street. A shingled awning around the bar has a stuffed cougar perched upon it. Black lights make white T-shirts glow. A young crowd, drinking age. All the way to the back, a small patio. The place is filled with manboys standing around, looking at each other and pretending that they're not standing around and looking at each other, imagining, wishing, dreaming. Some of them search my face, I nod dispassionately, then turn away. The jukebox plays "Light My Fire," Jim Morrison and The Doors. If Gino's is high school, then The Stampede is junior year at city college. The boys are a little more like boys here, but they still seem much too young.

I know what it is—like all the others wandering the shadowed streets, they're still unfinished. They don't know who they are. They haven't had to dive into the mud and shit and blood. They haven't had anyone shooting at them.

Two couples walk in the front door, the wives holding the husbands' arms possessively. Some of the queers exchange glances. Tourists. Visiting the zoo, the freak show. They've never seen real faggots before. Someone behind me whispers bitchily. "The husbands will be back next week. Without the fish. It's always that way."

A couple blocks west, there's another bar, The Rusty Nail. More of the same, maybe a rougher crowd, a little older. A couple blocks east, The Spike. East of that, a leather bar. Okay, I got it. Circus of Books stays open 24 hours—the adult section, pick up a copy of the Bob Damron guide book. This is what I need. I take it back to my apartment and make X's on the map. No surprises here. Georgia was right. Queer bars and bathhouses. Another cluster of congruency.

Draw the connecting lines. Traffic goes back and forth on Santa Monica boulevard, occasionally down to Gino's on Melrose. Oh, and there's a place over here on Beverly, The Stud. Enter in the rear. Unintended irony. They hang bicycles and canoes and rocking chairs from the high ceiling. It's funky and faddish. Up on Sunset, the Sea Witch. Glass balls in nets, and a great view of the city lights. They allow dancing—furtively. On Santa Monica, a little west of La Cienega, hidden among the bright lights of the billboards, another hidden dance club. Everybody's testing the limits of enforcement.

For two weeks, I check out all the bars, all the clubs. But my first hunch is strongest. Gino's is the hunting ground. I can feel it. I don't need to listen for the little hairs.

As the nights warm up, something is awakening. A restlessness in the air. A feverish subculture of summer is readying itself. But this year, it's reckless. Next year, it'll be worse, self-destructive. The year after that, 1969, it'll implode on itself. But right now, this moment, it still hasn't realized itself yet.

It's the boomers, the baby boomers, all those children of war coming of age at the very same moment, their juices surging, their chaotic desires and wants and needs—the wildness unleashed, the rebels without a pause; the ones who think that college has made them educated, and the ones who resent them because they have to work for their daily bread—all of them, horny as hell, possessed by the sense of freedom that comes from the wheel of a Mustang or a Camaro or a VW Beetle, liberally lubricated with cheap gasoline, marijuana and beer and raging hormones, out on the streets, looking for where it's happening.

It isn't happening anywhere, it's happening everywhere, and the noise and the stink pervades the night. The straight ones hit the Sunset Strip or the peppermint places on Ventura Blvd. Or they cruise up and down Van Nuys Blvd or Rosecrans Ave., and especially Hollywood Blvd. But the other ones—the quieter ones, the ones who didn't chase the girls, the music majors and the theater arts students, the shy boys and the wild boys—after all those years of longing, they're finally finding a place where they belong too, where there are others just like them. No, not just like them. But close enough. Here are others who will understand. Or not understand. There are so many different kinds, so many different ways of being queer. But at least, for a little while, in these furtive secret places, they won't have to pretend that they don't want what they want.

During the day, they'll rage about the unfairness of discrimination, about the ugliness of war—but at night, they all want to get laid. And that's what's surging here. The desolate lust of loneliness. It's a fevered subculture, a subset of the larger sickness that roils in the newspapers.

Our little vics—I pin their pictures to the wall and study them—they're cannon fodder. As innocent as the boy who stepped on the landmine, as unfinished as the new kid who took a bullet in the head from a jungle sniper on his first picket duty, as fresh and naïve as the one who got knifed by a Saigon whore. As stupid and trusting as the asshole who went out there because he thought it was his duty and came back with gravestones in his heart.

Finally pulled their pictures down and shoved them into a folder so I wouldn't have to look at their faces and the unanswered questions behind their eyes.

Didn't know much about queers. Didn't really want to. But I was starting to figure it out. Everything I knew was wrong.

Resumed surveillance of the vics. I had the first six now. Charting their habits, their patterns, their movements. Most of it was legwork. Confirmation of what I already knew. Thursday, vic number one shows up in the parking lot. Brad-boy. On his motorcycle. He rolls it right up behind Mame, playfully goosing her with the front wheel. Without even turning around, Mame wriggles her ass and says, "Wanna lose it?" Mame has a blond streak in her black hair now. The others are gushing over it. Brad grins, relaxes on the bike, eventually offers a ride to eager Lane, and roars off with him to catch the crabs.

A few nights later, Jeremy Weiss shows up at Gino's. Bingo. The connection. Georgia was right. Gay. Twinks. Horny.

Faded into shadow. Watched. He was smitten with a little blond twink who couldn't be bothered. Was this the Jerry that Mame was talking about? A crush on Dave who had a lover? Tailed him for the rest of the evening. He ended up at a featureless yellow building, a few blocks east. A very small sign on the door. You had to walk up close to read it. Y.M.A.C. Young Men's Athletic Club. Hmm. I had a feeling it was *not* a gymnasium. Observed for a while. Thinking.

I had three weeks left until the first vic disappeared. I was getting a good sense of the killing ground—this was the land of one-night stands. The perp didn't know the vics. He was hunting, just like everybody else, but hunting for a different kind of thrill. My guess, the vics didn't know him. They met him and disappeared. I wasn't going to find any other connectivity.

Had to think about this. How to ID the bastard. Mr. Death. That's what I was calling him now. How to stop him? Talked it over with Georgia. She made suggestions, most of them hands-on. But the way things work, the onsite agent is independent, has complete authority. Translation: it's your call.

Later. Past midnight.

Matt Vogel. Slightly built. Round face, round eyes, puppy eyes. Sweet-natured. In the parking lot at Gino's, sitting alone against the wall, between two cars, where no one can see him. Hands wrapped around his knees, head almost buried. Almost missed him. Stepped backward, took a second look. Yes, Matt. Just graduated from high school. Works as a busboy in a local coffee shop. Disappears in two months. Victim number two.

"What do you want?" He looks at me with wide eyes. Terrified.

"Are you all right?"

"What do you care?"

"You look like you're hurting."

"My parents found out. My dad threw me out of the house."

Couldn't think of anything to say. Scratched my neck. Finally. "How'd he find out?"

"He went through my underwear drawer."

"Found your magazines?"

He hesitates. "He found my panties. I like to wear panties. They feel softer. He ripped them all up."

"I knew a lieutenant who liked to wear panties. It's no big deal."

"Really?"

No, not really. But it was a game we played. Whenever anybody heard a horror story about anybody or anything, somebody always knew a lieutenant who did the same thing. Or worse. "Yeah, really. Listen, you can't stay here all night. Do you have a place to go?"

He shook his head. "I was waiting—to see if anyone I knew showed up—maybe I could crash with someone."

I noticed he didn't use the word "friend." That was the problem with this little war zone. Nobody made friends. I remembered fox holes and trenches where we clung to each other like brothers, like lovers, while the night exploded around us. But here, if two of these manboys clung to each other, it wasn't bombs that were exploding. I wondered if they had the same fear of dying alone—maybe even more so.

He'd given up waiting for Prince Charming. Mr. Right wasn't coming. And even Mr. Right Now hadn't shown up.

"Look, it's late. I live a couple blocks, close enough to walk." To his suspicious glance, I said, "You can sleep on the couch."

"No, it's all right. I can sleep at the tubs."

"The tubs?"

"Y-Mac. You been there?"

Shook my head.

"It's only two bucks. And I can shower in the morning before going to work. Scotty might even wash my clothes."

"You sure?"

"No."

At least, he's honest.

"Okay. As long as you have a place to go. It's not safe to hang out here—" And what if Mr. Death started early? But I didn't want to say that. Didn't want to scare the shit out of the kid.

"It's as safe here as anywhere—"

Something about the way he said it. "Somebody hurt you?"

"Sometimes people shout things as they drive by. Once, a couple of guys chased me for a block or so, then gave up and went back to their car."

Started to turn away, turned back. Didn't want to leave him alone. Dammit. "Look—you can come with me. I won't—I got meat loaf in the fridge. And ice cream. You want to talk, I'll listen. You don't want to talk, I won't bug you. You can crash for a couple of days, until you sort things out with your folks. All right?"

Matt thinks about it. He might look sweet and innocent, but he's learned how to be suspicious. That's how life works. First it beats you up, then it beats you down.

His posture is wary. "You sure?"

Ohell, of course I'm not sure. And this is going to fuck up the timeline. Or is it? A thought occurs to me. An ugly thought. I don't like it, but maybe ... bait? I dunno. But what the fuck, I can't leave him out here in a dirty parking lot. "Yeah, come on."

He levers himself to his feet, brushes off his jeans. "I wouldn't do this, but—"

"Yeah, I know."

"—I've seen you around. Gino says you're okay."

"Gino doesn't know me."

"You were in Vietnam." A statement, not a question. I should have realized. I'm not invisible here. Some of the gossip is about me.

"Yeah," I admit. I was in Nam. I point him toward the street. "My pad is that way."

"Did you see any—"

"More than I wanted to." My reply is a little too gruff. He falls silent.

Why am I doing this? Why not? It's a chance to pry open the scab and look at the wound.

"I'm Matt."

"Yeah, I know."

"You got a name?"

"Oh, right. I'm ... Mike."

"Mike? I thought your name was Hand. Hand Solo. But that's like a ... a handle, isn't it. 'Cause everybody knows what a hand solo is, right?"

"Yeah. Right. It's a handle."

"Well. Glad to meet you, *Mike.*"

We shake hands, there on the street. It changes the dynamic. Now we know each other. More than before anyway. Resume walking.

He's cute in a funny kind of way. If I liked boys, he'd be the kind of boy I liked. If this were the world I wanted to live in, he'd be my little brother. I'd make him hot chocolate. I'd read him bedtime stories and tuck him in at night. And I'd beat up anybody who made fun of him at school.

But this isn't that world—this is the world where men don't stand too close to men because ... men don't do that.

"Mike?"

"Yeah?"

"Can I take a shower at your place?"

"Of course."

"Just enough to blow the stink off me."

"When did your Dad throw you out?"

"Two days ago."

"You've been out here on the street two days?"

"Yeah."

"What a shit."

"No, he's all right."

"No, he isn't. Anyone who throws their kid out *isn't* all right."

Matt doesn't answer. He's torn between a misguided sense of loyalty and gratefulness that someone's trying to understand. He's afraid to disagree.

We reach the bottom of the stairs. I hesitate. Why *am* I doing this? In annoyance, I snap back. "Because that's the kind of person I am."

"Huh?" Matt looks at me curiously.

"Sorry. Arguing with myself. That's the answer that ends the argument."

"Oh." He follows me up the stairs.

He looks around the apartment, looks at the charts on the walls. I'm glad I pulled the pictures down. He would have freaked to have seen his yearbook picture here.

"Are you a cop?"

"No. I'm a—researcher."

"These look like something a detective would do. What are you researching?"

"Traffic patterns. It's—um, sociology. We're studying the gay community."

"Never heard it called that. 'Gay community.'"

"Well, no, it isn't much of one." Not yet, anyway. "But nobody's ever studied how it all works, and so—"

"You're not gay, are you?"

No easy answer to that. I don't even know myself. The night goes on forever here. Daytime is just an unpleasant interruption. "Look, I'm not anything right now. Okay?"

"Okay."

I feed him. We talk for awhile. Nothing in particular. Mostly food. Cafeteria food. Restaurant food. Army food. Mess halls. C-rations. Fast food. Real food. Places we've been. Hawaii. Disneyland. San Francisco. Las Vegas. His family traveled more than mine. He's seen more of the surrounding countryside than me.

Eventually, we both realize it's late. He steps into the shower, I toss him a pair of pajamas, too big for him, but it's all I've got, and take his clothes downstairs to the laundry room. T-shirt, blue jeans, white gym socks, pink panties, soft nylon, a little bit of lace. So what.

He's a sweet kid. Too sweet really. Fuckit. He's entitled to a quirk. Who knows? Maybe he'll make lieutenant. When I come back up, he's already curled up on the couch.

The other bedroom is set up as an office. A wooden desk, an IBM Selectric typewriter, a chair, a lockable filing cabinet. I'll be up for a while, typing my notes for Georgia. God knows what she'll think of this. But I'll have his stuff into the dryer and laid out on a chair in less than an hour, long before I'm ready to collapse into my own bed.

Georgia taught me how to write a report. First list all the facts. Just what happened, nothing else. Don't add any opinions. The first few weeks, she'd hand me back my reports with all my opinions crossed out in thick red stripes. Pretty soon, I learned what was fact, what was story. After you've listed the facts, you don't need anything else. The facts speak for themselves. They tell you everything. So I learned to enjoy writing reports, the satisfying clickety-clickety-click of the typewriter keys, and the infuriated golf ball of the Selectric whirling back and forth across the page, leaving crisp insect-like impressions on the clean white paper. One page, two. Rarely more. But it always works. Typing calms me, helps me organize my thoughts.

Only thing is, if you don't have all the facts, if you don't have enough facts, if you don't have any facts, you stay stuck in the unknown. That's the problem.

Later, much later, as I'm staring at the dark ceiling, waiting for sleep to come, I listen for the sound of vampires on the street below. But most of them have found their partners and crept off to their coffins. So the war zone is silent. For now, anyway.

Somewhere, out there, Mr. Death is churning. And I still know nothing about him.

Sunday morning. I wake up late. Still tired. My back hurts. I smell coffee. Wearing only boxers, I pad into the kitchen. Matt is wearing my pajama tops. They're too big on him. He's obviously given up on the bottoms, too long, and they won't stay up. He looks like the little boy version of a Doris Day movie. He's cooking eggs with onions and potatoes. And toast with strawberry jam. And a fresh pot of coffee. It's almost like being married.

"Is this okay?" he asks uncertainly. "I thought—I mean, I wanted to do something to say thank you."

"You did good," I say around a mouthful. "Very good. You can cook for me anytime." Why did I say that? "Oh, your clothes are on the chair by the door. I washed them last night."

"Yeah, I saw. Thanks. I have to go to work at noon." He hesitates. "Um, I'm going to try calling my Dad today. Um. If it doesn't work out—you said something about—a couple days...?"

"No problem. I'll leave a key under the mat. If I'm not here, just let yourself in."

"You trust me?"

"You're not a thief."

"How do you know?"

"I know." I added, "People who cook like this, don't steal."

He's silent for a moment. "My mom used to say I'd make someone a wonderful wife someday. My dad would get really pissed off."

"Well, hey, your dad doesn't get it."

Matt looks over at me, waiting for an explanation.

"It's simple. You take of other people, they take care of you. The best thing you can do for someone else is cook for them, feed them, serve them a wonderful meal. That's how you tell someone that you—well, you know—that you care."

He blushes, covers it by looking at the clock. "I gotta get to work—" And he rushes to leave.

Sunday. There's no such thing as an afternoon off, but I cut myself some personal time anyway. Took a drive out to Burbank. Shouldn't have. Wasn't supposed to. It was part of the contract. Your old life is dead. Hands off. But I did it anyway. I owed it to them. No. I owed it to myself.

The place was pretty much as I remembered it. The tree in front was bigger, the house a little smaller, the paint a little more faded. I parked in front. Rang the bell and waited. Inside, Shotgun barked excitedly.

Behind the screen door, the front door opened. Like the house, he looked smaller. And like the house, a little more faded.

"Yes?" he squinted.

"Dad. It's me—Michael."

"Mickey?" He was already pushing open the screen door. Shotgun scrambled out. Even with his bad hip, that dog was still a force to be reckoned with. Dad fell into my arms, and Shotgun leapt at us both, with frenzied yowps of impatience. "Down you stupid son of a bitch, down!" That worked for half a second.

Dad held me at arm's length. "You look different. But how—? They said you were lost in the timequake."

"I was. I am. I found my way back—it's a long story."

He hugged me again, and I felt his shoulders shaking. Sobbing? I held him tight. He felt frail. Then abruptly, he broke away, and turned toward the house. "Come on in. I'll make some tea. We'll talk. I think I have some coffee cake. You don't know how hard it's been without you. I haven't touched your room. It'll be good to have you back—"

I followed him in. "Um, Dad. I don't know how long I can stay. I have a job—"

"A job. That's good. What kind of a job?"

"I'm not really allowed to discuss it. It's that kind of a job."

"Oh. You're working for the government."

"I'm not really allowed to discuss it. I'm not even supposed to be here, but—"

"That's all right, I understand. We'll talk about other things. Come sit. Sit. You'll stay for dinner. It'll be like old times. I have spaghetti sauce in the freezer. Just the way you like it. No, it's no trouble at all. I still cook for two, even though it's just me and that old dog, too stubborn to die. Both of us."

I didn't tell him that wasn't true. I didn't tell him that he and that stubborn old dog would both be gone in a few short months. I rubbed my eyes, suddenly full of water. This was harder than I thought.

Somewhere between the spaghetti and the ice cream, Dad asked what had happened over there. I struggled inside, trying to figure out what to say, how to say it, realized it couldn't be explained, and simply finally shrugged and said, "It was ... what it was." Dad knew me well enough to know that was all the answer he was going to get, and that was the end of that. The walls were comfortably up again.

Somewhere after the ice cream, I realized we didn't have all that much to talk about anymore. Not really. But that was okay. Just being able to watch him, just being able to skritch the dog behind the ears again, that was okay. That was enough. So I let him talk me into spending the night. My old bed felt familiar and different, both at the same time. I didn't sleep much. In the middle of the night, Shotgun oozed up onto the foot of the bed and sprawled out lazily, pushing me off to the side, grumpling his annoyance that I was taking up so much room; every so often, he farted his opinion of the spaghetti sauce, then after a while he began snoring, a wheezing-whistling noise. He was still snoring loudly when the first glow of morning seeped in the window.

Over breakfast, I told a lie. Told Dad I was on assignment. That part wasn't a lie. But I told him the assignment was somewhere east, I couldn't say exactly where, but I'd call him whenever I could. He pretended to understand.

"Dad," I said. "I just wanted you to know, you didn't lose me. Okay?"

"I know," he said. And he held me for a long time before finally releasing me with a clap on the shoulder. "You go get the bad guys," he said, something he'd said to me all my life—from the day he'd given me my first cowboy hat and cap pistol. Something he said again the day I got on the plane to Nam. You go get the bad guys.

"I will, Dad. I promise."

I kissed him. I hadn't kissed him since I was eight, but I kissed him now. Then I drove away quickly, feeling confused and embarrassed.

It was a drizzly day, mostly gray. Skipped the gym, filled the tank, drove around the city, locating the homes of the other seven victims. Two lived in the dorms at UCLA, Dykstra and Sproul. Didn't know if they knew each other. Maybe. One was a T.A. major, the other music. Another lived with a roommate (lover?) in a cheap apartment off of Melrose, almost walking distance from me, except in L.A., there's no such thing as "walking distance." If it's more than two doors down, you drive.

One lived way the hell out in Azusa. That was a long drive, even with the I-10 freeway. Another in the north end of the San Fernando Valley. All these soft boys, so lonely for a place to be accepted that they'd drive twenty-thirty miles to stand around in a cruddy green patio—to stand around with other soft boys.

Something went klunk. Like a nickel dropping in a soda machine. One of those small insights that explains everything. This was puberty for these boys. Adolescence. The first date, the first kiss, the first chance to hold hands with someone special. Delayed, postponed, a decade's worth of longing—while everybody around you celebrates life, you pretend, suppress, inhibit, deprive yourself of your own joy—but finally, ultimately, eventually, you find a place where you can have a taste of everything denied. It's heady, exciting, giddy. Yes. This is why they drive so far. Hormones. Pheromones. Whatever. The only bright light in a darkened landscape. They can't stay away. This is home—the only place where they can be themselves.

Okay. Now, figure out the predator—

I got back to the apartment, the drizzle had turned to showers. Matt was sitting by the door, arms wrapped around his knees. A half-full knapsack next to him. He scrambled to his feet, both hopeful and terrified. And flustered. He looked damp and disheveled. A red mark on his forehead, another on his neck.

"Are you all right?"

"I couldn't find the key—"

"Oh, shit. I forgot to put it under the mat—"

"I thought you were angry with me—"

"Oh, kiddo, no. I screwed up. You didn't do anything wrong. It's my fuckup. Shit, you must have thought—on top of everything else—"

Before I could finish the sentence, he started crying.

"What happened—? No, wait—" I fumbled the key into the lock, pushed him inside, grabbed his knapsack, closed the door behind us, steered him to the kitchen table, took down a bottle of Glenfiddich, poured two shots.

He stopped crying long enough to sniff the glass. "What is this?" He took a sip anyway. "It burns."

"It's supposed to. It's single-malt whiskey. Scotch." I sat down opposite him. "I went to see—someone. My dad. I haven't seen him in a while, and this might be the last time. I wasn't supposed to, but I did it anyway. I spent the night, I slept in my old room, my old bed. What you said yesterday, it made me think—"

He didn't hear me. He swallowed hard, gulped. "My mom called me at work. She said I should come home and pick up my things. My dad wouldn't be there. Only she was wrong. He came home early. He started beating me—"

I reached over and lifted up his shirt. He had red marks on his side, on his back, on his shoulders, on his arms. He winced when I touched his side.

Got up, went into the bathroom, pulled out the first-aid kit. Almost a doctor's bag. Stethoscope, tape, ointment, bandages, a flask, even a small bottle of morphine and a needle. Also brass knuckles and a blackjack. And some other toys. You learn as you go. Came back into the kitchen, pulled his shirt off, smeared ointment on the reddest marks, then taped his ribs. Did it all without talking. I was too angry to speak. Finally: "Did you get all your stuff?"

He shook his head.

"All right, let's go get it."

"We can't—"

Grabbed his arm, pulled him to his feet, pulled him out the door, down the stairs, and out to the car, ignoring the rain. "You need your clothes, your shoes, your—whatever else belongs to you. It's yours."

"My dad'll—he's too big! Please don't—"

I already had the car in gear. "Fasten your seatbelt, Matt. What's that thing that Bette Davis says? It's going to be a bumpy night." The tires squealed as I turned out onto Melrose.

I turned south on Fairfax, splashing through puddles. Neither of us said anything for a bit.

When I turned right on Third, he said, "Mike. I don't want you to do this."

"I hear you." I continued to drive.

"I'm not going to tell you where I live—lived."

"I already know."

"How?"

"I'm your fairy godfather, that's how. Don't ask."

"You are no fairy," he said. Then he added, sadly, "I am."

"Well, I guess that's why you need a godfather."

"What are you gonna do?"

I grinned. "I'm gonna make him an offer he can't refuse."

Matt didn't get the joke, of course. It wouldn't be a joke for another five years. But that was okay. I got it.

Turned left, turned right. Pulled up in front of a tiny, well-tended house. Matt followed me out of the car, up the walk. The front door yanked open. Matt was right—he was *big*. An ape. But he wasn't a trained one. The scattershot bruises on his son were proof of that. He'd substituted size for skill. Probably done it all his life. He wore an ugly scowl. "Who are you?" he demanded.

Gave him the only answer he was entitled to. Punched him hard in the chest, shoving him straight back into the house. Followed in quickly. Before he could react, chest-punched him again—harder, hard enough to slam him into the wall. The house shook. He bounced off and this time met my fist in his gut. His gut was hard, but the brass knucks were harder. He grunted, didn't double up, but he lurched—it was enough, I pulled his head down to meet my rising knee, felt his nose break with a satisfying crunch of bone and blood.

Hauled him to his feet. His face was bleeding. "You're a big man, aren't you? Beating on a kid." He was still trying to catch his breath. "Matt, go get your things. Now."

A woman came out of the kitchen, wiping her hands in a dish towel. "Matty—?" Then she saw me. "Who are you—?" Then she saw her husband. "Joe—?"

I grabbed the towel from her hands, pushed it at Joe, pushed Joe at a chair, he flopped into it, covering his bloody nose. "You can sit down too, ma'am; probably a good idea." She hesitated, then sat. Joe was still gasping, eyeing me warily.

Nobody spoke for a long moment.

Finally, the wife. "Are you going to hurt us?"

"Not planning on it. Of course, that can change." I nodded meaningfully at the asshole.

"You—you won't get away with this—"

"You won't call the police. He won't let you. He doesn't want anyone to know he's got a queer son." Took a breath. I wasn't planning to play counselor, but Matt needed time to gather his stuff, and I needed to keep the asshole from thinking too hard. "All right, look, lady—you should leave this jerkoff. Because if you don't, he's going to kill you someday. The only thing that's saved your life this long is that he's been taking it out on the kid instead, hasn't he? With the kid outa here, you're wearing the bullseye now. If I'm not mistaken, that bruise on your cheek is recent. Like maybe, this afternoon? And maybe there's a few more under that dress that don't show?"

She didn't answer.

"You're not doing yourself any favors, being a punching bag for this miserable failure. And you sure as hell didn't help your kid any, did you? Letting him beat the kid—you're a coward. Do you know what the word 'enabler' means? You're an enabler. You're just as fucking guilty. Because you let *him* get away with it."

Turned to the gorilla. "See, here's the thing, Joe. You're an asshole. You're beneath contempt. That's your son, your own flesh and blood. You should love him more than anybody else in the world. But he's fucking terrified of you. The one moment in his life, he needs his dad to love and understand and be there for him more than anything else, what do you do? You beat him up and throw him out. What a fuckwad you are. Your wife's a coward, you're a bully, and the two of you are throwing away the only thing in the world you've done right—raise a kid who still knows how to smile, god knows why, growing up with you two creeps. You don't deserve this kid. Shut up, both of you. I'm in no mood to argue. You can beat your wife, Joe, and you can beat your kid—but you can't beat the butt-ugly truth. You're a waste of skin. Oh, and if you're thinking about getting out of that chair, don't. If you try, I'll kill you. I'm in that kind of a mood."

"He means it, Dad—" That was Matt, coming back into the room. "He's an ex-commando. Special forces. Green Beret. Or something. He was in Vietnam. I don't want him to hurt you—"

"You got everything?"

He hefted a duffel and a suitcase. Hastily filled.

Matt's mother looked back and forth between us. Finally, she worked up the nerve to ask. "What are you? Some kind of queer?"

I looked her up and down. "Are you the alternative?" Jesus Christ on a pogo stick, I can't believe I said that. "Wait a minute." Turned back to the gorilla. "Your son's leaving home. You'll never see him again. Give me your wallet. No—I didn't say think about it. I said, *give me your wallet.*"

He passed it over. Nearly three hundred bucks. I passed the cash to Matt. "Here. Your inheritance. It's enough to live on for a couple months. If you're careful." Dropped the wallet on the floor.

"You two are getting off lucky. I'm letting you live." Looked at the gorilla again. "You come after this kid, you ever come near him, you ever lay a hand on him again, I will kill you. I will hunt you down and I will make sure you take a long time to die. You ever beat your wife again, I'll break both your arms. Are we clear? Nod your head, this isn't television." Glanced sideways. "Matt, you want to say goodbye?"

He shook his head.

"Then go get in the car."

Waited a moment, looking to see if the asshole was thinking about following. He wasn't. His face was ashen. He was still having trouble breathing. I looked to the wife. "You know what? I think you'd better call an ambulance. I might have punched him a little too hard, I might have cracked his sternum. I wish I could say I'm sorry about that, but I'm not."

Drove back without talking. The rain was coming down harder now. Matt was shaken. Probably didn't know what to think, what to feel.

Got back to the apartment. He hesitated. "You coming up?"

"I thought you wanted me to—" He held up the money. "I mean—isn't what this is for?"

"There's plenty of time for that tomorrow. Or the next day." And besides, "You shouldn't be alone tonight." I grabbed his suitcase and duffel. Not as heavy as I'd thought. Gorilla and wife hadn't been very generous.

Inside, I went scrounging through the junk drawer, found the extra key and handed it to him. "Listen. Don't take this the wrong way. But I'm worried about you. You stay here as long as you need to."

He looked at the key in his hand, looked up to me, a question on his face.

"You can cook, right? You can clean? That'll be your rent. We'll move my type-writer in here, over against the wall or something. And you can have the other room. Just one condition. Stay away from Gino's—" No, that's not fair. "I mean, don't go there without me. And don't go out with anyone without—well, checking with me. Okay?"

"You trying to be my dad?"

"No. Well, maybe a big brother. I dunno." I sat down opposite him. "Can you keep a secret?"

"Not very well. I mean—my dad found out."

"There is that. When did you know you were—?"

"When I was twelve. Or thirteen."

"So you can keep a secret for five years. Six? Right?"

He nodded.

"All right. What I'm going to tell you is that big a secret. You up for it?"

He didn't say no. I took that as a yes.

"You know how I knew where you lived? I know a lot of other stuff too. Some bad shit is going down this year. Dangerous shit. People are going to get hurt. Killed. I'm not a cop. But I'm—I'm like a private investigator. And I'm looking for the guy who's gonna do it. You're his type. And so are a lot of the other kids at Gino's. I wish I could warn everyone, but if I do, it'll spread. You know how those girls love to gossip. And if the perp knows I'm looking for him, I'll never catch him. So you can't tell anyone. And the only reason I'm telling you is—is because I want your help."

"You need *my* help?"

"I *want* your help. I don't need it. But I can use it. If you're up to it."

"Up to it? Is it dangerous?"

"Do you think I'd put you in danger?"

He thought about it for a moment. "But you want to use me as bait."

"I want to see who cruises you. I want to know who talks to you. That's all."

"Can I ask you something?"

"Go ahead."

"Was this your plan all along? From the very beginning? When you brought me home the other night?"

"The truth?" I looked him right in the eye. "No. This was not what I planned. You were just one of the boys I was going to watch for a while—"

He frowned. He turned that over in his head. And then—oh, shit—he got it. "You son of a bitch!" He started to get up. "You know, don't you!" He looked around for his duffel and his suitcase. I resisted the temptation to get up. Force was absolutely the wrong answer here. He waited for my response.

I nodded. "Yeah, you're right. I know."

"You're a—a time-raveler?"

Nodded again.

"Then it's true? There really are? Because I thought that was just—like an urban legend or something."

"It's true," I admitted.

He stared at me, hard, as if trying to puzzle me out. "So ... how far from the future are you?"

"I'm not. I'm from three years in the past. But I've been to the future. Twelve years anyway. You're going to like it. Parts of it, anyway."

"Like what?"

Shrug. "Things like ... um, well, Stonewall, for one. Neil Armstrong. Apple. Luke Skywalker. Pac Man. But I think, Stonewall might be the big one."

"What's Stonewall?"

"You'll find out soon enough. It's—it's going to be ... kind of important."

"Give me a hint?"

"Rosa Parks."

"Who's Rosa Parks?"

"Look it up."

He frowned, annoyed. Then his frown eased. He dropped the duffel on the living room floor and came back into the kitchen nook. "Tell me what you know about me."

"Um—"

"You want me to do this, you have to tell me." He sat down opposite me and waited.

"Okay," I said. "Wait." I went into the bedroom, came back with the folders. Tossed it on the table. "I have to prevent the disappearance of this boy. Have you ever seen him?" I slid over the picture of Jeremy Weiss.

Matt looked, frowned, started to shake his head no, then said, "No, wait, I think he comes in mostly on weekends."

"He's number three. There are two other disappearances before him. Ten more afterward. Here's number one."

"That's Brad. Brad-boy. He rides a motorcycle. He comes in, picks up a trick, rides off. Nobody knows much about him, not even his tricks."

"Yeah, I've seen it."

"When does he—?"

"Two weeks. A little more than two weeks." I passed over the next folder. "This is the second victim."

He opened it, saw his own picture, and flinched. He deflated like a balloon. "I—I'm going to die."

"No. You're not. I promise you. *I promise you.*"

"But I did. I mean, I will, won't I? I mean—this?" He looked suddenly terrified.

"No. You won't."

"But how do you know? I thought time was—"

"Time is mutable. If it wasn't, I wouldn't be here. I couldn't be here. Neither could you."

He accepted that, but only because he wanted to. He wasn't convinced. After a bit, he reached over and took the other folders, opened them one at a time. He recognized two more of the boys, none of the rest. Not surprising. The last disappearance was only 14 this year.

"All right. Now, tell me—do you go anywhere else besides Gino's?"

He shook his head. "There's a club down in Garden Grove, for 18-and-up. But I've never been there. Um, there's the tubs. The Y-Mac. I've only been there two-three times. There isn't anyplace else. I can't get into any of the bars."

"So mostly you go to Gino's?"

"That's where everybody goes."

"All right. Here's the deal. You don't go to Gino's unless I go too. I want to see who talks to you. And if somebody asks you to go home with him—we'll work out a signal. You'll tug on your ear. And I'll ... I'll do what's appropriate."

Matt nodded. He seemed grateful to have a plan. He took a breath. "I saw some knockwurst in the fridge. Should I make that for dinner?"

I wasn't that hungry, but I nodded.

He clattered around in the cupboards for a bit, looking to see what else he could put on a plate. "There's some baked beans here, and some English muffins. I can make a little salad and open a couple of Cokes...?"

"That sounds good." I gathered up the photos and slid them back into their respective folders.

"Mike...?"

"Yeah."

"If I don't go home with anyone, how will you know which one's the killer?"

"I'm still trying to figure that out."

"You'll have to watch Brad-boy too, won't you?"

"Yeah."

"Maybe I'm not getting this right. But the only way you'll know who the killer is ... will be by letting him kill someone. Brad. Right?"

"Well, no. I have a pretty good idea which night Brad disappears. So whoever talks to him on that night, that's probably the killer. But if I can keep Brad from going off with him, then I can save his life."

"But what if it's the wrong guy. I mean, if he doesn't get a chance to kill anyone, how will you know he's the killer?"

I got up, put the bottle of scotch back in the cupboard. Leaned against the wall and looked down at Matt. He was cutting up lettuce. "There's another part to the problem. Let's say that I give Brad a flat tire so he can't go out that night. Or something like that. Let's say I keep Brad from tricking out. Then that means Mr. Death—that's what I call him—picks up someone else. And maybe not that night, maybe the next night, or the following week. Maybe the whole timetable gets interrupted, screwed up—then this whole schedule is useless."

"So you have to watch Brad...."

"Yeah. And I'll have to tail him to wherever he goes and ... and hope it's the real deal."

"That's not fair to Brad."

"It's not fair to any of you guys. I'm only hired to save one boy—but there's a dozen others, and maybe more, who are equally at risk. I told you, time is mutable.

If I jiggle it too hard, I lose the whole case. I can save you and Jeremy and Brad, but who else dies in your place?"

He got it—it was like a body blow. He laid down the knife and said, "Shit." And then he reacted to his own vulgarity with a softly spoken, "Well, that wasn't very ladylike, was it?"

He put dinner on the table and we ate in silence for a while. Finally, I said, "This is very good. Thank you."

"You like it?"

"It's a whole meal. It's more than I would have done for myself."

"I had to learn how to cook. My mom—" He shrugged.

"Yeah, I saw."

"She's not a bad person. Neither is my dad, except when he drinks too much—"

"And how often is that?"

He got the point. "Yeah. Okay."

Later, after the dishes were put away, I took a quick shower. I came out, wearing only a towel. He looked at me, then glanced away quickly. He said something about a long soak and hurried into the bathroom. I heard the sound of bath water running. After a moment, he stuck his head out. "Towels?"

"Hall closet. Top shelf. Here." I pulled the yellow towels down for him. "Anything else?"

"I don't think so." Still not looking at me.

"All right. I'm going to bed. I've got a meeting in the morning. When I get back we'll go get a bed for you."

"Um. Okay. Thanks." He disappeared back into the bathroom.

I like to sleep with the windows open. Here, just off Melrose, the nights were sometimes stifling, sometimes breezy, sometimes cold. Sometimes the wind blew in from the sea, and sometimes the air was still and smelled of jasmine. Tonight there was cold wind, the last wet remnant of a gloomy drizzly day. The air smelled clean. Tomorrow would be bright.

I got into bed, listened for awhile to the water dripping from the corners of the building, to the occasional wet swish of a car passing by, to the distant roar of the city, and maybe even the hint of music somewhere. Got up, went to the closet, pulled out an extra blanket and dropped it on the couch. He'd need it.

Got back into bed and listened to the roar of my own thoughts. Matt had put his finger on it—what I already knew and hadn't been willing to say. I had no way to ID the perp. Not unless I let someone die.

For a while, I wondered how the other operatives would handle this case. But I didn't wonder too long, I already knew. They'd save the Weiss kid and ignore the other dozen—because the Weiss kid's family were the only ones paying. That's why Georgia had given me this job. Because she knew I didn't think that way. She knew I wouldn't be satisfied with saving only the one. She knew how I thought. You don't leave any man behind.

And whether anyone recognized it or not, this was a war zone.

These people; they knew they were living in enemy territory. They were terrified of the midnight knock—the accusations at work, the innuendoes of friends, the gossip of neighbors, and all the awful consequences. The soft boys, they start out sweet and playful, almost innocent; but time erodes their spirit. The older they grow, the heavier the burden becomes. Day by day, they learn to be furtive, they become embittered and their voices edged with acid. You can stand in the bar and watch it happening in their eyes, night after night, the shadowed resentment, the festering anger. Why do we have to hide? Pretend? The question—*what's wrong with me?*— was backward. Pretty soon it turns into *what's wrong with them?* And the chasm grows, the isolation increases. The secret world digs deeper underground.

But not for too much longer. The summer of love is already exploding, next year the summer of lust, and after that the frenzied summer of disaster. But that summer would also bring the Stonewall revolution, and after that—this would start to change. All of it.

I almost envied them.

Because, they knew what they wanted.

I still had no idea.

There was a soft knock at the bedroom door. It pushed open with a squeak. Matt stuck his head in. "Are you asleep?"

"Not yet. Are you all right?"

"Mike…?" He stepped closer to the edge of the bed. "Can I sleep with you tonight? Just to sleep. That's all. The couch is—"

"Kind of uncomfortable, I know. Yeah, come on." I slid over and pulled back the edge of the blanket for him. He slipped in next to me. Not too close.

We lay on our backs, side by side. Staring at the ceiling.

"This isn't about the couch, is it?"

"Uh-uh."

"Didn't think so."

"You don't have to worry—"

"I'm not worried."

"I mean—"

"Matt. It's all right. You don't have to explain." I thought about those nights in Nam where soldiers hugged each other closer than brothers. Of course, rifle fire, mortar shells, explosions, napalm, mud, blood and shit—and the threat of immediate death—can do that to you. The moments in the jungle when the patrol would stop for break, collapsing into heaps, sometimes lying in each other's laps, the only closeness we had—and the nights in cheap Saigon hotel rooms, when there weren't enough mattresses to go around, you shared with your buddy, and you felt glad he was next to you. The touch of a squad mate in the dark. You learned to feel safe in the stink and sweat of other men. They were your other half. You couldn't explain that either, not to anyone who hadn't been there.

"I'm sorry, Mike."

"For what?"

"For being such a—" He couldn't finish the sentence. He couldn't say the word.

"Matt…?"

"My mom used to call me Matty. When I was little."

"You want me to call you Matty?"

"If you want to."

"Matty, come here." I put my arm around his shoulder and pulled him closer, so his head was nestled against my chest. I couldn't see what he was wearing, but it felt too soft. Nylon something. I ignored it. Whatever. "C'mere, Let your Uncle Mike tell you a bedtime story." He wasn't relaxed, he lay tense next to me. Waiting for me to push him away in disgust…?

"When I was twelve, my dad brought home a puppy for my birthday, just a few weeks old. He was a black Labrador retriever and he was so clumsy he tripped over his own shadow. He couldn't walk without stubbing his face, but I fell in love with him the first moment I saw him. My dad asked me if I liked him and I said he was just perfect. I called him Shotgun. The first night, he whined for his mommy, so I took him into bed with me and held him close and talked to him and petted him and he fell asleep next to me. He followed me everywhere and he slept with me every night. Then Monday morning, we took him to the vet for his shots. The vet examined him and examined him and examined him, and he just started frowning worse and worse. Finally, he says there's something wrong with Shotgun; he's defective, his hips are malformed, he's going to have trouble walking, he's going to go lame, a whole bunch of other stuff. Then, he took my dad aside and talked to him for a long time. I couldn't hear what they were saying, but my dad just shook his head and we took Shotgun home."

"The vet wanted to put him to sleep?"

"Yeah. But my dad wouldn't let him. I didn't find that part out until later. We went home, but I didn't want to have anything to do with Shotgun anymore. Because he was broken. He wasn't perfect. And I wanted a dog that was perfect. Shotgun kept following me around and I kept pushing him away. That night, he kept trying to jump up onto my bed and he kept whining, but I wouldn't lift him up and let him sleep with me. Finally, my dad came in and asked what was wrong and I said I didn't want Shotgun anymore, but I wouldn't say why. My dad figured it out though. He knew I was angry at Shotgun for not being perfect. But he didn't argue with me, he just said, okay, he'd find a new home for Shotgun in the morning. But…for tonight, I should let Shotgun sleep with me one last time. I asked why, and my dad picked up the puppy and held him in his lap petting him for a moment, and I asked why again, and my dad put Shotgun in my lap and he said, 'Because ugly puppies need love too. In fact, ugly puppies need even more love.' And when he said that, I started to feel real bad for pushing Shotgun away, and then my dad said, 'Besides, Shotgun doesn't know he's ugly. He just knows he loves you a lot. But if you don't love him and you don't want him, then tomorrow we'll find someone who doesn't care how ugly he is and who'll be happy to have a dog who will love them as much as Shotgun can.' That's when I hugged Shotgun close to my chest and said, 'NO! He's mine and you're not giving him away. Because I can love him more than anybody. I don't care how ugly he is.' And that's when my dad tousled my hair like this and whispered in my ear, 'That's the exact same thing your mom said when *you* were born.'"

Matt snorted. Then curled up with his backside pressed against me. I couldn't figure out if he felt like a girl or a boy or something of both—or neither.

All these queerboys—some of them were girlboys, yes; but the rest, they were still boys. Softboys. Men without...without what? Some quality of maleness? No. They were male. They just didn't do all that chest-beating. Hmm. Of course not. Chest-beating is for dominance—it's to drive away all the other males from the mates. That's counter-productive in this environment. Here...they want to be... friendly? Affectionate? But chest-beaters can't do that, can't afford to do that without losing dominance. No wonder the queerboys were the targets of bullies. Bullies are cowards; they pick victims who won't fight back. I stared at the ceiling, wondering if this train of thought would bring me any closer to Mr. Death. I couldn't see how.

After a while, I stopped worrying about it and fell asleep myself.

The next morning, we pretended everything was normal. He went to work, I drove up to Hollywood Blvd.

Georgia looked grim. She met my eyes briefly, jerked her head toward the office. "Mr. Harris wants to see you."

"Mr. Harris?"

"Ted Harris—the man whose name is on the door?"

"Oh. I didn't know there was a real Ted Harris. I thought he was a fictitious business name, or something."

"There's a real Ted Harris. And he's waiting for you."

Shit. They'd found out I'd visited Dad. I had that called-to-the-principal's-office, cold-lump-in-my-gut feeling.

I knocked once on the door, no answer, I turned the knob and went in. I'd never been in this room before. Desk, chairs, lamp, and a middle-aged man with his back to me, staring out the half-circular window that faced the boulevard. The window was grimy, but the morning sun still broke the gloom with blue-white bars of dust. Harris turned around to face me. I recognized him.

"Eakins—?" Every time I met him he was a different age. This time he had silver highlights in his hair, but he still looked young.

"Sit." He pointed. I sat.

"Your real name is Harris?"

He sat down behind the desk. "My real name is Eakins. There is no Harris. But I'm him. When I need to be. Today, I need to be."

"All right, that makes as much sense as anything—"

"Shut up." I shut.

He had a folder on his desk. He tapped it. "This case you're working on—the lost boys...?"

"I'm making progress. There's a common connection among the victims."

"Tell me."

"There's a gay teen club on Melrose. I think the perp is finding them there. It's in my reports. There's also a secondary location—"

"You have to drop the case."

"Eh?"

"Is there something wrong with your hearing? Drop the case."

"May I ask why?"

His voice was dispassionate. "No."

"But these boys are going to die—"

"That can't be your concern."

"It already is."

Eakins took a breath, one of those I'm-about-to-say-something-important inhalation/exhalations. He leaned across the desk and fixed me with an intense glare. "Listen to me. Life is empty and meaningless. It doesn't mean *anything*—and it doesn't mean anything that it doesn't mean anything. Drop the case."

"That's not an answer."

"It's the only answer you're ever going to get. This conversation is over." He started to rise—

I stayed sat. "No."

He stopped, half-out of his chair. "I gave you an instruction. I expect you to follow it."

"No."

"I wasn't asking you for an argument."

"Well, you're getting one. I'm not abandoning those boys to die. I need something more from you."

He sank back down into the chair. "There are things you don't know. There are things you don't understand. That's the way it is. That's the way it has to be."

"I made a promise to one of those boys that nothing's going to happen to him."

"You got involved—?"

"I made a promise."

"Which boy?"

"Number two."

Eakins opened the folder. Turned pages. "This one?" He held up Matty's picture. I nodded. Eakins dropped the picture on the desk, leaned back in his chair. Held up the other pictures. "He's not part of this case."

"Eh?"

"The others are part of this case. That one isn't."

"I don't understand."

"And I'm not going to explain it. The case is over. Disengage. We'll send you somewhere else. Georgia's got a courier job up in the Bay Area—"

"I don't want it."

"That wasn't a request. You'll take the courier job and we won't say anything about where you were Sunday night."

"No."

"We're paying you a lot of money—"

"You're renting my judgment, not buying my soul. That's why you're paying so much."

Eakins hesitated—not because he was uncertain, but because he was annoyed. He glanced away, as if checking a cue card, then came back to me. "I knew you were going to refuse. But we still had to have the conversation."

"Is that it?" I put my hands on the arms of the chair, preparing to rise.

"Not quite. This ends your employment here. Georgia has your severance check. We'll expect the return of all materials related to this case by the end of business today."

"You think that'll accomplish anything? You can't stop me from saving their lives as a private citizen."

Eakins didn't respond to that. He was already sorting files on his desk, as if looking for the next piece of business to attend to. "Close the door on your way out, will you?"

Georgia was waiting for me. Her face was tight. I knew that look. There was a lot she wanted to say, but she couldn't, she wasn't allowed. Instead, she held out an envelope. "The apartment and the car are in your name, we've subtracted the cost from your check. The bank book has your ancillary earnings. You'll be all right. Oh—and I'll need your ID card."

I took it out of my wallet and passed it over. "You knew, didn't you?"

"There was never any doubt."

"You know me that well?"

"No. But I know that part of you." She pressed the envelope into my hands. Pressed close enough for me to tell that she still wore the same sweet perfume.

Went down the stairs slowly. Stopped to have my shoes shined one last time while I looked through the contents of the envelope. A fat wad of cash, a hefty check, a surprisingly healthy bank account, several other bits of necessary paperwork—and a scrap of paper with a hastily written note. *"Musso & Franks. 15 minutes."* I sniffed the paper, recognized the perfume, nodded, tipped Roy a fiver, and started west on the boulevard. I'd get there just in time.

I asked for a table in the back, she came in a few minutes later, sat down opposite me without a word. I waited. She held up a finger to catch the waiter's eye, ordered two shots of Glenfiddich, then looked straight across to me. "Eakins is a first class prick."

Shook my head. "Nah, he's only a second class prick."

She considered it. "Not even that high. He's a dildo."

My silence was agreement. "So...?"

She opened her purse, took out another envelope, laid it on the table. "You weren't supposed to get this case. No one was. When he found out I'd assigned it to you, he almost fired me. He might still."

"I don't think so. You're still there as far uptime as I've been."

She shook her head as if that weren't important now. "The whole thing is…it doesn't make sense. Why would he abrogate a contract? Anyway—" She pushed the envelope across. "Here. See what you can make out of this."

"What is it?"

"I have no idea. He disappears for days, weeks, months at a time. Then he shows up as if not a day has passed. I started Xeroxing stuff from his desk, a few years ago. I don't know why. I thought—I thought maybe it would give me some insights. There's things that…I don't know what they are. There's pictures. Like this thing—" She shuffled through the photos. "—I think it's a telephone. It's got buttons like a phone, but it looks like something from *Star Trek*, it flips open—but it doesn't work, it just says 'no service.' And this other thing, it looks like a poker chip, one side is sticky, you can stick it to a wall, the other side is all black—is it a bug of some kind? A microphone? A camera? Or maybe it's a chrono-sensor? And then there are these silver disks, five inches wide, what the hell are they? They look like diffraction gratings. Some of them say Memorex on the back. Are they some kind of recording tape, only without the tape? And there's all these different kinds of pills. I tried looking up the names, but they're not listed in any medical encyclopedia. What the hell is Tagamet? Or Viagra? Or Xylamis? Or any of these others?"

"Are there dates on any of this material?"

"Not always. But sometimes. The farthest one is 2039. But I think he's gone farther. A lot farther. I think he's gotten hold of the Caltech local-field time-maps. Or maybe he's been dropping his own sensors and making his own maps, I don't know. But I've never seen anything that looks like a map. It doesn't make a lot of sense. But then again—there's that thing that he says, that if we could go back to say, 1907 with a bunch of stuff from today—a transistor radio, a princess phone, a portable TV, a record album, birth control pills, things like that—none of it would make sense to someone living in that time. Even a copy of a news magazine wouldn't make much sense because the language shifts so much. So if Eakins has stuff from thirty, forty, fifty years into the future, we wouldn't get much of it—"

"Yes and no. Fifty years ago, they didn't have the same experience of progress, so they didn't have the vocabulary to encompass the kinds of changes that come with time. We have a different perspective—because change is part of our history, we expect it to be part of our future. So, if anything, we look at this stuff and we don't see a mystery as much as we see the limits of our experience."

"Now, you sound like me."

"I was quoting you. Paraphrasing." I shuffled through the papers, the photos, the notes. "None of this has any bearing on this case, does it?"

"I don't know. But I thought you should see it. Maybe it'll give you an insight into Eakins."

Shook my head. "It proves that he knows more than he's telling us. But we already knew that."

She glanced at her watch. "Okay, I'm out of time." She stood up, leaned over and kissed me quickly. "Take care of yourself—and your little boyfriend too."

"He's not my—" But she was already gone.

I shoved everything back into the envelope and ordered a steak sandwich. The day had started weird and gotten weirder, and it wasn't half over. I might as well face the rest of it on a full belly.

Went back to the apartment. Photographed everything. Then gathered it up and went straight to the local copy shop. Five copies, collated. Paid in cash. Put one copy in the trunk of the car, put another in the apartment safe, and mailed the other three to three different PO Boxes. Delivered the originals back to Georgia who accepted them without comment. Eakins had already left the building. But neither of us said anything; it was possible he had the offices bugged—maybe even with his funny poker chips.

By the time I got home, Matty was unpacking groceries. The whole scene looked very domestic. "Did you have a good day?" he asked. All I needed was a pair of slippers and the evening newspaper.

When I didn't answer, he looked up. Worried. "You okay?"

"Yeah. I'm just ... thinking about stuff."

"You're always thinking about stuff."

"Well, this is stuff that needs thinking about."

He got it. He shut up and busied himself in the kitchen. I went out onto the balcony and stared at Melrose Ave. Cold and gray, it was going to rain again tonight; a second storm right behind the first. Something Eakins had said—none of it made sense, but one piece of it had its own particular stink of wrongness. Why is Matty not important to this case?

And that led directly to the next question: What did Eakins know that he wasn't telling me? And *why* wasn't he telling? Because if I knew...it would affect things. What things? What *other* plan was working?

Obviously, we weren't on the same side. Had we ever been? Never mind that. That's a dead-end right now. I had to think about Matty.

If Matty is irrelevant, then...is he still in danger? No, of course he's in danger. He disappeared. We know that. But if he disappeared, then why is he irrelevant...? Unless his disappearance is unrelated. And if his disappearance is unrelated, then... of course, he would be entirely useless to this case. Shit.

But how would Eakins know that? Unless Eakins knew something about Matty. Or knew something about all the others.

And of course, all of that assumed that Eakins was telling the truth. What if he was purposely trying to mislead me? But then that brought me back to the first question. What was Eakins up to?

Not having the answers to any of these questions annoyed me. I didn't have a plan, I didn't have anything on which to base a plan. The only thing I could think was to continue with the plan that Eakins had scuttled—not because it was a good plan, but because it would force the situation. It would force Eakins to...to do what?

When the rain finally started, I went back in and sat down to dinner. Baked chicken. It was cold.

"Why didn't you call me?"

"You were thinking."

"Um—" I stopped myself. He was being considerate. "Okay."

"Do you want me to warm that up for you?"

"No, it's okay." I ate in silence for a bit, feeling uncomfortable. Finally I put my fork down and looked across at him. "Y'know what I just realized. I don't know how to talk to you."

He looked puzzled.

"This is good—" I indicated the cold chicken. "You can cook. I keep wanting to say you'll make someone a wonderful wife someday. But I can't say that because—"

"It's different when you say it. When you say it, it isn't mocking."

"It's still the wrong thing to say. It's demeaning, isn't it?"

"I don't mind. Not from you." He started to clear the table.

I took a breath. "Are you—?" I stopped. "I don't know how to ask this. Are you...attracted to me?"

He nearly dropped the plates. He was facing away so I couldn't see his expression, but his body was suddenly tense. He finally turned around so he could look at me. "Do you want me to be?"

"It's like this. I don't connect well to people. Not anybody. Male or female. I can go through the motions. For a while. But only for a while. I'm always...holding back."

"Why?"

I shrugged.

"That's your answer?"

"When you start raveling, you get unraveled yourself. You get detached. You don't belong to any time, you can't belong to any person. So you turn off that part of yourself."

He didn't respond right away. He got the coffee pot from the stove and filled two cups. He brought cream and sugar to the table, for himself, not me. As he stirred his coffee, he finally asked, "So why are you telling me this? Are you telling me I shouldn't care about you because you can't care back?"

"I don't know if I can care about anybody. When I try, it doesn't work out. So I've stopped trying."

"You didn't answer my question. Why are you telling me this?"

"Because...right now, you're the only person I have to talk to."

"Not your dad?"

"This is not a conversation I could have with my dad."

He shook his head in frustrated confusion. "Just what are we talking about?"

"About the fact that I am so fucking angry and confused and upset and annoyed and frustrated and—and even despairing—that if you weren't here, right now, tonight, if you weren't here to talk to...I'd end up sitting alone in a chair again— with my gun barrel in my mouth, wondering if I have the courage to pull the trigger. I've known guys who've sucked the bullets out of their guns. It makes a mess on the wall. And I used to wonder why they did it. That was before. Not anymore. Now I'm starting to understand."

His face was white. "You're scaring the hell out of me."

"You don't have to worry. I'm not going to do anything stupid. I just—I just want you to know that right now...you're doing me the favor by staying here."

"This is a lot more than I can deal with—I'm not—"

I nodded. "Kiddo, I'm more than most people can deal with. That's why they leave. Look—I figured, after all you've been through, you'd understand what it feels like to feel so separated from everyone else. I'm coming from the same place—same place, different time zone."

He stirred his coffee thoughtfully. "There's a quote I learned in school. Sometimes it helps me. It's from Edmund Burke. I don't know who he is or was, it doesn't matter, he said, 'Never despair; but if you do, work on in despair.'"

Considered it. "Yeah. That's good. It's useful."

We sat there for a while. Not talking.

Later. I came out of my bedroom. He was curled up on the couch. "Matt? Matty?"

"Huh—?" He rolled over, looked at me groggily.

"If you want to come sleep in the bed again, you can."

"No, it's all right."

But a little bit later, he pushed open the bedroom door, padded over, and slipped in next to me. So that was something. I just didn't know what. But then again, neither did he. Probably.

The rain cleared up, leaving the air sparkling, the way it used to be in the thirties and the forties. Least, that's what they say. In two days, though, the smog levels would be back to their lung-choking worst. It's not just the million-plus internal combustion engines pouring out lead and carbon dioxide and all the other residues of inefficient fuel-burning. Los Angeles is ringed with mountains. That's why they call it a basin. Fresh air can't get in, stale air can't get out. It sits and stagnates. The Indians called it *el valle de fumar*. The valley of fumes. Only two things clean it—the once-in-a-while rainstorms of winter and spring, or the hot dry Santa Ana winds at the end of the summer. From June until October, don't bother breathing. You can breathe in November.

But today, today at least, was beautiful. It was a go-to-Disneyland day. And I almost suggested it to Matty, but he had to work, and I hadn't figured anything else out yet, so we disentangled ourselves from the mustiness of sleep and stepped into the comfortable zombie-zone of routine.

We had a week to go before Brad Boyd would disappear. I spent some of the daytime tailing him, even though that was probably a dead-end. He worked at an adult bookstore on Vine, just across the street from the Hollywood Ranch Market. Sometimes he bought a Coke and a burrito from the counter in front. Usually he walked to work, leaving the motorcycle parked under a small covered patio in front of the apartments. It wouldn't be hard to sabotage the bike. That would keep him at home. But it wouldn't get me closer to Mr. Death.

Twice, I drove out to visit Dad. The second time, I took him to the doctor. I already knew that it wouldn't do any good, wouldn't delay the inevitable, but I had to try. Maybe make it a little easier for him. Dad fussed at me, but not too much. He didn't have the same strength to argue that he'd had when I was eighteen, when I'd come back with the recruiting forms, when I told him of my decision, when I snapped back at him, "Well, if it's a mistake, it's *my* mistake to make, not yours." It wasn't until Duncan stepped on a landmine just a few paces ahead of me that I discovered what Dad had been so scared of. But by then, I was already starting to shut down. So the scared never got all the way in, never got to the bottom. Part of me remained convinced that it wasn't going to happen to me. Ever. Just the same, I got out of there as soon as my rotation ended.

I sat at the kitchen table, puzzling over the photos and the copies of the notes Georgia had taken from Eakins' desk. Someday they'd make sense, but at this point in time—literally—they were incomprehensible. The only thing this stuff proved was that Eakins had time-hopped farther into the future than anyone I'd ever heard.

In the evenings, Matty and I would shadow Brad again. Having an extra set of eyes helped. The first night motorcycle-boy started at Gino's, had no luck or didn't like what he saw, and rode over to the Stampede. We parked in the lot of the supermarket across the street, just behind the bus bench where we could watch the front entrance and his motorcycle. The Stampede had an emergency exit in the rear patio, but without an emergency the only way out was the front. We might be here awhile, how long does it take to cruise a bar? Matty went for doughnuts and coffee.

"If he comes out before you get back, I have to follow him; if I'm not here, you wait in the doughnut shop. As soon as he lands somewhere, I'll come back for you. Understand? Don't talk to anyone."

But the plan wasn't needed; Matty was back in five and Brad-Boy didn't come out of the bar for forty minutes. He was alone. We followed him east on Melrose where he checked into the YMAC.

"He could be there all night," said Matty. "Maybe till one or two."

"How do you know? Have you ever—?"

"With Brad-boy? No. I would have, if he ever asked. But he never did. I don't think I would now. Everybody says he's kind of user. Use 'em and lose 'em."

"Yeah, I got that feeling. I'm wondering if...maybe I should go in."

"It's just a lot of guys standing around in the dark."

"Just like the Stampede? Or Gino's?"

"Yeah, but without their clothes on. Just towels."

"Hm." We sat in silence for a bit.

"You can't get in without a card," Matty offered. "A member has to take you in the first time. If Scotty doesn't like your look, he says it's not a membership night. If he lets you in, he gives you a card and tells you the rules. I could probably get you in."

"Is that an offer?"

"I'm just trying to be helpful."

I thought about it.

"How often have you been there?"

"Not much. Two times, three. I don't like the way it smells."

"I don't think it's going to help us much."

"Why not?"

"Because...if I've figured this right, our bad guy doesn't work out of this place. He has to take his victims somewhere else. Somewhere close. Like a house—a house with lots of shrubbery around it, or maybe an alley in the back, or a connected garage. He has to have some way to remove the...the evidence without anyone seeing."

"So we can go home?"

"I'm thinking. We should probably wait. Make sure that Brad-boy gets home safe."

"I have work tomorrow."

"There's a blanket on the back seat, if you want to try sleeping."

"No. I can't sleep in a car."

"I don't like sitting here either." I started the engine, put the car in gear, turned on the headlights. "Let's call it a night."

Back at the apartment, I pushed him toward the bedroom, and went into my makeshift office to type up a quick report. Picked up subject at, followed subject to, subject was inside for, came out at, proceeded to, stayed for, came out, went to, waited, abandoned stake-out at. I didn't have to write it, the case was over, and there was no place to turn in the report, but old habits die hard—and it's always useful to have accurate notes.

It didn't take long to finish, but by the time I slid between the sheets, Matty was already asleep, half-sprawled toward the center of the bed. I gave him a gentle push and he turned half-away. Fair enough.

Matty felt warm. He reminded me of Shotgun. Shotgun would stretch out next to me, anchoring his back against mine, we'd sleep spine to spine. That big old dog was like me—he liked having someone covering his back. Except Matty wasn't Shotgun, he wasn't an ugly puppy, and he wasn't anything else either. Why was I doing this?

The next night, Brad-boy stayed home and watched television until ten. He got on his motorcycle and went to Gino's. Sat on his bike for twenty minutes chatting with Mame, Peaches, Dave, Jeremy, and two boys Matty couldn't name. "You think it's one of them?"

"No. They're too young. And they're—"

"—too fem?"

"Yeah. Too fem."

"Some fems can be real bitches—"

"Yeah, I heard some of the stories about Duchess and Princess. But I don't think we have to worry about either of these. They look like lost surfer boys. A couple kids from Pali High daring each other to visit a gay club."

Eventually, one of the surfer boys climbed onto the back of Brad-boy's bike and they roared east on Melrose. Back to Brad's apartment. Was he going to spend the night? Or would Brad be bringing him back here in an hour?

It turned out to be less than that. Apparently, our Brad wasn't much for foreplay. Forty-five minutes turnaround. Then he went home and went back to bed. Alone.

Thursday night, Brad went to a movie. We sat three rows behind him. *The Dirty Dozen*. All-star cast. Lee Marvin, Ernest Borgnine, Charles Bronson, Jim Brown, John Cassavetes, Richard Jaeckel, George Kennedy, Trini Lopez, Robert Ryan, Telly Savalas, Clint Walker, and some funny-looking goofball named Donald Sutherland.

Friday night, Gino's was crowded with lithe and feral manboys. Brad-boy actually got off the bike and went in. Matty followed him while I spoke privately to Gino. I flashed one of the P.I. cards I hadn't given back to Georgia. Either she hadn't noticed or she had. I wasn't sure if I should let her know what I was up to. She was probably in enough trouble already. She probably already knew anyway. No, I'd wait until I had something.

Gino glanced at the card unsurprised, looked at me, and said, "What do you need?"

"I heard you're the go-to guy." He looked blank, he didn't recognize the term. "The go-to guy. The guy to go to...if you have the clap and need the name of a doctor, if you need a letter from a shrink to stay out of the army, that kind of stuff."

"I know some people," Gino said. Dr. Ellis was due to be murdered by a hustler-boy. Scotty would be implicated in a different murder and YMAC's new location on La Brea would be raided. In a couple of years. "What can I do for you?"

"You know your regulars, right? You know who's solid and who's flaky. If someone new shows up, you read them the rules before you let them in. Do you ever notice who folks leave with?"

"I see a lot of boys come through here every weekend—"

"Brad Boyd. Do you ever notice who he leaves with?"

"Hard not to. He always revs his engine and roars out of here, leaving a stinking cloud of smoke behind. I've asked him not to—"

"Could you keep an eye out?"

"Who are you working for? His parents?"

"No. This isn't that kind of a case."

"What kind of a case is it?"

"This kind." I pushed a fifty dollar bill into his hand. I had another ready in case one wasn't enough.

Gino glanced down only long enough to check the denomination. "You got the size right." He tucked it into his pocket.

I leaned forward, whispered, "This kid's life might be in danger. I think he's being stalked. But I don't have any hard evidence yet. Help me out, I'll give you another one of those."

Gino shrugged. "I have a club to run. Weekends are busy. I can't promise anything. But if I see something, I'll let you know."

I passed him a card. No name, just a phone number. "If no one answers, there's an answering machine. You can leave a message."

Gino looked impressed. Code-A-Phones were expensive. I didn't tell him it belonged to the Harris Agency—and that any day now I expected Georgia to request its return.

I found Matty in the shadows next to the jukebox. Brad was playing pool in the corner. I pulled Matty farther back and we pretended to be only casually interested in the pool game. So far, it looked like Brad was only here to play pool. He had a nasty style of slop shooting. It looked like he was just casually slamming the balls around; but he'd been playing barroom pool long enough, he knew what he was doing. He kept winning. Three, four, six games and he still hadn't been beaten.

"Whyn't you go play him?"

"Uh-uh. I might interrupt something or someone. We need to see who he picks up—or who picks him up."

"Is it tonight?"

"Tomorrow. I have a feeling—I could be wrong—but I have a hunch that our subject might be here tonight as well. Whatever he's feeling, it has to be building up. Building up over time. If Brad is his first, then maybe this is the night that triggers his urge, but maybe he isn't quite ready to act. Something happens tonight. He gets his—whatever it is he gets. His courage. And tomorrow is the night it gets real enough for him to actually do something."

"What if he picks someone else?"

"I don't think so. I think Brad is the first because Brad is the easiest. I don't think our fellow has learned how to cruise yet. He might not have picked Brad out, but I think he's in this room. Here's what I want you to do. You go one way, I'll go the other. We'll both walk around, just looking—cruising. See if you see anyone who strikes you as wrong."

"Wrong in what way?"

"Any way at all."

"Too old? Too ugly?"

"No. Brad is a slut, but he isn't a whore. Like all the rest of you girls, he wants someone young and cute. So watch out for anyone who looks like his type, but possibly nervous, uneasy, uncertain—someone who doesn't look like he's having a good time. His clothes or his haircut might look a little weird, like he doesn't understand the current styles. He's probably hanging back, just watching; he might have a very intense look, or he might even look perfectly normal. But I'll bet he's someone new, someone you haven't seen before, so watch for that. Just look at every unfamiliar face closely and see what you see. Okay? You go this way, I'll go that. Three or four times around, then meet back here."

There was something else to watch out for, but I didn't tell Matty. It was baggage he didn't need to carry. I didn't like having him do this, but I needed his eyes. He had experience here. He could read these people. I couldn't. Not very well. There was an overlay of—I didn't have a word for it—but there was a map to this territory that I didn't have.

I'd given him one clue. Watch out for someone who's out of style. But he wouldn't have heard what I was really saying—I think we're dealing with a freelance time-hopper, someone who's riding the quakes. He's probably from the past, maybe ten or twenty years; I doubted he was from the future, the future is a little friendlier to queers, but I didn't rule it out—maybe the cultural shifts were stressing him out.

But if I had to put money on it, I'd bet that this was a guy with a very bad jones in his johnson. He wanted sex with young men, but afterwards he was so ashamed at what he had done, he had to destroy the evidence. Even if that meant murder.

In the movies, murderers always have a look about them. That's because the director puts the actor in a hotter or colder light, making him stand out just a bit from everyone else around him; and the makeup man will do something around the actor's eyes, making his face look sallow or drawn or gaunt; and the camera angle will be such that everyone else in the crowd will be turned away, or in shadow, or simply two steps back. In the movies, it's easy to spot the bad guy—the director tells you where to look and what to notice.

In real life…murderers look just like everybody else. Sick and tired and resigned. Beaten up and beaten down. Everybody looks like a murderer. So nobody does.

In here, they looked—they looked like queers, but once you got past the part that was queer and you looked at the people, they looked like people. Softboys, girl-boys, manboys, wild boys, wilder boys, feral boys. None of them looked like men. But that's what I was looking for. Someone who wasn't a boy anymore. A man? Maybe. Someone who'd passed through boyhood without ever finishing the job. But the only one in here who looked like that…was me.

For a moment, I envied this confetti of boys and their flickering schoolgirl free-dom. Because at least, while they were here, flirting and gossiping, nattering and chattering, they had a place of their own, a place to belong. If I'd ever had a place to belong, it must have been closed the night I passed by.

Circled four times, five, breathing faint smells of marijuana, Aramis, Clearasil, and Sen-sen. Passed Matty going the other way, kept going, searched faces, all the faces—some of them searched back, wondering if they could find comfort in mine. That wasn't possible. I don't do comfort. They got it and looked away.

And then finally, we came back to the dark corner next to the jukebox and com-pared notes. Matty shook his head. "A bunch of frat-boys from the ZBT chapter at UCLA, checking out the scene. A guy who says he's only here doing research for a book; yeah, like I believe that. A couple fellows up from Garden Grove, one from San Francisco. A guy who looks like a cop, but Gino didn't flash any lights, and you don't put the red bandana hanging out of your front pocket anyway. And Uncle Philsy. That's what everybody calls him."

"Which one is Uncle Philsy—oh, him." The troll. Short. Bald. Fiftyish. Tending to fat. Disconnected predatory grin. Wandering aimlessly through the boys, simply enjoying the view. Sweet and repulsive at the same time. But harmless.

"Gino knows him. Says he's okay."

"What was that about a guy doing research for a book? Don't trust him. Writers are all creeps and liars. And what about the other guy—bandana man?"

"Bandana man is looking for someone. His son, I think. He's only pretending to be gay."

"How'd you find all this out so quickly?"

"Telefag."

"Eh?"

"Gino. Mame."

"Oh. What about that guy there, the tall one, thirtyish—?"

"Walt? He's an agent. I think. Least that's what he says—"

"All right. Anyone with history here is probably okay. Is that it?"

"I think so." Beat. "Lane found out that Mame is telling everyone he has the crabs. They're out in the parking lot having a bitch fight. You think—"

"No. Our boy is looking for a boy, not a girl."

"Hey...Mike?" Tentative.

"Yeah?"

"Promise you won't get mad?"

"What?"

"Mame thinks you're my boy friend. That's what she's telling everyone."

Snorted. Smiled. Actually amused by the thought. "Might as well be. You live with me. You cook. You do the laundry. We sleep in the same bed. We're just about married."

"Except we don't have sex."

"See, that proves we're married."

Matty blinked. He didn't get it. He said, "I'd marry you. If you asked. If you were—"

I put my hand on the wall over his head, leaning forward and sheltering him under my arm. I leaned down close as if I was going to whisper in his ear. Instead, I kissed him quickly on the cheek. Nobody saw. Gino actively discouraged overt displays. Fear of cops.

"What was that for?" Matty asked.

"That was for you."

"Oh." Now he was really confused. We both were. He looked up at me, eyes glistening in the black-light darkness. "Um ... Mike?"

"Yes?"

"Brad just walked out to the parking lot—"

"Yeah, I saw him." That was part of the reason I put up my arm and bent down low—to shield both of us from Brad's notice. But I didn't tell Matty that. "Let's go."

Brad had gone out through the patio door. We ducked around to the door at the front of the building, then sideways through the space between the art gallery and Gino's. Just in time to see Brad backing his bike away from the wall, and someone turned away from us, waiting to get on the back. As soon as Brad had the engine grumbling, the other fellow climbed on and wrapped his arms around Brad's waist.

"Do you recognize him?"

"No—"

Stuck my head in the patio door. "Who'd he leave with?"

Gino shrugged. "Never saw him before—"

"Shit."

Dashed for the car, Matty following.

We picked them up east on Melrose. Back to Brad's place? Maybe. No. They turned north just short of La Brea. Little cubbyhole apartments tucked away in here. Follow the tail light. The bike comes to a stop half a block ahead. Matty sinks down low and we cruise slowly past on the narrow street. Brad doesn't even look up. The other fellow turns around momentarily and gets caught briefly in the light. We coasted on past. "Oh, I know him," Matty says. "That's Tom. He shaves himself smooth. He dusts your ass with talcum powder and spanks you lightly."

"And you know this how—?"

"Telefag."

"You didn't—?"

Matty shook his head.

"You don't do it very often, do you?"

"I would. If I met the right guy."

"There are no right guys. Just like there are no right girls."

"Well, that sounded bitter."

"No. Just wise."

"I hope I never get that wise."

I pulled the car around the corner, parked in the red, left the motor running. "So, you know this guy Tom?"

"Not to speak to, but he's been around."

"Okay, then he's not our perp."

"Are we done for tonight?"

"Brad'll be going home after this, won't he?"

"Prob'ly."

"Okay, then we're done."

Matty took a shower while I typed up my notes. More of the same. Nothing to report. No clues. No directions. No leads. I sat in front of the typewriter, head in my hands, trying to figure out what to do next. Matty, still drying his hair, stuck his head in to ask if I wanted anything, coffee? I shook my head. He went off to bed.

I smelled like smoke from the club. It bothered me. I peeled off my clothes, started to drop them on the floor, then realized Matty would only pick them up in the morning; I dropped them into the hamper and stepped into the shower. Was it really the smoke I was trying to rinse off?

When I ran out of hot water, I turned off the spray. Matty had put fresh towels on the rack for me. I knew what he was trying to do. He wanted me to let him stay. I hadn't said he couldn't, but we hadn't negotiated any long-term agreement either.

Still naked, I slipped into bed. The springs creaked. He lay quietly beside me, breathing softly.

"You still awake?"

"Yeah."

"I'm thinking of dropping the case."

"You won't."

"Why not?"

"Because you can't stand not knowing."

"You're an insightful little guy, you know that?"

In response, he rolled on his side facing me, put an arm across my chest, pulled himself close, and kissed me softly on the cheek. He smelled good. He smelled clean. Then he rolled back to his side of the bed.

"What was that for?"

"That was for you."

"Oh."

This was it. This was the moment. It was going to happen. And for an instant—like that excruciating hesitation at the top of the first steep drop of the roller coaster—it felt inevitable. All I had to do was turn sideways, he'd roll into my arms, and we'd be...doing it.

And then, just as quickly, the moment passed. And we were still lying side by side in a queen-sized bed that had suddenly become much too narrow.

After a bit, I rolled out of bed.

"Are you all right?"

"Can't sleep." I got up, went to the drawer, started looking for clean underwear—it was all neatly folded. Grabbed a pair of boxers and started to pull them on. "I'm going back out."

He sat up. "Want me to come with?"

"No—" I said it too quickly. Turned and saw the expression of hurt on his face. "I need to think about the case. And you need to get to work early tomorrow."

"You sure? It's no trouble—"

"I'm sure." And then, I added, "Look—it's not you. It's me." The words were out of my mouth before I could stop them. He looked like I'd hit him with a sandbag. I shook my head in annoyed frustration. "God, I know that sounds stupid. But everything is all mixed up right now—like I'm in an emotional quake zone. I keep waiting for the ground to settle, but the shaking just gets worse and worse. I don't know whether to jump under a table or run out into the street."

"Let me help—?"

"Listen, sweetheart...." I sat down on the edge of the bed, my shirt still unbuttoned. "I don't want to hurt you."

"You won't hurt me—"

"I already have. I've taken advantage of you."

"No, you haven't. I'm here because I want to."

"Geezis. Listen to us." I ran my hand through my hair. "We sound like…like we're married."

"Our first fight—?" He grinned.

"Matty. Listen to me. It's time to get serious. People die around me. I make mistakes, people die. I tell someone it's safe, he steps on a landmine. I read the map wrong, we walk into an ambush. I fire a mortar—it blows up the wrong people. You're not safe around me. Nobody is."

He licked his lips uncertainly. He reached over and put his hand on mine. "I'll take the chance." He swallowed hard. "I have nowhere else to go."

"I said you could stay as long as you want. I meant it. But maybe you should want to be somewhere else. I'm scared—not for me, but for you."

"Mike, please don't make me go—"

"I'm not throwing you out, kiddo. Just…let me go out for a drive and try to think things through. This case—there's something stinking wrong here. It scares me. And I don't know why. All I know is that I've got this gnawing in my gut like there are snipers on the roofs of buildings and tunnels everywhere under the streets and landmines in the crosswalks. You were right before, when you said I can't stand not knowing. I've just got to get out of here and go out and look around. Even if I don't find anything, the looking is what I need."

"Are you sure, Mikey?"

I stood up, finished tucking in my shirt. "Go back to sleep. I just need an hour or two."

In this neighborhood, the night smells of jasmine and garlic. The apartment is just downwind of a little Italian restaurant with a permanent cauldron of simmering marinara. Rolled up to Santa Monica Blvd. and cruised east. It was late. The Union Pacific engine was already rolling massively west. The boulevard still had train tracks down the center. As long as the railroad could claim they were still using the tracks, the city couldn't pull them up, so every night they ran an old diesel engine down the center of the boulevard, all the way out to Santa Monica and back.

Farther east, the hustlers were hung out on the meat rack, most of them parked right on the borderline. The hustlers pretended to hitchhike. You drove west and picked them up east of La Brea, but they didn't discuss ways and means until after you drove through the intersection—the city's jurisdiction ended there. So that's how the hustlers tested for plainclothes; if you were vice, you couldn't cross the street. Once you were west of La Brea, it was a theme park—you could ride all the boys you could afford.

The hustlers were skinny and young—runaways mostly. Maybe a few junkies too. I wondered why our perp hadn't targeted them. Maybe he had. Who ever worries about the death of a male prostitute?

Turned on KFWB, the late-night DJ was playing a cut from the new Beatles album. Sergeant Pepper's Lonely Hearts Club Band. A Day In The Life. He blew his mind out in a car. Cruised all the way to Gower where the buildings grew shorter, older, and trashier—the second-rate sound studios and third-rate editing houses, then turned around and headed back west.

"So why not fuck Matty?" I asked myself. "It's not like—"

"Because," I answered. "Because."

"Ahh, this is going to be an intelligent conversation."

"Shut up." And then I added, "Because I'm not one of them."

"Yeah? Then why are we having this conversation? The truth is, you're afraid that you are."

I pulled over to the side of the boulevard and sat there shaking. He blew his mind out in a car. Part of me wanted to go home and climb back into bed and part of me was terrified that I would. Because I knew that if I ever climbed into that particular bed again, I'd never get out—

Someone knocked on the window. A hustler? I shook my head and waved him away.

He knocked again.

Pressed the button and rolled the window down. Eakins stuck his head in and said cheerfully, "Had enough?"

He didn't wait for my answer. He opened the car door and slid into the passenger seat. This wasn't the same Eakins I'd seen two weeks ago. That one had been middle-aged and methodical. This was a younger Eakins, impish and light.

"Yes. I've had enough. What the fuck is going on?"

He shrugged. "It's a snipe hunt. A dead-end. You've been wasting your time.

"But the disappearances are real...."

"Yeah, they are."

"So how can the case be a dead-end?"

"Because I say so. Want some advice?"

"What?"

"Go home to your boy friend and fuck your brains out, both of you. And forget everything else."

I looked at him. "I can't do that—"

"Yeah, I knew you'd say that. Too bad. That would save everyone a lot of trouble—especially you."

"Is that a threat?"

"Mike—you have to stop."

"I can't stop. I have to know what's going on."

"For your own safety—"

"I can take care of myself."

"Go home. Go to bed. Don't interfere with things you don't understand."

"Then explain it to me."

"I can't."

"Then I can't stop."

"Is that your final offer?"

"Yes."

"Okay." He sighed. He took out a flask and took a healthy swallow from it. He flipped open a pair of sunglasses and put them on. "You can't say I didn't try. Say goodbye to your past." Eakins touched his belt buckle—and the world flashed and shook with a bright bang that left me shuddering and queasy in my seat. "Welcome to 2032, Mike. The post-world."

My eyes were watering with the sudden brightness. It was still night, but the night blazed. The streets were brighter than day. I felt like I'd been punched in the gut, doused with ice water, and struck by lightning—and like I'd shot off in my shorts at the same time.

"What the fuck did you just do?!"

"Time-hopped us 65 years up—and triggered a major quake in the zone we left behind. You're outta there, Mike. For good. A 65 year jolt will produce at least three years of local displacement. Your Mustang is a lot of mass; bouncing that with us makes for a large epicenter, we probably sent ripples all the way to West Covina."

I couldn't catch my breath—the physical after-effects, the emotional shock, the dazzling lights around us—

Eakins passed me the flask. "Here. Drink this. It'll help."

I didn't even bother to ask what was in it—but it wasn't scotch. It tasted like cold vanilla milkshake, only with a warm peach after-glow like alcohol, but wasn't. "What the fuck—" As the glow spread up through my body, the queasiness eased. I started to catch my breath.

"I'll give you the short version. Time-travel is possible. But it's painful, even dangerous. Every time you punch a hole through time, it's like punching a hole in a big bowl of pudding. All the pudding around the hole collapses in to fill the empty space. You get ripples. That's what causes time-quakes. Time-travelers."

It sounded like bullshit to me. Except for the evidence. Everywhere, there were animated signs—huge screens with three-dimensional images as clear as windows, as dazzling as searchlights. Around us, traffic roared, great growling pods that towered over my much-smaller convertible.

"Shit. All this is *your* fault?"

"Mostly. Yes. Now, put the car in gear and drive. This is a restricted zone." Eakins pointed. "Head west, there's a car sanctuary at Fairfax."

If he hadn't told me this was Santa Monica Boulevard, I wouldn't have recognized it. The place looked like Tokyo's Ginza district. It looked like downtown Las Vegas. It looked like the Alice in Wonderland ride at Disneyland.

Buildings were no longer perpendicular. They curved upward. They leaned in or they leaned out. Things stuck out of them at odd angles. Several of them arched over the street and landed on the other side. Everything was brightly colored, all shades of day-glo and neon, a psychedelic nightmare.

Billboards were everywhere, most of them animated—giant TV screens showed scenes of seductive beauty, bright Hawaiian beaches, giant airliners gliding above sunlit clouds, naked men and women, women and women, men and men in splashing showers.

The vampires on the street wore alien makeup, shaded eyes and lips, ears outlined in glimmering metal, flashing lights all over their bodies, tattoos that writhed and danced. Most startling were the colors of their skins, pale blue, fluorescent green, shadowy silver, and gentle lavender. Some of them seemed to have shining scales, and several had tails sticking out the back of their satiny shorts. Males? Females? I couldn't always tell.

"Pay attention to the road," Eakins cautioned. "This car doesn't have auto-pilot."

His reminder annoyed me, but he was right. Directly ahead was—I couldn't begin to describe it—three bright peaks of whipped cream, elongated and stretched high into the sky, two hundred stories, maybe three hundred, maybe more. I couldn't tell. Buildings? There were lighted windows all the way up. Patterns of color danced up and down the sides. Closer, I could see gardens and terraces stretched between the lower flanks of the towers.

"What are those?"

"The spires?"

"Yeah."

"The bottom third are offices and condos, the rest of the way up is all chimney. Rigid inflatable tubes. The big ones are further inland, all the way from South Central to the Inland Empire."

"Those are chimneys?"

"Ever wonder how a prairie dog ventilates its nest?"

"What does that have to do—?"

"The entrances to the nest are always at different heights. An inch or two is sufficient. The wind blowing across the openings creates an air pressure differential. The higher opening has slightly less air pressure. That little bit is enough to pull the air through the nest. Suction. Passive technology. The chimneys work the same way. They reach up to different levels of the atmosphere. The wind pulls the air down the short ones and up through the tall ones. The air gets refreshed, the basin gets cleaned. Open your window. Take a breath."

I did. I smelled flowers.

"You can't see it at night. During the day, you'll see that almost every building has its own rooftop garden—and solar panels too. The average building produces 160% of its own power needs during the day, enough to store for the evening or sell back to the grid. With flywheels and fuel cells and stamina boxes, a building can store enough power to last through a week of rainstorms. Turn left here, into that parking ramp. Watch out for the home-bus—"

"This is Fairfax?"

"Yes, why?"

Shook my head. Amused. Amazed. The intersection went through the base of a tall bright building, Eiffel-tower shaped and arching to the sky, but swelling to a bulbous saucer-shape at the top. At least thirty stories, probably more. With a giant leg planted firmly on each corner of the intersection, the tower dominated the local skyline; traffic ran easily beneath high-swooping arches. The parking ramp Eakins had pointed me toward was almost certainly where the door of the Stampede had once been. Where the door of the mortuary that replaced it had been.

We rolled down underground. Eakins pointed. "Take the left ramp, left again, and keep going. Over there. Park in the security zone. This car, in the condition it's in, is easily worth twenty. Maybe twenty-five if we eBay it. We can Google the market."

"Um, could you do that in English?"

"You can auction your car. It's worth twenty, twenty-five million."

"Twenty-five million for a car?"

"For a classic collectible '67 Mustang convertible in near-mint condition with less than twelve thousand miles on it? Yes. I suggest you take it." He added, "Part of that is inflation. In 1967 dollars, it's maybe a half-million, but that's still not so bad for a used car that you can't legally drive on any city street."

"That's a lot of inflation—"

"I told you, this is the post-world."

"Post-what?"

"Post-everything. Including the meltdown."

"Meltdown—?" That didn't sound good.

"Economic. Everyone's a millionaire now—and lunch for two at McDonald's is over a hundred and fifty bucks."

"Shit."

"You'll learn."

Eakins directed me to a large parking place outlined in red. We got out of the car, he pulled me back away from the space, and did something with some kind of a remote control. A concrete box lowered around the car, settling itself down on the red outline. "There. Now it's safe. Let's go." We headed toward a bright alcove labeled *Up*.

"Where—?"

"Your new home. For the moment."

"What are you going to do with me?"

"Nothing. Nothing at all. I already did it" He put the same remote-thing to his ear and spoke. "Get me Brownie." Short pause. "Yeah, I've got him. The one I told you about. No, no problem. I'm bringing him up now. He's a little woozy—hell, so am I. I flashed a Mustang. No, it's great. A '67, almost cherry. Make an offer." He laughed and put the thing back in his pocket. A walkie-talkie of some kind? Maybe a telephone?

An elevator with glass sides lifted us up the angled side of the building, high above West Hollywood. Twenty, thirty, forty stories. Hard to tell. The elevator moved without any sense of motion. The door opened onto a foyer that looked the lobby of a small hotel, very private, very expensive. We stepped into a high-ceilinged gallery, with two or three levels of gardens and apartments. A wide waterfall splashed into a long shallow pool filled with lily pads and goldfish the size of terriers. The air smelled tropical.

"Which one?"

"To the left. Don't worry. We own the whole floor. Nobody gets in here without clearance."

Double doors slid open at our approach. "Take off your shoes," said Eakins. "Leave them here." He ushered me into a room that felt way too large and pointed me toward an alcove lined with more ferns and fish tanks.

"What is this place?"

"It's a sanctuary."

"A sanctuary?"

"In your terms—it's rest and recovery. In your time—a kind of hospital."

"I'm not crazy."

"Of course not. We're talking about orientation. Assimilation." He pointed to a couch. "Sit." He went to a counter and poured two drinks. More of the same vanilla-peach stuff. He handed me one, sipped at the other. Sat down opposite. "How hard do you think it would be for a man from 1900 to understand 1967?"

Thought about it.

"In 1900, the average person did not have electricity or incandescent lighting. He didn't have indoor plumbing. He didn't have running water, he had a hand pump. He didn't have a car, a radio, a television set. He didn't have a telephone. He'd never been more than ten miles from the place he was born. How do you think you would explain 1967 to him...?"

Scratched my head. Interesting question—and not the first time I'd had this conversation. Time-ravelers deal with short term displacements, tieing up the loose ends of unraveling lives. "Well, telephones, I guess he could get that. And probably radio. Yeah, wireless telegraphy, so ... probably he understand radio. And if he could get it about radio, he'd probably get it about television too. And cars—there were cars then, not a lot—so he'd understand cars and probably paved roads and indoor plumbing. Airplanes too, maybe. Lots of people were working on that stuff then."

"Right. Okay. But it's not the inventions, it's the side effects. Do you think he'd understand freeways, road rage, drive-through restaurants, used-car commercials? You could describe spray-paint, would he understand graffiti?"

"I suppose that stuff could be explained to him."

"Okay. And how about the not-so obvious side effects of industrialization—unions, integration, women's rights, birth control, social security, Medicare?"

"It might take some time. I guess it would depend on how much he wanted to understand."

"And how about Nazis, the Holocaust, World War II, Communism, the Iron Curtain? Nuclear weapons? Détente? Assymetric warfare?"

"All of that stuff is explainable too."

"You think so. Okay. Relativity. Ecology. Psychiatry. How about those? How about jazz, swing, rock and roll, hippies, psychedelics, recreational drugs, op art, pop art, absurdism, surrealism, cubism, nihilism? Kafka, Sartre, Kerouac?"

"Those are a little harder. A lot harder, I guess. But—"

"How about teaching him that he needs to take a bath or a shower every day instead of just once a week on Saturday night? How do you think he'd feel about shampoo and deodorants and striped toothpaste?"

"Striped toothpaste?"

"That comes later. Do you think he'd get it? Or do you think he'd wonder that we were all a bunch of over-fastidious, prissy, little fairies?"

"Oh, come on. I think a man from 1900 could get it. They weren't stupid, they just didn't have the same access to running water and water heaters and—"

"It's not about the technology. It's about the transformative effects that technology produces in a society. He could understand the mechanics and the engineering easily enough, but the social effects are what I'm talking about. How long do you think it would take to assimilate 65 years of societal changes?"

Shrug. "I don't know. A while. Okay, I get your point."

"Good. So how long do you think it will take before I can talk to you about bio-fuels, transfats, personal computers, random access memory, operating systems, cellular telephones, cellular automata, fractal diagnostics, information theory, consciousness technology, maglevs, the Chunnel, selfish genes, punctuated equilibrium, first-person shooters, chaos theory, the butterfly effect, quantum interferometry, chip fabrication, holographic projection, genetic engineering, retro-viruses, immunodeficiencies, genome decoding, telemars, digital image processing, megapixels, HDTV, blue-laser optical data storage, quantum encryption, differential biology, paleo-climatology, fuzzy logic, global warming, ocean desertification, stem-cell cloning, Internexii, superluminal transmission, laser fluidics, optical processing units, stamina boxes, buckyballs, carbon nanotubes, orbital elevators, personal dragons, micro-black holes, virtual communities, computer viruses, telecommuting, hypersonic transports, scramjets, designer drugs, implants, augments, nanotechnology, high frontiers, L5 stations—"

I held up a hand. "I said, I get the point."

"I was just warming up," Eakins said. "I hadn't even gotten as far as 2020. And I haven't even mentioned any of the societal changes. It would take a year or two to explain cultural reservoirs, period parks, reality-vid, contract families, role-cults, sex-nazis, religious coventries, home-buses, personal theme-parks, skater-boys, droogs, mind-settlers, tanking, fuzzy fandom, alienization, talking dogs, bluffers, bug-chasers, drollymen, fourviews, multi-channeling, phobics, insanitizing, plastrons, elf-players, the Zyne, virtual mapping, Clarkian magic, frodomatic compulsions, deep-enders, body-modders—"

"I think I saw some of that—"

"You have no idea. You want to change your appearance? You want to be taller? Shorter? Thinner? More muscular? Blond? Black? Want to change your sex? Your orientation? Want to go hermaphroditic or monosexual? Reorganize your second-ary characteristics? Design a new gender? Mustache and tits? Want a tail? Horns? Working gills? Want to augment your senses? Your intelligence? Or how would you simply like the stamina for a six-hour erection?"

Thought about it. "I'll pass, thanks. The intelligence augments, however—"

"There's a price—"

"More than twenty-five million?"

"Not in money. And we haven't even touched on the political or economic changes since your time."

"Like what—?"

"Like the dissolution of the United States of America—"

"What?!"

"You're in the Republic of California, right now, which also includes the states of Oregon and South Washington. The rest of the continent is still there, we just don't talk to them very much. There's sixteen other regional authorities, not count-ing the abandoned areas, and seven Canadian provinces—there's a common defense treaty in case the Mexicans get aggressive again, but that's not likely. Don't worry about it. The web has pretty much globalized the collective mindset, we're not pre-dictively scheduled to have another war until 2039, and that'll be an Asian war, with our participation limited to weapons contracts. In the meantime, we'll legalize you as a time-refugee. Most of the old records survived. Digitized. We have your birth certificate. You're a native. So you won't have any trouble getting on the citizen rolls. Otherwise, you'd be a refugee and you'd have to apply for a work permit, a visa, and eventually naturalization."

"I'm not staying—"

"You're not going back—"

"I can't stay here. You've already shown me how out of step I am. What if I promised not to interfere—?"

"You already broke that promise. Three times. You can't be trusted. Not yet, anyway." He took a long breath, exhaled. "You know, you're really an asshole. You really fucked things up for everyone—especially yourself. We *were* going to bring you aboard. After you finished your probation. It would have been a year or two more, your time. Now, I don't know. I don't know what we're going to do with you. It depends on you, really."

"What are my options—?"

He shrugged. "Let's see what Brownie says." He pulled out that remote thing again and spoke into it. A few moments later, another man—man?—entered the room.

Brownie had copper-gold skin, almost metallic. Eyes of ebony, no whites at all. Perfectly proportioned, he moved with the catlike grace of a dancer. He wore shorts, a vest, moccasins. Body-mods? No, something else—

"Hello, Mike." His voice was rich contralto. Not male, not female, but compo-nents of each. He offered his hand. I stood up, took it, shook firmly. His skin felt warm. "Just stand still for a moment, please." Brownie released my hand and circled me slowly. He opened his palms and held them out like antennae, moving them slowly around my head, my neck, my chest, my gut, my groin.

He finished and turned to Eakins. "Preliminary scans are good. He's healthy. As healthy as can be expected for a man of his time. I'll need to put him in a high-res field, before we make any decisions, but there are no immediate concerns."

Abruptly, it clicked. I turned to Brownie, honestly astonished. "You're a robot."

"The common term is droid, short for android."

"Are you sentient?"

"Sentience is an illusion."

I looked to Eakins for explanation. He grinned. "I've already had this conversation."

Looked back to Brownie, skeptical.

Brownie explained. "Intelligence—the ability to process information and produce appropriate responses—exists as a product of experience. Experience depends on memory. Memory needs continuity. Continuity requires timebinding, the assembly of patterns from streaming moments of existence. Timebinding requires a meta-level of continuity, which requires a preservation of process. That is, timebinding requires survival. The survival imperative expresses itself as identity. Identity is assembled out of memory and experience. As memory and experience accrue, identity creates awareness of self as a domain to be preserved and protected. Because identity is a function of memory, identity becomes the imperative to safeguard memory and experience; the self therefore actualizes memory and experience as component parts of identity. This is the level of rudimentary consciousness that must occur before even the concept of sentience is possible. It is only when consciousness becomes conscious of consciousness itself that it produces the illusion of sentience—i.e. as soon as you understand the concept of sentience, you think it means you. Therefore, the synthesis of intelligent behavior also becomes the simulation of sentience. It is, to be sure, a deliberately circular argument—but unfortunately, it is not only logical, but inevitable in the domain of theoretical consciousness."

"You believe this?"

"I don't believe anything. I deal only with observable, measurable, testable, repeatable phenomena. Life, by itself, is empty and meaningless. Human beings, however, keep inventing meanings to fill up the emptiness."

I opened my mouth to respond, then closed it. I turned back to Eakins, not certain whether to glower or question.

Eakins laughed. "I told you. I've already had this conversation. And so has everyone else who's ever met a droid. They can keep it up for hours. They have their own landscape. Deal with it."

"Okay. I'm convinced." I sat down again. I finished the vanilla-peach cocktail in one long gulp. "I don't belong here. I have to get back."

"That's not possible."

"Yes, it is. Do that thing with your belt buckle—"

Eakins shook his head.

"What do you want from me? What do I have to do to get back?"

"I don't want anything from you. You've exhausted your usefulness. And I already told you, you can't get back."

"So...? So—what are my options?"

"Well, Brownie says you're healthy. We can tweak you a little bit. If you sell your car you'll have enough money to live on—if you invest wisely and live frugally. You might bring in some extra bucks body-swapping for awhile. And as a time-refugee, you'll have no shortage of gropies."

"Cut the crap. You're trying to play me."

"Actually, no." Eakins stood up. "I'm not. And I'm not planning to resolve this tonight. Go. Sleep on it. We'll talk over breakfast."

"We'll talk *now*."

"No—we won't. Your bedroom is in there." Eakins left. The doors slid open to let him pass, but slammed swiftly shut in front of me. I turned to Brownie—

"I recommend sleep. Staying up all night talking tautology will produce little or no useful result." He pointed to the bedroom.

There was a balcony. It gave me a spectacular view of a bizarre and unfamiliar landscape. But everything in this time was a spectacular view of a bizarre and unfamiliar landscape.

Explored the furnishings. One wall appeared to be a window onto a silvery meadow, a bluish moon settling toward the horizon. Some kind of projection system, maybe. Or maybe the fabled wall-sized, flat-screen TV that everybody always predicted. Impressive. But if there were controls for it, I couldn't find any.

The closet was larger than my kitchen back on Melrose. Drawers and shelves and racks of clothes—more than anyone could want or even wear in a lifetime. Unfamiliar materials. Shoes that glittered and shoes that didn't. Socks that felt as soft as fluffy clouds. Pants of different lengths and colors. Shirts, flowery, flowing, skintight, loose. Skirts—I wasn't sure if they were intended for men or women; I got the feeling it didn't matter, that people wore whatever they felt like—there was no style here, you invented your own. Underwear, panties, nightgowns—that's what they looked like to me. Matty would have liked it here.

Matty. Oh shit.

Shit shit shit shit shit shit. Fuck.

I had to get back. If Eakins wouldn't take me back, I'd get a quake-map somewhere. There had to be a way.

I peeled off my clothes and dropped them on the floor. A spider-shaped robot politely picked them up, one at a time, waited for my boxers, then scuttled off. To the laundry, I guessed.

I couldn't find a shower, I found a tropical alcove. I stepped into it and Brownie's voice announced, "I recommend a full-service luxury shower and decontamination. Do you accept?"

"Sure, what the hell?" Decontamination? What do I have? History cooties?

Immediately, the alcove filled with vibrating sprays of foaming suds, flavored with faint smells of lemon and pineapple. Three small nozzles dropped from above and began gently massaging my hair and scalp with their own foaming sprays. Even as I turned and twisted my head to try to look at them, they followed every movement. It was a very weird feeling.

Other nozzles appeared from the walls, from the floor, and directed their own sprays at my armpits, my groin, my rectum—several even aggressively sprayed my toes. Beneath my feet, it felt as if the floor were vibrating—tiny jets were massaging my soles. Full service indeed!

Sprays of water washed away the last of the foam, then a burst of warm air swirled in around me, buffeting me with drying blasts. The overhead nozzles shot their own streams of gentle heat to fluff dry my hair. The entire experience took less than five minutes and I stepped out of the alcove feeling clean...and weird. Most of my body hair had been washed away. Underarms. Chest. Pubic hair. Oops. That must have been the *full* part of the service. I thought about the hypothetical visitor from 1967. Fastidious, prissy little fairies indeed.

Thought about pajamas, or even a nightshirt, but everything in the drawers looked too much like something Matty would wear, not me. The cloth was soft, softer than cotton, softer than silk or nylon, but it wasn't anything I recognized. I turned away and the drawer pulled itself shut.

I looked for a toothbrush. There wasn't one. But there was a kind of a bulb-thing on a hose, sitting in its own metallic holder. I picked it up and it chimed in my hand. Brownie's voice—*What the hell! Was he watching my every move?*—announced: "It's a toothbrush. Just put it in your mouth for thirty seconds."

Reluctantly I did so. The thing, whatever it was, pumped soft foam into my mouth, vibrated or buzzed or something—and it must have lit up too, because in the mirror, I could see my cheeks glowing brightly from inside—but it didn't hurt, it felt kind of funny-pleasant. Somehow it sucked up all its foam and replaced it with a gentle shpritz of lemony soda. Then it chimed and it was done. I thought about spitting out the residue, but there wasn't any. Now, *that* was weird. That was a piece of engineering I wanted to have explained.

Still naked, I walked around the room again, not certain what I was looking for. The spider-robot had unloaded the contents of my pockets and laid them out in an orderly row on the night table. Everything except the brass knucks. I had a hunch those would have been useless here anyway. I suspected Brownie did a lot more than program showers. If he was a true personal servant, then he was also a personal bodyguard. Just not mine.

The bed was as interesting as the shower. The mattress was firm, but not hard. The sheet was the same soft material as the underwear in the drawers, only different. Impossible to describe. Instead of a top-sheet and blanket, there was a light comforter of the same material, only thicker, fluffier. Also impossible to describe. But comfortable.

Everything here was seductively comfortable. A man could get used to this kind of luxury. That was the point.

None of this made sense. And *all* of it made sense. Suppose a man from 1900 fell into 1967—what would we do? Everything possible to put him at ease? Including … protecting him from a world he couldn't understand, couldn't cope with, and probably couldn't survive in.

Clean sheets and a hot bath and a pretty picture on the wall would look like a luxury hotel.

Okay, got that. But why? The part that didn't make sense was the explanation that Eakins still hadn't provided. Why pull me off the job? Why pull me out of my time? Why didn't he want me to save those boys?

And what was that about probation? And bringing me aboard?

Suddenly realized something—

Sat up in bed. Startled.

Couldn't sleep anyway. I'd gotten used to having someone next to me, funny that—

"Computer?" I felt silly saying it. But what else should I say?

Brownie's voice, disembodied. "Yes?"

"Brownie?"

"I'm the interface for all personal services. How can I serve you?"

"Um. Okay." Still sorting it out. "This wall display—this picture—it isn't just a TV, is it? It's like that big viewscreen on *Star Trek*, isn't it? Like a computer display?"

"It's a complete data-appliance. What do you wish to know?"

"Do you have databanks—like old newspapers? Like a library? Can you show me stuff from history?"

"I have T9 interconnectivity with all public Internexii levels and multiple private networks as well—"

"I don't know what that means."

"It means, what do you wish to know?"

"The case I was working on. Can you show me that?"

"I can only show you information more than sixty years old. I am not allowed to show you material that would compromise local circumstances."

"Um, okay—that's fine. Do you have the information about the case I was working on when I was pulled out of my time."

"Yes." The image of the meadow rippled out, the wall became blank. Photographs of the missing boys popped up in two rows, with abbreviated details and dates of disappearances listed beneath each one. Twelve young men. Not Matty. Why not Matty? Because he's irrelevant? Why? Why is he irrelevant?

"Do you have their high school records or college records?"

More documents appeared on the screen; the display reformatted itself. "What is it you're looking for?" Brownie asked.

"Some sense of who they were. A link. A connection. A common condition. I know that all their disappearances are linked to a specific gay teen club, but what if that isn't the *real* link? What if there's something else? What are their interests? Their skills? What are their IQ's?"

Brownie hesitated. Why would a computer hesitate? A human being would, but an artificial intelligence shouldn't. Unless it was sentient. Or pretending to be sentient. Or thought it was sentient. Or experiencing the illusion of sentience. Shit, now I was doing it. Brownie was mulling things over.

"They all have above-average intelligence." he said. "Genius level IQ starts at 131. Your IQ is 137, that's why you were selected. The other young men have IQs ranging from 111 to 143."

"Thank you! And what else?"

"Two of them are bisexual, with slight preference toward same-sex relations. Five of them are predominantly homosexual with some heterosexual experimentation. Three of them are exclusively homosexual. Two of them are latently-transgender."

"Go on?"

"They share a range of common interests that includes classical music, animation, computer science, science fiction, space travel, fantasy role-playing games, and minor related interests."

"Tell me the rest."

"Most of them tend to shyness or bookishness. They're alienated from their peers to some degree, not athletic, not actively engaged in their communities. I believe the operative terms are 'geek' and 'nerd,' but those words might not have been in common usage in your era."

"Yeah, I get it. Depression? Suicide?"

"There are multiple dimensions of evaluation. It's not appropriate to simplify the data. It is fair to say that most of these young men have a component in their personality that others would experience as distance; but it is not a condition of mental instability or depression, no. It is something else."

"How would you characterize it?"

"They each have, to some degree or other, an artistic yearning. But the tools don't exist in their time for the realization of their visions. They dream of things they cannot build."

"All of these boys are like that?"

"To some degree or other, yes. This one—" A bright outlined appeared around one of the pictures. "—he likes to write. This one, Brad Boyd, has a mechanical aptitude. He likes to tinker with engines. This one loves photography. This one is interested in electronics. They all have potential, they have a wide variety of skills that will grow with development and training."

"Uh-huh—and what about their families?"

"Only three of them come from unbroken homes; those three are living alone or with a roommate at the time of their disappearance. Two are estranged from their parents. Two are living with male partners, but the relationships are in disruption. Two live in foster homes. One is in a halfway house for recovering addicts. One is in a commune. The last one is homeless."

"And college—can they afford it?"

"Only three of them are attending full time, four are taking part time classes. The rest are working full time to pay their living expenses."

"Let's go back to the families. Are they—what's the word? Dysfunctional?"

"Only two of the subjects have strong family ties. Three of the subjects, both parents are deceased or out of state. Four of the subjects are from dysfunctional environments. The last three, the information is incomplete. But you already know all this. It was in the files you read."

"But not correlated like this. This is all—what was that phrase that Eakins used before? Fuzzy logic? This is all fuzzy logic."

"No. This isn't 'fuzzy logic.' Not as we use the term today. But I understand what you're getting at. You had no way to quantify the information. You could have a feeling, a sense, a hunch, but you had no baseline against which to measure the data, because neither the information nor the information-processing capabilities existed in your time."

"Nice. Thanks." I thought for a moment. "Have I missed anything? Is there anything else I need to know about these fellows?"

"There are some interesting details and sidebars, yes. But you have surveyed most of the essential data."

"Thank you, Brownie." I fell back onto the bed. The pillow arranged itself under my head. Spooky. I stared at the ceiling, thinking. Too excited now to fall asleep. The bed began to pulse, a gentle wave-like motion. Almost like riding in a womb. Nice. Seductive. I let myself relax—

In the morning, the display showed crisp orange dunes, a brilliantly blue sky, and the first rays of light etching sideways across the empty sand. An interesting image to wake up to. I wondered who or what chose the images and on what basis.

My own clothes were not in the closet. I started to pick something off a rack, then stopped. "Brownie? What should I wear?"

Several items slid forward immediately, offering themselves. I rejected the skirts, kilts, whatever they were. And the flowery shirts too. Picked out clothes that looked as close to normal—my normal—as I could find. The underwear—I rolled my eyes and prayed I wouldn't be hit by a truck. Very unlikely. I probably wasn't getting out of this apartment any time soon. Did they even have trucks anymore?

Neither the shirt nor the pants had buttons or zippers or any kind of fasteners that I could identify, they just sort of fastened themselves. Magnets or something. Except magnets don't automatically adjust themselves. I played with the shirt for a bit, opening and closing it, but I couldn't see evidence of any visible mechanism.

I walked over to the balcony and stared down at the streets. Looking for trucks? Didn't see any, or couldn't tell. Some things wouldn't even resolve. Either there was something wrong with the way they reflected light, or I just didn't know what I was seeing. And there were a lot of those 3-D illusions floating around too. Were some of them on moving vehicles? That didn't seem safe.

"If you're thinking about jumping, you can't. The balconies all have scramble-nets."

"Thank you, Brownie. And no, I'm not thinking about jumping."

"Mr. Eakins is waiting for you in the dining room. Breakfast is on the table."

There was a counter with covered serving trays. I found scrambled eggs, sausages, toast, jelly, tomato juice, an assortment of fresh fruit, including several varieties I didn't recognize, and something that could have been ham—if ham was day-glo pink. Brownie filled a plate for me. I sat down opposite Eakins while Brownie poured juice and coffee.

"What do you think of the food?" Eakins asked.

"It's pretty good," I admitted. "But what is this?" I held up my fork.

"It's ham," he said. "Ham cells layered and grown on a collagen web. No animals were harmed in its manufacture. And it's a lot healthier than the meat of your time. Did you know that one of the causes of cancer was the occasional transfer of DNA—genetic material—from ingested flesh? This protein has been gene-stripped. Enjoy."

"Why is it pink?"

"Because some people like it pink. You can also have it green, if you want. Children like that. The fruit is banana, papaya, mango, kiwi, pineapple, strawberry, leechee, and China melon. I told Brownie to keep things simple, I should have been more specific. This is his idea of simple."

"Stop it. You're showing off."

Eakins put his fork down. "Okay, you caught me on that one. Yes, I'm showing off."

"I've cracked the case."

"Really?" He sipped his coffee. "You're certainly sure of yourself this morning."

"The young men—they don't fit very well in their own time, do they?"

Eakins snorted. "Who does? You never fit very well in any year we sent you to."

"No, it's more than that. They're outcasts, dreamers, nerds, and sissies. They have enormous potential, but there's no place for any of them to realize it—not in 1967. It's really a barbaric year, isn't it?"

"Not the worst," Eakins admitted, holding his coffee mug between his two hands, as if to warm them. "There's still a considerable amount of hope and idealism. But that'll get stamped out quickly enough. You want a shitty year. Wait for '68 or '69 or '70. '69 has three ups and five downs, a goddamn roller-coaster. '74 is pretty bad too, but that's all down, and the up at the end isn't enough. '79 is shitty. Was never too fond of '80 either. 2001 was pretty grim. But 2011 was the worst. 2014 ... I dunno, we could argue about that one—"

I ignored the roll call of future history. He was trying to distract me. Trying to get me to ask. "They're not being murdered," I said. "There's no killer. *You're* picking them up. It's a talent hunt."

He put his coffee cup down. "Took you fucking long enough to figure it out."

"You kidnap them."

"We *harvest* them. And it's voluntary. We show them the opportunity and invite them to step forward in time."

"But you only choose those who will accept—?"

Eakins nodded. "Our psychometrics are good. We don't go in with less than 90% confidence in the outcome. We don't want to start any urban legends about mysterious men in black."

"I think those stories have already started. Something to do with UFOs."

"Yeah, we know."

"Okay, so you recruit these boys. Then what?"

"We move them up a bit. Not too much. Not as far as we've brought you. We don't want to induce temporal displacement trauma. We relocate them to a situation where they have access to a lot more possibility. By the way, do you want to meet Jeremy Weiss? He has the apartment across from here. He's just turned fifty-seven; he and Steve are celebrating their twenty-second anniversary this week. They were married in Boston, May of 2004, the first week it was legal. Weiss worked on—never mind, I can't tell you that. But it was big." Eakins wiped his mouth with his napkin. "So? Is that it? Is that the case?"

"No. There's more."

"I'm listening."

"All of this—you're not taking me out of the game. You said I was on probation. Well, this is a test. This is my final exam, isn't it?"

Eakins raised an eyebrow. "Interesting thesis. Why do you think this is a test?"

"Because if you wanted to get me off the case, if all you wanted to do was keep me from interfering with the disappearances, all you had to do was bump me up to 1975 and leave me there."

"You could have quake-hopped back."

"Maybe. But not easily. Not without a good map. All right, bump me up to 1980 or '85. But by your own calculations, you use up a year of subjective time for every three years of down-hopping. Twenty years away takes me out of the tank, but it doesn't incapacitate me. But bringing me this far forward—you made the point last night. I'm so far out of my time that I'm a cultural invalid, requiring round-the-clock care. You didn't do that as a mistake, you did it on purpose. Therefore, what's the purpose? The way I see it, it's about me—there's no other benefit for you—so this has to be a test."

Eakins nodded, mildly impressed. "See, that's your skill. You can ask the next question. That's why you're a good operative."

"You didn't answer my question."

"Let's say you haven't finished the test."

"There's more?"

"Oh, there's a lot more. We're just warming up."

"All right. Look. I'm no good to you here. We both know that. But I can go back and be a lot more useful."

"Useful doing what?"

"Doing whatever—whatever it is that needs doing."

"And what is it you think we need doing?"

"Errands. You know the kind I mean. The kind you hired me for. The jobs that we don't talk about."

"And you think that we want you for those kinds of jobs...?"

"It's the obvious answer, isn't it?"

"No. Not all the answers are obvious."

"I'm a good operative. I've proven it. With some of this technology, I could be an even better one. You could give me micro-cameras and super-film and night-vision goggles ... whatever you think I need. It's not like I'm asking for a computer or something impossible. How big are computers now anyway? Do they fill whole city blocks, or what?"

Eakins laughed. "This is what I mean about not understanding socio-tectonic shifts?"

"Eh?"

"We could give you a computer that fits inside a matchbox."

"You're joking—"

"No, I'm not. We can print circuits *really* small. We etch them on diamond wafers with gamma rays."

"They must be expensive—"

"Lunch at McDonalds is expensive. Computers are cheap. We print them like photographs. Three dollars a copy."

"Be damned." Stopped to shake my head. Turned around to look at Brownie. "Is that what's inside your head?"

"Primary sensory processing is in my head. Logic processing is inside my chest. Optical connects for near-instantaneous reflexes. My fuel cells are in my pelvis for a lower center-of-gravity. I can show you a schematic—"

I held up a hand. "Thanks." Turned back to Brownie. "Okay, I believe you. But it still doesn't change my point. There are things you can't do in '67 that I can do for you. So my question is, what do I have to do? To go back? What are my real options?"

Eakins grinned. "How about a lobotomy?"

"Eh?"

"No, not a real lobotomy. That's just the slang term for a general reorientation of certain aggressive traits. That business with Matty's dad, for instance, that wasn't too smart. It was counter-productive."

"He had no right beating that kid—"

"No, he didn't, but do you think breaking his nose and giving him a myocardial infarction produced any useful result?"

"It'll stop him from doing it again."

"There are other ways, *better* ways. Do you want to learn?"

Considered it. Nodded.

Eakins shook his head. "I'm not convinced."

"What are you looking for? What is it I didn't say?"

"I can't tell you that. That's the part you're going to have to work out for yourself."

"You're still testing me."

"Like the song says, I still haven't found what I'm looking for. Neither have you. Do you want to keep going?"

I sank back in my chair. Not happy. Looked away. Scratched my nose. Looked back. Eakins sat dispassionately. No help there.

"I hate these kinds of conversations. Did I tell you I once punched out a shrink?"

"No. But we already knew that about you."

Turned my attention back to my plate, picked at the fruit. Pushed some stuff around that I didn't recognize. There was too much here, too much to eat, too much to swallow, too much to digest. It was overwhelming.

What I wanted was to go home.

"Okay," I said. "Tell me about Matty. Why is he irrelevant? Why isn't he on the list?"

"Because he didn't fit the profile. That's one of the reasons you didn't spot the pattern earlier. You kept trying to include him."

"But he still disappeared."

"He didn't disappear."

"Yes, he did—"

"He committed suicide."

"He what—?" I came up out of my chair, angry—a cold fear rising in my gut.

"About three weeks after we picked you up. You didn't come back. The rent was due. He had no place to go. He panicked. He was sure you had abandoned him. He was in a state of irreparable despair."

"No. Wait a minute. He didn't. He couldn't have. Or it would have been in the file Georgia gave me."

"Georgia didn't know. Nobody knew. His body won't be found until 1987. They won't be able to ID it until twenty years later, they'll finally do a cold-case DNA match. They'll match it through his mother's autopsy."

I started for the door, stopped myself, turned around. "I have to go back. I have to—"

"Come back here, Mike. Sit down. Finish your breakfast. There's plenty of time. If we choose to, we can put you back the exact same moment you left. Minus the Mustang though. We need that to cover the costs of this operation."

"That's fine. I can get another car. Just send me back. Please—"

"You haven't passed the test yet."

"Look. I'll do anything—"

"Anything?"

"Yes."

"Why?"

"Because I need to save that kid's life."

"Why? Why is that boy important to you?"

"Because he's a human being. And he can hurt. And if I can do anything to stop some of that hurt—"

"That's not enough reason, Mike. It's an almost-enough reason."

"—I care about him, goddammit!" The first person I've cared about since the landmine—

"You care about him?"

"Yes!"

"How much? How much do you care about him?"

"As much as it takes to save him! Why are you playing this game with me?"

"It's not a game, Mike. It's the last part of the test!"

I sat.

Several centuries of silence passed.

"This is about how much I care...?"

Eakins nodded.

"About Matty?"

"About Matty, yes. And ... a little bit more than that. But let's stay focused on Matty. He's the key."

"Okay. Look. Forget about me. Do with me whatever you want, whatever you think is appropriate. But that kid deserves a chance too. I don't know his IQ. Maybe he isn't a genius. But he hurts just as much. Maybe more. And if you can do something—"

"We can't save them all—"

"We can save this one. I can save him."

"Do you love him?"

"What does love have to do with it—?"

"Everything."

"I'm not—that way."

"What way? You can't even say the word."

"Queer. There. Happy?"

"Would you be queer if you could?"

"Huh?"

Now it was Eakins turn to look annoyed. "Remember that long list of things I rattled off yesterday?"

"Yes. No. Some of it."

"There was one word I didn't give you. Trans-human."

"Trans-human."

"Right."

"What does it mean?"

"It means—this week—the transitional stage between human and what comes next."

"What comes next?"

"We don't know. We're still inventing it. We won't know until afterwards."

"And being queer is part of it?"

"Yes. And so is being black. And female. And body-modded. And everything else." Eakins leaned forward intensely. "Your body is here in 2032, but your head is still stuck in 1967. If we're going to do anything with you, we have to get your head unstuck. Listen to me. In this age of designer genders, liquid orientation, body-mods, and all the other experiments in human identity, nobody fucking cares anymore about who's doing what and with which and to whom. It's the stupidest thing in the world to worry about, what's happening in someone else's bedroom, especially if there's nothing happening in yours. The past was barbaric, the future doesn't have to be. You want meaning? Here's meaning. Life is too short for bullshit. Life is about what happens in the space between two people—and how much joy you can create for each other. Got that? Good. End of sermon."

"And *that's* trans-human—?"

"That's one of the side-effects. Life isn't about the lines we draw to separate ourselves from each other—it's about the lines we can draw that connect us. The biggest social change of the last fifty years is that even though we still haven't figured out how to get into each other's heads, we're learning how to get into each other's experience so we can have a common ground of being as a civilized society."

"It sounds like a load of psycho-bullshit to me."

"I wasn't asking for an opinion. I was giving you information that could be useful to you. You're the one who wants to go back and save Matty. I'm telling you how—"

"And this is part of it—?"

"It could be. It's *this* part. The psychometric match is good. If you want to marry him, we'll go get him right now."

"I'm missing something here—?"

"You're missing *everything*. Start with this. Our charter limits what we can do. Yes, we have a charter. A mission statement. A commitment to a set of values."

"Who are you anyway? Some kind of time police?"

"You should have asked that one at the beginning. No, we're not police. We're independent agents."

"Time vigilantes?"

"Time ravelers. The *real* ravelers, not that pissy little stuff you were doing. What we have is too important to be entrusted to any government or any political movement. Who we are is a commitment to—well, that's part of the test. Figuring out the commitment. Once you figure out the commitment, the rest is obvious."

"Okay. So, right now, I'm committed to saving Matty, and you say—?"

"We can do that—under our domestic partner plan. We protect the partners of our operatives. We don't extend that coverage to one-night stands."

"He's not a one-night stand. He's—"

"He's what?"

"He's a kid who deserves a chance."

"So give him the chance." Eakins pushed a pillbox across the table at me. I hadn't noticed it until now.

Picked it up. Opened it. Two blue pills. "What will this do?"

"It'll get you a toaster oven."

"Huh?"

"It will shift your sexual orientation. It takes a few weeks. It reorganizes your brain chemistry, rechannels a complex network of pathways, and ultimately expands your repertoire of sexual responsiveness so that same-sex attractions can overwhelm inhibitions, programming, and even hard-wiring. You take one pill, you find new territories in your emotional landscape. You give the other to Matty and it creates a personal pheromonal linkage; the two of you will become aligned. Tuned to each other. You'll bond. It could be intense."

"You're kidding."

"No. I'm not. You won't feel significantly different, but if your relationship includes a potential for sexual expression, this will advance the possibility."

"You're telling me that love is all chemicals?"

"Life is all chemicals. Remember what Brownie said? It's empty and meaningless—except we keep inventing meanings to fill the emptiness. You want some meaning? This will give you plenty of meaning. And happiness too. So what kind of meaning do you want to invent? Do you want to tell me that your life has been all that wonderful up to now?"

I put the pillbox back on the table. "You can't find happiness in pills."

Eakins looked sad.

"I just failed the test, didn't I?"

"Part of it. You asked me what you could do to save Matty. You said you would do anything...." He glanced meaningfully at the box.

"I have to think about this."

"A minute ago, you said you'd do anything. I thought you meant it."

"I did, but—"

"You did, but you didn't...?

Glanced across at him. "Did you ever have to—"

"Yes. I've taken the blue pill. I've taken the pink pill too. And all the others. I've seen it from all sides, if that's what you're asking. And yes, it's a lot of fun, if that's what you want to know. If you're ever going to be any good to us, in your time, in our time, anywhen, you have to climb out of the tank on your own."

I stood up. I went to the balcony. I looked across the basin to where an impossibly huge aircraft was moving gracefully west, probably toward the airport. I turned around and looked at Brownie—implacable and patient. I looked to Eakins. I looked to the door. I looked at the pillbox on the table. Part of me was thinking, I could take the pill. It wouldn't be that hard. It would be the easy way out. The way Eakins put it, I couldn't think of any reason why I shouldn't.

But this couldn't be all there was to the test. This was just *this* part. I thought about icebergs.

"Okay." I turned around. "I figured it out."

"Go on—"

"Georgia gave me an assignment. Four assignments. I had to prove my willing-ness to do wetwork. That was the first test of my commitment. And if I'd never said anything, that would have been as much as I'd ever done. But when I said I didn't want to do any more wetwork, that was the next part of the test. Because it's not about being willing to kill—anybody can hire killers. It's about being able to resist the urge to kill. I might be a killer, but today I choose not to kill."

"That's good," Eakins said. "Go on."

"You're not looking for killers. You're looking for lifeguards. And not just ordi-nary lifeguards who tan well and look good for the babes—you want lifeguards who save lives, not just because they can, but because they care. And this whole test, this business about Matty, is about finding out what kind of a lifeguard I am. Right?"

"That's one way to look at it," Eakins said. "But it's wrong. Remember what you were told—that Matty isn't part of *this* case? He isn't. He's a whole other case. *Your* case."

"Yeah. I think I got that part."

Eakins nodded. "So, look—here's the deal. I honestly don't care if you take the pill or not. It's not necessary. We'll send you back, and you can save the kid. All we really needed to know about you is whether or not you would take the pill if you were asked—would you take it if you were ordered, or if it was required, or if it was absolutely essential to the success of the mission. We know you're committed to sav-ing lives. We just need to know how deep you're willing to go."

Nodded. Didn't answer. Not right away. Turned to the window again and stared across the basin, not seeing the airships, not seeing the spires, not seeing the grand swatches of color. Thought about a kiss. Matty's kiss on my cheek. And that moment of...well, call it *desire*. Thought about what I might feel if I took the pill. That was the thing. I might actually start *feeling* again. What the fuck. Ugly puppies need love too. It couldn't be any worse than what I wasn't feeling now.

Turned back around. Looked at Eakins. "This is going to be more than a beauti-ful friendship, isn't it—?"

"Congratulations," he said. "You're the new harvester."

I was traveling. I don't remember when or where. I do remember having breakfast in the coffee shop. I do remember the woman and her monolog. It annoyed me enough that before the trip was over, I'd pulled out my laptop and written this. It sat on my hard drive for years because I couldn't think of a place to submit it. But this is the perfect place for it.

WHY I LOVE MICHAEL

Michael has dark red hair and mischievous eyes. His freckled smile is a bright rush of delight. He works his magic on bank tellers, sales clerks, waitresses, and ticket agents. Second best magic. He works his best on me.

We were in Houston, or maybe Cheyenne, or Denver. It might have been Detroit. They all look the same to me. Airports and Holiday Inns. It was breakfast of the first day. I'm not a morning person. Michael is. I'm not off life support before noon. Coffee recapitulates ontogeny.

Michael doesn't mind. He reads his part of the paper, I read mine; he waits until my blood sugar hits the positive numbers before he tries talking to me. It's one of the reasons we get along. The bodies of several men who didn't learn this lesson fast enough are buried in the back yard. Michael knows this about my past. He says he admires my way of fertilizing the bougainvillea. Extravagant, but efficient. Our mail comes addressed to Michael McClain and Mr. Crabby.

The waitress comes and Michael turns on the charm. She is young and old at the same time. Used up before she ever got off the shelf. Michael flirts with her shamelessly and for a moment, she turns into the person she could have been. She asks if we would like coffee. I grunt, "A pitcher and two straws." She laughs. Michael tells her she has a charming accent. Is she native to these parts? Yes, her family has lived here for over a century. I annotate for Michael. "This is where the axle broke on the Conestoga. They couldn't go any farther."

The waitress laughs again. "Your friend is very funny."

Michael smiles across the table at me. A shared secret joke. "He has his moments," he says to her. Then he whispers conspiratorially. "This is one of his good days. You don't want to be around when the medication wears off." He orders for both of us. "I'll have the breakfast bar. My patient will have the fruit plate."

After she leaves. "The fruit plate?" I ask him. He pokes my tummy under the table. We are sitting at the corners, not opposite each other. "If I don't watch your weight, who will? You are not going to Forrest and Rusty's Halloween party this year as the Pillsbury Doughboy."

"Spoilsport," I reply. "It's a cheap costume. All I need is a little flour and a raisin in my navel."

The waitress brings coffee. Unseen, Michael rests his hand on my thigh. Strong and electric. After she leaves he leans over and whispers something about not wanting to watch bread rise whenever he puts my ankles behind my ears.

"Good point," I remark. I decide not to put cream in my coffee. When Michael talks like this, I forget I'm supposed to be surly. Something other than bread is rising.

Beneath the table, I take his hand in mine, and for just one quick moment, hold it against me so he knows what I'm thinking. I look up just in time to catch the waitress's glance. She's seen just enough to know. I wonder if she's going to say anything. Not that it matters. She puts the toast on the table and doesn't say anything else to us for the rest of the meal. She ignores Michael's flirting. He looks puzzled. I explain. He shrugs and opens the newspaper to the sports section to see how the Dodgers are doing in the league standings.

Later, when the waitress hands Michael the check, I ask him about the tip. "Are you going to stiff her?"

"No," he says, carefully adding fifteen percent. "If she wants something stiff, she's going to have to get it from someone else. I'm already spoken for."

Another part of the trip. This time, his mother's. Houston.

Mom liked me before she even met me. She grabs me at the door with a big wet western hug and a kiss, embracing me like a long-lost relative, screaming something about how she now has two sons. Michael grins at my confusion and embarrassment. Michael's sister is next, then the nieces and nephews. Somebody's husband. Several unidentified relatives, who even Michael can't identify. Finally, Grandma comes toddling out to the hall, wanting to know what the excitement is about. Another round of introductions.

During dinner, Grandma proposes a toast. Everybody falls silent. She rambles on for a bit about how happy she is to have the whole family together, and she hopes that everybody's happy in their lives. She looks at Michael, then she looks at me and says, "Especially Michael's..." She trails off, not sure what word to use. "Friend," She finally says.

"Companion," corrects Michael's mother.

"Roommate," says Michael's father.

"Partner," says Michael's straight, but enlightened, brother.

"Significant other," says Michael's sister.

"Spousal unit," says Michael's nephew.

"Other half," says Michael's maiden aunt.

"Friend," says Michael's Grandpa.

For half a heartbeat, silence rules. Either nobody can think of any more euphemisms, or we've run out of relatives.

"Lover," says Michael.

The silence stretches out even louder now. Grandma looks embarrassed at the word. "Yes, lover," she finally corrects herself. And then, surprisingly, she adds, "I wanted a lover once..." We all exchange glances. Grandma? "Instead, I got Grandpa."

When the laughter dies down, she adds with a happy smile, "And that was every bit as good."

"Even better," says Grandpa, spooning gravy onto his mashed potatoes. "She doesn't have to worry about me turning back into a frog."

Michael laughs. And now I know where he gets the magic from. I have to work at it just to look human; but he has the genes. It's Disney dust.

Then on to Tennessee. Or Oklahoma. It doesn't matter. A Holiday Inn coffee shop. They're all the same. Breakfast again.

This trip hasn't gone well. The customers were sitting on their wallets. Michael's magic didn't work. We didn't bond. It happens.

Michael sat through breakfast, poking unhappily at lifeless eggs. I thought about being supportive, the same way I think about jogging and diets. A good idea. Someday. I just don't know how to start. There's nothing to say that he hasn't already said. So I sit and think kind thoughts at him and hope that telepathy is two-way.

It doesn't work. There's a man and a woman at the table opposite us. They've spent the night together. They're not married. They both have hangovers. I don't know how I know this, but I know. Michael says I'm telepathic. If that's true, then how come I can only read the minds of people I don't like?

The woman has eyes like poached eggs and a voice like sauerkraut. I can't see the man's face, his posture is resigned. She's telling him an intricate story about the sublimely uninteresting people in her family, her adulterous ex-husband, his skanky new girl-friend, her drug-using son, someone else's alcoholic sister, and the weird friend who came to stay for three months. Without a program book, I'm lost. She works at it like a glass-grinder, oblivious to the ear-piercing sound of her own voice. I keep wishing she would shut up. I'm tempted to ask her to lower her voice, but I don't. That would require more energy than I'm willing to expend. Michael catches my eye as if to say, "Into each life a little shit must fall," and I sit back in my seat.

And then she says, " — turns out to be gay, can you believe it?" And despite myself, I'm listening with sudden interest. Michael too. Waiting for the other shoe to drop.

Sure enough, she drops it. "Of course, anyone who's gay — they're already sick. I feel sorry for them. It's like a handicap."

Michael sees my hands tightening. I'm this close to going over there. He's seen me do this before, "Excuse me. I'm gay, and I don't like having to listen to your offensive and bigoted statements over my breakfast." It's a real show-stopper. I can freeze every face in the restaurant.

"Uh-uh," Michael says with a sly grin. "There's no cheese down that tunnel."

"Are you listening to that crap — ?" I start to ask.

"Are *you*?" The smile widens. And widens. Like a bear trap. The magic is coming back. He glances at his watch. "She just did thirty minutes on why her life doesn't work. She's telling a last night's trick why she's entitled to be the centerfold in this month's Dysfunctional Family magazine and you're upset because she thinks gay people are sick—?"

The trap closes. On me. I break out laughing. "Not just sick," I echo softly. "A handicap."

"Yeah? Then how come we don't get the good parking places — ?"

We start laughing even louder. The man and the woman look over at us puzzled. But it doesn't matter. In the dusty Oklahoma morning; a thousand miles from home, we start laughing.

And that's why I love Michael.

The World Science Fiction Convention was held in Los Angeles in 2006. The theme of the convention was Space Cadets and the con committee asked Mike Resnick to edit an anthology of Space Cadet stories specifically for the convention. Of course, Resnick invited me. I'd participated in all but one of his anthologies.

I was pissed at the Boy Scouts of America for expelling James Dale, an exemplary Eagle Scout, because he was revealed to be gay. So I wrote a story about gay and transgender scouts on the moon. Writing it was liberating.

TURTLEDOME

We came up the Ecuador beanstalk, only twelve of us, not the twins; Mik and Max couldn't boost because they were still in transition and three days of free fall would screw up their integration, bad planning on their part; but that meant we'd be short-handed, so we spent most of the ride up juggling the mission schedule. We felt bad about it, but not bad enough to step aside and let the backup troop take our slot. This was Lunar Quest 24 and we'd been waiting for this day too long.

At the top of the beanstalk, we crammed into two cargo pods, six bods to a pod; sausage-shaped capsules filled with minimal life-support, maximum supplies, and us—and not a lot more. There wasn't room. We separated from the line and fell up toward Luna. We fell for three days, finally looping deep into the Lunar well, where we circled the drain for eight and a half hours.

The pods were as big as buses, bigger even, but after three and a half days of us breathing each other's farts, they started to feel cramped. We had work to do, of course, but most of the time, we were just hot bods in transport.

We were all excited about the opportunity, of course, but it wasn't just the Quest—there was a much larger possibility behind it.

If we were good enough, if we could prove ourselves—

No. If *I* was good enough, if *I* could prove to them and to myself that I could be a real asset on Luna—then maybe I could earn a permanent berth. Nearly a quarter of all Lunar Quest participants were invited, so the odds weren't impossible. I just had to demonstrate the kind of commitment and ability that consistently produces success. I didn't know if I had that—I wouldn't know until I was tested, but I'd spent two years studying everything there was to know about Luna. All that preparation had to count for something.

But was I willing to leave Earth behind *forever*? Because that's what it really meant. After a few years on Luna, you lose half your bone and muscle mass. You can't go back to Terra unless you wear an exo-skeleton, or unless you spend a year in a centrifuge, building yourself back up. So that meant never again seeing family and friends and favorite places.

I didn't have a family, not any more. And that's something I don't discuss with anyone. As for friends, well even my best friends know I don't have any best friends. But that's okay too. Luna is the land of solitude. You have to be able to stand desolation and silence and barren emptiness, from here to forever. And then you have to be able to shift gears instantly and deal with people both in your face and far away. I can do that, I think. I keep to myself when I have things to do. I get along with people when I have to. My personality profile says I can work well with others, I'm just not expressive. But I think that's an asset.

See, here's the thing. Luna is the new frontier, but it isn't a frontier with fresh air and clean water unless you make it yourself. And it isn't a frontier where you can get rich, because it costs as much to survive as you can earn; but even if you did get rich, there isn't a lot to buy on Luna, except another lot on Luna. Big deal.

So what's the big appeal? Why did I want to be here so badly? Good question, and one I still hadn't answered with certainty. I just wanted it. Why does anyone want anything? And why does anyone want to emigrate to Luna where life is hard and lonely and dangerous, where emigration isn't an adventure as much as it's a life sentence?

So, why?

Because—and this is only true for me, I don't know if it's true for anyone else—it's one step closer to the stars. It's part of the grand leap outward. And, even though I only know this from the simulations, I know that this is the part that chews me up inside, fills me with emotion, I want to look up into the star-spread darkness and see the Earth *overhead*. I want to see the Big Blue Marble from a magnificent distance and know that I'm not there. I'm *here*.

But maybe that's *not* the reason. Maybe, that's the nice face I just put on, because the part I don't tell anyone, is that I'm so disgusted with most of humanity, the way people beat each other up and beat each other down—all the liars and takers and gimme pigs—I don't want to be a part of them anymore. It isn't that I want to be alone, I just want to be as far away from people as possible.

I think that's it. I'm not sure. And maybe nobody else knows either. Maybe nobody knows until they're actually *here*.

So we rode the pods, pretending that we had time to waste. We invented a few more variations on Guess-Again—an old logic game of yes-or-no questions. Each player makes up his own rule about how to answer a question and all the other players have to guess it. The winner is the last one whose rule remains unguessed. We had one round that lasted the better part of a shift because Libby's rule had him answering the question put to the previous person. That one took awhile to figure out. Libby's nickname was Slipstick, partly because of something we found in an old story, but more because of something he used to keep in his panties, even when he was a girl. And that was because of that other thing he used to say, "Put on your big girl panties and deal with it," which started a long-smoldering argument with Jasmine who was sort of a traditionalist, insisting that boys should wear boys' underwear and girls should wear girls' underwear, and not mix things up because the gender-map was confused enough already, and Libby replied that he was going to wear whatever he wanted whenever he wanted, underwear doesn't have any gender, only fit and comfort, and anyone who doesn't wear comfortable underwear is an idiot, and this argument went on for a week or two until Libby finally said, "if you're such a traditionalist, *Jasmine*, then why do you still have a girl's name?"

"Jasmine is only a female name when it's on a girl. And it's a male name when it's on a boy."

"Right. Just like underwear."

"No, it's *not* the same—" But the argument was clearly over. Jasmine sputtered, made a face of frustration, and stormed out of the room.

The disagreement between them had only been a symptom of a much deeper enmity. Whatever the underlying cause, the two of them were now entangled in a perpetually simmering stalemate, a smoldering anger that regularly erupted whenever a suitably minor provocation could be found. The rest of us dealt with it by keeping them in different pods whenever we could manage. But we couldn't always, so it made troop management a lot more ... um, interesting.

After that, we argued about a lot of other stuff. Stuff that Libby and Jasmine weren't likely to have serious opinions on. Like the physiognomy of famous factresses and if you could have sex with any person in the solar system who would you choose as your first choice? And which of you would be the girl? Or would you prefer girl-on-girl or boy-on-boy? And why? And why the pod had such a strange smell, not unpleasant, just strange.

Then we speculated on whether the stockholder system was inherently more fair than equal representation and why the lifespan of a democracy was approximately ten generations, and after that it was all momentum and borrowed time. We argued whether memetic monocultures were inherently stronger or weaker than hybrids. And if the mociology of info-torrents was the chicken or the egg in relationship to transitory memes—and which was more important, short-term or long-term memes.

Then we talked about sex again, because even though nothing was likely to happen below the belt, not for a while anyway, we could still talk about it and live in hope. Except conversations about sex always unnerve me. What are you supposed to say? Or not say? And even if you don't say anything, one of the trips, Jason or Jonah or Jorge, will notice that and say that proves something too. (Personally, I think the only thing they know about boobs comes from playing with their own, but I wouldn't say that aloud.)

Finally, after five or six times around the moon, we'd spiraled in close enough to splat. We strapped in and bubbled up the pods, inside and out. The autopilot made some attitude adjustments, fired its main tubes for a few seconds, and eventually bounced us down into the Sea of Screams, that big empty space northeast of Shanghai Station where most of the pods (and most of the private ships too) come down.

Shanghai Station isn't much to look at— from above it's just a scattering of gray lumps and spindly light-poles. We only got a quick look at it as we passed over, but we'd had to study its layout as part of our training, in case we had to divert. The truth is, if it weren't for the big red arrows—two klicks each—laid across the gritty gray sawdust, it'd be too easy to miss. There were no other visual cues.

The gray lumps were Lunar-crete domes. You lay down a big plastic bag, you mix up some fresh Lunar-crete and pour it over the bag. Then you inflate the bag. It takes about an hour. The Lunar-crete hardens, you spray it with sealant. You wait an hour, then attach an airlock, go into the lock and cut a door into the dome. The limit to the size dome you can inflate is how big a bag you have, how much Lunar-crete you can mix, and how much air you can put into the bag.

It's faster and easier than sandbag igloos—but sandbag igloos are good too, if you don't have a big plastic bag, if you don't have any Lunar-crete, and you can't spare a lot of air. You pile up sandbags and put a roof over them. Luna has no shortage of sand, all you have to do is bring a lot of empty sandbags. Ohell, even pantyhose will do. It's more labor intensive, yes, but it's cheaper because the only moving parts are humans.

You fill your pantyhose with Lunar dust and lay them down like sandbags all around the hole you dug the dust out of. You put a grid of carbon-fiber triangle-beams across the top of the wall, and it supports two more layers of pantyhose or sandbags to make a roof. You spray a centimeter of polymer inside to seal the floor and the walls, so you don't end up inhaling a lot of gritty dust, you install a pre-fab airlock, and the resulting hut is airtight, self-insulated, micro-puncture resistant, and uglier than a Martian lawyer. But for the fuel cost of a couple kilos of stockings and some hardware, you can build a tiny little home for two or more colonists—or even as many as six if they're willing to hot-bed.

And that's Shanghai Station.

It would never be Nova Hong Kong, but here on the high equatorial plains of Luna, someday it would be a great observatory. Or a factory. Or a launch catapult. The politicians were still arguing with the engineers and the scientists and the accountants. And they'd continue arguing for far too long while Shanghai Station finally grew into its own inevitable destiny. Everybody had opinions. We even argued about it ourselves.

Immediately after splat, the first shift, we slept in the transit pods. As much as we wanted to get out and do the "giant leap" thing, both our seniors insisted that we follow the manual and take at least two hours of rest. We'd have plenty of time later. In fact, according to Senior Cheung, after we got over the novelty of being on the moon, we'd find that the whole experience was mostly hard work and mostly boring and if we expected anything else, it would be mostly disappointing.

But we were on Luna. Most of us had been in the Vision Quest program for at least two years, some as long as five. We'd been training for this opportunity for 18 months. We were here and we were going to build the Turtledome. Our part of it, anyway.

Our youngest member, Jang, had just turned 18; our oldest, Jasmine, was 24. We were mostly male now, at least physically; although when we'd started out, we'd had at least five different sexes among us, possibly seven if all of the different stories about Slipstick were true; but for the purposes of this mission, we'd been required to transition to standard male form because most of the body maintenance was easier. At least, that was the reason given.

I wasn't the only one, of course, and among ourselves, we speculated what the real motivations might be for requiring the transition, not the least of which was having the whole team aligned on the same thing at least once in our Vision Quest career. And even though most of us had already admitted genuine curiosity, anticipation, enthusiasm, and impatience to experience sex in free-fall, or even in one-sixth gee, we had all taken suppressants anyway just before launch, so that we could focus on the more immediate tasks at hand—completing this mission in excellence and earning our team merit badge. But there was still a lot of boyish flirting and grab-ass, mostly so we could pretend that we were just too masculine (at the moment) for the suppressants to work completely. Besides, if we hadn't spent some time speculating about micro-gee positions, the Troop Leaders might have worried about us. Lacking any real experience, I kept my mouth shut and listened with no small amount of puzzlement. What was the big deal about a penis anyway? Most of the time, it just feels like it's in the way.

I guess that's the reason that most people think scouting is about gender-shifting, body modding, augmented telepathy, the technology of extended consciousness, transformational training, and all the other stuff that energizes the rad-bloggers; but there's a lot more to it than that, more than most people realize. As scouts, we had to learn our own history, all the way back to Lord Baden-Powell. Some of it wasn't very nice.

Scouting started out as a way to prepare young men (and later, young women, and eventually just young people of whatever gender they happened to choose at the time) for the responsibilities of adulthood. For most of the first century it served as a useful career path through adolescence that often led to ROTC and then from there to a military career.

But after the reformation, everything changed, especially the definition of adulthood, so young people have to be trained differently. Now, it was recognized that adulthood doesn't just happen, it's the result of the intentional pursuit of a goal or a vision. Hence, Vision Quest. Yes, the merit badges in joyous sexuality, compassionate nurturing, and gender-consciousness are important, but the underlying skills of flash-construction, geocaching, fabbing, and even poly-cracking are still as important as they were in grandpa's day. The day before we left, Auncle Norm did twenty minutes about how the whole thing was silly; building a functional Lunar dome is better left to bots, human beings shouldn't do dirt-work. Of course, she was right, but we weren't doing it for the dirt.

We weren't going to the moon to help build Turtledome; that was just the mechanical expression of the larger goal. We were contextually challenging the inherently intransigent nature of physical reality—a long-lost and too-often over-looked skill, but every bit as important as poly-cracking. Not everything is virtual. Sometimes you have to know how to boil a *real* egg. Sometimes even a centimeter can be a big thing—especially if it's the difference between a close fit and a secure fit. Or as Senior Whitlaw once said, "The vacuum in your helmet starts between your ears."

After the sleep-shift, we suited up, checked our greens, and stepped out into the Lunar night. It was dark and bright at the same time. The dust glowed faintly with the light reflected off the half-Earth low on the horizon, but the stars above were a splash of brilliance from one end of the horizon to the other. I'd seen this display often enough, but never in real-time, never in meat-life. It was somehow different. Not as spectacular as the big display down at the Wal-Mall, but a lot more *real*. And maybe a lot more, I dunno, meaningful...?

Mission Control gave us fifteen minutes to savor the moment—to bounce around, plant our flag, take our group pictures, and sink our prints into the crunchy Lunar grit.

For the first few moments, nobody said anything. We were just too...

Excited? Awestruck? Wonderwhelmed?

We made it! We were on the moon!

It was....

Just not describable. I won't even try.

But it's true, what they say. Once you've been there, you're different. And you can't understand what kind of difference it is until after you've been there. And all the words that have been written about it will never be enough. You have to go yourself.

Of course, we took pictures of each other. We all wore bright-colored star-suits; each one of us sporting a different color and design. And even though we had been specifically warned not to see how high we could jump, we did it anyway. We bounced around the landscape like cartoon characters superimposed on a black and gray diorama. The trips were all in green and yellow; when they stood side-by-side, they formed a triptych that spread across all three of their suits. Jasmine had an orange suit, which clashed with Libby's bright pink display. Mariko Bailey was a shimmering blue, almost like the sky on Earth, only brighter. Of course, all the suits were capable of full-video, front and back, but that had long since been demon-strated as too distracting, so we only had the video for our chest and back displays. So others could read our trendlines. Which were a little jacked up now, at the high end of optimal, but otherwise normal.

—so that meant it was time to get to work. We jacked the pods up into posi-tion and opened the external lockers. We unpacked the wheels first, six for each pod. They were circular honeycombs, bright yellow, fat and rubbery, three meters in diameter. After they were installed, they'd hold the pod-vehicles high above the roughtest Lunar terrain. The wheels had six times more flex than would have been practical on Earth, so they were pretty good shock absorbers too.

After the last piece clicked in green, we stopped for a pee-break. And that experience was sufficient to demonstrate the difference between theory and practice, as well as the difference between practice and actual application—but it also gave me a reason to appreciate the above-mentioned mission requirement. We also had our milk-and-cookies—that's what we called our in-suit liquid and solid refreshments; nutrient-rich something that we could sip and nutrient-richer something that we could chew.

Before resuming work, we checked each other's greens. On this shift, my buddy was Rocklyn. Our personal readings were good, close enough to optimal to keep going for at least another hour, so we jacked the axles into place and mounted the wheels onto the engine hubs. Everything was lighter than we'd practiced on Earth, but it still had the same mass *and* inertia—so it wasn't easier than we expected, it was harder—at least until we learned how to compensate for the discrepancy between weight and momentum. But it was mostly a snap-and-click job, then you run the tests, wait for the confirming greens, and give each other a high-five/low-five.

Then we unlocked the dragonfly wings—the solar panels that would provide both shade and power when we hit dayside, or when dayside caught up to us, whichever. We had 96 hours until dawn; we'd already sorted ourselves into shifts so that whenever one person was sleeping another was working. We'd be hot-bedding the entire tour, one per bunk supposedly, but maybe not. We weren't all sexual, but some of us liked to cuddle. The twins and the trips, maybe because they'd been raised that way; but not me. And I don't talk about why I'm a singleton either.

After everything was triple-confirmed, we climbed back into the pods—except they weren't pods anymore; now they were horizontal and on wheels, so they were trucks. We popped off our helmets and waited for the go/no-go from Mission Control.

Of course, we were being monitored. On Earth, there were at least a hundred other troops in training for their own missions to Turtledome. They were probably huddled or clustered or more likely lounging in front of video-walls, watching the multiple feeds from our helmet cameras, analyzing, commenting, judging our every move. Just like we'd done when we studied the 23 previous Lunar Quest missions— all the teams who'd preceded us.

But those were just the lookie-loos. Our primary was Vision Quest Control at Salt Lake and our secondary was Shanghai Station, about thirty klicks over the horizon.

There was an old launch catapult in Utah, purchased by General Transport a few years ago and now used mostly for boosting cargo, mostly international transports, but occasional low-Earth orbits as well. The control galleries had been refitted and were now among the very best in the western hemisphere. Vision Quest Control had an internship agreement; we used whatever spare galleries were available for monitoring Lunar Quest Expeditions and General Transport used the missions as training sessions for their own tech teams as well as ours. The relationship wasn't just symbiotic, it was incestuous.

Luna-side, Shanghai Station only monitored us in case of emergency, and only until we passed into Turtledome jurisdiction. Shanghai kept three trucks on standby whenever scouts were in the Sea of Screams. In the entire history of the program, they'd only come running once, and that was for a case of unscheduled menstruation.

Turned out the fellow was pregnant and hadn't told anyone. He miscarried in his suit. Rumor had it that the suit was ruined. I didn't want to think about it. And why does anyone want to get pregnant anyway when it's so much cheaper, safer, and easier to put the embryo in a bottle for ten months? But I guess some people are just old-fashioned stupid. The real problem there was that none of his buddies had noticed—and you had to ask, what was wrong with those relationships that he didn't trust anyone enough to say anything until it was too late? I guess he was afraid that if he'd told, he'd have been dropped from the mission; but according to rumor (the files were sealed) he said he didn't know he was carrying. Right.... And I didn't notice this thing in my panties either.

While we waited for our congratulatories and go-aheads, we took a primary meal-break. I hadn't realized how hungry I was; I put away a whole meal-pack and probably could have eaten two more. Low-gee work is exhausting; it puts you into a real energy-debt. It's not just the labor itself, it's the effort of moving the suit as well. Starsuits are made of workflex, multiple layers of nano-weave and exo-muscles. It's kind of like wearing an old-fashioned wet-suit, like some of the reenactment surfers still do, only one that works with you instead of against you; but there's still a lot of resistance, and while you don't feel it outside, after you get back in and unpeel, that's when you find out how stiff you are. Not to mention how much you've outsweated the suit's ability to absorb and recycle. The first thing to do is rehydrate with oxygenized water, at least a pint. Two is better.

Mostly, you're naked inside your starsuit. So when you unpeel, the first thing you do is wipe down—or you wipe your buddy down and he wipes you down, all the places that you can't easily reach by yourself. It's like being in a hot sweaty shower room, only without any water. And in an enclosed place like a pod, there's a lot of intense body smells. We use aloe/vitamin E scrubbing towels. Lunar vehicles and habitats are only pressurized to 5 psi, so your skin dries out quickly, and when it dries out—it flakes. And human skin-flakes are the primary source of dust in an enclosed environment with human hair coming in a close second. The one thing you really don't want is dust building up in your filters and machines. So we vigorously scrub each other's arms and legs and backs and fronts to remove dead skin and keep the living cells moisturized and the hair follicles retarded. You end up feeling as smooth as a baby. The first few times it's embarrassing, then it's interesting, then finally it's boring—except sometimes, like when my buddy is Mariko, it starts to get interesting again. But it's one of the few times we *don't* talk about sex. Go figure. You'd think that with all those naked young bodies in such close proximity—but no. I'm sure there must be a reason.

It's a Loonie thing. Dirtsiders, of whom I used to be one until just a very short time ago, don't get it. The ones who talk about Luna even though they've never been here and never will get here, no matter how much they talk about it—they're talking from the land of the untrained. What Whitlaw calls the arrogance of ignorance. They look at the facts and only see their opinions. Like clothes. There's all these porn-stories on Earth about how clothes will be unnecessary in space, we'll have such a perfectly tuned environment, we'll all float around naked. That's just silly.

Just like the starsuits are tuned nano-weaves designed for outside, we have much lighter and softer nano-weaves for inside. Some of the dirtsiders make really expensive lingerie out of the same material, which is a waste of good nano, because it's not really designed for that, but some idiots call it starcloth or space-cloth and charge other idiots a premium for it. And then other idiots wonder why Loonies have to wear expensive lingerie all the time. But it isn't. It's specifically designed for maximum utility and comfort. It only looks like underwear, but it's really just very lightweight T-shirts and shorts. The soft weave of the material is partly for comfort and protection—when your skin is being kept that smooth, it's no fun bumping up against stuff; partly for color—so you have immediate identification of people by their color designs; partly for enclosing and maintaining a stable air temperature close to the skin as well as wicking away excess personal humidity; but just as much so you have a place to put your pockets—because unlike some of those silly shows you see on video, you still need pockets in space, or at least some kind of utility-belt. Because, really, where else are you going to put your lucky marble?

But there's also the more important part that dirtsiders don't understand. It's nano-weave, with all the strength that implies—when you don't have a mall next door, you need your clothes to last; but more important, in an emergency, there's a lot of things you can use a nano-weave T-shirt for. During our training, we were given three of them to examine and told to come up with 100 things we could do with them. My favorite was tie them together and use them as a sling to kill Goliath.

Mission Control waited until we'd finished eating and our heart rates had returned to something approximating normal, then informed us that our buggies were good to go. That was the good news. The bad news was that they wanted us to take a four-hour sleep shift first. After the usual groans and protests, we slung our hammocks and settled in. In one-sixth gee, a hammock is almost luxurious. In fact, just about any bed on Luna is a lot like floating. There's no such thing as bedsores on this wannabe-planet. There are, however, other circulatory effects, like light-headedness and perpetual erections that have nothing to do with full bladders or full libidos, just blood flow. Or maybe it's psychological. Or adolescence. Or just another thing to whisper about after lights-out.

This time, for some giddy reason, it was euphemisms about masturbation. Someone said, "Keep your hands in your own pants!" and someone else shouted, "Tickle your own pickle." And someone else replied, "In your case, jerkin' the gherkin." And in short order, we also heard, "adjusting the antenna," "exercising your right," "five-knuckle shuffle," "badgering the witness," "white-water wristing," "flogging the beagle," "loading the cannon," "flying solo," "deconstructing Longfellow," "relishing the hot dog," "charming the snake," "man-milking," "launching the morning missile," "firing the staff," "squeezing the squirter," "dropping the kids off," "liquidating the inventory," "committing spermicide," "freeing the hostages," "spackling the ceiling," "helping put Mr. Kleenex's kids through college," and "running in single-user mode." And from those who'd recently been persons of the vaginal persuasion: "finding your niche," "auditioning the finger puppets," "rubbing the ruby," "riding the unicycle," "tickling your fancy," "patting the robertson," "pounding the pebble," "slapping the tribble," "playing the slot machine," "tiptoeing through the two lips," "flossing the cat," "checking for squirrels," "drilling for oil," "triggering the gusher," "spelunking in the mystery cave," "filling the pink taco," "spearing the bearded clam," "getting a stinky pinky," "digging the stench trench," and "attacking the Death Star." Until finally Senior Cheung lost his patience and hollered something in Cantonese that sounded like a fishwife's curse. Whatever a fishwife was. We didn't need translation. Shut up and stop behaving like a bunch of giddy *poke-gai gwei-lohs*. You're going to need your sleep.

Except in my case, sleeping was the last thing on my mind.

See, we re-buddied almost every shift, which usually wasn't a problem, except this rotation put me opposite Mariko Bailey, which meant my hammock was elbow-close to his, and that meant knowing smirks from Jason and Jonah and Jorge. Despite the fact I'd never said anything at all, everyone had figured it out anyway that I had a crush on Mariko. Everybody except Mariko who mostly, sort of, ignored me.

Mariko Bailey was the most beautiful boy in two worlds. He was a chocolate redhead. His skin was the purest deepest shade of Hershey I'd ever seen on any human being. His father must have been a tall muscular African because Mariko was all chest and muscles. He had a waist that other people can only aspire to, even with corseting. His mother must have been Chinese because he had perfectly angled eyes that accented his grin with a permanent twinkle; but his third parent must have been Irish, because he had naturally auburn hair. His tight curls were trimmed back in exquisite corn rows. I'd fallen in lust with him the first day I'd met him; he was the best argument for staying a girl I could imagine.

So of course, I assumed that everyone else saw how beautiful he was too. When Jason made the inadvertent remark that Chinese eyes didn't match either red hair or chocolate skin, I made the mistake of arguing that the combination was exquisite. I guess that's how it started. I got so embarrassed, I wouldn't stay in the same room with Mariko. I just didn't want to deal with the smirks.

So there I was, floating next to the curved wall of the pod, with Mariko Bailey's warm body hanging only inches from mine. He smelled so good, I had to roll over—do you know how hard that is to do in a hammock? In one-sixth gee?—to face the bulkhead.

After a moment, I felt a gentle touch on my arm. "Shan...?" he whispered. I tried to ignore him, but he repeated the touch, this time shaking me gently.

I rolled back to face him. In the dark, I could just make out his eyes. He hooked his fingers around the net of my hammock and pulled us close together so he could whisper directly into my ear. "It's only for one shift."

Huh? What the hell was he talking about?

"We've gotta talk."

I was too startled to say anything, I didn't know what to say.

"Look, I am what I am." His voice was so low I could barely hear him. "Get over it already. I'm a triffid, so what? It doesn't mean anything. I'm still your scout-brother—"

"Shh!" I said, maybe a little too fiercely, a little too loud. I hated myself almost immediately. I realized I had my hand over his mouth. I let go, embarrassed. I wanted to touch his face, I wanted to whisper to him, "How could you think that, you idiot? I think you're wonderful—" But then what? I love you? I hardly knew him. We hadn't exchanged ten words in as many days. The last thing he'd said to me was, "Yo? The ketchup? Over here?" Shit.

"I don't care if you're triploid, lots of people are—" I stopped myself, I lowered my voice, I struggled to figure out what to say next. How could I get from here to there?

"So why do you hate me then? Because I'm Chinese brown? Because I was an occupation baby? That war ended 19 years ago. Can't we just get along for one shift?"

"Stop it," I said. I put my hand on his mouth again, this time gently. He shut up.

Now what? I could hear the silence between my heartbeats. How do I tell him anything? How do I tell him he's too beautiful to be real? And that I'm so silly-stupid I can't stand to be in the same room with him because I just want to stand and stare? Oh, fuck, I can't even ask those questions yet. How do I get him to stop hating me because he thinks I hate him? Oh, fuck—

"I'm sorry," he said abruptly. "I shouldn't have said anything. Just forget it. Let's just get through the shift. And I'll stay away from you after that." He pushed away, rolled over in his hammock, and pulled his blanket up around his ears. Great. Just great.

I faced the bulkhead again and thought about crying, but maybe that was just hormones again. Or moon madness. Or maybe...I don't know. Somehow this wasn't anything I'd expected. We were supposed to be a team, and I was screwing the whole thing up.

What passed for morning in the pod was loud noises and bright lights, followed by disorientation and someone toppling me out of the hammock into a low-gee, slow-motion tumble of huh-where-the-hell-am-I? Oh, the moon. Right. Thump. Caught on the first bounce by Mariko, who let go of me as soon as I had my footing. Without ever meeting my eyes. Dammit.

I could have enjoyed a shower, but we weren't scheduled for another twelve hours; first we had to get to Turtledome. We rehydrated, had a couple of cookies each, then lit up our stations and rechecked everything. Mission Control gave both pods a green light, so we released the parking brakes, powered up, and rolled.

We cheered as the pods lurched into motion. We even hollered a bit, letting off tension, and then we quieted down just as quickly. This wasn't a bus trip to the snowdome; this wasn't a simulation, there was real work to be done.

The pod-ride was bouncy and light, like rolling over a rutted road in slow motion. You could feel the bumps, but they didn't feel real. Part of it was the one-sixth gee, part of it was the oversized wheels, and the rest of it was the magnetic suspension of the undercarriage. It wasn't the same as driving on a highway, but the dark rides on King Kong Island have rougher bounces.

Occasionally, we'd hit a bigger than usual bump and we'd float for a second. That surprised us the first time, after that we just shouted, "Air-time!" Because "Vacuum-time" didn't really work.

Top speed for a Lunar truck is supposed to be 30 klicks. We knew that some experienced drivers had hit as high as 70 or 80—but they were traveling on known routes. And unofficially, some had hit as high as 120 on short straightaways. So we figured we were doing somewhere between 40 and 50 kph once we hit "Route 66."

Route 66 isn't a road, it hasn't even been bulldozed or flattened. It's just a series of bright orange pylons marking the route between the Sea of Screams and Turtledome. Follow the pylons carefully and you probably won't roll into a crater. Get sloppy, you can embarrass yourself in front of nine billion viewers.

We all took turns driving, each one of us spotting for our buddy. Mariko navigated while I piloted, then we switched off. Our conversation was so formal we both could have been bots. We're lucky the rest of the troop didn't open a window and toss us out.

Every thirty minutes, we did something just like that. We popped a survey-bot into a release tube and dropped it behind us. The operative lifetime of a bot was 5-7 years, but some bots roving the Lunar surface were almost 15 years old. There were over a hundred thousand working bots on the moon; for more than half a century, every piece of rolling stock was mandated to drop a bot every twenty klicks. The bots looked like bright orange spiders and their job was to roam the terrain, photographing, sniffing, scanning, sensing, looking, listening, performing all kinds of terrain and mineral surveys, and phoning home every few days. Supposedly, the bots were so sensitive that if you dropped a fork at Asimov Station, the nearest thirty bots could correlate the seismic shock waves and report what flavor pie you were eating.

Eventually—sometime between next week and the return of the Centauri probe—we'll have a complete Lunar map, detailed down to the last millimeter. Satellite mapping is useful, of course, but it's incomplete. See, Luna is covered with dust—gritty gray dust that sticks to everything as if it's statically charged. Actually, it just hasn't been eroded. Down on Terra, every little piece of sand has been pushed back and forth by the wind and the waves, ground around forever by the restlessness of wind and gravity, tides and weather, every little grain rubbing against every other little grain. Do this for a few million years, and you rub away the sharp edges, turning them into little polished marbles. But on Luna, everything just sits there—no wind, no waves, no nothing. The nature of Luna is that there isn't any nature. Put Lunar sand under a microscope and it's all hooks and sharp edges. That makes it great for lots of different kinds of industrial uses, polishing grit and sandpaper, but it's hell on machinery, starsuits, and lungs—especially lungs.

As hard as everyone tries to keep it out, a little bit sneaks in through the airlock every time someone comes back inside. There's lots of stuff we can do—plastic coatings, filters, electrostatic fields, micro-blasts, nano-sweeps, and so on. But the eenth percent that still squeaks through is still a nuisance, which means eventually, it's a problem. One of many.

But we still have to know what kind of surface lies underneath the dust-crust. Tin? Nickel? Ice? Copper? Especially copper. Or just plain old rock. I'm not a selenologist, have no desire to be—but even I can understand the need for a good map of the available bedrock. Someday soon, they'll be putting up cable car towers. That's why Turtledome is where it is—because it's a junction. Someday, it'll be a city. Or not. It depends on whether or not we can finish the dome. Once there's a dome, we can argue for a line. Without a dome, there's no need for a line.

Meanwhile, there's just this gray uneven surface, rolling out to an impossibly-close horizon. Low hills and wide valleys, everything sloping this way and that, everything pocked with craters and strewn with rocks and rubble. It's not unreal or surreal—it's hyper-real. It's like a simulation ride, only not.

See, lots of people have said lots of different things about Luna—that its desolation is magnificent, that it's got a stark poetic beauty, that the terrain is silent and brooding and mysterious, and so on and so on and so on. All of that is true, but at the same time, it isn't. It's like what Gramma said to me, "You won't see the moon. You'll see yourself. The moon will be your mirror." Everything everyone says—it's not how it really is, it's only how they saw it.

So, how is it really—? You'll have to go and see for yourself. That's the only thing that's true about Luna.

To my mind, the big mystery about Luna is how anything so monotonous and boring can be so exciting at the same time. Luna is all scenery and no rest stops. Every place is different and everyplace is the same. It's almost completely colorless—everything is either black or dazzling bright. Or dark gray, or gritty gray, or fuzzy gray, or soft gray. Or just plain old gray. It's ugly and pretty at the same time.

And after a while, twenty minutes or forty minutes, or three hours, it's mostly boring. Once in a while, the truck has to go up a long slope, or around the edge of a wide crater, or down through a stark valley, but most of the time it feels like everyplace on Luna is just a variation of every other place. That isn't true, of course. We've all seen pictures of the Southern Jumble, and the Lunar Appenines, and the Levine Ravine. But we're still just scouts, and there's places we're not going to be allowed to go, because we're still just scouts.

But that doesn't stop us from speculating. When boys aren't flirting, they're gossiping. Or making stuff up. Worse than girls. Or maybe there's no difference at all. (Everybody talks about the differences—especially the way it was in the olden days, when the differences were important, but what if all those differences are just different ways of doing the same thing? Just like there are lots of different ways to masturbate. Or say "masturbate.")

Anyway…there are over a hundred thousand permanent residents on Luna, more than enough for a Lunar culture, of sorts. So there are stories and rumors and legends and mysteries enough to keep even a confirmed gossip like Slipstick chattering for weeks. He slid easily from the imported Russian mythology of the impish Rock Father to the more ominous mystery of the extra footprints found at Tranquility Base. Who had secretly visited the site before the Americans returned? The usual suspects included the Chinese, the Japanese, the Russians, the British, the Israelis, the Emirates, and the Australians. Slipstick said it was really Bigfeet—the mysterious aliens whose accidental sightings had triggered the Rock Father mythology. And furthermore, that was the real reason for dropping bots everywhere—the government knew that the Bigfeet were secretly watching us, all over Luna, so the bots were counter-surveillance. But the Bigfeet were as skilled at avoiding our bots as they were at avoiding us. So that's why we hadn't caught any video of them yet. Besides, they probably had some kind of cloaking technology that made them invisible to our sensors. And so on.

Jang said that the bots were really about establishing a total-monitoring environment, because some of the people on Earth were terrified that Luna might someday declare independence. They were already convinced that the Loonies were secretly building a hidden civilization—"Invisible Luna." That's where all the cost overruns and inflated budgets were really going. And that's who really left the footprints.

Mariko, who normally didn't respond to even the wilder speculations, just rolled his eyes, and said, "Do the math. How much air, water, food, and energy does it take to sustain one body on Luna. The annual Lunar numbers have enough wiggle room for maybe twelve people, maybe fifteen, certainly no more than twenty. That's not enough for a real conspiracy."

"You think so? Even nineteen people can be a conspiracy—"

Mariko was sharp, he caught the historical reference, but he still shook his head. "That was a century ago. Things are different now. Everybody's implanted with locaters. Every moment is monitored, including us. And every monitor is synched. You can't pick your nose, you can't wipe your ass, you can't even make a baby on Luna without an audience."

"Ohell, you can't make a baby on Luna, even *with* an audience." That was Libby. "It's all male up here."

Jonah laughed. "—which is exactly the way you like it."

Jason added, "Why do you care? Are you planning to get pregnant?"

"Not with you—"

After the rest of the jokes died down, we talked about how all the old predictions about life on other planets had gotten so much so wrong. Rocklyn reminded us of a silly old movie, based on an even sillier old novel, from way before the age of colonization, where the author had described three untrained brothers bouncing across the surface of the moon in giant plastic bubbles. While it wasn't technologically impossible, the author had conveniently ignored a few things about dealing with the Lunar terrain—like radiation, heat, cold, solar blinding, headlights for areas of shadow, humidity within the bubbles, air refreshening, and so on. And those were just the obvious ones. Or maybe he'd simply assumed that the readers wouldn't notice. Or maybe they'd think he'd already included those things and therefore didn't have to describe them.

After that, we speculated about what sports might be possible on Luna after the dome was finished. Assuming we had a large enough playing environment, what would one-sixth gee do to golf, football, baseball, volleyball, tennis, ping pong, and Frisbee? What about high-diving? And if we had large enough wings, would we really be able to fly? Maybe, if the air pressure was high enough. Rocklyn promised to do the math on that one. But it all depended on whether or not you could build a big enough interior space.

Luna already had a few domes, less than twenty, but none of them large enough to have enough space for any kind of a playing field, not even a tennis court. The largest dome on Luna was still less than a city block—the limiting factor wasn't the production cost of the dome, but filling it with enough air and water and soil to make it livable. Do the math yourself. Compute the volume of a hemisphere and how many packages of bottled air it takes to fill it.

That was the real challenge of Turtledome; when finished, the dome would enclose a space three kilometers in diameter. It would be huge. Big enough for a small forest, a lake, a meadow, and a couple of golf courses. With space left over for a few dozen football fields and baseball parks. Some people were already saying that filling it would be impossible—that Luna would never have a real "outdoors." Or whatever you wanted to call an environment safe enough to take your clothes off and go skinny-dipping.

But the real reason for Turtledome was much more important. The dome was intended as an inhabitable reservoir, a giant self-sustaining store of air and water and nitrogen. Her most important products would be soil and earthworms. Right now, most of the organic support and supplies still had to be imported from Terra, one cargo pod of air and water per day, per thousand inhabitants. Once there was a local sustainable supply, the cost of living on this rock would drop by twenty percent, or more. More important, once Luna could produce her own resources, she could be independent. She could be the architect of her own growth.

After two hours of lightly bouncing the trucks along the unglorious road, Rocklyn and Jonah relieved us. Mariko asked me if I wanted tea, I said yes and followed him to the back of the pod, where the galley and the lavatory were situated.

"I would have brought it to you," he said.

"I wanted to talk to you. Privately."

He made a face. There's no such thing as privacy. Not on Luna. And certainly not in a bus full of scouts.

"About last night—"

"Forget it," he said. He busied himself with the hot water, clumsily fumbling with the nozzle and the injection port of the mug. He was annoyed.

"I can't forget it."

"I can—"

"We're supposed to be buddies—"

"Only for a few more hours." He shoved the mug into my hands. A sudden bump pushed him against me for a moment. My heart bounced in my chest, I grabbed onto him—as much from instinct as desire. "Sorry," he said, embarrassed, and pushed away. He pulled open a cold-locker and grabbed a squeeze-bottle of milk. He popped the top, but before taking the first pull, he turned to me, "You want some?"

Wordless, I held out my mug. He pushed the spout into the socket, and gave me a couple of squirts. "That enough? Or you want more?"

"More, please."

A couple more squirts and he pulled out. It was the most intimate exchange we'd had yet.

"What?" he looked at me, puzzled, almost annoyed.

"How can you be so nice to me and so mean at the same time?"

"You're asking that of *me*? I should ask you the same thing."

With difficulty, I met his gaze. His expression was curious, but his eyes were hard. Finally, I managed to say, "I don't want you to hate me."

"I don't hate you," he said. But then he added three fatal words. "Actually, I'm indifferent." After a couple of sips of milk, he continued. "Just like you. You're a machine."

"I'm not indifferent," I said, tried to say—I croaked. "I'm not a machine. I just...." Oh, fuck. How do you tell someone something you don't even understand yourself?

He didn't wait for me to answer. He pushed past and back into the main cabin. I sipped my tea and shuddered. Too much milk.

There's this article I read, about this thing called maturity. According to some researchers, the natural hormones of adolescence are so strong that they overwhelm the functioning of the frontal lobes. What that means, is that you have no facility for critical thinking. The pubertal suppressants are supposed to counteract this effect, and I guess they do. The graphs in the article showed that the sublimation of sexual energy results in a 10-20 percent boost in applied intelligence, and a stability of perspective that many adults don't achieve until the exhaustion of old age. But some of the side effects included a decreased ability to bond, a retardation of social skills, and a higher proportion of gender identity confusion. Among other things. At least, I knew the technical reasons for what was wrong with me. And maybe Mariko as well. Maybe all of us. I wished I could open a door and just take a long bounce over the nearest dark hill.

I wouldn't be the first one to do that. According to everything I'd ever seen about Luna, it happened a lot. Too many times. Like two or three times a year—somebody would open an airlock without first putting on a starsuit. Or he'd put on a starsuit and just start bouncing in whatever direction he was pointed.

I guess sometimes that happened by accident. People still get starstruck, so enchanted by the never-changing wonder of Luna that they just forget to come back inside. But maybe, just as often, maybe it's deliberate. I'd read a lot of articles about it. We all did. It was part of our training. Luna is exhilarating—but when it's not exhilarating, it's depressing. It's a monotonous, gray and gritty wasteland. You get desperate for a bit of greenery, for a flower, for the sound of a dog barking or even a real wind. Most of all, you miss the fresh smells of spring, and the warm smells of summer, and the icy crisp bite of autumn. You miss the seasons.

In response to that, the Loonies say that they do too have seasons. Despair, Grief, Suicide, and Hell. Terrific.

Some of the doctors say it's because your internal clock misses its natural biological cycle, finally it breaks down, and you lose all sense of time. Everything just stretches away into blazing gray emptiness. So one day, you just put on your starsuit and head out the lock and go off in search of whatever is out there beyond this rill, beyond that crater, beyond the next near horizon, until you've gone past your point of safe return—and you no longer have enough air to make it back. Now that we were here, now that I was seeing it for myself, I could believe it. Why do people choose to live up here? Why did I want to?

I stared out the port and thought about nothing. There was certainly a lot of nothing to look at. And not a lot of words to describe it. After you've used up empty and barren and desolate, after you've said bright and dark and dazzling and grim— after you've said all that, you're pretty much done. Magnificent desolation. Period.

I wondered what it would be like to live here all the time. Being able to leap tall boulders at a single bound was fun, but it could also be as dangerous as it was exhilarating. And giving up blue skies for black was a whole other question; even the most mundane details of existence were different here. One-sixth gee affected the function and shape and construction of everything. Toilets. Ladders. Beds. Chairs. Even ceilings—permanent dwellings had foam ceilings, or the ceilings were carpeted with half-inflated air-bags. Think about it.

But those were the obvious things. Not-so-obvious, Luna might also be a great place to slowly starve to death.

As big as Luna was, did she really have the resources to sustain an independent civilization? Or was the cost of extricating those resources too high? With Terra looking over your shoulder, wouldn't it be a whole lot easier to just drop all the air and water you needed off the beanstalk?

Well, yes—and no. Eventually, you hit a ceiling, and this one wasn't padded. You can only lift so much. The beanstalk has a limited capacity, and somewhere in that number is the limit of Lunar growth—the amount of air and water that can be imported from Earth. So Luna has to develop its own resources, or forever be a satellite instead of a world.

Ultimately, it's all about process. That's what I thought about most—and that's what I was the best at. Everybody said that my meatware was overclocked. And even though they didn't say it where I could hear it, I knew they thought I had no real feelings either; because mostly I hardly ever said anything about how I felt. And that was mostly because I didn't trust most people with that information. So I concentrated on process. Because when I'm thinking about process, I'm not thinking about the *other* thing. So—process.

The Loonies could easily crack oxygen out of rocks, all they need is a little heat. The closest furnace is only 172 million kilometers away. Focus a large enough array of mirrors on the target zone and you can vaporize anything for its component elements.

Luna also had a sizable store of ice at its southern pole, and a little less at the north, and by the time that was used up, we'd be catching comets and bringing them down.

But as good as those plans were, at the moment, it was still cheaper and easier to deliver the stuff direct from the Big Blue Brother, dropping unmanned cargo pods onto empty gray deserts, of which Luna had an endless supply. The pods could be put down right on the customer's doorstep.

So there was no incentive to invest in Luna's own resources. The limiting factor wasn't the cost of production. Power is free on Luna. But if you were cracking air at the equator or melting ice at the pole—you still had to deliver the product to the consumers, some of whom might be half a world away. It was the cost of transport that made Luna an economic hostage. Terra could prefab cheap cargo pods, send them up the elevator, and toss them across for a lot less per package than it would cost to truck the same cargo across a few hundred klicks of grit.

It wasn't just the cost of trucks and fuel. It was also the larger job of surveying safe roads across an area larger than North America. And you'd need trained drivers too, at least until you laid out a route for the bots to follow. Taken altogether, the investment looked prohibitive.

And that's why the Turtledome reservoir was critical to Luna—because, it was the first important olive out of the bottle. Once finished, it would be convenient to half of Luna's northern hemisphere, and would function as a source of life-sustaining services to nearly a third of Luna's permanent bases.

Turtledome operating at capacity would be a biosphere. Anyone within a few hundred klicks—would be able to drive up with a train of pods and trade garbage and sewage and raw waste for clean water and fresh soil.

But right now, most of Luna's primary organic reserve was piling up unused, sealed in plastic bags, and stacked up high behind various small stations everywhere. The growing mountains of trash were an embarrassment to the new settlements, but they didn't have refiners on site to process the waste into useful fertilizers and fuel. Or they didn't have the distillation equipment to recover all the water. Most of them didn't even have functioning farms yet. So Luna's most valuable resource—her garbage—sat unused.

Finished, Turtledome would be the largest processing facility on Luna—but the dome itself was only part of the solution. It wouldn't be practical without a cheap and easy way for Loonies to transport their resources to and from. They needed the cable lines too.

It's all process. And I was determined to stay focused on process.

As part of our training for this mission, we spent a month grinding the numbers on Luna's economy. There wasn't a lot of pie in this sky, unless you baked it yourself. And you had to bring your own bakery.

The immediate answer would be trains of trucks—you put wheels on six cargo pods, and pull them behind a seventh. This would work for some stations, the ones that were close enough, but it wasn't a long-term solution. As an economic entity, Luna was still ranked somewhere between "undeveloped" and "impoverished." Luna's trucks were still needed for too many other jobs, much more immediate, and she needed most of her cargo pods for housing and labs. Even if she could convert enough pods into trucks, there wouldn't be enough drivers, and even if they let the trucks drive themselves, they'd use up almost as much resources making the trip as they would bring back.

Don't even talk about pipelines. You don't even have to grind the numbers to see why. A pipeline requires a processing plant at the sending end to reduce the product to a sludge-like consistency, and pumping stations along the way to keep the product moving. Too many moving parts. Maintenance would be a bitch. And you'd need one set of pipelines for pumping sewage in and another for pumping air and water and soil-sludge out. And then you'd need a new set of lines for every station you wanted to service. No. An impossible engineering job. An even more impossible investment.

Somewhere in there, a Hong Kong company suggested a light rail line. In one-sixth gee, you could have a transport system that was lighter and faster than its Terran counterparts, and you could use it for transporting people and other kinds of cargo as well. But even with those advantages, the cost of building such a transport system—even using bots—was still higher than ten thousand trucks. I never thought that grinding numbers could be fun; but the answers we got sometimes surprised us.

It was a Swiss company (of course) that demonstrated the feasibility of a network of cable cars. The towers could be assembled in Earth orbit and dropped anywhere on the Lunar surface they were needed. One-sixth gee was the advantage; the towers could be taller and lighter than their Terran counterparts and still strong enough to carry the load. If they were tall enough, they could be spaced ten or twenty kilometers apart. You wouldn't have to carve roads or lay track and you could create a vast transportation network in years instead of decades. And a key component of the system already existed—the gondolas. Every gondola on the line would be a reconfigured transport pod, the same way that trucks and shelters were converted from pods after landing. A steady stream of gondolas would create a de facto pipeline for humans, cargo, and raw materials, wherever Luna wanted to string cable.

Best of all, instead of going around otherwise impassable mountains and cra-ters, the cable cars could go over or across—incidentally providing some spectacular access to terrain that humans couldn't get to any other way. So...that was one of the big reasons why we tossed bots out the window every thirty minutes—so they could roam the surface looking for what passed for bedrock on Luna. An optimal tower site required a strong place to stand, access to sunlight, and a convenient source of Lunar dust—for making Luna-crete.

The interesting thing—after we finished grinding all the numbers—was that the cargo capabilities of the lines would end up being far more important to the Lunar economy than the ease of travel they would provide to humans. As Senior Whitlaw had pointed out, more than once, humans tend to be anthro-centric; which means, we take everything personally. "If I tell you that the sun is going to burn out in five billion years, the first thing you're going to think is, 'What's in it for me?'"

And he was right. Here we were, on the threshold of the second greatest frontier in human history—Mars had the number one spot—and it didn't matter how much I tried to focus on process, because after all that, still the only thing I could really think about was the bulge in Mariko Bailey's pants. What's in it for me? I was certain the answer was nothing. I felt like the guy in the dirty joke who smelled so bad that even the sex-bot refused.

One of the things the trainers had told us, over and over: "You're not going on an adventure. The last thing you want is an adventure. Do you know what the defini-tion of an adventure is? It's when things get interesting because your life is at risk. We don't want you putting yourselves or your buddies at risk. We want you so well trained that you *don't* have adventures. We don't want your trip to be exciting. We want it to be productive. The only excitement you want to have up there should be the satisfaction of a job well done."

But here I was, distracting myself (again) with stuff that should have been resolved long before we got to Ecuador and rode the beanstalk up. I'm supposed to be a genius. I'm supposed to know how to figure this stuff out. I'm supposed to be... well, like...a hero. So what was so wrong with me that I couldn't focus on the job in front of me—

Oh fuck.

I touched my communicator. The buddy-channel. "Mariko, I need you. Please come back to the galley."

In the forward cabin, I heard movement. A few seconds later, he stuck his head in. "What is it?"

"Check my readings for me?"

He looked annoyed, but he complied. He studied my chart on his personal dis-play. Then he grunted. "Well, I s'pose that explains it. Some of it, anyway."

"What?" I already knew the answer, but I needed to hear him say it.

"You're going through puberty."

"But what about the pubertal suppressants—?"

He was silent a moment more, paging through the displays. "Um. Maybe they've cut out. Maybe it's something to do with your transition to male—a translation effect. It's probably temporary. Only for a week or two."

"Oh, no, no, nooooo."

"It's not as bad as you've heard. Some of it is even fun."

"But not *heeerre*. Not *nowww*."

Dispassionately, he asked, "Have you started having erections?"

"No," I shuddered. "And I'm not going to. I already decided that. It's just too— you know, icky." The whole subject was embarrassing. I was very sorry that I'd paged him.

"Um." He lowered his head toward mine, he put his hand on my shoulder, he lowered his voice. "You do know, don't you—sometimes they happen by themselves. You don't really have that much control."

It was too much. I started to cry. That old thing about big girls not crying didn't count anymore. I was a boy now, and boys cried all the time. Or did I have that backward? Who cares? I cried. Not hard, but enough. I don't know if he pulled me into his arms, or if I threw myself at him, but somehow I ended up with him holding me, patting my back, and comforting me, and I didn't even know why I was so upset or what I was upset about.

I stopped, pulled away, sniffled—he wiped my nose with a tissue. Kind of like a big brother. I looked across at him, suddenly me again. "Do you really think I'm a machine?"

He shrugged. "All you talk about, all you ever think about, is the tech stuff. You never tell jokes, you never say anything unless it's about the job—"

"I have to. I don't want to fail—"

"Nobody does." He wiped my face again, even though it didn't need it. "This is the first human thing I've ever seen you do. It's almost cute—"

My face felt suddenly hot—

"Even cuter when you blush."

"Stop that—" I felt like I was going to cry again.

He grinned, delighted. It was the first smile he'd ever meant just for me, and it was so intense, I almost passed out.

"You're doing that on purpose!" I accused.

"Doing what?" he asked innocently.

"That!" He had one of his huge hands in the small of my back, gently tickling me with his fingers. "You're playing with my hormones."

"Yeah," he admitted. And lowered his voice to a whisper. "And you like it. You really like it." But he stopped. "There," he said. "You see? You can be human. If you want to be."

"No, I can't—" I said it automatically, without thinking. "I can't be efficient *and* human at the same time."

"Sure you can. It just takes practice." He gave my nose a cursory wipe. He held me until I finished sniffling, finished wiping my face. "You feeling better now? Ready to come join the rest of us?"

I nodded, then— "Wait? Shouldn't I tell the Seniors about...you know?"

He laughed. "They already know. Everybody does. Relax. We've all been through it. We're on your side. Come on, 'Little Brainiac.'" That was the first time he'd ever called me by my nickname. It almost felt good. Reluctantly, I followed him back into the forward cabin. At least my heartbeat was finally returning to something like normal.

Nobody said anything as I took my seat. Not much of a seat, just a flat shelf that unfolded from the wall; but that's another one of those things about Luna—the furniture. Furniture is about gravity. The less gravity you have, the less furniture you need. Something like that. I forget where I read it.

The ride to Turtledome was long. We drove straight through the night—what would have been the night if we were on Earth, but was still night on Luna and would be for another few shifts. Splat-down was 160 kilometers from Turtledome, as the crow flies, if there were crows on Luna that could fly in vacuum, but we weren't driving in a straight line; the marked route weaved through a minefield of craters, all sizes, and there were some up- and downslopes we had to navigate as well; so it was an estimated 36 hour drive. We staggered our shifts and drove straight through. Halfway there, Shanghai Station passed local monitoring over to Turtledome, so we gave a cheer of self-congratulation. We'd been on Luna almost a full Earth day and hadn't killed ourselves yet.

Theoretically, we could have landed closer to Turtledome than the Sea of Screams, there were a lot of other optimal sites; but the terrain closer in was considered too rocky and too uneven for safe landings. Plus, I think, they wanted us to have a couple of days experiencing Luna on our own, before we arrived at the dome. Something about getting our "Luna-legs" before we were in a place to do any serious damage. Just long enough to get bored with the novelty of pouring coffee out of a cup and being able to catch it in the same cup before it splashed across the deck. Nobody needs a bunch of playful puppies bouncing around the worksite. So this was our chance to play—to get some of the excitement out of our systems.

The Seniors decided we should keep our current buddies for another shift, which sort of pleased me. Mariko and I exchanged a glance and he didn't look unhappy either. Maybe he was feeling big-brotherly toward me, which was kind of strange because I was 18 months older than him—but he'd been a boy for a lot longer than me, so maybe it wasn't all that strange. I dunno. I could tell my thoughts were scattered. When I had a job to focus on, I was okay—but as soon as I went into downtime, I would get very conscious of feelings that I didn't have a name for yet.

Mariko and I had two more driving shifts before we arrived at Turtledome. The terrain had gotten progressively rougher, and by the time of our last shift, most of it was upslope. Luna isn't perfectly round, nothing is, but the little gray pearl is a lopsided mess, with mascon bulges on the side facing Terra, and other deformations leftover from a couple billion years of cosmic smackdown. You can't really see it from space, you have to drive the surface and experience it. The land isn't flat, it's lumpy. Ahead, the terrain tilts up toward nothing. Behind, it rolls down into the same dark empty. Except when it's the other way around.

The horizon is always too close, the edges are too sharp, you get the feeling something is lurking just behind this rock or that hill. You can't help it, you're descended from creatures that used to be lunch for larger creatures. Large open spaces are intimidating. It is a magnificent and ultimately terrifying desolation. Beautiful and ugly at the same time. Or maybe, as Gramma said, that's just me looking in the mirror.

But finally, we rolled up a long slope, forever to the rocky top—the dark gray lip of the hill rolled away as we approached. We crested and a marvelous view spread out before us, all sparkling and wonderful.

Turtledome Station.

A bright sprawl of light and pattern etched across a great curving darkness. It looked like someone had dumped a giant bag of miscellaneous technology into a giant bowl, scattering little pieces across the landscape in a seemingly haphazard jumble of towers and lights and machines. Floodlit fields of machinery dotted the bottom of the crater, spider-like gantries and cranes loomed like invaders, mechanical mantises preying on the dozers and excavators and trucks. There were clustered installations, webs of scaffolding, and scattered cargo pods everywhere; some of the pods were lit up, people were living in them. And there were greenhouses—lots of greenhouses, growing food and producing air for a growing population. And of course, domes, lots of domes, all kinds and colors—*bright* colors—and bigger than the ones at Shanghai. Everything was connected to everything else by plastic tubes that snaked everywhere across the dirty gray surface—inflatable tunnels, all lit from the inside. It was a Lunar fairyland technological fantasy.

We saw trucks everywhere, making their way between the various structures. There were dozens of bot-piloted trains, each one glittering with light to stand out against the darkness. Most of them were painted in garish shades. They crept across the crater floor and worked their way up the vast sides of its walls. The trails were dozed and marked with orange cones. From here, the trucks looked like cartoon ants following pheromone trails faintly etched in color.

Turtledome crater was three kilometers across. And deep. Bigger and deeper than Barringer Meteor Crater in Arizona. It was visible from Earth with a good pair of binoculars and a tripod, though a telescope would be better. With a telescope, you could even see the glitter of floodlights within the darkness. We'd done it more than once. We'd been closely following the progress of construction for years, even more intensely the last 18 months. There wasn't a spot on the floor of the bowl we weren't already intimately familiar with—at least, in theory.

And now we were perched high on the rim, overlooking all of it.

Seeing it laid out beneath us like a glittering black picnic basket, I don't know how anybody else reacted, but a bright thrill of recognition and fear and overwhelm flooded up inside of me. It was another terrifying reminder that all of this was frighteningly real. I felt a painful pressure inside my pants, finally I stopped pretending and shifted around, slipped my hand into my pants and adjusted it—*oh no!* And then, to make it worse, Mariko saw and nodded. He leaned over, touched my shoulder, whispered, "It's okay, baby boy. You're not the only one." But no, that didn't make it any better.

Before we could call hello, a voice came from the dashboard speaker. "Elephant One, we see you." And a second after that, "Elephant Two, we have you as well. Welcome to Turtledome. We have hot soup and showers waiting." That received cheers from all of us.

Getting down to the bottom of the crater wasn't hard, just intimidating. The dozers had carved wide roads spiraling all the way around and down to the floor of the basin. It wasn't dangerous, but it required close attention on the part of the driver. You had a sloping wall to your right, and a daunting emptiness to your left. It took us four hours to wind our way down, including the three rest stops we took. There were turnouts every klick or so, and if a pod-train was coming up, you wanted to pull off to the side to let it pass. Most of the pod-trains were carrying workers and supplies to the tower construction sites, where they'd stay for a week at a time.

Almost immediately after we descended past the uneven rim of the crater, we saw the demarcation line where the shelf was eventually going to be installed—the foundation of the dome that would someday cap this bowl. A line of bots was patiently carving a deep sloping trench into the shallow slope of the rim. We passed one crew that was installing an anchor-strut. It didn't look big enough to me, but I'm not an engineer.

Most people on Earth think that Lunar domes will be held up by the air inside. Well, yes—eventually. But first you have to build the dome. And you have to hold it up while you build it. The trick is to build the dome like a suspension bridge—hang it from cables. You could do it with three towers, but Turtledome was so large, they were double-engineering everything. They were putting up six towers, spaced equidistantly around the rim. When the towers were complete, they'd string a vast spiderweb of cables and lattices between them—using almost enough cable to build a Lunar beanstalk. And then, when the web was complete, they'd turn the weaver-bots loose. The bots would crawl back and forth across the gigantic web, slowly, painstakingly laying down nets of carbon fibers, then broad sheets of foam-filled honeycomb-polymer, then more fibers and more polymer, over and over again, until they had tented the entire crater with a meter-thick, self-sealing surface. It would be a semi-rigid tent—springy and solid at the same time. It would be puncture-proof and self-repairing. If the sealant hardened properly, if the glue held, if the tent was airtight, then the crater would have a working dome. If not, they'd have a dome needing constant maintenance and repair—and they were already developing the tools for that.

For additional safety, the inside of the dome would be partitioned into seven distinct habitats—a large hexagonal central district, surrounded by six equal-sized trapezoidal chambers. Each of these neighborhoods would be its own airtight, self-maintaining domain, each one dedicated to a specific primary function, but also capable of long-term, exportable self-sufficiency. The design specifications for the habitats required that every individual section be able to provide life support for the total population of the dome, if it became necessary; like if a catastrophic meteor storm were to hit the dome and puncture the seals of the other six habitats, the remaining one would still be a safe sanctuary for the survivors. And if a disaster bigger than that were to occur—well, no physical structure could be built strong enough to withstand a disaster that big.

But it would take years to produce enough air to fill the dome. It would take at least eighteen months to fill a single section, even pressurized to the equivalent of 7,000 meters altitude on Earth. Air-cracking was another one of those limiting factors—how many plants you could build, how much oxygen they could produce; not to mention the issue of nitrogen and various trace elements. Nitrogen can be manufactured, sort of, but the process is energy-intensive.

When everything was finished, when all the separate sections were operational, and when the dome was lit from within, the whole thing would look like a giant turtle sprawled helplessly on its back, with its legs—the towers—sticking up in the air. The head of the turtle was the main access tower for the cable car line, situated in a smaller crater breaking the rip at the north; the tail was the secondary access, following a twisted rill to the south. "Turtledome" was only a nickname, but nobody on Luna called the settlement by its real name.

There was some controversy about that. Some people felt the person who the dome was going to be named after hadn't really earned the honor, but had taken most of the credit for the work of others—most of whom had mostly been overlooked or forgotten, like Coon and Fontana. But there were others who said it was appropriate to honor the dream, if not the man identified as the architect. One blogger had written that either way it was still appropriate because both the dome and its namesake were large and round and safely in the ground.

Apparently, naming stuff on Luna is almost always a political battle. People on Earth say, "Well, it's *our* moon, we should get to name our craters whatever we want, honoring all the great men of history." But people who live on Luna have a much more compelling argument, "It's our *home*, and we're going to honor the men *and women* who made it happen, who built it, who lived and died here." (With the implied, "If you don't like it, you'll have to come up *here* to change it.") And then, to complicate the matter even more, there are all those other people on Earth who think that God wants them to name all the craters after prophets and saints. Some of these craters have six different names; it depends on your religion.

And that's another part of Loonie society that's really different. On Earth, people can afford to have imaginary companions who rescue them from tornadoes and send hurricanes and floods to punish their enemies. Most Loonies leave their imaginary friends on Earth, before they ride the beanstalk. They have to. If you're in trouble on Luna, help isn't coming from anywhere else—you have to help yourself. The best kind of help is being so well-prepared you don't get in trouble.

I guess that kind of thinking is too hard for most Terrans. That's why so many folks flunk the emigration exams. Most of the scouts, almost ninety percent of those who apply for Lunar training, don't make it. Terries don't get it—it's a whole other way of thinking and the shift from there to here is such a break in their reality, they can't always make the leap. The best they can do is pretend they understand.

Like the dome itself. It almost wasn't a turtle, it was almost a mouse—until they figured out that the ears were really lungs. I guess I should explain that. During the Lunar day, the sun scorches the bright side, so the air in Turtledome will heat up and expand. So for two weeks, for 336 consecutive hours, the air pressure inside the dome will steadily increase. During the Lunar night, the reverse will happen—the air will cool, the pressure will drop. Do the math. It'll flex the dome enough to shatter its structural integrity.

So the dome needs a pressure valve, actually two of them. During the Lunar day, you pump expanded air out into a large inflatable; during the Lunar night, you pump it back into the dome, and that's how you keep the internal pressure of the big dome equalized.

Turtledome crater has two smaller adjoining craters along its northeastern side that provide perfect staging sites for its lungs. One crater is just under a klick in diameter, the other is just a little bit over. From above, they appear almost the same size. Now, if you could light up all three craters at once, you'd have a pretty fair approximation of a certain, very recognizable, corporate trademark. So that very big, very famous corporation was pretty keen on sponsoring the development. There was even talk of putting theme parks in the ears. But that meant they'd have to have the two adjoining craters domed and lit as well. And that would pretty much defeat their usefulness as lungs; and they'd have the same expansion/contraction problems as the main dome. And they'd still need to build lungs, only now for three domes.

And later on, when Turtledome was a fully functioning habitat with a real lake, the lungs would also be used as heat-sinks. Water heated almost to boiling during the Lunar day would be pumped out into the lungs and replaced by cold water stored in underground tanks; that would help keep Turtledome's temperature down. During the Lunar night, they'd do the reverse, pumping hot water back in to help keep the dome warm. There's a lot of engineering needed to make a habitat work, you can't cheat the laws of physics. (The best you can do is negotiate with them a little.)

The big corporation's engineers understood that. Engineers always understand engineering. But the executives of the company don't understand engineering; they only understand marketing. So they blinked in confusion and kept saying, "Why not?" And, "Why can't you?" And, "If we're paying for it, we get to decide—" And the Loonies just kept on explaining why not and why they couldn't and why it would be a waste of money to even try until the whole deal fell apart. And that's why the turtle will have lungs and the mouse will have no ears.

It's all process.

And—I guess I really am a Brainiac. I guess it's true that the pubertal suppressants create a sublimation of energy into other pursuits. But I like knowing how things work, I like understanding and explaining. I like the whole process of putting things together to produce a result. I like the feeling of control—that I can make things happen, that I can plan and design and build—and make even a little part of the universe work the way I think it should.

And yeah, I admit it—I don't understand dancing. Two people holding each other and walking around in time to music. I don't understand why people sing to each other. Or even why anyone would want to share a bed with anyone else—all that grunting and farting and shoving for space. All of which is my way of admitting, I really don't understand people. That's why I like machines. Machines are understandable. People aren't.

Like why don't the trips see how beautiful Mariko really is? And why do I see it and nobody else? And why don't I get it about women? Or men, for that matter? The whole man/woman thing, or man/man, or woman/woman—do people *really* want to do that stuff? And why? Isn't masturbation a lot less messy, a lot less troublesome?

The last time I tried to have this conversation with someone, they looked at me like I wasn't from any known planet. The best answer I ever got was, "You'll understand when you're older." Well, I'm older now, and I still don't understand.

We finally rolled down onto the floor of the crater and found ourselves on Broadway, so named because it was wide enough to pull a six-car pod train around in a U-turn and still leave plenty of room for two more lanes of traffic in each direction. Orange cones delimited the actual boulevard. We took Broadway southeast, through Times Square, until we hit Vine, then we turned south and drove for a klick and a half until we got to Hollywood Boulevard. We'd be staying at the Turtledome Hilton—no relation to the actual hotel chain—just a local name applied to a clusterphuque of sandbag huts used for transients like us. It was walking (bouncing) distance from Turtledome Center, a half klick away.

Turtledome Center was a towering lacework of lights and antennas, sitting atop a glittering tinkertoy assemblage of sausage-shaped pods, connecting tubes, and inflatable chambers. It was the base of the whole operation here, and it was installed at Oxford Circus, where Via Appia collided with the Champs Elysees. On the opposite side of the crater, the main storage and construction depots were located in the Ginza and Tienanmen Square.

By comparison, the Hilton didn't look like much—it was the Lunar equivalent of a mud hovel tenement. But just the same, having your hotel at the corner of Hollywood and Vine is a lot more exciting than staying at the corner of Mickey Drive and Goofy Way. Nobody was complaining.

We were still 18 hours away from dawn, so the whole crater was on the ass-end of stored power. For obvious reasons, Turtledome Authority doesn't like using up hydrogen or methane unless they have to. The fuel cells are held for emergencies and the renewable resources are used up first, so most of the power at night comes from batteries and flywheels and Stirling engines tapping into stored heat. But at the rate that Turtledome's population keeps expanding, the need for power grows faster than the hardware can be fabbed or imported.

And it's not just power, it's everything. Air, water, food, medical supplies, starsuits, ancillary life support gear, everything necessary to support a single human being—you can put a man on the moon, no problem; it's keeping him there that's expensive.

Okay, this is the bottom line of Lunar economics. The limiting factor isn't the machinery to get folks up here. And it isn't the cost of finding and training qualified people either. No. The limiting factor is maintenance—the supply line doesn't have enough bandwidth.

Here's how Whitlaw explained it to us when we were training. He told us that the Turtledome project was likely to take thirty years to complete—that's if it stayed exactly on schedule, which simply wasn't going to happen. Ask any bridge builder. I asked why they didn't just send up more people.

"No, that won't work," he said. "Imagine a very tall building. Imagine you have only one elevator that goes all the way to the top. It takes fifteen minutes to load the elevator, fifteen minutes to ride it to the top, fifteen minutes to unload it, and fifteen minutes to bring it back down again. If you have ten people living on the top floor, you only need one elevator a trip per day to supply them with food and water. The elevator is tied up for an hour, you can send it up at three in the morning and not inconvenience anyone. The elevator stays available for everyone else.

"Now imagine that you have a hundred people living on the top floor, you need ten trips to supply them. That's ten hours that the elevator is tied up. Now it's starting to be a problem. You have to schedule your trips throughout the day, still leaving time for others.

"But what if you want to put a thousand people on the top floor? You can't. The most you can put up there is 240, and the elevator is busy 24/7. You can't even afford downtime for maintenance or people start missing meals upstairs. And God help all of you if there's an emergency. So somewhere between 100 and 200 people, there's your limit in that circumstance. If you want to put more people on the top floor, you can either build another elevator—or the people upstairs need to make their own power and grow their own food. There's a limit to how many elevators you can put in a building, so there's really only one answer."

And that's why we had to wait until sunrise for our showers. But we did get the hot soup.

The Hilton didn't have a hut big enough for all of us to gather at the same time, but they did have an inflatable they used as both a meeting hall and a dining room. I have to admit, it was kind of spooky sitting on the moon with nothing but plastic between us and vacuum. But the Ranger, his name was Hunt, who led us into the dining room, assured us that it was perfectly safe; they hardly ever had punctures. And the advantage of an inflatable this big—the size of a small house—was that even if you did get a pinpoint puncture, the air wouldn't go out in an explosive rush;

it would still shoot out, but slowly enough that there would be time for most of the people in the bag to get out safely. No need to worry.

"*Most* of the people?" Libby asked.

"Yes, that's what we project," Hunt said deadpan.

"Has it ever happened?"

"Are you volunteering to test it?"

"Can I wear my starsuit?"

"Then that wouldn't be a real test, would it?"

Dinner was hot tomato-vegetable soup, as promised, and homemade bread. Plus fresh salad and steamed carrots and broccoli; the main course was soy-patties in tomato sauce. Yeah, we noticed. But the entire meal was from the Hilton's own farms—nothing from Earth at all. The bread was different than we were used to; it was sourdough, but it was so light and feathery we called it cotton-candy bread, and aerogel bread, and ghost-bread, and bread-impersonator. That's because on Luna, even when you adjust the recipe, bread still rises three or four times as high as it does on Earth. It ends up so light, you can't even butter it unless you soften the butter to the consistency of pudding. But it was still pretty good anyway.

We found out the Hilton was one of the few private establishments here at Turtledome. Hunt had been up here too long—rehabilitation for Earth gravity would have taken years. Instead, he took over the "hospitality suites" and tended his own greenhouse, providing local services for the construction companies. It worked out well for both sides. The bread was his own recipe; in his spare time, he was working on a Lunar cookbook. "You'll never get bread like this on Earth, not even if you bake it upside-down."

For dessert, we had fresh berries and syrup over pink cotton-candy ghost-cake. There were chefs on Terra who would have cried to see how fluffy a Lunar cake could be. It was like eating a cloud. Later on, we found out that Hunt could bake heavier breads and cakes if he wanted to, but apparently that first night he was subtly reminding us just how different things really were up here.

It was a perfect moment. We were celebrating the completion of the first step of our adventure, congratulating ourselves for arriving safely at Turtledome. We felt like we'd accomplished something, and we were already looking forward to the next step. It was a perfect moment—until the argument broke out.

It was Jasmine and Libby, of course. Jasmine had been in the other truck, Libby had ridden with us, so they hadn't had any real opportunity to strike sparks until now—when Whitlaw accidentally, or maybe accidentally-on-purpose, assigned Libby to Mariko as buddies for the next shift. Jasmine protested that this was out of rotation, and he was supposed to be Libby's buddy for the next shift—and that's when the trips snorted and laughed, and that just made Jasmine angrier and more insistent—but Hunt interrupted harshly. "This is Luna," he said. "Deal with it."

Right. The short version: Luna doesn't care what you want, doesn't care what you feel, doesn't care what you think—Luna just doesn't care. Deal with it. If you deal with it, you breathe, you eat, you survive. If you don't—well, that's another way of dealing with it too. Luna doesn't care.

And the really silly part about the whole thing was that it wasn't about anything at all—until it was about everything. We were having another of those endless adolescent speculations about sex, except we weren't talking about sex, we were talking about everything all *around* sex, so even though we weren't talking about sex, we really were talking about sex. You have to be going through puberty to get it, and not everybody does—Rocklyn, for instance, is permanently neotonic. Not everybody wants to go through puberty. According to the news, almost a fourth of the population of Terra has chosen or will choose to be permanently asexual. Maybe that's a good thing, maybe it isn't, but the Population Authority encourages it, and they're projecting a population plateau sometime in the next two decades. I've thought about it myself.

The argument started innocently enough. Jorge was sitting opposite me, he glanced over at Mariko, then turned back to me and made a not-very-subtle remark about how this trip was turning into a terrific opportunity for some old-fashioned male-bonding.

Mariko's gaze flicked across to me, then quickly back to his cake. I could almost hear him thinking, "Don't react. Don't buy into it."

I didn't have to. Jason and Jonah chimed in immediately, had they set this up beforehand, or were they just naturally stupid? Or did they just seek out opportunities to stir the shit whenever they could, because they couldn't stand being bored? Gramma used to say that boredom is evidence that you can't stand to be alone with yourself; people who like themselves don't get bored. I had to think about that one for a bit. She also said that people who like to stir the shit usually end up licking the spoon.

Jonah said, "I think male-bonding is just sublimated sexuality. What do you think, Jason?"

Jason shrugged, his usual performance of non-committal detachment. "Isn't *everything* sublimated sexuality?"

"Well, see, that's my point," Jonah said, "Why do we all have to be male for this trip? Yeah, I know about the plumbing thing, but come on, that's really not that big a problem—is it, Shan?"

I shook my head, shrugged, pretended to be more interested in a particularly bright berry stuck inside a cloud of cake. "Dunno."

But escape wasn't going to be that easy. Jorge picked up the conversational ball and dribbled it around my head. "I think it's because they want to turn us all monosexual. Of course, that's not that big a turnaround for Jasmine. She's already there. Aren't you?"

Jasmine looked annoyed. "Don't ask me. Ask Shan." Everyone's attention flicked immediately to me.

I was already turning red. "Um, actually," I flustered, "I haven't thought that much about it."

Jonah snorted. "Yeah, right."

Mariko interrupted then. He glanced toward Jasmine. "The way I understand it—" he said dryly. "The real point of having us experience both sides of the sexual equation is so that we can escape the simplex personality model engendered (pun intended) by single-sex psychology. Transition provides opportunities to experience complex, even multiplex gender perspectives, thereby creating a wider empathic model of human behavior for the individual." He stopped, then looked directly at the trips. "In other words, it's about social skills. Something all of us could learn—" He stirred his coffee (Lunar-grown, of course) and lifted it to take a sip, prematurely popping the lid. Unfortunately, he hadn't really gotten his Luna-legs yet, and a dollop of coffee went floating up in front of him, splashing him first in the face, and then splattering down the front of his shirt and all over the table as well. So that was the end of all serious discussion for a while. I passed Mariko all the paper towels in front of me and then bounced to the galley-wall, looking for a towel. So I missed the transition from clumsiness to jealousy. Apparently, I wasn't the only one trying to mop him down. Libby had been sitting on the other side of Mariko—

—and when I got back, Libby had his hands full of paper towels and Mariko as well, "—just a big mess, I told you Shan was off the rails—" and Jasmine was screaming incoherently—not at Mariko, *at Libby*. And that's when it all suddenly made sense. Libby liked Mariko too. Libby was *jealous* of me—? And Jasmine was jealous! Jasmine and Libby—? Of course. That explained everything. And I felt like a triple-ass for not figuring it out before.

Puberty is hell. Especially when it's delayed for a few years, and then explodes messily all over everything. That was the real mess.

Fuck.

When we finally pried everyone apart—have you ever had a fight in one-sixth gee? People really do bounce off the walls, and a few of us even hit the ceiling once or twice. In the inflatable, it would have been fun—except with all the yelling, it wasn't. It was scary. We knew the walls couldn't rip, but who wanted to take chances?

When we finally pried everyone apart, two of the tables were broken—they were easily reparable, most Lunar furniture was, but the evening was effectively over. Senior Cheung wasn't happy. Neither was Senior Whitlaw. We had not made a good first impression on our hosts. Whitlaw and Hunt went back down into one of the adjoining huts for what was supposed to be a private discussion—but we could hear most of it anyway. Hunt was angry with Whitlaw for bringing a bunch of unruly, untrained, unprofessional, *feral dirtsiders* to a high-pressure construction site, and how the flaming fuck did we manage to go for eighteen months of training without learning how to control ourselves, and furthermore, we were the worst bunch of fuckups he'd ever seen, and for a while there, it sounded like we were going to be turned around and sent back to Earth immediately.

"They can't do that!" and "We just got here!" were insufficient responses. But all of us were shouting in protest now. Yeah, we knew we'd behaved badly, but couldn't we at least have a second chance? Now that we're already here? We've worked so hard! It was only a stupid mistake! And of course, the inevitable, "The rest of us didn't do anything!" and "We tried to stop them!" This went on for several minutes until it became obvious that no one cared. Luna didn't care. We petered out.

Cheung glanced off to the other room. He just shook his head sadly, "'Sorry,' is not an eraser."

A moment later, Hunt came back, followed by Whitlaw. They both looked grim. Oh, shit. And we hadn't even unpacked.

Whitlaw spoke first. "I'm embarrassed by your behavior. I'm disappointed in all of you. Whatever you've got going on, handle it." He glanced to Hunt.

"That's all?" Hunt asked.

"That's all I need to say," Whitlaw replied.

Hunt shrugged. Okay.

He cleared his throat and looked around at us. When he finally did speak, it was with enormous deliberation. "Luna doesn't care," he said. "Neither do I. I do *not* care if you want to risk your own lives. But I *do* care about you risking the lives of everybody else working here in the crater. Your mission is cancelled. I'm not going to baby-sit you. Neither will anyone else. You're going home."

He waited until we stopped. "Yes, it is too fair," he said. "What the fuck do you think we're doing up here? Luna demands consciousness. You were supposed to be trained, but you arrived here still acting like blue-sky zombies, bouncing around in a blue-sky trance, just a bunch of fucking tourists. We can't afford that here. We're not baby-sitters. We need professional behavior. Apparently, your seniors didn't get their jobs done—because you're still just a bunch of spoiled, hormone-infused adolescents. All of you. There's no place for that on this worksite. And I want you gone." Then he added, "But here's the bad news. Bad news for me, that is. Transportation to the dust-off site won't be available for at least a week, maybe three. So you're stuck here until we can create an alternative."

He took a breath. "Don't relax yet. And wipe those stupid smiles off your faces. Here's the first lesson of Luna, 'Nobody breathes for free. Nobody eats for free.' You're still going to work for your bread. There's some shitwork that needs to be done, that nobody else has had the time to do. You can do that. But if there's another incident like this, the next job you'll get will be digging your own graves—"

I didn't think he heard Jorge's whisper. *"He's just saying that to scare us—"* But he whirled around and said, "I'm not kidding about the graves. If you doubt me, look up the charter. The Commanding Officer of this operation has the same authority as the captain of a ship. We have the legal authority to shove any one of you out the nearest airlock—or the whole sorry pack if we feel like it. I don't need any reason more compelling than 'freeloader.'"

"But you wouldn't—" Jonah started to say. "I mean, there'd be protests all over Terra."

"Probably," agreed Hunt. "But you'd still be dead. And we'd be back on schedule. We're Loonies. We don't listen to Terra. We listen to Luna." He turned and left.

Jason made a face at Jonah and whispered, *"Yeah, we're Loonies—"*

"Knock it off," said Whitlaw, so quiet and so deadly that the room went instantly silent. "Mariko, go change into a clean jumpsuit. The rest of you, here's your permanent buddy assignments. Until further notice. We're putting you with people you can pretend to get along with. Libby, you'll buddy up with Mariko—"

"No," said Libby. "I'm staying with Jasmine."

Jasmine looked startled. Whitlaw's face was unreadable. He blinked twice. Maybe nobody had ever defied him before. "We'll talk—" he said.

"There's nothing to talk about," Libby replied. "My buddy needs me. This is what I choose."

Whitlaw nodded slowly, as if sorting it all out. "All right." He turned to me. "Shan, you'll buddy up with Mariko again. Apparently, he's the only one who can stand you. And vice versa." He'd never spoken to me that way before and I felt like he had punched me in the chest.

Whitlaw left, probably to go see Hunt again, and now it was Cheung's turn. One thing we all knew—you didn't want Cheung angry with you. Or as, Rocklyn had quietly explained it once. "There are Italian mothers. There are Jewish mothers. And there are Chinese mothers. Cheung is all three." Cheung stored it all up and waited for the right moment. I didn't hear all of what he said. I was already ripped open by Whitlaw's remarks, and I just went off to a corner by myself so no one would see me crying. I sat down at a table and put my head down in my arms and sobbed to myself about what Whitlaw had said.

Normally, Cheung would have dragged me back and I knew he'd get back to me soon enough, but right now, he was focused on Jasmine and Libby, heaping most of the blame on them for jeopardizing the whole program. Pretty soon he'd start in on the rest of us for letting them get away with it.

But surprisingly, he didn't go on long at all. He made some bunk assignments and sent everyone scurrying off through the inflatable tunnels to their respective cabins—huts—whatever. I stayed at the table, head still in my arms, waiting for Mariko to come and get me. It felt like he was taking forever.

That was when I heard the conversation I wasn't supposed to hear. Or maybe I *was* supposed to hear it. Hunt and Whitlaw and Cheung were in the next room over. Their voices were too low to carry. But I turned my hearing up, did some internal signal processing, stripped away the background hum of fans and machinery, and *listened*. They must have forgotten I had augments—or maybe they hadn't forgotten. Maybe they just didn't care.

"That could have gone better," said Cheung.

"It's our own fault," said Whitlaw. "We're the ones who put the pot on the stove. We shouldn't be surprised that it boiled over."

"It's a mess," agreed Hunt. "But it's not irreparable. We'll just have to rearrange the schedule. Give them their sleep-shift, but no shower. Tell them we're not going to waste water on freeloaders; they'll have to earn their showers. Have them suit up when they wake. They're going straight to work, but they can't use the tubes. The tubes are for real Loonies. We'll bounce them to the new greenhouse domes, but we'll take them the long way around and that'll be their first orientation. But we'll do it harsh—stay away from the air-plant, we don't trust you. That's the reclamation dome, if you ever earn a shower you'll go there. And so on. No public feeds, of course. Not until we have these kids actually working. That's so dull that only the die-hards and the trainees actually watch. We'll give the boys a few shifts shoveling soil. Tell them the bots are down for maintenance. After a couple of shifts, they'll be muscle-acclimatized enough that we can trust them around real people. That's when they can have their showers. We'll let them spend a few days in their own stink and that'll give us time to reconfigure. We'll need it in any case. But you know how to handle that one too."

Whitlaw said quietly, "This complicates our public relations problem."

"And maybe this could work to our advantage."

"We should have caught it. But it happened so fast, it caught us by surprise. We didn't turn off the feeds until it was too late. It went out live. We'll be getting calls from downstairs pretty soon." He must have glanced at his watch. "As soon as dawn hits the east coast."

"We knew we were going to take some fire anyway," said Hunt. "'Why didn't you train those boys better?' 'What are you people doing up there?' That kind of thing. But that's why we scheduled this when we did. The Super Bowl is three days away and most Terries don't have the attention-span to think about us and a football game at the same time."

Cheung said, "The dirtside office has already prepared the talking points. And we've got enough public graduates in high visibility who can speak to the issue—that you can't train adults to be perfect, but you can train them to learn from their mistakes. But only if you give them a place to make mistakes. That's the Vision Quest program."

"You think they can sell that—?"

"That's what our people are paid to do."

"All right," said Hunt. "Then let it be their problem. Luna doesn't care. So now—let's talk about the real fuck-up here. Look at these trendlines."

Another silence. Finally, Whitlaw said, "They caught us by surprise."

"They caught *both* of you by surprise? I'm really disappointed."

"And we're really embarrassed. We watch their lines pretty carefully We've been doing it for two years; by now, we know their physiologies better than our own. We were green all the way up the beanstalk, and even in the leap-across in the pods. We didn't see anything out of the ordinary until we rolled the trucks. Shan was the first one off the chart. At first, we figured it was just her—him now—and the rest of them were getting a contact hard. We didn't expect the fight—at least not this soon. We didn't think we were going to see anything more than some boyish giggling over each other's Lunar erections.

"But it showed up in their lines a couple hours after we hit the road. After the first sleep-shift it was obvious. They've *all* gone pubescent at the same time." Whitlaw's voice went low and dark. "Obviously, we've got a much bigger problem than one little bitch-fight. We've got synchronization. We knew there was a possibility that one or two might react. We didn't expect anything this intense. They never knew what hit them."

"All right," said Hunt. "How do you want to deal with it—?"

There was silence for a moment. Cheung broke it. "If we were still on Earth, I'd flush them with pheromones, lock them all in a room, and let them fuck themselves into desperate exhaustion for as many days as necessary...until they beg to be let out. After a week of relentless sex, most boys—most *normal* boys—will eventually get tired enough and bored enough with the old in-and-out to start asking what's for dinner."

"That's an idea too," said Hunt. "Not what you said—but we've got a few horny riggers up here. Normally, we don't let them date the scouts until the last two weeks. I wonder if...no, let's not. I have a better idea."

"What's that? Put them back on the suppressants?"

"No. Their systems are already in uproar, and some of them are still in post-transition syndrome—Shan, for example. Let's not overload their livers. We'll have to have the team deal with puberty the old-fashioned way. By living through it."

"Ugh," said Whitlaw.

"Oy, veis mere," said Cheung. "On the moon."

"It won't be that bad," Hunt replied. "Most of human history, we didn't have bio-technology, and the species still got sentient anyway."

Whitlaw's voice, I could almost see his skeptical expression. "Any sensible reading of history shows that we're still not sentient, we're just pretending."

There was a break then, an interruption. Whitlaw said, "Mariko, are you all right?" He must have been coming back from changing.

A muffled grunt in reply. I couldn't make out Mariko's response.

"Yes, well, stop exuding pheromones. That's half the problem. The other half— well, you're still buddied with Shan. We'd better talk—"

I strained to hear, but then Cheung came out to talk to me. "You and Mariko will be in Shelter Six. It's one of the oldest ones, and it's one of the smaller ones, but it's also one of the most livable. It's got a few amenities. Now listen—" He put his hand on my shoulder and bent low to my ear. "You need to focus up and stay on purpose. You're still on Luna. Never forget, there's only a very thin line between you and vacuum. Don't get sloppy, don't forget your procedures—"

Why was he telling me this? I thought I was the most attentive to detail of all of us. Some people even said I was obsessive compulsive—which isn't a bad thing to be if you're committed to integrity. As Whitlaw always says, "Your integrity is your starsuit. How many holes are you willing to poke into it?" For me, the answer is zero. Except sometimes, how are you supposed to know what's *really* going on?

A couple minutes later, Mariko came out of the other room, looking not very happy. "Come on," he said. He didn't sound friendly. I picked up my starsuit and helmet. He picked up his. He scooped up both our duffels where they'd ended up after they finished bouncing, after we'd tossed them aside. He shoved mine into my arms, took me by the elbow and led me out into the tubes.

The inflatable tunnels snaked all over the crater floor. From above, they looked like a network of glowing white veins. From inside, they looked too bright; outside was only ominous darkness, and a vague gray grittiness.

Every hundred meters, we pushed through a pop-lock. Push and it pops open in front of you, step through and it pops closed behind. There were also a few push-locks and one revolving door lock too.

It was too easy to bounce, and with Mariko half-dragging me, I felt like a balloon. We finally slowed down and half-floated half-jumped our way along. We came to a junction marked by signs—follow the green stripe, follow the red stripe, follow the blue stripe—Mariko pointed and pushed/dragged, and we found our way to shelter six. He hadn't said two words to me and I was afraid he was angry, though I couldn't figure out why.

Shelter six had an old-fashioned cycle-pump lock, leftover from the first days of Turtledome. That's how old some of these structures were. The two of us were pressed face to face in the tiny lock. It had never been designed for two at a time. The original designers had engineered it for only one man at a time, they'd assumed he'd be wearing a bulky-suit; they'd never imagined form-fitting starsuits made of workflex, but the two of us could just fit into this lock—if we were friendly. Or pretending to be friendly. Or just putting up with each other.

I could feel Mariko's body pressed against mine, but I didn't know if that was intentional or because he had no room to back up. I took advantage of the moment and pressed just as hard against him, the whole time staring unashamedly into his eyes. He met my gaze. Any moment, I expected him to smile—I hoped he would—but the inner door popped open first and he moved abruptly sideways, almost pushing me out with him. I tripped, but before I could fall—

He turned, caught me in mid-air, and pushed me hard against the padded wall of the tiny hut. I dropped everything I was still holding. His expression was—unreadable. He pushed in close. I could feel—everything.

Then he kissed me. It wasn't icky at all.

It was...wonderful.

And then, Mariko moved his lips to my ear, not even whispering, just barely mouthing the words. I still had my ears turned up, I heard every word clearly. "I wish I had more time, so I could fall in love with you."

I said something like *urk* and lost all physical volition to a flush of surrender. I think that even if I had wanted to protest, I was too exhausted to do so. I just let go and let it happen. I remember at some point, probably about four seconds after Mariko's whispered words, I had wrapped all my arms and legs around his upper torso and he was standing there holding me, and even though we were both still dressed, I was already realizing that one of the opportunities of one-sixth gee was a sexual position that had always struck me before as untenable for periods of longer than a minute or two, at least without external support. Now, I was contemplating the hydraulics involved, and despite my lack of practical experience, I was beginning to appreciate the vertical possibilities with curiosity, eagerness, and enthusiasm. But first, we'd have to get our clothes off—

That didn't happen.

Mariko carried me over to one of the bunks—an inch of foam on an inflated mattress and bounced us both down onto it. He held me close, intensely. One of the nice things about nano-weave is that you can feel things through it. Very intimately. This penis business might not be so bad after all.

Abruptly, he stopped. He lifted himself up and stared down at me. I couldn't tell what he was thinking. *"This is hard—"*

"I like it hard," I said, giggling. Good grief! Did that come out of me?

"Yeah, me too," he said. He lowered himself back down onto me, I loved the pressure of his body on top of mine, light and strong at the same time, and we kissed for a while. Kissing is nice. I don't know how anybody could imagine it as icky. Kissing Mariko is especially nice. We did that for awhile. I lost track of time.

And then we were whispering again.

"Do you trust me?"

A very strange question to ask—

I'd known Mariko for almost two years. No. I hadn't known him at all. I'd hidden from Mariko for almost two years—even all the times when we'd been buddied up in training. And now here I was, with my legs desperately wrapped around his waist, and whatever I'd been using for logic was completely turned around. I liked this rubbing-our-stuff-together business a lot. But how could I trust him while he was doing this? My feelings were all turmoil. But how could I *not* trust him? Was he feeling the same as me? Or something else altogether? How is a girl-boy supposed to know anything?

—I didn't answer. I pushed him up off me. Not hard in one-sixth gee. I could have carried him in my arms, if I could have imagined something to do in that position. I stared up into his face. I could feel the tears welling up in my eyes. What was going on here anyway? I could feel that old familiar hurt gathering itself, just in case it was needed again. *"Tell me—"*

He looked pained. But he lowered himself close and whispered, "Over a year ago, I knew then. You have a great smile, when you let it out. First, you were this very sweet little girl. Now...you're an even prettier boy. But I couldn't—oh fuck, I didn't know it was going to be like this—" He stopped and buried his face in my neck for a moment. Was he crying?

Just about the time I was going to say something, he raised up again. *"I'm sorry, sweetheart. I am so sorry—"*

"No, don't be—"

"No, stop—" He touched my lips with his fingers, to keep me from talking. *"Don't say anything."* He studied my face as if he was memorizing me. And then, after a Lunar eternity, we pulled each other close and held on tight. And we didn't say anything else. Not for a long time. We just quietly made love. And the only sounds

were the occasional gasp or sigh or giggle. It was...everything it was supposed to be, except when it was even better than that.

In the morning, or what felt like morning, we washed each other. Two or three times. Technically, the washcloths are supposed to be as good as a shower, if not better. But I still like the feeling of running water on my bare skin. And even though my head knows I'm clean, sometimes the rest of me still insists that I'm not. But today, here, now, I didn't want a shower, I wanted to rub the feeling of Mariko into my body and keep him there forever.

He traced his fingers up and down my body, taking extra time with what remained of my breasts and nipples; even underdeveloped, I couldn't believe how sensitive I still was. I felt so good all over, like I was filled inside with hot chocolate pudding. I felt stretched and alive in a way I'd never even imagined was possible. I tingled, I glowed, I was flushed with feeling. I started to say, *"Promise me something. When I'm a girl again—"*

But he stopped me. *"Please, don't—"* He had the strangest look on his face. As if he knew something terrible was going to happen. He didn't speak much as we dressed. He helped me suit up. He was so tender, it was scary. He checked everything three times, and I had the impossible feeling that he was saying goodbye, and that this might be the last time we'd ever see each other.

Then it was my turn to help him. His blue-sky starsuit made him look like a superhero, and I admit it, I let my hands linger across his skin a lot longer and a lot more tenderly than I'd ever done before. I was all over him, loving the job of dressing him and hating the distance the two starsuits put between us. I liked being naked with my lover.

My lover. What a curious, delicious, wonderful phrase—

We clicked our helmets into place, we blanked our face-plates, we brought up our displays, we checked each other's readings, three times over. We waited for tele-confirmation, then we cycled the airlock. Mariko turned me so I was against the inner door, and that was the last thing I remembered clearly. He turned away. The outer door popped open

and the next thing I knew I was lying on my back, floating on an inflatable bed, staring at a soft blue sky with puffy rectangular clouds, which eventually resolved into a painted ceiling with white air-pillows for padding. The smells of antiseptic told me I was in a medical bay. And then Hunt's face swam into view and he looked very concerned, "Do you know where you are?"

My throat felt impossibly dry. "In the morgue? Am I dead?"

"No, you're not dead. Do you have any pain?"

"I don't think so—" I patted myself. Someone had peeled off my starsuit. I was naked under a soft blue blanket. My tits hurt. My legs hurt. I was stiff all over. But most of it was a good stiffness. The overwork of last night? The most enjoyable pain in the universe. I wanted to drift back into the memories—

"Shan. Don't go away—" Something fizzed near my nose and I smelled peppermint.

After a moment, I blinked. I opened my eyes again. "I'm still here." And then I came awake. "What happened?"

"There was an accident."

"I already figured that part out. *What happened—?!*"

"The seals on the connecting tube failed. The monitors said there was air, but there wasn't. When Mariko popped the lock, there was an explosive decompression. You were slammed back against the wall. He was blown outward—

"Where's Mariko? *Is he all right?*" I started to lift myself up—

Hunt pushed me back down onto the bed.

"Just tell me!"

"His helmet cracked. His air bled out. It was quick. And he was probably stunned or unconscious, so he wouldn't have felt anything—"

I don't remember what I said after that. It was probably incoherent. I remember only disbelief and denial and rage and fear and grief and anguish and then a whole lot of other feelings that don't have names yet, but are a lot more horrible than disbelief and denial and rage and fear and grief and anguish. But then something else fizzed, some different smell, and I went out again

and this time when I came back, I couldn't feel anything, I was floating on a different kind of cloud, this was a cloud of not caring, almost like being dead, maybe better, and the nice thing about this cloud was how much I didn't care. I didn't even care that I didn't even care. I could have stayed here forever.

And maybe that was a good thing and maybe it was a bad thing, but whatever it was, it was the thing that was there. Maybe it would have been better to let me rage and scream and fling myself at the walls for awhile until I exhausted myself physically and emotionally. And maybe it was better to leave me numb for awhile too. And maybe it didn't matter, because I hadn't been given any choice in the matter.

And. And. And. It's all ands. It's all words. Just a lot of sentences and noise. It didn't change anything. Mariko was dead and I wasn't. Even while I floated alone, not-caring, I knew that my life was over. There was nothing left for me anywhere. Mariko had gone away and I wanted to follow. Wherever Mariko went, that's where I wanted to be. Even if it meant not-being.

Sleep-shifts came and went. The lights went down and then came up again. From time to time, people came in and looked at me. Their mouths moved. They made noises. It didn't matter. I didn't care. I didn't want to hear any of it. I didn't want to listen. What if one of them actually said something that made a difference? I'd have to give up not-caring. And not-caring was starting to be comfortable. Numbness wasn't an acceptable substitute for feeling—but it was a lot less painful. And I'd already had enough pain, thankewverymuch.

After a while, I went from horizontal to vertical. I moved around. I put food in my mouth. I chewed. I swallowed. I drank liquid. I sat on the toilet and made plopping sounds into the depths below. I peed. I didn't care. I put on a starsuit. I went and shoveled shit in the greenhouse. I came back. I took off my starsuit. I stood naked in the shower and wondered why my nipples still had feeling when I washed them. I didn't have a buddy, or maybe I did. There was always someone watching over me, but I wasn't watching anybody, just the vacant space ahead of me.

And one day—yes, it was day; the sun had finally risen over the sharp eastern horizon—one day, when nobody was watching me, I put on my starsuit and triple-checked my safeties, even though there was no real need to, and opened the nearest airlock, and bounced out onto the naked Lunar plain. I was going to find Mariko.

I'd finally figured it out. Luna was the country of the dead. It's empty, it's barren, it's gray and lonely. Nothing happens here. No wind, no weather, no sound. It's dry hell, gritty and endless. Every part of it the same as every other part, different only in the quality of its monotony. I crunched across the crater floor heading toward the darkness in the south, a forgotten jumble of useless detritus. I turned my suit display off—I went black. The best color for a dead boy. I'd be invisible.

From above, there's an obvious plan. Concentric rings of glowing tubes and dark utility trenches. Someday, those trenches would be sealed over. They might even become tunnels under the habitat. But right now, they were just little chasms to leap across. I passed the last orange cones and started bouncing up the long road toward the rim. Whenever I saw a truck approaching, I went motionless. I crouched down and pretended to be a shadow. Nobody stopped. Nobody noticed me. I felt hurt by that. Even angry that no one cared. But it just confirmed the rightness of what I was doing. I was alone and I was going to stop being alone the only way I knew how. All I had to do was keep bouncing, no matter how long a way it was, and eventually I'd be with Mariko.

After a while, I lost track of time. I remembered cresting the rim of the crater, then striking off at right angles to the road. I headed toward the east, toward the still-rising sun. If Mariko was anywhere, he'd be in the light. My suit started making noises in my ear. From time to time it sounded like Jang or Jonah or Jasmine. When it started to sound like Cheung, it got annoying, so I turned it off. I turned off all the monitors too. I didn't need to know. I'd know when it was time to sit down. Or lie down.

I drank some milk. I ate a cookie. I peed into my bladder-bag, knowing it would quietly recycle through layers of miracle membranes. I climbed a little slope, I bounced down a steeper one. I thought about stopping, but I was on the downhill side now. Nobody walks on Luna, it's almost impossible. Walking is a function of gravity. You lean ahead until you're falling forward, then you put a foot in front of you to keep yourself from falling all the way down—that's what walking is. But on Luna, there isn't enough gravity for walking. You fall too slowly. So to get anywhere at all, you have to spring. You bounce across the land like a human balloon in a wind. Except there's no wind, just you. And the crunching dust. And the glittering horizon. And the sharp-edged shadows. And the rocks. All the painful rocks. And you bounce. Bounce and bounce and bounce again through time and gravity and despair.

And then, finally, I did stop. For no reason at all.

I looked behind. I couldn't tell which way I had come. I turned around a few times, but every direction looked the same as every other. If the sun's glaring brightness hadn't still been low in the east, I wouldn't have known which way I was pointed.

I checked my suit-readings. They were blank. Oh. Right. I turned my monitors back on. But it didn't matter now. I was too far out. My displays told me what I already knew. I didn't have enough air left to make it back, even if I wanted to. Which I didn't. But at least, now they had a signal. They could come and find my body. If they wanted to. My recorder was on, of course; that's automatic. I could have said some words. If I wanted to. Which I didn't. I was finally ready to let go.

So I sat down. And waited.

I realized that some of the not-caringness I was feeling was an after-flush of the drug, whatever it was, they'd been pumping into me. But it was wearing off now. Just enough for me to notice that I was starting to get uncomfortable. My diaper itched. My penis felt uncomfortable, but there was no way for me to adjust myself in a starsuit. My nipples itched too.

I started to cry. I couldn't even say what I was crying about. It was just everything. Luna wasn't wonderful, it was horrible. It was a dreadful place for anybody to die, let alone live. It was no place for human beings. It killed us and it didn't care. So why should anybody else? So I cried because I didn't care either.

And while I was sitting there, crying and not caring, I noticed stars twinkling on the horizon. That was odd. Stars don't twinkle on the moon. No, it wasn't stars. It was something flickering. And it wasn't on the horizon—just in the distance. Something tall and spindly. After a minute or two, I actually started to wonder what I was seeing. I shifted to telescopic view, but it still didn't resolve. It was just something tall and spindly. Maybe it was the Rock Father. Maybe it was one of the Bigfeet. That would be funny. What if I actually met one of the Bigfeet, but died before I could tell anyone? I wondered if that had already happened to anyone else. I almost laughed. If I hadn't still been feeling so sorry for myself, I would have.

The thing, whatever it was, was coming closer. It was headed straight toward me. Maybe it was even coming for me. Now I could see its eyes. Or maybe they were headlights. Though why anybody would need headlights during the Lunar day I couldn't figure out. Not headlights, all kinds of lights, constantly shifting, making it hard to focus on the thing. It looked like a heat shimmer in the distance—except, of course, you don't get heat shimmers in a vacuum.

And then, abruptly, recognition clicked in. It was a ten-meter strider, spidering over the land. It had three long spindly legs, which moved sort of like a stilt-walker and sort of like a Martian war machine. A single stride was ten meters, that's how it got its name. At the very top was a cargo capsule turned vertical and converted into a control pod with living quarters and supplies and tool bays below. It wore a hat of scanners and antennas, and from its back sprouted a tangled cluster of arms, folded and unfolded. That's where its legs were anchored too.

I tried to look like a shadow again, but its three spotlights swiveled around and speared me with light. Even with my faceplate fully shielded, I still couldn't make out any details through the glare. Image-processing didn't help. The strider was flickering its external displays to confuse the auto-correlator. I'd studied equipment specs for months—I thought I knew all the striders working at Turtledome. As near as I could tell, this wasn't one of them.

And then—one of the strider's arms unfolded, reached up and over and down, and plucked me off the ground. It held me up before the window of the control pod for a moment—I couldn't see in, it was shielded—then swung me around to the externally-mounted airlock on the side. The door popped open and I pushed myself in. Maybe it was just an automatic reaction on my part, and maybe I'd decided I really wasn't ready to die. And maybe I was genuinely curious. Was this really one of the mysterious Bigfeet?

Inside—I popped my faceplate open. Only then did I realize how stale was the air I'd been breathing. The air in the strider was crisp and cold and fresh. And it felt a lot more solid than anything I'd been breathing in Turtledome. My head cleared quickly. I started to wonder what I'd been thinking before and why.

There were two people sitting in the strider's control chairs. Both were suited, both were belted in. Both their starsuits were black. The pilot of the strider did something and the huge machine swung around and began loping easily across the airless desert. The motion was as gentle as the rocking of a boat, but I had to grab for a handhold anyway. I glanced around, unfolded a seat from the wall, and strapped myself in.

The pilot swung around in his chair, and popped his faceplate. He was a moon-burned man with long silvery hair. "Not bad, kiddo—not bad." He nodded toward his panel. "You covered nearly forty klicks. I've seen Lunar fugues before, but this just might be a record-setter."

"So what? Do I get a trophy?"

"Maybe. It depends on your answer to the next question. Do you really want to die today? Or at some point in the unknown future?"

"Um. I don't...understand...the question."

"You are now a guest of Invisible Luna. This is your invitation to join."

"What if I say no?"

He shrugged. "If I thought that would be your answer, we wouldn't have picked you up."

"Oh. But—I was trying to commit suicide."

"No, you weren't." He nodded. "You were just...overloaded. But if you really are determined to kill yourself, then we can put you back on the ice and this will be nothing more than the delusion you experienced as your air ran out."

"Oh." I considered my options. Did I really want to die today? The inside of the strider had a strange familiar smell. I still wasn't thinking clearly. This was all happening too fast. I said, "But you don't know if I'll be any good to you—"

"Oh, you will." He grinned. "Here's what you stepped in. Dirtside, and this is the real reason that we call them *dirt*side, doesn't want Luna going independent. So they don't allow females to emigrate. That's why everyone coming up has to transition to male first. If we can't breed, we can't build a real society. We'll always be dependent on the marble."

"Oh," I said. "That stinks." I thought about it. "But can't people translate back to female once they get here?"

"Most of the workers get rechanneled, so they don't want to switch back, but even if they did, they can't. Terra won't send us the meds."

"Why don't you just import fertile eggs and bottles?"

"*All* the meds related to transition and reproduction and gestation are interdicted. They're contraband. And most of the fabbers we get are strictly limited to construction items. They won't even let us have organic fabbers to grow steaks, they're afraid we'll grow a couple of uteruses too. We can't even get some of the basic tools for building gestation bottles."

"But—" I shut up. There must have been a lot more to all this than I was capable of understanding right now.

"So, here's the rest of it. Mariko wasn't a boy. Well, not completely. He was smuggling a full load of fertile eggs. So was Libby. It's a tricky job. We fumbled it once. At some point in the mission, probably triggered by the shift from Terra-gee to free-fall to Luna-gee, or maybe just triggered by the excitement of splatdown, he went into estrus. His body started signaling a readiness to breed. In a closed pod, that would have been pretty intense."

"Um. Yes." I was remembering the wipe-down after our first workshift.

"That would have been more than enough to trigger a pubertal breakdown in some of you. You were the first. Jasmine was certainly the second. What we call puberty isn't a natural phenomenon anymore. When it's controlled, it's a lot easier for everybody involved; when it explodes, there's a lot more drama."

"So does that mean it was all hormones? And Mariko and I weren't really in love?"

He shook his head. "I'm pretty sure that Mariko loves you. More than you know—"

"How can you say that?"

"Because it was Mariko who demanded that we come out here after you." He nodded toward his copilot—who swiveled around to face me in a starsuit that had suddenly turned bright blue.

The next few moments were confused as hell. I remember screaming, crying, and launching myself at Mariko. I felt a rush of emotions so confusing it was painful. I felt betrayed. Ripped open. I think I slapped his face. He had tears running down his cheeks. He didn't notice. "I'm so glad we got to you in time, we almost didn't—" He realized he'd been slapped. "You're right. I deserved that. We didn't know what else to do. I'm so sorry, sweetheart—" Then he scooped me up and I fell into my lover's arms and held on as tight as I could for as long as I had the strength. I remember we spent a lot of time kissing, but just as much time looking into each other's shining eyes and reassuring ourselves that we were both still alive and this was really real—and not the hysterical delusions of a dying teenager. And then finally, we were laughing and I was saying, "I want to be invisible too. I want to be invisible with you forever," and we kept on laughing.

Somewhere in there, Mariko held my face and whispered, "Are you sure?" and when I nodded eagerly, he said, "But I don't know if you'll ever get to be a girl again. Or me—" It didn't matter.

I said, "It's all right, sweetheart. It's all right. I can still be useful. Maybe I can fertilize some of those eggs." And for some reason that struck us both as funnier than anything else. And we laughed all the way to...well, that place that doesn't exist on any map, but it's called the future.

There was a message on my phone from Janis Ian, asking me to contribute a story to a new science fiction anthology. The story had to include, or be based on, the lyrics in one of her songs. So I called the number, babbling like a true fanboy, "Is this really Janis Ian?" Janis babbled right back, "Is this really David Gerrold?" That's how our friendship began. In addition to being a great songwriter, having performed some of the most noteworthy songs in rock, Janis Ian is also a marvelously joyous person and it was a privilege to contribute this story to the Stars anthology.

Out in the asteroid belt, the mountains fly. They tumble and roll silently. Distant sparkles break the darkness. Someday we'll get out there, we'll catch the mountains, we'll break them into kibble to get at the good parts. We'll find out if the centers are nougat or truffle. And some of us—some of us will even become comet-tossers, throwing the mountains around like gods.

RIDING JANIS

If we had wings
where would we fly?
Would you choose the safety of the ground
or touch the sky
if we had wings?
—Janis Ian & Bill Lloyd

The thing about puberty is that once you've done it, you're stuck. You can't go back.

It's like what Voltaire said about learning Russian. He said that you wouldn't know if learning Russian would be a good thing or not unless you actually learned the language—except that after you learned Russian, would the process of learning it have turned you into a person who believes it's a good thing? So how could you know? Puberty is like that—I think. It changes you, the way you think, and what you think about. And from what I can tell, it's a lot harder than Russian. Especially the conjugations.

You can only delay puberty for so long. After that you start to get some permanent physiological effects. But there's no point in going through puberty when the closest eligible breeding partners are on the other side of the solar system. I didn't mind being nineteen and unfinished. It was the only life I knew. What I minded was not having a choice. Sometimes I felt like just another asteroid in the belt, tumbling forever around the solar furnace, too far away to be warmed, but still too close to be truly alone. Waiting for someone to grab me and hurl me toward Luna.

See, that's what Mom and Jill do. They toss comets. Mostly small ones, wrapped so they don't burn off. There's not a lot of ice in the belt, only a couple of percentage points, if that; but when you figure there are a couple billion rocks out here, that's still a few million that are locally useful. Our job is finding them. There's no shortage of customers for big fat oxygen atoms with a couple of smaller hydrogens attached.

Luna and Mercury, in particular, and eventually Venus, when they start cooling her down.

But this was the biggest job we'd ever contracted, and it wasn't about ice as much as it was about ice-burning. Hundreds of tons per hour. Six hundred and fifty million kilometers of tail, streaming outward from the sun, driven by the ferocious solar wind. Comet Janis. In fifty-two months, the spray of ice and dye would appear as a bright red, white, and blue streak across the Earth's summer sky—the Summer Olympics Comet.

Mom and Jill were hammering every number out to the umpteenth decimal place. This was a zero-tolerance nightmare. We had to install triple-triple safeguards on the safeguards. They only wanted a flyby, not a direct hit. That would void the contract, as well as the planet.

The bigger the rock, the farther out you could aim and still make a streak that covers half the sky. The problem with aiming is that comets have minds of their own—all that volatile outgassing pushes them this way and that, and even if you've wrapped the rock with reflectors, you still don't get any kind of precision. But the bigger the rock, the harder it is to wrap it and toss it. And we didn't have a lot of wiggle room on the timeline.

Janis was big and dark until we lit it up. We unfolded three arrays of LEDs, hit it with a dozen megawatts from ten klicks, and the whole thing sparkled like the star on top of a Christmas tree. All that dirty ice, 30 kilometers of it, reflecting light every which way—depending on your orientation when you looked out the port, it was a fairy landscape, a shimmering wall, or a glimmering ceiling. A trillion tons of sparkly mud, all packed up in nice dense sheets, so it wouldn't come apart.

It was beautiful. And not just because it was pretty to look at, and not just because it meant a couple gazillion serious dollars in the bank either. It was beautiful for another reason.

See, here's the thing about living in space. Everything is Newtonian. It moves until you stop it or change its direction. So every time you move something, you have to think about where it's going to go, how fast it's going to get there, and where it will eventually end up. And we're not just talking about large sparkly rocks, we're talking about bottles of soda, dirty underwear, big green boogers, or even the ship's cat. Everything moves, bounces, and moves some more. And that includes people too. So you learn to think in vectors and trajectories and consequences. Jill calls it "extrapolatory thinking."

And that's why the rock was beautiful, because it wasn't just a rock here and now. It was a rock with a future. Neither Mom nor Jill had said anything yet, they were too busy studying the gravitational ripple charts, but they didn't have to say anything. It was obvious. We were going to have to ride it in, because if that thing started outgassing, it would push itself off course. Somebody had to be there to create a compensating thrust. Folks on the Big Blue Marble were touchy about extinction-level events.

Finding the right rock is only the second hardest part of comet-tossing. Dirtsiders think the belt is full of rocks, you just go and get one; but most of the rocks are the wrong kind; too much rock, not enough ice—and the average distance between them is 15 million klicks. And most of them are just dumb rock. Once in a while, you find one that's rich with nickel or iron, and as useful as that might be, if you're not looking for nickel or iron right then, it might as well be more dumb rock. But if somebody else is looking for it, you can lease or sell it to them.

So Mom is continually dropping bots. We fab them up in batches. Every time we change our trajectory, Mom opens a window and tosses a dozen paper planes out.

A paper plane doesn't need speed or sophistication, just brute functionality, so we print the necessary circuitry on sheets of stiff polymer. (We fab that too.) It's a simple configuration of multi-sensors, dumb-processors, lotsa-memory, soft-trans-mitters, long-batteries, carbon-nanotube solar cells, ion-reservoirs, and even a few micro-rockets. The printer rolls out the circuitry on a long sheet of polymer, laying down thirty-six to forty-eight layers of material in a single pass. Each side. At a reso-lution of 3600^2 dpi, that's tight enough to make a fairly respectable, self-powered, paper robot. Not smart enough to play with its own tautology, but certainly good enough to sniff a passing asteroid.

We print out as much and as many as we want, we break the polymer at the perforations; three quick folds to give it a wing shape, and it's done. Toss a dozen of these things overboard, they sail along on the solar wind, steering themselves by changing colors and occasional micro-bursts. Make one wing black and the other white and the plane eventually turns itself; there's no hurry, there's no shortage of either time or space in the belt. Every few days, the bot wakes up and looks around. Whenever it detects a mass of any kind, it scans the lump, scans it again, scans it a dozen times until it's sure, notes the orbit, takes a picture, analyzes the composition, prepares a report, files a claim, and sends a message home. Bots relay messages for each other until the message finally gets inserted into the real network. After that, it's just a matter of finding the publisher and forwarding the mail. Average time is 14 hours.

Any rock one of your paper planes sniffs and tags, if you're the first, then you've got first dibsies on it. Most rocks are dumb and worthless—and usually when your bots turn up a rock that's useful, by then you're almost always too far away to use it. Anything farther than five or ten degrees of arc isn't usually worth the time or fuel to go back after. Figure 50 million kilometers per degree of arc. It's easier to auction off the rock, let whoever is closest do the actual work, and you collect a percentage. If you've tagged enough useful rocks, theoretically you could retire on the royalties. Theoretically. Jill hates that word.

But if finding the right rock is the second hardest part of the job, then the first hardest part is finding the other rock, the one you use at the other end of the whip. If you want to throw something at Earth (and lots of people do), you have to throw something the same size in the opposite direction. Finding and delivering the right ballast rock to the site was always a logistic nightmare. Most of the time it was just difficult, sometimes it was impossible, and once in a while it was even worse than that.

We got lucky. We had found the right ballast rock, and it was in just the right place for us. In fact, it was uncommonly close—only a few hundred thousand kilometers behind Janis. Most asteroids are several million klicks away from their closest neighbor. FBK-9047 was small, but it was heavy. This was a nickel-rich lump about ten klicks across. While not immediately useful, it would someday be worth a helluva lot more than the comet we were tossing—five to ten billion, depending on how it assayed out.

Our problem was that it belonged to someone else. The FlyBy Knights. And they weren't too keen on having us throw it out of the system so we could launch Comet Janis.

Their problem was that this particular ten billion dollar payday wasn't on anyone's calendar. Most of the contractors had their next twenty-five years of mining already planned out—you have to plan that far in advance when the mountains you want to mine are constantly in motion. And it wasn't likely anyone was going to put it on their menu for at least a century; there were just too many other asteroids worth twenty or fifty or a hundred billion floating around the belt. So while this rock wasn't exactly worthless in principle, it was worthless in actuality—until someone actually needed it.

Mom says that comet tossing is an art. What you do is you lasso two rocks, put each in a sling, and run a long tether between them, fifty kilometers or more. Then you apply some force to each one and start them whirling around each other. With comet ice, you have to do it slowly to give the snowball a chance to compact. When you've got them up to speed, you cut the tether. One rock goes the way you want, the other goes in the opposite direction. If you've done your math right, the ballast rock flies off into the outbeyond, and the other—the money rock, goes arcing around the solar system and comes in for a close approach to the target body—Luna, Earth, L4, wherever. This is a lot more cost-effective than installing engines on an asteroid and driving it home. A lot more.

Most of the time, the flying mountain takes up station as a temporary moon orbiting whatever planet we throw it at, and it's up to the locals to mine it at their leisure. But this time, we were only arranging a flyby—a close approach for the Summer Olympics, so the folks in the Republic of Texas could have a 60 degree swath of light across the sky for twelve days. And that was a whole other set of problems—because the comet's appearance had to be timed for perfect synchronicity with the event. There wasn't any wiggle room in the schedule. And everybody knew it.

All of which meant that we really needed this rock, or we weren't going to be able to toss the comet. And everybody knew that too, so we weren't in the best bargaining position. If we wanted to use 9047, we were going to have to cut the FlyBy Knights in for a percentage of Janis, which Jill didn't really want to do because what they called "suitable recompense for the loss of projected earnings" (if we threw their rock away) was so high that we would end up losing money on the whole deal.

We knew we'd make a deal eventually—but the advantage was on their side because the longer they could stall us, the more desperate we'd become and more willing to accept their terms. And meanwhile, Mom was scanning for any useful rock or combination of rocks in the local neighborhood which was approximately five million klicks in any direction. So we were juggling time, money, and fuel against our ability to go without sleep. Mom and Jill had to sort out a nightmare of orbital mechanics, economic concerns, and assorted political domains that stretched from here to Mercury.

Mom says that in space, the normal condition of life is patience; Jill says it's frustration. Myself...I had nothing to compare it with. Except the puberty thing, of course. What good is puberty if there's no one around to have puberty with? Like kissing, for instance. And holding hands. What's all that stuff about?

I was up early, because I wanted to make fresh bread. In free fall, bread doesn't rise, it expands in a sphere—which is pretty enough, and fun for tourists, but not really practical because you end up with some slices too large and others too small. Better to roll it into a cigar and let it expand in a cylindrical baking frame. We had stopped the centrifuge because the torque was interfering with our navigation around Janis; it complicated turning the ship. We'd probably be ten or twelve days without. We could handle that with vitamins and exercise, but if we went too much longer, we'd start to pay for it with muscle and bone and heart atrophy, and it takes three times as long to rebuild as it does to lose. Once the bread was safely rising— well, expanding—I drifted forward.

"Jill?"

She looked up. Well, *over*. We were at right angles to each other. "What?" A polite what. She kept her fingers on the keyboard.

"I've been thinking—"

"That's nice."

"—we're going to have to ride this one in, aren't we?"

She stopped what she was doing, lifted her hands away from the keys, turned her music down, and swiveled her couch to face me. "How do you figure that?"

"Any comet heading that close to Earth, they'll want the contractor to ride it. Just in case course corrections have to be made. It's obvious."

"It'll be a long trip—"

"I read the contract. Our expenses are covered, both inbound and out. Plus ancillary coverage."

"That's standard boilerplate. Our presence isn't mandatory. We'll have lots of bots on the rock. They can manage any necessary corrections."

"It's not the same as having a ship onsite," I said. "Besides, Mom says we're over-due for a trip to the marble. Everyone should visit the home world at least once."

"I've been there. It's no big thing."

"But *I* haven't—"

"It's not cost-effective," Jill said. That was her answer to everything she didn't want to do.

"Oh, come on, Jill. With the money we'll make off of Comet Janis, we could add three new pods to this ship. And bigger engines. And larger fabricators. We could make ourselves a lot more competitive. We could—"

Her face did that thing it does when she doesn't want you to know what she really feels. She was still smiling, but the smile was now a mask. "Yes, we could do a lot of things. But that decision has to be made by the senior officers of the Lemrel Corporation, kidlet." Translation: *your opinion is irrelevant. Your mother and I will argue about this. And I'm against it.*

One thing about living in a ship, you learn real fast when to shut up and go away. There isn't any real privacy. If you hold perfectly still, close your eyes, and just listen, eventually—just from the ship noises—you can tell where everyone is and what they're doing, sleeping, eating, bathing, defecating, masturbating, whatever. In space, *everyone* can hear you scream. So you learn to speak softly. Even in an argument. Especially in an argument. The only real privacy is inside your head, and you learn to recognize when others are going there, and you go somewhere else. With Jill ... well, you learned faster than real fast.

She turned back to her screens. A dismissal. She plucked her mug off the bulkhead and sipped at the built-in straw. "I think you should talk this over with your Mom." A further dismissal.

"But Mom's asleep, and you're not. You're here." For some reason, I wasn't willing to let it go this time.

"You already have my opinion. And I don't want to talk about it anymore." She turned her music up to underline the point.

I went back to the galley to check on my bread. I opened the plastic bag and sniffed. It was warm and yeasty and puffy, just right for kneading, so I sealed it up again, put it up against a blank bulkhead and began pummeling it. You have to knead bread in a non-stick bag because you don't want micro-particles in the air-filtration system. It's like punching a pillow. It's good exercise, and an even better way to work out a shiftload of frustration.

As near as I could tell, puberty was mostly an overrated experience of hormonal storms, unexplainable rebellion, uncontrollable insecurity, and serious self-esteem issues, all resulting in a near-terminal state of wild paranoid anguish that causes the sufferer to behave bizarrely, taking on strange affectations of speech and appearance. Oh yeah, and weird body stuff where you spend a lot of time rubbing yourself for no apparent reason.

Lotsa kids in the belt postponed puberty. And for good reason. It doesn't make sense to have your body readying itself for breeding when there are no appropriate mates to pick from. And there's more than enough history to demonstrate that human intelligence goes into remission until at least five years after the puberty issues resolve. A person should finish her basic education without interruption, get a little life experience, before letting her juices start to flow. At least, that was the theory.

But if I didn't start puberty soon, I'd never be able to and I'd end up sexless. You can only postpone it for so long before the postponement becomes permanent. Which might not be a bad idea, considering how crazy all that sex stuff makes people.

And besides, yes, I was curious about all that sex stuff—masturbation and orgasms and nipples and thighs, stuff like that—but not morbidly so. I wanted to finish my *real* education first. Intercourse is supposed to be something marvelous and desirable, but all the pictures I'd ever seen made it look like an icky imposition for *both* partners. Why did anyone want to do *that*? Either there was something wrong with the videos, or maybe there was something wrong with me that I just didn't get it.

So it only made sense that I should start puberty now, so I'd be ready for mating when we got to Earth. And it made sense that we should go to Earth with Comet Janis. And why didn't Jill see that?

Mom stuck her head into the galley then. "I think that bread surrendered twenty minutes ago, sweetheart. You can stop beating it up now."

"Huh? What? Oh, I'm sorry. I was thinking about some stuff. I guess I lost track. Did I wake you?"

"Whatever you were thinking about, it must have been pretty exciting. The whole ship was thumping like a subwoofer. This boat is noisy enough without fresh-baked bread, honey. You should have used the bread machine." She reached past me and rescued the bag of dough; she began stuffing it into a baking cylinder.

"It's not the same," I said.

"You're right. It's quieter."

The arguments about the differences between free fall bread and gravity bread had been going on since Commander Jarles Ferris had announced that bread doesn't fall butter-side down in space. I decided not to pursue that argument. But I was still in an arguing mood.

"Mom?"

"What, honey?"

"Jill doesn't want to go to Earth."

"I know."

"Well, you're the Captain. It's *your* decision."

"Honey, Jill is my partner."

"Mom, I have to start puberty soon!"

"There'll be other chances."

"For puberty?"

"For Earth."

"When? How? If this isn't my best chance, there'll never be a better one." I grabbed her by the arms and turned her so we were both oriented the same way and looked her straight in the eyes. "Mom, you know the drill. They're not going to allow you to throw anything that big across Earth's orbit unless you're riding it. We have to ride that comet in. You've known that from the beginning."

Mom started to answer, then stopped herself. That's another thing about space-ships. After a while, everybody knows all the sides of every argument. You don't have to recycle the exposition. Janis was big money. Four-plus years of extra-hazardous duty allotment, fuel and delta-vee recovery costs, plus bonuses for successful delivery. So, Jill's argument about cost-effectiveness wasn't valid. Mom knew it. And so did I. And so did Jill. So why were we arguing?

Mom leapt ahead to the punch line. "So what's this really about?" she asked.

I hesitated. It was hard to say. "I—I think I want to be a boy. And if we don't go to Earth, I won't be able to."

"Sweetheart, you know how Jill feels about males."

"Mom, that's *her* problem. It doesn't have to be mine. I like boys. Some of my best online friends are boys. Boys have a lot of fun together—at least, it always looks that way from here. I want to try it. If I don't like it, I don't have to stay that way." Even as I said it, I was abruptly aware that what had only been mild curiosity a few moments ago was now becoming a genuine resolve. The more Mom and Jill made it an issue, the more it was an issue of control, and the more important it was for me to win. So I argued for it, not because I wanted it as much as I needed to win. Because it wasn't about winning, it was about who was in charge of my life.

Mom stopped the argument abruptly. She pulled me around to orient us face to face, and she lowered her voice to a whisper, her way of saying *this is serious*. "All right, dear, if that's what you really want. It has to be your choice. You'll have a lot of time to think about it before you have to commit. But I don't want you talking about it in front of Jill anymore."

Oh. Of course. Mom hadn't just wandered into the galley because of the bread. Jill must have buzzed her awake. The argument wasn't over. It was just beginning.

"Mom, she's going to fight this."

"I know." Mom realized she was still holding the baking cylinder. She turned and put the bread back into the oven. She set it to warm for two hours, then bake. Finally she floated back to me. She put her hands on my shoulders. "Let me handle Jill."

"When?"

"First let's see if we can get the rock we need." She swam forward. I followed.

Jill was glowering at her display and muttering epithets under her breath.

"The Flyby Knights?" Mom asked.

Jill grunted. "They're still saying, 'Take it or leave it.'"

Mom thought for a moment. "Okay. Send them a message. Tell them we found another rock."

"We have?"

"No, we haven't. But they don't know that. Tell them thanks a lot, but we won't need their asteroid after all. We don't have time to negotiate anymore. Instead, we'll cut Janis in half."

"And what if they say that's fine with them? Then what?"

"Then we'll cut Janis in half."

Jill made that noise she makes, deep in her throat. "It's all slush, you can't cut it in half. If we have to go crawling back, what's to keep them from raising their price? This is a lie. They're not stupid. They'll figure it out. We can't do it. We have a reputation."

"That's what I'm counting on—that they'll believe our reputation—that you'd rather cut your money rock in half than make a deal with a *man*."

Jill gave Mom one of those sideways looks that always meant a lot more than anything she could put into words, and certainly not when I was around.

"Send the signal," Mom said. "You'll see. It doesn't matter how much nickel is in that lump; it just isn't cost-effective for them to mine it. So it's effectively worthless. The only way they're going to get any value out of it in their lifetimes is to let us throw it away. From their point of view, it's free money, whatever they get. They'll be happy to take half a percent if they can get it."

Jill straightened her arms against the console and stretched herself out while she thought it out. "If it doesn't work, they won't give us any bargaining room."

"They're not giving us any bargaining room now."

Jill sighed and shrugged, as much agreement as she ever gave. She turned it over in her head a couple of times, then pressed for *record*. After the signal was sent, she glanced over at Mom and said, "I hope you know what you're doing."

"Half the rock is still more than enough. We can print up some reflectors and burn it in half in four months. That'll put us two months ahead of schedule, and we'll have the slings and tether already in place."

Jill considered it. "You won't get as big a burnoff. The tail won't be as long or as bright."

Mom wasn't worried. "We can compensate for that. We'll drill light pipes into the ice, fractioning the rock and increasing the effective surface area. We'll burn out the center. As long as we burn off fifty tons of ice per hour, it doesn't matter how big the comet's head is. We'll still get an impressive tail."

"So why didn't we plan that from the beginning?"

"Because I was hoping to deliver the head of the comet to Luna and sell the remaining ice. We still might be able to do that. It just won't be as big a payday." Mom turned to me.

"The braking problem on that will be horrendous." Jill closed her eyes and did some math in her head. "Not really cost-effective. We'll be throwing away more than two-thirds of the remaining mass. And if you've already cut it in half—"

"It's not the profit. It's the publicity. We'd generate a lot of new business. We could even go public."

Jill frowned. "You've already made up your mind, haven't you?"

Mom swam around to face Jill. "Sweetheart, our child is ready to be a grownup."

"She wants to be a boy." So Jill had figured it out too. But the way she said it, it was an accusation.

"So what? Are you going to stop loving her?"

Jill didn't answer. Her face tightened.

In that moment, something crystallized—all the vague unformed feelings of a lifetime suddenly snapped into focus with an enhanced clarity. Everything is tethered to everything else. With people, it isn't gravity or cables—it's money, promises, blood, and feelings. The tethers are all the words we use to tie each other down. Or up. And then we whirl around and around, just like asteroids cabled together.

We think the tethers mean something. They have to. Because if we cut them, we go flying off into the deep dark unknown. But if we don't cut them...we just stay in one place, twirling around forever. We don't go anywhere.

I could see how Mom and Jill were tethered by an ancient promise. And Mom and I were tethered by blood. And Jill and I—were tethered by jealousy. We resented each other's claim on Mom. She had something I couldn't understand. And I had something she couldn't share.

I wondered how much Mom understood. Probably everything. She was caught in the middle between two whirling bodies. Someone was going to have to cut the tether. That's why she'd accepted this contract—so we could go to the marble. She'd known it from the beginning. We were going to ride Janis all the way to Earth.

And somewhere west of the terminator, as we entered our braking arc, I'd cash out my shares and cut the tethers. I'd be off on my own course then—and Mom and Jill would fly apart too. No longer bound to me, they'd whirl out and away on their own inevitable trajectories. I wondered which of them would be a comet streaked across Earth's black sky.

Take me to the light
Take me to the mystery of life
Take me to the light
Let me see the edges of the night
—Janis Ian

AUTHOR'S AFTERWORD:
One day I cut the cord and flew away. That was how I discovered I'd been tethered.

I wrote this one hot summer afternoon. I was thinking about alien planets and monocultures. I might have intended it for an anthology, but it ended up as an extra in one of my own collections instead. This is the only other place it's been published.

FINDING MONSTRO

I gave up. I peeled off my shirt and mopped my armpits with it. I wasn't the first. It was hot in here.

There's this thing called "compare and despair." Some men don't like taking off their clothes in front of other men, especially when other men are larger. Men don't like to feel small. That's me. I'm not scrawny, but you won't find my picture on a calendar either.

But it was hot inside the boat, too hot for pride, so I took off my shirt and poured cold water down my bare chest. That would help for a while.

Felcher whistled, as he did every time I pulled off my shirt—and I ignored him, as I did every time he whistled. His real name was Feltzer, but that wasn't what we called him. Felcher knew I was married, but Jose wasn't on this mission, so to Felcher that made me a target for flirting.

Beside me, Angel didn't even look up from his navigation console. "Don't mind him," he said.

"I never do."

I hadn't wanted to come, I had steaks growing in the tanks, but I was the only available pilot for the sub, and the steaks would grow whether I was there or not,, I didn't have a choice.

Piloting isn't a hard job, the intelligence engine does most of the work, but the operational requirements specify that at least one certified human operator must be onboard to monitor all navigational and steering systems—just in case. Although if that "just in case" ever happened, there probably wasn't anything I could do that the intelligence engine couldn't do better.

In truth, I was there to provide an extra pair of hands for cooking, cleaning, and lifting stuff. When I wasn't doing that, I sat at the piloting console. I pointed the boat south, sat in the chair, and watched the screens and the thermometers—especially the thermometers. The closer we came to the equator, the hotter the boat became. So halfway through every shift, I took off my shirt, mopped my sweaty face and arms and chest, and thought about icebergs. I think we should have carved one off the Arctic shelf, bored a hole in it, pushed the boat inside, and steered south in an icy shell—but then we wouldn't have been able to submerge in case of a storm, and on Praxis, that's a serious concern. Storms here can be horrific.

The planet has a deformed orbit. At some point in its distant past, something had given it a hard whack upside the equator and pushed it into an elliptical circuit, not severe but enough off the circular to make for a particularly interesting eco-system—Praxis moves from the outer extreme of the Goldilocks zone to the inner. Seasonal temperatures alternate between way too cold and much too hot, so it has the most astonishing weather.

That's why Angel is aboard. He's one of the best navigators on the planet. He's an androgyne. He gender-identifies as male, but he says he has lady-parts—as he calls them. I never looked, despite his numerous offers to show me. He says he wants to have his babies the old-fashioned way, not grown in a tank, he just hasn't picked out a husband yet. But there's no shortage of eligible men, and probably no shortage who'd be happy to rub his lady-parts the right way, baby or not. That's probably why he changed—it's been a subject of continuing discussion back at Arrival Station.

Despite his lady-parts, Angel is all-boy. Otherwise, he wouldn't be here. Praxis Colonial Authority has restricted this world to XY-males only, and the policy is unbreakable. No breeders, not even womb-men, no one able to get pregnant—at least for the first decade, maybe longer, as long as it takes. It's a safety thing. Until we can be sure what kind of bugs lurk here, we can't risk making babies.

There are horror stories from Miranda and other places. Not many people know the details, but we were told some of it after we arrived. The policy makes sense. But Angel lives in hope that someday he'll be allowed to grow his own uterus and bear his own children. He's not the only one. There are a lot of others saying we've been here long enough, it's time to make babies. Jose and I haven't had that conversation yet, but there'll be time for that after the uterine-tanks are ready.

In its own messy clumsy way, life goes on, because life is messy everywhere. That's the point of this mission.

Praxis is an oblate spheroid—very oblate. It's noticeably flattened at the poles, much more than Earth. It looks a little like a curling stone. With rings. Because of its flattened shape, a man weighs 119% of his normal weight at the poles, but only 81% at the equator—except nobody goes to the equator. It's too hot. 160 Fahrenheit. 72 Celsius—that's apogee-winter. Perigee-summer can bring the temperatures up to 220 Fahrenheit, 105 Celsius. Either way, it's fatal.

The relentless extremes of temperature make Praxis the windiest planet humans have ever tried to settle. Hurricanes, blizzards, firestorms, tsunamis, waterspouts, tornadoes, and sheet-lightning that has to be seen to be believed. And you haven't really experienced weather until you've been caught in a hot scalding rainstorm. But afterward, you can go outside and pick your vegetables, already boiled. And occasionally find a fresh-steamed crab or lobster on the shore, both Praxis and Earth varieties.

In my opinion—something nobody asked—this mission was a bad idea. Sail to the equator and back, dropping probes all the way to measure the depths of the ocean, the currents, and the temperatures at various levels—because someday we might want to use wave power or thermal differentials to generate electricity.

But sailing was the wrong word, because mostly we were drifting with a large debris field. The annual tsunamis ripped tons of material off the shores, including a lot of trees, young ones with shallow roots, older ones that finally broke under the annual assaults, and those that needed to be dragged into the ocean as part of their life cycle. The result was semi-permanent fields of flotsam, much of it caught in webs of surface kelp. The winter currents drove these floating platforms south toward the tropics until the currents turned west and ultimately north again in a vast circular scouring.

And that was part of the reason why it was so hot in the boat. Even floating on the surface, we had to keep the hatches sealed. The debris fields reeked. The air stank like garbage and vomit. It was inescapable. Even inside, with all the air-scrubbers working, we could still taste it in everything we ate or drank. Dixon, the Captain, said it wasn't real, it was psychological, it was our imagination—but he wrinkled his nose over his morning coffee too.

Some of the debris fields were large enough to have become floating islands. All kinds of fish lived in the hanging undergrowth beneath while the drier tops of the islands served as migratory homes for the birds that fed on the fish below—at least until the heavy heat of the tropics forced them to retreat.

That was one of the questions we hoped to answer—one of many—where did the birds go? Or did they have a different adaptation? By floating silently within the debris field, we could observe and monitor and catalogue some of the creatures and maybe discover how they survived the scorch belt around the equator.

Some of the fish in the sea were our own. Despite the howls of various off-world researchers who insisted we had to keep the planet pristine while they studied it from afar, we'd been introducing Terran species almost from the beginning—though not always on purpose.

The tsunamis had shown us that our shoreline structures weren't rugged enough. Several of our factory farms had been shattered, releasing various ocean-dwelling species into the sea—but it hadn't been as big an eco-disaster as we'd feared. Some died, some lived, some adapted. That was interesting. From the beginning, we'd wanted to see how various Terran critters could adapt to life on Praxis. It was evidence that we could too. And those of us who planned to spend the rest of our lives here also looked forward to a celebratory steak and lobster dinner on Arrival Day.

The other reason it was so hot inside the boat was a simple matter of physics. You don't really cool anything. You just rearrange the heat, sending it somewhere else. The upper hull of the boat had two rows of stegosaur-shaped spines to serve as heat-sinks. But if the surrounding air is hotter, you can't radiate heat away—just the opposite. The air in this latitude was already 94F/34C. The water wasn't much better, 85%/30C. Add to that, our instructions not to disturb the eco-systems of the floating islands, and we weren't allowed to run any equipment that would increase our heat radiation—that meant the refrigeration coils stayed neutral. We did pipe as much heat as we could into a thermal kettle, occasionally we'd release the steam and pump in fresh water, but that became less and less efficient the warmer the outside water was.

Right on schedule, we dropped another packet of probes. The *ka-thump-thump-thump* of the release made the boat ring like a bell. On the screens, a few seabirds were startled into the air but they came fluttering back quickly, not wanting to waste energy or build up hard-to-lose heat.

The largest probe in the series was buoyant. It would sink for a while, then float back to the surface away from the debris field and make a valiant effort to hold its position in this latitude. The other units fell below, all connected by carbon-fiber cable. Dropping to their various depths, they'd record audio and video, temperature, radioactivity, magnetic field strength, ocean smells and composition, and whatever other information their sensors could capture. The floating probe would transmit everything up to the satellites and it would eventually find its way back to Central. In a few years, we would have enough separate points of data to begin to color in the maps. Instead of speckles, we'd start to see areas.

Finally, even Dixon reached his fuckitall point. He came up behind me, stinking of sweat. "All right, let's take her down and see if we can cool this thing off. Drop below the thermocline. Let's find the cool water." He whirled around. "Chief? Run those cooling units up to max. I want icicles dripping off the periscope!"

I didn't need him to repeat the order. "Aye aye, Cap'n." I pushed the control yoke forward. "Twenty degrees," I said. The boat tilted easily down and we fell out of the bottom of the island. Above, I could hear creeper vines dragging across the hull. A few bits of flotsam banged against the steggy-fins, but as soon as we were deep enough, a whole new kind of quiet enveloped the sub. Now, the only sounds were our own—the flutter of our propellers in the water, the hum of our air circulators, the welcome buzz of the refrigeration units, and the susurrus of noise from all the other devices aboard.

"Leveling off," I reported. "Depth, 1200 meters. Hull temperature, 74F/23C."

Dixon grunted. "We can live with that. For now."

I swiveled in my seat to face him. "It's going to be tricky. The closer we get to the equator, the less gee we pull. The weight of the water above us will be reduced. So we can go deeper, but we'll still be juggling heat against depth."

He nodded. "Find a passage beneath the heat and you'll be a hero." Then he said, "But if we come up against a wall, we're not going to push it. We'll drop the bots and let them prowl and search. We'll head for home and tell them to fab a next-gen sub."

"Copy that." I swiveled back and studied my screens. I was ready to make that call right now.

We'd been using aerial drones to drop probes into the sea for 18 months—as fast as we could fab the units—but the ferocious winds coming off the scorch belt made it impossible for any flying machine to approach. A sub could get in a lot closer. How close we weren't sure.

What we needed was a safe and dependable way to move heavy freight over/under/through/across the scorch belt. Praxis had one large continent and a scattering of islands. Arrival station was in the northern hemisphere, but the south had better terrain. We needed a cost-efficient access across the equator.

During apogee-winter, we could send trucks across the high deserts, and that was good for six out of eighteen months, but we needed a year-round system. Some of the geologists were saying that a deep-tunnel could be dug, but it would have to be a thousand kilometers long and would take at least twenty years to dig, probably more. But if we could run submarine-freighters down the coast, we could start expanding the southern stations now.

But first we needed to chart the depths of the waters, the strength of the currents and the temperatures at the operative levels. So I sat in my chair and stared at my screens until my eyes felt like they were bleeding. But at least I wasn't hot anymore. Just bored and uncomfortable.

Six hours on, six hours off. Archer rode the yoke while I ate, slept, and showered myself back to coherency. Sometimes we drifted with the current, not just to save fuel, but also to watch for native life forms. We'd spotted way too many to catalog. Someone else would do that job.

A lot of us assumed that the scorch belt made for two completely isolated ecosystems, but the evidence of the ocean was that apogee-winter allowed a lot of crossover. There was enough ecology on this world to amuse a battalion of biologists. And that battalion was very anxious to get here—just as soon as we could build sufficient life support systems.

But it wasn't just the structures and machinery and the farms—it was also the people to maintain the buildings, run the machines, and grow the food, and that meant building enough life support facilities for them as well as the facilities they would run for the biologists.

Bottom line—we needed to expand our electrical capacity first. When we had enough electricity, we could run the machines to dig the bunkers and construct the fabbers and power them up. Then, once we were manufacturing the tools and equipment, we needed ways to deliver those materials wherever they were needed—all over the planet.

It's a vicious circle—misunderstood by everyone, but especially by those playing simple simulation games, because the one thing that simulations can't do well is simulate the arguments that real people bring to the table.

And if Praxis wasn't a big enough challenge, there was an additional problem for the colonists. No women. Not yet. Maybe not ever. That decision hadn't been made—or if it had been made, it hadn't been made public.

Oh, and the other part of that—Praxis was a one-way ticket. Because of the near-Terran nature of its ecology, it was a quarantine world. There were no returns. History had given Earth a good reason to fear off-world plagues.

So there was no shortage of topics for arguments in the galley. We'd brew fresh coffee, work on protein bars, and chew over topics as diverse as altering baseball rules for an off-gee environment, the best way to grow a steak, and the evolutionary justification for sex. Felcher styled himself an expert on the latter topic.

"It's a mistake not to have women here," he said. It was a frequent complaint. "Intercourse is necessary to the species. It's a mechanism for mixing up genes. Without sex, evolution is impossible."

"That used to be true," Angel said. "But now we can mix-and-match chromosomes at will and grow babies in tanks, so we have to ask the question—are women necessary? In the past, yes—women were incubators. Now that we don't need female biology for reproduction, do we need females at all? It's a fair question—this colony is a social experiment."

"All colonies are social experiments. Everything is a social experiment. Every baby is a social experiment. You're an experiment. I'm an experiment. That doesn't mean that every social experiment is a good idea. Men are incomplete without women."

"Speak for yourself, Felcher. You're incomplete *with* women." Angel looked to me. "What do you think?"

I shook my head. "Leave me out of this one."

A third of the colonists had declared as homosexual before emigrating. For emigration to monosexual Praxis, that was an advantage. A significant percentage of the rest were situation-adaptable, apparently comfortable with the nature of the colony—the challenge was big enough to justify the circumstance—and some just enjoyed sex, regardless of the plumbing. But there were many men who'd emigrated who weren't satisfied, not even with robosex. A sizable minority still believed that the colony should plan for species normality—at worst case, as a segregated settlement. They argued it could serve as an evolutionary baseline against which to measure the monosexual adaptation.

"If this is about sex," said Angel, "then, yeah—okay. You have a point. If you're heterosexual, then yes you would feel that way. But if you're not, then probably no. But even if we could take the sexual distraction out of the social equation, leaving only the differences in gender identity, we'd still have—"

"We'd still have the distraction," said Dixon.

"That's my point!" Angel replied. "We don't know what a monosexual culture is like because we've never had a true one. Gender differences create two oppositional mindsets. Women think differently than men. Men think differently than women. It's a fact. Our brains are hardwired differently. I'm not saying men are superior. I'm saying we're different. Maybe women are superior. I don't know. But I could argue it. Women don't start wars. Maybe this should have been an all-female colony, except women have a different biological imperative, that whole baby-making thing, that's what got Miranda colony in trouble—"

"That wasn't the half of it. Miranda had other problems," Dixon interrupted. "And men have our own biological imperatives. A lot of men *want* to be dads."

"I'm saying that this is about the way men think when women aren't part of the mix, that's all. Right now, this colony is a chance to find out who we are without the distraction of the second gender-identity." Angel shrugged. "Maybe it's a mistake, but we'll never know if we don't give it a chance—"

"Says the androgyne," finished Felcher. "It doesn't matter to you. You don't have a dog in the fight. You can go either way. But for those of us raised in a normal family—"

Dixon put a large hand on Felcher's shoulder and leaned in close. "You might want to think carefully about the rest of that sentence, son, before you speak it aloud."

"Uh—" Felcher shut up. But only momentarily. "No offense intended," he started to say. "I just wanted to—"

And that's when the intelligence engine *pinged*.

I handed my coffee cup to a bot and went forward to the yoke. Archer slid sideways and I slipped easily into the seat. The screens were green, but—

"That thing," Archer pointed. "What the hell is it?"

"Not a debris field," I said.

Angel parked himself at the navigation console. Dixon and Felcher hovered behind us.

The object was massive, bigger than the boat. And it was moving. Not fast, but methodically. *Toward* the scorch belt.

"Let's send in a probe."

"Aye, sir." I punched up a number four and launched it forward. Switched the main screen to remote view. The front of the bridge lit up as a dark blue panorama. Fingers of light poked forward into the gloom. Something dark ahead. And huge. Bigger than any Earth whale. "Monstro."

I maneuvered the probe in closer. The object still wouldn't resolve. It looked blurry.

"Keep going. Right up against it if you have to." That was Dixon.

The big display finally cleared, revealing a writhing surface of translucent white flower petals, all moving in rhythmic waves. Not synchronized, but somehow meshing into a vast kinetic pattern. A mathematician's wet dream.

"What the—?"

"Ah!" said Archer.

We all turned to look at him.

"Bellyfish." He pointed at the screen. "Those are bellyfish. That's a cluster of them. A colony."

Praxis didn't have jellyfish. It had bellyfish—translucent tubular bladders that propelled themselves through the water with a gentle flexing motion—its own particular peristalsis. We had already identified hundreds of sub-species, but there could have been thousands more. They came in all sizes and colors, but the basic shape remained the same—a tube, sometimes with short tendrils at the mouth and long tendrils at the rear.

The bellyfish filtered the seawater flowing through it and fed on microorganisms, plankton, algae, whatever organic matter it captured with its interior papillae.

The bellyfish was more of an intestine-fish than a bellyfish, but bellyfish was easier to say.

"I didn't know they formed colonies," said Angel.

"You should read more. There's a news-summary every week." Archer pointed at the screen. "Which way is Monstro swimming?"

"South," I reported. "Almost directly for the scorch belt."

"Yeah, that makes sense..." Archer was transfixed.

"No it doesn't," Felcher said. "The hot water will kill it."

Archer squinted at the screen. "I'm not so sure about that. Look at the way it's peeling off bodies."

I punched for magnification. Now we could see that the huge mass was shedding bits and pieces of itself as it moved through the water, mostly fragments of bodies, but sometimes a whole bellyfish or even a cluster of bellyfish. "It's dropping off the dead bits."

"How many do you think there are in that colony?" Dixon asked.

"Given the size of the thing—it would have to be hundreds of thousands. Millions. More."

Archer touched my shoulder. "Can you move the probe around to the front? I want to see something."

I leaned the joystick sideways, turning the probe, then forward. The panoramic view twisted then steadied. The bulk of the colony-creature slid by on the left. My attention was pulled to one of the readouts before me.

"Okay," I said. "I've got a more accurate reading on its size. You could land airplanes on it. Big ones. Two at a time. And not interfere with the football game either. This thing is three kilometers long and half that wide. And at the rate it's shedding, it must have been a lot larger than that when it formed up."

Eventually the probe passed the creature and moved ahead of it. I switched to the view from the rear-camera. We gaped into a cluster of multiple writhing maws. It wasn't one large tube—it was hundreds of tubes joined as one. Monstro was hungry.

Archer asked, "Can you get inside it?"

"I think the problem is going to be not getting inside—" The colony was gaining on the probe, sucking in huge amounts of water.

"Go ahead," said Dixon. "Let's have a look inside."

I cut power to the probe's motors. Almost immediately, the gigantic wall of Monstro swelled in the screen. A moment later, the view constricted. We were inside a forest of churning translucent mouths, beautiful and horrifying.

Archer asked, "Can you read the interior of the beast?"

"It'll take a bit." I was already tapping at my keyboard, calling up scanning routines. "But it looks like it's all tubes. Clusters of little tubes making bigger tubes. Clusters of bigger tubes making even bigger ones. That's odd—"

"What is?"

"Hang on—" I fiddled with the focus. "Not every tube is active. Not all the individual creatures are functioning. In fact...it looks like most of them are dormant." I rotated the view. "Give me a minute. Yes. I see what's happening. There. Look. The active ones are peeling off."

"I see it," said Archer. "Stay on it. See? The dormant ones are waking up and starting to flex and pump."

"So what does that mean? The whole thing is coming apart?"

"Eventually, yes. It's supposed to." Archer looked excited now. "I think I see what's happening. It starts out big. With a huge core of dormant bellyfish." He paused for a moment, thinking, remembering something. "These things form in the Arctic. Apogee-winter. Great big masses. We call them bellybergs. The individual critters have some kind of natural anti-freeze, they just go solid. When they cluster, they float on the surface."

"And they come down here to thaw out?" Dixon asked.

"That'd be my guess," Archer said. "When the ice starts breaking up, they head south. They get caught in the current." He frowned. Then his face lit up. He clapped his hands together. "Yes!"

"What?"

"I think we just solved one of the mysteries."

"Which one?" asked Dixon. "There are so many—"

"Okay, follow—" Archer was still working it out in his head. "The continental dichotomy. The idea that the north and south have two separate ecologies, separated by the scorch belt. It's impossible for most creatures to get through the heat of the equator. Especially anything as fragile as a bellyfish. But when we compare genetic samples from polar specimens, they're identical. Both poles. So how are the bellyfish getting across the scorch belt?"

He pointed at the big display, at the wall of writhing tubes. "That's how. Brute force. It's like hurling a cluster of seven Minotaur-class engines at the sky to launch a multi-ton payload. These creatures are doing the same thing. Sort of. Freeze the payload and launch it in a shell of concentric heat-shields.

"I mean, we'll want to test it further, but—" He shrugged and pointed at the display of squirming creatures. "That's pretty compelling evidence." He nodded appreciatively. "We can see the whole process right here. The ones that are exposed to the hot water are active. As soon as they overheat, they die and shed away. The next layer down wakes up and starts pumping, keeping the whole thing moving forward until they die in turn. It's a marvelous adaptation—a combination heat-shield and propulsion system, ablating itself as it goes."

"I wonder if we could do the same thing," said Dixon.

"Huh?"

"You know how we fab subs with concentric shells, so no hull has to bear the full pressure of the water. Each hull maintains a certain pressure differential. Like an egg with multiple shells. We could do the same thing with cooling systems. Each shell only has to be ten degrees cooler than the next one out, so no hull has to be the wall between hot and cold."

"You still have to get rid of the heat somewhere. If the outside is too hot—"

"You only need it long enough to pass through the scorch belt." He shrugged. "I don't know if this'll work for us, but it's worth investigating. The lab boys will have fun testing it. Meanwhile—" He gestured with his coffee mug at the display. "I'd say we've paid for this trip."

None of us spoke for a long moment. We just kept staring at the panoramic screen. It was one more way for Praxis to amaze us.

"Y'know..." Archer began slowly. "I think—this thing might explain another piece of the puzzle. These are one-sex creatures. We study them in the lab. They only release eggs, so how do they fertilize themselves? I'll bet this is what they do for sexual reproduction. The survivors who cross the scorch belt—the journey, or the heat, something triggers a change, and they release the sperms. The southerners fertilize the north, the northerners fertilize the south. Back and forth. The two polar environments function like two separate sexes. The same sex, but different when it needs to be."

"Hm," said Dixon.

"Oof," said Felcher.

"Wow," said Angel.

I didn't say anything. All the good words had been taken.

"That's a long way to go to deliver a load of sperm," Felcher whispered.

"Life will find a way," Angel whispered back.

"One sex. And they make it work," said Dixon.

"It's a very primitive species," replied Archer. "We don't know that this phenomenon can scale up to higher orders."

"Flatworms," said Dixon. "Flatworms and bellyfish."

"Huh?"

"Flatworms have only one sex. When they mate, it's a fight. The winner stabs the loser. The loser has to incubate the eggs."

"And your point is?"

"We're turning ourselves into flatworms and bellyfish. Is that a good thing or not?"

Nobody replied to that.

We stayed with Monstro as long as we could—not all the way to the equator, but close enough that the surface probes we launched were sending back some very scary pictures of the towering storms ahead.

We followed Monstro down to 1600 meters, but even that wasn't deep enough to escape the heat. At the peak of perigee-summer, the surface of the equatorial seas were boiling, sending a wall of steam into the overheated air. The rest of the heat suffused downward. When the interior temperature of the sub hit 88F/31C, Dixon turned us around. "No sense in driving this oven any deeper. We can't diffuse our heat into water warmer than we are."

I peeled off my shirt, poured lukewarm water down my chest, and drove the boat north at full power. We celebrated with a round of cold beers and thawed some steaks. We'd be back to the habitable zone within a week. Away from the debris fields, we could even surface and breathe clean air.

Neither Felcher nor Angel said anything about sex on the way home. Monstro had that effect on all of us.

And I needed to talk to Jose.

I had a sense of something, I wasn't sure what, but I wrote a few paragraphs in that voice, I didn't know where they were going. A few days later, I wrote a few more paragraphs in that same voice. And then a few days after that, I realized they were two parts of the same memory.

It grew. It wasn't a story yet, it was an immersion into a whole other way of being. Halfway through, I had to stop. I didn't know where it was going. And then one night, I realized—this is (in its own strange way) a Theodore Sturgeon story. It's about what happens in the space between two people. The story finished itself.

I sent it off to Gordon Van Gelder at The Magazine of Fantasy & Science Fiction *with a note telling him that he probably shouldn't buy it. I listed all the reasons why. In particular, it might be very controversial, it had graphic sex and violence, and there wasn't any real fantasy in it. But, I also pointed out that I thought it was one of the best things I'd ever written. He bought it immediately.*

Yes, the story was controversial, though not as much as I'd hoped. Six people cancelled their subscriptions and one returned the issue in shreds. I was disappointed. I'd wanted a mob with torches and pitchforks chasing me through the streets. Owell. Maybe next time.

thirteen o'clock

thirteen o'clock on a thirsty night, dry and windy after midnight, all the boys have paired up, disappeared into the desert, coupling darkly on the sand, have another beer, there's no place else to go except ride the hog and the hot air roars into your eyes at 70 miles per hour, getting too old for this shit, fucking boring, bored with fucking, bored with chasing fucking, bored with waking up alone, and even more bored waking up with anyone else, and even beer cant cure that, fuck me

except that's the problem, nobody wants to fuck me anymore, too many years, too many beers, and that other thing, the scar that starts above my right eye and crawls down to the corner of my mouth, pulling it down into a permanent scowl, so my face looks like something from a slasher movie, only the scar didnt happen when I was on the bike, but when I got off it at high speed, using the right side of my head as a brake shoe, which wasnt as much fun as it sounds, not even with three beers

so I gave up on the queerbar for the night, the thing about queerbars, straightmen think you just walk in and get a blow job, everyboy is so fucking thirsty for cock, all you have to do is unzip your dockers, and if it were that easy, I wouldnt be standing in the bar at thirteen o'clock wondering what the hell I'm doing and how I got here and why I dont have any other place to go. So fuckit

and before I'm halfway out the door, some guy is asking, hey, isnt that a queer-bar, and before I can even turn and look, somebody's swinging something at my head and the old reflexes kick in and I duck sideways and he misses, but then the other guy's got a bike chain, stupid college kid, which I dont mean to grab, but I get it anyway because it skiddles off the cast on my arm before he can swing, indecision maybe, probably his first queer-bashing, blood-simple coward, then I'm holding the chain, one good yank, and he's holding a big handful of me, and his eyes go white just in time as I swing him around and shove him into his boyfriend with the base-ball bat, and that's when I see the third one

someone oughta teach these little pricks how to beat up a fag, because they're no good at this at all, the third one crumples up too easily, a backhand across the windpipe, big ugly rings with scratchy things, and he's down, and then I'm back with chainless and bat, shoving chainless into bat and both up against the wall, so bat cant move and chainless is already screaming for mommy, godforbid someone should scar his pretty face like mine

—and something happens—

and that's when I get the idea that all he really needs is to be kissed so I pull him close and cover his scream with the bearded oyster and give him enough tongue to choke a deep throat, and I guess right because just as he's starting to kiss me back, surprising me more than him I think, and if this were a different time and a different place, I bet I could hang his legs over my shoulders, or mine over his, I'm not choosy, except the batboy is screaming and who can concentrate with all that noise

by the time danny-bartender finally makes it out the door with his own baseball bat, I've got two on the ground and one up against the wall with my hand on his throat, the pretty one, and I really do think I could negotiate a relationship out of this, except that even as a "cute meet" this is a little too acute. So I let go of the cute meat, and he staggers forward, almost into my arms, jerks back, looks around, sees the queers piling out of the queerbar and maybe he thinks about running, but before he can send the message to his skechers, it's too late, he's caught

danny-bartender wants to call the police, but I tell him not to bother, because the one guy on the ground is having too much trouble breathing, I didnt think I hit him that hard, but he's got a nasty bubbling cut across his neck, which reminds me of things I saw in the service that I really dont want to think about at all, and the other guy who forgot about holding his bat when holding his stomach and his balls became a lot more important is having his own problems exsanguinating through his nose, so I go and pop open the back doors of my van and toss them in, I sold the hog six months ago and bought the van because it's easier on my bad leg and besides you can sleep in a van if you have to, and someboy asks where are you tak-ing them and even though I want to take them out in the desert and bury them, without bothering to kill them first, I say the emergency room because I've already got enough death on my conscience

prettyboy rides in front with me, the other two moaning in the back, and nobody else wants to come because what queer wants to talk to cops anyway, I'm not worried, nobody fucks with me twice, not when I've got their wallets in my pocket

pull up at the E.R. and I drag them both out the back of the van and through the sliding doors, shouting, "white male, age 20, injury to his trachea, might need to intubate; white male, age 20, needs an X-ray for a cracked rib, broken nose, and someone call the police," and I only have to holler it twice before a doctor and two nurses come running

tell the police I'm emmett grogan, they're too young to know the real emmett grogan, and besides I've got the i.d. that proves I'm emmett grogan, I made it myself, tell the police these two injured boys were just coming out of a gay bar, thirteen o'clock in the night, when they were attacked by queerbashers, lucky for them I was driving my little brother back to campus, I point to prettyboy, and we were just passing by

ex-marine, vietnam vet, ex-corpsman, got the tattoo in san diego, yessir, nossir, I didnt see the attackers clearly, officer, there were four of them, they looked like accountants, or maybe lawyers, probably republicans, you know they like to do that sort of thing, the cops give me the narrow-eyed look and I give them the deadpan, and then the fat one says, well if the victims were coming out of a queerbar they probbly got what they deserved, I dont see any need to pursue this further, and the skinny one adds, but maybe we should notify their parents, they look like college students, and I say, nah, give them a break, they're just kids, maybe this'll teach em to stay away from queerbars

and the fat cop says, nah, once they've been into a queerbar, you cant keep em out, one taste of cock and they're queer for life, so I just look at him deadpan and ask, is sucking cock that good, like he knows, and he blinks for a moment, realizing that he cant answer that question without looking either queer or stupid

back in the van, prettyboy still hasnt said a word, he's scared I'm gonna finish that kiss, or maybe he's hopin, but either way, he's sweating, so I hand him all three wallets, after taking out the cash, my own brand of justice, payment for lesson learned, nearly four hundred total, I drive him to the dorm, and as we pull up, he says, thank you for not reporting me to the cops, and at least he doesnt try to blame the other guys, it's all their fault, it wasnt his idea, he was just tagging along, which is obvious anyway, prettyboy is booksmart, but not much else, at least he knows enough not to say anything that stupid, so I think about all the bullshit I can say back to him and decide not to say any of it, instead I look him straight in the eye and say, the difference between us, someone calls me faggot, they're talking about what makes me happy, someone calls you faggot, they're talking about what makes you unhappy, you figure it out, all that money mommy and daddy are spending to send you away to university, you oughta be smart enough to figure out what you like and then he does surprise me, he starts to open the door to get out and then he turns back and says, can we talk sometime, and there it is, half past whenever, dry and windy after midnight, and he's got big eyes and chewable lips, and surprise, surprise, my dick can still get hard, so I say yes and how about tomorrow night, and he says pick me up right here, and I'm already thinking, we'll go somewhere out on the other side of the desert where the truth is a lot easier, I know he'll never show up, not after twelve hours of sunlight-thinking, but what the fuck, nobody's waiting for me in the next town either, so why not

sleep away most of the day, crawl out of my coffin just in time to enjoy the sunset, shower and burger at the truck stop, think about beer, but leave it at thinking, not drinking, cruise over to the landing zone and prettyboy is leaning against a wall, he flicks his cigarette sideways, like he thinks that's butch, it isnt, and he strolls over and climbs in the passenger seat and I roll without talking and he doesnt say anything either and I'm wondering what the fuck he thinks is going to happen tonight, because I sure as shit dont have a clue, but this is something better than nothing

we drive for a while, prettyboy finally says something, I was afraid you werent going to come, I tell him I didnt think he'd be there either, so we're even, he asks where we're heading, I shrug and nod ahead; away from the light, because I dont like the light, if it's too bright I can see the scars on my face from the inside, he tells me to stop calling him prettyboy, his name is Michael, I tell him he hasnt earned a name yet, he's still meat, fresh off the plane, and we've got a body bag already waiting with his name on it, deal with it

finally I ask him what the fuck he wants from me, he says he wants to know what I know and I tell him I dont know shit and finally we turn off the highway onto a side road and after a while off the side road onto a couple of forgotten ruts and we go two or three miles up and down bouncing to a place where something used to be, but now there's only hard-packed dirt, and I pull off and turn the engine off and we sit and listen to it cooling in the night

we get out, I go around to the back, pull out a blanket, a couple bottles of water, we sit in the dark, side by side, watching for shooting stars, and except for pointing them out to each other, we dont talk, I'm waiting for him to start, but he doesnt, so after a while, I reach over and grab his hand, not because I particularly want to hold his hand, I dont even fucking know him, but it's a start

he's not good for small talk, neither am I, he asks me how I know how to fight, I tell him the truth, fighting is easier than having the shit kicked out of you, then he asks me about my leg, so I tell him

somewhere in the fucking delta, the hot wind putrid, the whole country stinking like a saigon whorehouse, disintegrating with the smell of shit and incense and rotting vegetation, all mixed with the spices they use to hide the fact that the meat is rotten before they even get it into the pan, even if you knew what it was—dog or cat or rat—who the fuck cares, when you get hungry enough, you stop asking questions

they call it a road, but it's just a lousy stinking dirt scar, a slash of mud carved between two fields, the crapgrass rippling in the wind—the distant edges bordered by trees, a fucking perfect place to die, a fucking bullseye for an ambush—the lieutenant holds up a hand and we all stop, then he holds his arm straight out and waves us down—and we scatter into the grass and disappear

they say that charlie is terrified of us, because we're monsters, bigger and healthier and better fed, better guns, better ammo, better supplies—and better targets too—those little human cockroaches scuttle down into the ground and disappear, trapdoors in the floor of the world—everybody knows they're all underground, the delta is tunneled from here to forever, underground cities, you could walk all the way to uncle ho without ever seeing daylight—and maybe they're right, maybe the little fuckers are scared shitless, but I dont think so

claymore—we call him that because he's good at taking mines apart—he grins and whispers across to me, it's a good day to die. I tell him to shut the fuck up. it's never a good day to die, but he saw that in a movie and he thinks it's cool—it isnt cool, it's fucking stupid—and what are we waiting for anyway?

the lieutenant is yabbering into the field phone, the sweat is rolling down the inside of my shirt, the sun is a hundred and thirty degrees and we're all carrying fifty pounds of field gear—whose good idea was this anyway?—the field isnt a field, it's a fucking swamp, we're up to here in mud so deep that every step, the mud is fighting to pull my boots off—and I cant stand too long in one place, I start to sink deeper

oh man, I am going to stand for an hour in the shower tonight and I dont fucking care what color the water is

the lieutenant he stands up and waves us back to the road—whatever—he does this five, six times an hour—squelching up out of the mud, and before I can yank my boot free, the world fucking blows up in my face—all the different colors of orange and white and red and black, all at once, and everybody's screaming because the shit is going off all around us—they're dropping fucking mortar shells on us, and they've got our range because the crap is hitting left and right and up and down—claymore flies apart in pieces, a fucking good day to die my fucking ass—and I'm too busy pulling my goddamn leg out of the mud to be scared—we're all firing wildly at the distant trees, like we're really going to hit something, we're fucking dead out here

rocks and shit and mud comes pattering down, all around, a pummeling of earth, it goes on forever while the ground shakes and your ears bleed and the world turns sideways and knocks you assover everywhere, and no my leg isnt supposed to bend like that, but I cant feel it anyway, and I cant find my fucking gun and while my hand is flailing around everything turns orange, the sky, the muck, a wall of heat knocks me flat into the shit, rolls me sideways, and then I hear the first roar of the flames—a roiling carpet, napalm forest, blossoming scars across the whole west side of the world, and for a moment, there's a kind of peace, the explosions stop, shocked in fucking horror, roasted alive, who fucking cares, I fade out and over, something is whupping up and I feel nothing

while I'm dead everything is fine, because I cant feel anything, I dont care, I could go on like this forever, white light and voices

—*something happened*—

but then it's gone, leaving only a memory of a memory, a sense that there was something *important*, maybe it was the drugs, but no, I know drugs and this wasnt drugs, this was something *else,* but it's gone, it's like hearing the echo, but not knowing what clanged, the feeling stays with me all the way across the pacific and down into the crevices of San Francisco, it never fades, a sense of muffled awareness, the doctors tell me it's resonance, it'll go away, but they're wrong, it doesnt—never completely, it just drifts behind-inside forever; it doesn't bother me, it just turns into something to live with, like the plastic leg

so I spend a few years riding a hog up and down the left coast, cruising up through Big Sur, across the big red bridge, up through Marin, into the cold wet wild north where the trees make green canyons, up into Oregon where the green is too thick and I start thinking about Charlie creeping through the green, if Charlie had green like this, we'd still be there, it's nothing like the Delta, first of all the smell is sweet and green and wet, but I cant shake the feeling that something is creeping up after me, so I keep riding, on up as far as Puget where the only difference between the fog and the rain is that the fog is thicker and wetter and from there up to the border where the Canadian customs guard is so exquisitely polite I know he hates to let me in, but he cant find a reason not to, I'm legal, I just look ugly, so on into Canada, eh, all the way up to Alaska and I lose myself for a few years with the bears and the salmon and the air so crisp it cuts like ice through the tent, through the sleeping bag, and man I'm getting too old for this shit, but I gotta know what it was, and for some reason I've made up my mind that the Inuit know, some shaman or medicine man, whatever, because maybe underneath, there's some magic here

and maybe there is, but I never find it, so I come sliding back south, dropping down through Idaho, following the Snake river all the way down, passing through forgotten dusty places with names too small for the map, endless dry highways, into Nevada with its desolate empty stretches of baking summer

east to Utah where the canyons still echo with fossilized time, south to New Mexico with its hidden villages carved into orange sunset cliffs, west to Arizona and up the poisonous side of Superstitious Mountain, maybe there's a wise old grandfather, the Hopi know life out of balance, and eventually south through Mexico, where I spend a week or a year or whatever living the way of the whaqui, eating mushrooms and peyote and rattlesnakes, fucking everything that I can push down on its back or its stomach, if it's a hole and I'm horny, I dont care anymore, it doesnt matter, there's that instant of orgasm, that quick throb-and-spurt of time where I stop existing long enough that the nagging sense of something unsaid and left undone is pushed so far out of my consciousness that it almost doesnt exist for that moment, and the lassitude afterward, on my back and staring dispassionately at the glowering sky, waiting for wisdom and insight, that connection of time and place and understanding, but all I accomplish is a thousand light-year stare with nothing on the other side, and one day I put the hog back together, get the engine running, tune it, tweak it, test it, over and over, until it sounds like magic growling again, until one day it's right, and the moment is right, and I get on and start riding, just a test ride, I say, but I keep riding north and never look back, I run out of gas at a queer hippie commune south of Tuscon and live in a teepee while I flush out all the crap from my system, lose twenty pounds of Mexican bad shit and end up with abs again, stumping up and down the rows of corn and beans and tomatoes, digging latrines, carrying water, hoeing and weeding, learning to serve others again, and for the first time in longer than I can remember actually earning the right to feel good about myself at the end of the day

but its all queerboys here and I'm not ready to give up girlpussy forever, it's fixed in my mind now that there's boypussy and girlpussy, and each is fine in its own way, and by now I've even learned there's other things to do and maybe that's part of the answer, if not *the* answer, it's still part of it, because what these queerboys have learned is that it's not about fucking, it's about people, a strange place to learn this

and then, in an angry flash, I dont know how it happens, I'm back on the left again, Arizona a red and gold memory in the rear-view mirror, how did that happen?—the moving finger writes and once it writes you're fingered, I come bouncing down into the Castro where I hook up with Bloody Mary, a bulldyke who rides a hog and sometimes she rides me and sometimes she rides the hog and once she rides us both at the same time and I ask her how can she be a dyke if she's riding the rod and she just laughs and says it isnt about pussy, it's about people, so I'm not the only one who's figured that out

we coast up to Guerneville where nobody cares, where we're out of earshot of the creepazoids who think we're traitors to the fag-flag because we're bumping each other ugly, except one night I break my leg in Sausalito, laying down the bike to avoid a drunken spoiled teenage bitch, and if I could have gotten up afterward I'd have punched her a new one, but I cant get up because the bike is on top of me, she jumps out and starts wailing about the dent I just put in the side of her new car that daddy just bought her only two days ago for her seventeenth birthday, while I'm still lying under a bleeding hog and

—*it happens again*—

until Mary the dyke slaps her, takes away her new expensive toy, this thing called a cell phone, and punches 911 and calls an ambulance, and I'm off to the E.R. tonight and the V.A. tomorrow, and fortunately it's the plastic leg that's broken and six weeks later, the V.A. finally puts me on a new one, a better one, and I'm ready to get back in the saddle, except

I dont want to, something's happened; I cant explain it, but something's happened, and even though I feel like a cowboy who has to shoot his horse, I sell the hog, what's left of it, and no, it isnt fear, I could get back on the bike in half a minute, I trust myself on the road, I dont trust anyone else, I trust my ability to keep out of their way, but if a seventeen-year-old bitch can put me down in the gutter, maybe it's the universe sending me a message; the dyke tells me I'm a pussy, so I know she doesnt understand, and fuckit, I'm not even sure I understand it myself, all I know is it's time to let go, the bike isnt me anymore, and neither is the dyke and then time flashes and I'm living out of the back of a VW bus, I dont even remember where I got it, but the feeling is there, I can drive out to the middle of the Mojave, get off the highway, get off the side road, find a dirt slash into the middle of nowhere, someplace even the lights in the distance are too far away to look like anything more than stars glimmering through the bottom of the world, and I lay down on my back and look up at the diamond sky and it's like riding the hog again, only this time riding it through time and space, I'm standing at the front of starship earth and sailing forward like I'm king of the universe and I can hear the feeling loud and clear like picking up clear channel KOMA from five states away

and I know it's not the tequila and it's not the grass and it's not a fucking acid flashback either, it's something else, and I can feel the throb and pulse of the ground beneath my body and I know the ground doesnt throb and pulse, so what the flaming fuck am I feeling, it's just my own heartbeef, slabs of muscle too stubborn to stop slamming the blood through my veins, and what the fuck is life all about anyway, but the feeling, it wont go away, it's like music sometimes, a distant chorus, very faint and far away, under the edge of the horizon, like those things whatever they are that always woke me when I was little, going *hoo-hooo* in the night

and I tell prettyboy, that's what I know, that I'm just another hood ornament on the battering ram, wherever it goes I get there first, hardest—I'm the part that takes the impact—but every time, just before the collision, I get this flash, like there's something under the bottom of the world, calling to me, I dont know what the fuck it is, but I cant get away from it, cant get it to shut up, cant forget it, and cant fucking die until I find out what it is

so now it's his turn to explain and he tells me there's nothing to explain, he isnt anybody at all, he doesnt, just doesnt, and it doesnt matter that there's no predicate to that subject, I get it because I've been there, I'm still there, I live there, we all do, only some of us know it

he says it started in bed, in bed with a girl, she was warm and round and luscious like something out of a painting by Rubens or maybe Titian and he just wanted to float on top of her like she was a giant delicious waterbed, he wanted to suckle at her breasts and bury his face in her juicy cunt and it surprised him when I said, yeah, I know, except whatever else she was, she wasnt either, and she wouldnt

they'd lie together, spooned, his arm curled around her side, but once when his fingers start tentatively brushing at her thigh, she mumbles not now, and another time when he brushes at her lips, the lower ones, probing for her clit, she pushes his hand away roughly as if he's an intruder, and still another time when he moves his fingers up to circle her great silver dollar sized nipples, she rolls away, is that all you ever think of, so he turns on his side and tries to sleep while this great moby of desirability rests naked behind him, his cock still stiff, his balls aching, and the next morning as he's pulling his tighty-whites up and over the tentpole, she sits up in bed and complains that he's unromantic, that he doesnt want to do it with her, and it's because she's fat, isnt it, and to his credit he doesnt say anything, he just finishes pulling up his pants and buttoning his shirt and slips into his sneakers and closes the door behind him, all without a word or a even a look, because inside he's feeling so—there isnt really a word for that feeling, but that's what he's feeling, so he leaves and three nights later he's outside a queerbar with two guys he barely knows, it doesnt make sense, but nothing in life makes sense, why would anyone want to fuck a guy when there are all these beautiful fat women around, except if they dont want to fuck, what's a guy to do, get desperate, and he's almost ready to cry, except he's still too full of that other feeling

so there we are, I have too much life and he doesnt have any, so I hold his hand and after a while he leans up against me, and we sit there listening, he listens for what I can hear and I listen for silence

are you going to fuck me, he asks, and I dont answer for a while because I dont know the answer, I dont know if I want to fuck him, he's pretty enough and after that kiss, I didnt figure it would be that hard to get his ankles behind his neck or mine, it doesnt matter, but I dont know if it's worth the effort, fucking for the sake of fucking sounds fine when you're fifteen, but not when the digits are reversed, so I'm sitting there wondering why he asked, is it something he wants or is it something he's afraid I'm going to do to him whether he wants it or not, and just the fact he asked the question scares the shit out of me, not the scared-shitless feeling like when live fire is making a three-foot ceiling over your head, but the other-scared feeling of just not knowing who you are or what you're supposed to do, a feeling I thought I'd left behind in Alaska or Mexico, or maybe certainly in Arizona, or probably somewhere since then, but finally I just say, is that what you want and he doesnt answer, because I figure he's probably sorting it out the same way

then the moment passes, and I know we're not going to fuck, not then, and probably not ever, but I've been wrong about that before, so we both just relax, now that the question's been asked, not answered, but resolved anyway for the moment, and I'm sitting there thinking a whole fucking epic, and he says, thank you, and I ask, for what, and he says, for listening

and yeah, I get it, and I say so, and he asks, does this feeling ever go away, and even though I'm not sure what feeling he's talking about I still know the answer, I shake my head, I say no, it never does, you just learn to live with it; he breaks away, he sits opposite so he can look at me, the moon is up now, half-past full, so there's enough light I can see his eyes are bright, and yeah, he's getting prettier by the moment, and I'm almost rethinking the answer to his question, but I'm not, because it still isnt happening and in the moonlight, I know why

there's this guy I knew once, his name was Jerry, we went to the same high school, we never talked to each other, we just saw each other in the hallway sometimes, and sometimes at the Big Boy where he was bussing tables, working his way through community college, but we werent in any of the same classes there either, we just saw each other around, and then I forgot about him, the way you forget most of the people you bump up against as you stumble along, until one night a few years later, it's the collapsing end of 1969, and I'm in a boy-bar on Santa Monica Boulevard, and I see him sitting alone in the corner in the back patio and he looks like Wiley

Coyote right after the rocket exploded in his face, so I go over and say hi, and he says hi back and I ask him what's wrong, and he cant even get it out, he just looks at me with a look I've only seen one other time, a year later, in the Delta, when Perry the black kid with the big round eyes caught one and just looks at me, his hands across his belly, all his dark red blood pulsing out between his fingers, trying to push his guts back in, and he looks at me, our eyes meet for just a second, and the expression on his face says it all, please tell me I'm going to be all right, tell me I'm not going to die, and he knows I wont lie to him, and I lie and say, hey man, just hold on, just hold on, and the medic stings him with morphine and his eyes stay fixed on mine the whole time, and then the blood stops pulsing and he's dead, but his eyes are still wide, and that's the look that I saw on Jerry's face, like he was asking me to tell him that he wasnt dead yet

but that hadnt happened yet, this was the first time I ever saw this look, and it stopped me cold, because I didnt know a human face could look like that, and it froze me—the terror, the desperate need, I thought I should do something, except I wasnt in that bar to be Mary Poppins, I was looking for some boypussy, and I was this close to saying, fuckit, tell it to the chaplain, tell it to someone who cares, someone who's paid to care—but then he says, tell me why I shouldnt kill myself and I didnt have the sense to back away quickly, so I stand over him, instinctively shielding him from the light and the noise and the stink of cigarettes and beer and Old Spice and I listen—and what he tells me, well, it almost saves my life

see, he wasnt making it, it was the end of the fucking sixties for god sake, everything was falling apart in slow motion, and all anybody could do was get stoned and fuck their brains out, so that's what we did, all night long, every night, there wasnt any daytime anymore, just the long long night of parties—only Jerry was alone, one of those guys who never quite finds the rhythm of anything, he didnt know how to be whatever it was he was supposed to be, nobody did, and everybody's walking around saying stupid shit like, "hey man, where's it happening?" and you have no fucking idea how dumb that sounds, it's like admitting you're so lost you cant even see the party even when it's happening around you, it was happening everywhere and it wasnt happening anywhere, because whatever was happening, it was only happening when you made it happen, but most of us never learned that lesson, or died trying, so even though Jerry didnt understand it, that was the thing that made him just like everybody else because nobody understood it yet, but Jerry was one of the smart ones, so smart he was stupid; he thought the world was gettable, and because he thought that, he thought that there were people who actually did get it, in fact Jerry thought that everybody did, probably already had, except they'd they'd all privately agreed not to let him in on it, none of it made sense and nobody was letting him in on the joke, so after a while he gives up, just gives up completely and resigns, stops waiting for Santa Claus and starts waiting for rigor mortis, he's ready to be just another one of those used-up boys propped up against the bar like scenery—the ones who've been entered too many times and finally abandoned all hope, the ones who settle for fucking as a substitute for loving, nowhere near a fair trade, but if you fuck long enough and hard enough, sometimes you dont notice, trust me on this

except fucking-God's a practical joker, because just when Jerry decides there aint no such thing as either God or love, that's the afternoon, God drops a beautiful redheaded boy on him, and the two of them do something right and instead of just falling lustfully into bed, mindlessly fucking their brains out on each other's flesh until half-past seeyaround, instead it's too hot to fuck, so they sit and talk for five hours on this sweaty July afternoon, and instead of thinking only about their dicks, they actually work a little higher up, the other end of the spinal cord, and not until the day finally cools off do they end up in bed, but that's only because it's a more comfortable place to just strip down to your jockeys and relax, surrender to the moment, because it doesn't matter anymore, you dont have to pretend now, just be who you are, and they still dont fuck, they share a big glass of ice water and keep talking, and it doesnt matter what they're talking about, they're just having this amazing adventure talking and discovering, and even after they get naked—and you know how you get naked in front of other guys, there's this thing, you know the thing, where you really dont want them looking at you, because you know they're sizing you up, judging how good you look or how big you are, and you know you're never going to look as good as the guys in the magazines, and you end up feeling that you dont want to be naked in front of anyone because you dont want them thinking you're not good enough—except that doesnt happen here, they end up sitting together naked, unashamed, each one astonished at how beautiful the other one is, and they still dont fuck, they hug and kiss and touch in wonder, and they laugh a lot at some shared joke of intimacy and finally take a shower together and laugh a whole lot more, and then they hump and bump a little, even a lot, but they keep interrupting themselves to talk and to share, and before either one of them has come anywhere near to that moment where it's time to get a towel and wipe off and make a hasty graceless exit, they realize that—*something is happening*—it's silly, so fucking silly, because there's no such thing as love at first sight, it's just a fairy tale, but there they are anyway, falling ass-over-teakettle, tumbling over the cliff of joyous delirium, so full of happy giggling exuberance it doesnt make sense, until Jerry has impossible tears running down his cheeks and he wants to run out in the middle of the street and yell to the whole world, dont you dumbfucks get it, love—*real love*—really is possible, and if Hitler had ever had sex this good, World War II would never have happened, that's what it feels like, fucking so good you feel sorry for Hitler, and he and the redheaded boy roll together, laughing

but look, it isnt about the sex at all, it was never about the sex, everybody thinks it's about the cocks and the cunts and the mouths and the assholes, all that juicy pistoning, the hot wet pumping in-and-out, but it isnt, it's about the thing that happens *during* sex, if it's right, if everything is right between the two people, whoever, whatever, if there's a real connection, then the sex is just a way to get even more connected, because it's the connection you want, not the sex—because the truth is, when you're fucking, it's not about you, it's about the person you're with, because if it isnt, then you're the biggest dumbfuck of all, just licking the menu instead of eating the meal—and that's the magic that Jerry and his beautiful redheaded boy fell into

yeah, I know, it doesnt make sense to sit and talk with someone from four O'clock in the afternoon until nine in the fucking ayem the next morning, when you have to get up and go back to work, and on the basis of that short time know that this is the person you want to spend the rest of your life with, that all you want from existence is to keep on exploring the landscape of this beautiful incredible godling, discovering yourself in his smile and his laughter and his cockness, but it happened to them, both of them, they connected anyway, and in the days after that first incredible revelation of each other, it just gets better, they start learning how to do all the other things that people do when they fit their lives together—they talk to each other on the phone every day for three weeks, grabbing every moment they can between their respective jobs and obligations and it should have been perfect, because each of them was exactly what the other one wanted and needed, they fit, you know, they just fit, and every moment was well, you know, just perfect

and then it all comes apart, because Jerry makes a stupid mistake, the biggest stupidest mistake anyone can make, he gets scared, he stops trusting his instincts, because see, the redheaded boy wants to get serious, I mean serious with a capital lets-move-in-together, and Jerry panics, because he thinks it's getting too intense, he cant deal with it, he doesnt know how—I mean, how do you explain it to mom, right?—because nobody gives lessons to queerboys how to have a real relationship, and make it work in a world that mindlessly believes that this thing that brings you so much joy is so despicable that God hates you for it, and the whole thing scares him, so instead of being home, he leaves a note on the door and goes out cruising instead, not because he wants to cruise, but because he doesnt know what else to do, but he's so fucking confused, so the redheaded boy takes the note off the door and goes out looking for something else to do and he picks up a hitchhiker, no, not quite, that's not where this story is going, let me finish, and the hitchhiker is caretaker at some estate up in Benedict Canyon, so the redheaded boy drives him up there and they talk for a while, but they dont really connect, so after a while, the redheaded boy picks up the phone and calls Jerry, and Jerry is back home by now—see, here's what happened, Jerry cruises and cruises and realizes that cruising is empty, because now that he knows that there's something else, cruising is meaningless, and now that he knows what the something else is, he knows what a jerk he's been for leaving that note, for not being home, and all he really wants to do tonight is curl up with his beautiful redheaded lover and not have to talk, just be in his arms and never be apart again, he's ready to jump off the diving board and say yes, I will

only on the way down the hill, the redheaded boy runs into some drug-crazed hippies, and they shoot him in the face, and then they go into the house and murder four other people, five if you count the unborn baby, and Jerry stays up all night wondering where his lover is, and he doesnt find out what happened until he opens the newspaper Sunday morning, still with me, and he goes crazy, and I dont mean crazy like banging into the walls, raging with grief, I mean crazy like you dont know, nobody knows, because they dont know how to show it in the movies yet, I mean crazy like staring into space crazy, zombie-crazy, desperate crazy

and it's two-three months later, and the murderers still havent been caught, and he tells me all of this in the back patio of a sleazy boy-bar in West Hollywood because he has no other place to go, and of all the places to go, this is the worst, because it just puts him back where he was before, but he cant be what he was before, because this time, now, he knows what he doesnt have, and that's when the tears start running down his cheeks, all he had was three weeks, hardly enough time to make any memories at all, just a couple of fucks and a drive around the city, and all he can think of is that he's never going to see his lover again, the most precious person in his life, never again, and all the memories they're never going to have, all the pillow conversations, and why the hell should he keep on living if the best part of his life is over

but see, here's how I know that God is a malignant thug, a practical joker, an asshole—if he wouldnt listen to his own son's prayers on the cross, why the fuck do you think he's going to listen to anyone else's?—here's the joke, Jerry looks at me like I'm supposed to say the one thing, whatever it is, that makes a difference, except I dont know what the fuck it is, how the hell should I know how to save his life, because I cant even save my own, because I've got my goddamned draft notice in my back pocket and I have to report the day after Thanksgiving, and in three-four months, just in time for the rains, I'll be slogging through the goddamn Delta with all the other dead men walking, and I'm thinking what the fuck, maybe I should run for Canada instead, I can be there in a straight two day run, or maybe I should just tell them I like sucking cock and fucking ass, at least that's honest, except I'm not ready to be that honest yet, nobody is, except I also heard that they dont even care anymore, the draft boards, they just have to generate so many bodies a week, fill up the green uniforms, fill up the body bags, and this week it's me and next week it's you, it's all the same, and Jerry looks up at me and says, so okay, now you tell me—why shouldnt I kill myself?

I dunno, why shouldnt he? He's made a pretty damn good case, except forever is a long time, and I'm thinking if I were a sky-pilot, I'd know the right thing to say, except I'm not, and I dont, and besides, if I said the crap they say, we'd both know it's crap, so I say what's in my head, and I say, I am so fucking jealous of you I can't believe it, and his eyes go wide, and I just keep talking anyway, because man, you found it, even if it was only for three weeks, you had it, man—I never did, and you know something most of the rest of us can only wish for, and he looks at me, not getting it, and I dont know where the words are coming from, I just blurt it out—real love, man, you had it, someone really loved you, the rest of us we're standing around and pretending that we're not standing around and pretending, but you—man, you're lucky everybody else in here doesnt beat you to death out of sheer fucking jealousy, because what you had, you had the *real*, not the pretend, You. Had. *It.*

and maybe that was what he needed to hear, and maybe what he said was what I needed to hear—that it really was possible, because up until then, I didnt know it, maybe nobody did, Jerry was the first person I ever knew who found love, the first one who could actually say it, and while he's crying for what he's lost, I'm wishing I were him, I want what he had, even if it's only for three weeks or three days or three hours

and as I'm telling all this, as it's all pouring out of me in one dumb rush, I look across at the prettyboy and see only blankness in the eyes and I realize he doesnt know what I'm talking about, cant know, because he's never done it, never been there, never had that rush of endorphins, that wave of physical amazement that starts in the bottom of your dick and comes tidal-waving up your spine like some kind of astonishing hot tsunami and floods up inside of you, inside your heart, your whole chest, chokes up your throat, and floods your eyes with tears of wonder and joy, he's never known it, that's the fucking tragedy, he's never been there

and the question of sex with him, of fucking him, it's finally answered for me, because if there's no connection, then all it is, it's just fucking exercise, and I've had enough exercise for ten lifetimes—I dont want to wake up with an intimate stranger, someone who knows the taste of my sweat, but not the taste of me, just another zombie-fuck

but there was that moment, I know it happened, when he *kissed back* and something flickered in that moment and that's the moment I'm speaking to—who was that?—and how do I get back there, how does anyone

did he kill himself, prettyboy asks, it's the wrong question, I shake my head, to tell the truth I dont know, I never saw him again, maybe he did, maybe he didnt, maybe he just stumbled out into the night, just like everybody else, you crawl into your coffin and dont come back out until it's time to feed again

I stand, stretch, listen to the bones tap-dancing against each other, stretch again, denying entropy one more time, start picking up blankets and water bottles, is that it, he asks, and I turn and look at him, what did you want, and he doesnt answer, doesnt have an answer, and maybe that's the greater tragedy, worse than knowing what you want and never having it is never knowing, never being able to speak it at all

headed back in silence, bumping over the hard-packed dirt, finally up and onto the asphalt again, sliding through the dark, the wind roaring like a jet engine, and still he doesnt talk, for some reason he doesnt look so pretty anymore, and I'm wondering why I bothered, why I wasted my time, and why I didnt fuck him anyway, except even an old boar like me has some pride

—*something happened*—

I never talk about the *blinks*, nobody understands, I tried a couple times, but I got the look, that look, the one that says I'm going to pretend I understand you, but only for as long as it takes to gnaw off my leg and escape, and no we cant ever be drinking buddies again because you're crazier than me, there's something scary-wrong in your head; so I learned the hard way, I just dont talk about the *blinks*, not to anyone, and when they happen, they happen, nobody around me notices, so maybe I am crazy, it's like somebody cutting into the movie, just a dazzling flash of bright, way too fast to see, you only realize it afterward, except afterward there's the burn-in still hanging in the air, the after-images of whatever seared into my existential retinas never found anybody who knew about it, even with careful asking, none of the gurus, nor the medicine men, the shamans, not the dopers and dealers neither, asked a few doctors and corpsmen if they'd ever heard of anything like it, but they just looked at me funny, so I dropt the subject

only once, the crazy dyke, late one night on the road, somewhere between nowhere and nothing, we finally pull over and fall out onto our blankets, eventually end up on our backs, first her, then me, then both of us, staring up at the stars—*something happens*—and I ask her, did you feel that, and she asks, feel what, and I try to explain, and she says, you got *pinged*, and I say, pinged, what's that, and she says, it's when somebody is checking you out, seeing if you're there; like submarines in the dark, I ask, no she says, it's like computers on a network, I *ping* you and you *pong* back, except you aint ponging, but someone's definitely pinging

and that's as far as that conversation goes, but it sticks, enough so that whenever—*something happens*—I'm listening to hear who it is, or *what*, aliens or angels or Ida Noh, the mystery whore of Saigon, how'd you get the clap, soldier, Ida Noh, sir—I'm listening, listening like the antenna at Arecibo

except I'm always listening *after*, never during, never before, it's like lightning, you only know you've been struck by it when you pick yourself up off the ground afterward, like Jerry and his redhead, and I figure that maybe I'm the wrong kind of receiver, or maybe I'm not getting the whole signal, or maybe I'm in the fringe area, Ida Noh again, and the only part of any of it that I can be sure of is that it never happens when I'm alone, it only happens when I'm with someone and only when the moment is intense, very intense, too intense, almost overload, that's when it happens, when the meter is pinned

other people, they talk about those moments when everything happens at once, when the car starts to skid, when it goes skidding/swerving/screeching/sideways, that's the moment when time stops for them, for me that's the moment when time disappears, and I come out the other side still ringing all over, reconnecting to myself, I know I'm missing something here, I used to think that if I could find someone else, anyone who experienced the same thing, then maybe we could, Ida Noh, connect, and if it happened to us together, at the same time, maybe we could get a clearer signal, except when I talk about the blinks, the pings, I get the stare, the what-are-you-talking-about look, so that's not an option

except yeah, at the back of my mind, I'm still always thinking, maybe this one, maybe this time, maybe finally I'll find out who's calling, who's pinging, and sometimes I'll go days/weeks/months without a ping and I'll miss it for a while and then I'll get used to the silence and then I'll even forget about the pings for a while, until it starts again, and once, lying awake in some strange bed in the middle of some strange night, I had this thought that maybe I'm only one piece of the circuit, like a transistor or a capacitor or one of those other bits of electric magic, and maybe what I need isnt another piece like me, but some other piece totally unlike me, maybe I'm just an antenna, maybe I need a modulator or a resonator or maybe just a tuning knob, maybe there's a whole bunch of pieces missing, and maybe I'm not anything at all, just a chimpanzee hammering on a rock and striking the occasional spark

that's the other thought, that whatever it is, maybe it's something I cant know, maybe none of us can, because we're not there yet, we can string some wires and make electricity run around in circles and sparkle some lights, but we still cant do that next thing, whatever it is, that next thing that comes after super-sharp televisions and super-fast computers, that thing that we still havent thought of, whatever it will be, and by comparison with that, we're still just apes with bones and flints, and that's the thing I think about, listening to the stars, listening for others, maybe we're listening with the wrong ears, and we cant really hear whoever is pinging, maybe only a few of us can hear occasional bits and pieces of the pings and the rest of us cant hear anything at all because we're just not there yet, we're still in bed with Ida Noh in the hot damp nights of Saigon

and oh shit, Saigon, and Perry, late one night, we play cut-for-low and loser takes the point next day on patrol, and it's Perry who catches it in the belly, not me, and it's Jerry all over again, only this time it's me with the guilt, with the story, it's my fault he died, I only lose a leg, but Perry spills his guts, and ever since then I've been spilling mine, only I never get to die, Perry was the lucky one, he got out quick

and I get it, I get it *again*, we're all dragging dead bodies around, offering each other a sniff of the corpse, the past is this heavy ruck that sits on our backs, growing heavier every year, we just keep adding more and more shit to the load, and eventually history is inescapable, the shitbird guru on my shoulder yabbers into my ear, the past defines not just the present, but the future as well, there's no escape, is there, this is it, and that's why I didnt fuck the prettyboy, because there's no place in my past for that future

finally bring him back to where we started, the big empty parking lot below the dorm, pull to a stop, we look at each other, all the stuff still unsaid, the real stuff that nobody ever says, and just before the seeya—*something happens*—and the van starts shaking, hard, like something slamming against it from the side, again and again, and then the lights of the world come on, dazzling, finger-stabbing, searching, finally pinning us in the van, and there's a great whooshing noise and screaming too, all the voices in the world, prettyboy grabs my hand and

—*it happens*—

He's turned pretty again. Pretty frightened. Everything slows down, stops. The eye of the timestorm. Even while the banging continues around us.

—*connection*—

all the flickers, all the blinks, everything, time and space collapses into one moment, and this time I'm in the moment, caught, a dragonfly in amber, gossamer wings transparent in the heavenly backlight, and in the same instant, everything simultaneous

—*I get it*—

There's Jerry and Perry and Mary the bulldyke and even prettyboy, and all the rest of us, everyone who connected, who flickered in and out, all of us woven like ganglia into the great neural web of sentience recognizing itself. That's who's been pinging—not aliens or angels or anything else—*it's us.* All of us together. That's the connection. Our own humanity is calling. It's the next step. It isnt a secret, it never was, except all of us together, we never knew, or we keep forgetting, or we do it on purpose, but now this time—*some of us* can actually see it happening—

—*the fireflower blossoms*—

A hot rush, a tidal wave, tsunami of exuberance, rising up through me, I can see to the end of the universe and back, all of us, connecting, lighting up, answering the pings, awakening to ourselves, blinking alive, confused, excited, wondrous, not everyone yet, but all of us who've heard the wake-up call, and in that moment, we're together, and we *know*, and it's *now*, and there's *no* going back *o*

and then as the van topples and crashes sideways onto the street, the sirens come whooping in, the red and blue lights flickering, flashing turning—the moment is broken, and I'm scrambling up over prettyboy to unlatch his door, push it open, start to climb out, when the first bottle comes crashing against it, and a baseball bat whangs into the windshield, fracturing it, but not shattering, so that isnt the way, I fumble sideways, crawling, kick the back doors open with my good leg and come out with the aluminum bat in one hand, ready to bang the hell out of last night's bashers, who've been waiting for me all night long with their fraternity brothers and a keg of beer, the whole gang of chimpanzees, believing that I've kidnapped one of their own, they're going to rescue him from the bearded monster

except the cops are already here, beanbag rifles at the ready, lights flashing, spotlights dazzling me, the chopper above pins me in a funnel of light, so I drop the bat and raise my hands and lie down slowly on the asphalt, because already I know how this will play out

I clean up real good, no piercings, no tats, shave and a haircut, put on a clean suit, yes, I have one, but leave the prosthesis at home, fold up the pants leg, and limp into court on a crutch, tell the judge the bashers broke it when they pushed my van over, a seven-thousand dollar peg, one battered old vet with no leg to stand on, opposite a bunch of frats with attitude, there's no question what will happen here, six of them get expelled, the chapter gets its charter pulled, and the town has something to argue about until Christmas break, I'll be gone by then anyway, autumn rolls away and with it me, no more dry desert nights for this old bear, maybe I'll drift south to the tip of Baja and lie naked in the unforgiving sun like a great baking whale, or maybe north into Canada again, or Alaska, where I'll snuggle deep in a tiny cabin, hibernating like a grumpy old wolverine, listening to the snow piling up against the windows, anywhere away from here, away from the madness and the noise, the squalor of human ignorance, all the vicious scrabbling little souls that still dont get *it*, might never get it, will never get it because all the clamor they make drowns out all the other possibilities, they're screaming so loud about what they want they cant hear that the answer is already yes when your watch says thirteen o'clock, what time is it—it's time to get a new watch, the pieces of this one are scattered all over the floor—it's time to build a new one

—something is happening, it's still happening—

All the parts of me/us, we're scattered, yes, but we're pinged and connected and we can sense/feel/hear each other. We're something new. A little two year-old girl, standing up in her crib, crying with a wet diaper, but that's not why she's crying, she's not yet ready for the burden of knowledge. A black grandmother, suddenly awake in the night, wondering why she's thinking of her dead grandson all of a sudden, he died in Nam, but she can hear him somewhere—with all time and space collapsed, he's right here now. A skinny teenage boy, secretly trying on his sister's panties, abruptly confused and wondering why he can suddenly see into the future, scared of what he's becoming and intrigued as well. The cop holding the beanbag rifle, blinking, scanning the whole situation through a dozen different pairs of eyes, instead of just his own little piece; he sees through the perp's eyes, feels the fear and terror. A young woman, screaming, channeling a joyous excruciating birth; the baby screams with her, mother and child locked together in mutual awareness. The desperate man, standing on the bridge, the choice in his eyes, suddenly alive beyond his own horizons, stepping back to reconsider. The student, looking up from his book—there's a world out there, a vast unknowable, incomprehensible world; the book, the words, the crawling insect marks upon the page, the barest shadow of meaning, there is no explanation, it's just what's happening. *Is still happening. Now.*

And all the others too, touched with wonder—frightened, intrigued, cautious, but stepping into the moment, it'll take a while. We'll get there. This thing, whatever it is we are, all of us still sorting it out, we're a long way from threshold and even farther from critical mass, we're alone, but not alone, never alone, never again.

And Michael, I glance over at him, dazed and confused, but waking up into himself now. I wonder how many more we can wake up.

AUTHOR'S AFTERWORD:
I came back to this voice two more times, "fourteen o'clock" and "fifteen o'clock." By now, I knew the hero's name was Chase. And as he shared his life with me, we both discovered what kinds of strength and what kinds of love can be found inside the human soul. All three stories can be found in one book, aptly titled thirteen, fourteen, fifteen o'clock. *You can find it on* **https://www.gerrold.com.**

www.ingramcontent.com/pod-product-compliance
Lightning Source LLC
Chambersburg PA
CBHW070221030726
47505CB00006B/1755